DIRTY BAD

CHANCE

NEW YORK TIMES AND USA TODAY BESTSELLING AUTHOR

JASINDA WILDER

DIRTY BEASTS:

CHANCE

1

From the Frying Pan Into the Fire

Annika

THIS IS A STUPID IDEA.

All available evidence points to this new guy being just a different form of torture than dealing with fucking *Alvin*. Yes, his name is actually Alvin. Not only is Alvin ugly, stupid, mean, and a meth-addicted drug dealer, his name is *Alvin*. Like that asshole cartoon rodent—and honestly, they're similar, Alvin and Alvin.

All that and still, here's me, owing his ugly, stupid, mean, meth-addict-ass twenty-five grand. Therefore, unless I would like to very quickly find myself on the really nasty end of his infamously short temper—and by that I mean dead with a bullet in the skull—I'm obliged to do what he says.

Because I do not have twenty-five thousand dollars, or twenty-five thousand of any currency.

Therefore, here I am, in a swank, exclusive, anything-goes nightclub in Las Fucking Vegas, fetching his slimy tweaker-ass drinks like I'm like his bitch.

I'm not his bitch. I'm no one's bitch.

Except that's not true, is it? Because here I am, in this club, covered in spilled beer and vodka-Sprite, humiliated, angry, desperate, hungry, exhausted, and ready to collapse, doing his bidding.

Then, this colossal brute comes to my rescue. He knocked Alvin off his feet with a *finger.*

Alvin, as previously stated, is stupid. I don't mean that figuratively. I mean it literally—he's lacking in IQ, as well as education. He's the worst kind of stupid—where he's smart enough to not realize he's stupid. He thinks he's a master manipulator, a master businessman, a god among men. He thinks this, truly. He thinks this because he's managed, so far, to deal drugs and stay alive and accumulate a bit of a reputation for being a slimy, snaky little shit with bad products and worse prices; he's under the impression that he's a big, swinging-dick player on the dealer scene.

He's not. He's a joke. He's who the desperate go to when they've got nowhere else to turn for their next fix. He's this because he'll take payment in non-currency form. You're a male, he'll give you drugs if you work for him—transport his product, cook his product, package his product, beat up people who owe him money or haven't come through on their end of the bargain. You're a woman, well…I suppose that's obvious: if you don't pay him in dollars, you suck or fuck him and his friends, or he'll shoot you in the face himself, and no one has quite figured out what he does with the corpses.

Such is my fix. I owe him. I refuse to suck or fuck him or his friends. Therefore, here I am, doing his bidding. Which, I realize, is one short step up from the nasty alternative.

Back to Alvin and his idiocy. He gets tweaked, gets high on blow, gets drunk, or gets some combination of the above, and he forgets he's a tiny pathetic worm of a man. He thinks he can say "fuck off, fatso" to a man the size of this Chance and get away with it. He assumes everyone knows who he is and he thinks he's Pablo Escobar—untouchable.

This Chance brute hung him over the side of a balcony one-handed and didn't seem to strain in the slightest. Just lifted him clean off the floor, one-handed, like he was a bad little puppy being grabbed by the scruff.

So the question I have to answer for myself is, leave the club, and know that eventually Alvin will find me? Because he will. He's slimy like that. Can't spell his own name, and I'm not entirely certain that's an exaggeration. But he's street-smart. He knows people. He knows the power of the dollar and he knows the power of addiction; and somehow, despite his own plethora of addictions, he's managed to stay alive and carve out a little niche for himself, and therefore he knows people. Bad, dangerous people. Alvin himself couldn't find the bottom of a pot if he was pissing into it, but he can pay people in drugs or money to find me for him.

If that sounds like a lot of contradictions, that's because Alvin is exactly that—a walking contradiction. Smart yet stupid, dangerous yet pathetic.

I'm fully aware that very, very soon he's going to quit accepting my refusal to perform sexually for him. He'll put a gun to my skull and tell me to start sucking his dirty little cock or he'll pull the trigger. That, or give him twenty-five thousand dollars he knows damn well I don't have. I know this is what he'll do, because I've watched him do it. I've made myself useful, so far, but useful only goes so far with a worm like Alvin. Eventually, he'll get tired of me being useful and decide he just wants me for the fact that I'm a female and will take what he wants.

That's the known.

Then, there's the unknown.

Chance.

A man who must be at least five or six inches taller than me, and I'm six-three. Taller than most men, it's rare to find a man I literally have to tilt my head to look up at. Making him rarer still, he's as brutishly muscular as he is tall. Those arms are the size of my thighs, and I'm no skinny waif myself, which means they're *thick*. Having seen him lift Alvin's 120 pounds with one of those giant arms, it's obvious it isn't just fat making them big. His shoulders are as dense, hard, and massive as the cliffs along the Pacific Coast Highway.

He's far from ugly. His skin is brown and smooth, his face is handsome, with a hard jawline enhanced by a short beard that's more stubble gone long, deep brown eyes that are almost black, and long thick black hair bound back at his nape in a loose ponytail. He's just a damned good-looking man, on top of being an absolute unit.

It's trouble, him looking the way he does and thinking he's got some mission to protect damsels in distress or whatever his issue is. Trouble for me, and trouble for him. Because sure he's big. Sure, he can squash little Alvin with a thumb. But it doesn't matter how big you are, someone rolls past with an automatic and fills you with holes, you're now just big and dead.

And I can guarantee you, he's made a mortal enemy of Alvin Robertson.

I have a decision to make. Because Chance has made me an offer—one he's disguised as a command: Go with him.

Go where? I don't know.

Do what for him, in exchange for his protection? I can only assume, and I assume he wants what Alvin wants. What every man wants, the moment he knows I'm desperate.

I can leave. I can tell Chance will allow me to walk out, if I insist. But if I do, I'm right back where I started—under Alvin's thumb, waiting for him to get sick of wanting and not having me. And since I am, as mentioned, flat broke, that leaves only the second option. And as also mentioned, it's not far from the truth to say I'm strongly considering just letting him kill me—because there's no way in hell I'm touching him or letting him touch me.

Which leaves me with one real choice—go with Chance.

If only because he's good-looking and if I'm going to jump out of the frying pan and into the fire, it may as well be in the company of a gigantic, handsome, damsel-rescuing sort. If I'm going to have to use my body to get out of trouble, I'd rather it be with a man I find attractive.

He's staring down at me with those big, deep, brown eyes—they're hard eyes. He's a man who's seen and done some shit. "Come with me." His voice is equally deep, and equally hard as his eyes.

My temper flares, because I *hate* being told what to do. "Maybe you could rephrase that as a question."

He just blinks down at me, and then his enormous paw slides around my waist and pulls me into motion. I have no option but to move as directed or fall, so I start walking—I drop my cane into my hand and lean on it. Just the relatively short walk through the crowd without my cane left my knee throbbing something fierce, so I'm forced to lean on it rather heavily as I follow him through the crowd. *Follow* isn't quite the right word—accompany is closer. He stays right beside me and slightly in front of me, clearing a path through the heaving, shifting throng of dancing patrons with both his massive bulk and an outstretched arm. People take one look at who bumped them, then look up, and up again, see him scowling down at them, and clear out of the way *fast*. His other hand remains at the small of my back, applying gentle but firm pressure. There's no struggling through the crowd for me, this time, which I must admit is sort of nice.

We reach the bar running roughly parallel to the wall, and he lifts a section of the bar up, moves through, holds it for me, and then lowers it back in place. Once through, he fishes a keycard from his pocket, touches it to a reader on the wall, which turns green. The door, which was disguised as merely part of the wall, pops open. Again he holds the door for me and closes the door behind himself. The moment the door is pulled to, the noise and clamor and thudding music fades to a muffled throb. I let out a breath I hadn't realized I was holding, ducking my head and sucking in a breath.

"Chaotic out there, yeah?" His voice, here in the quiet of a service corridor, is deep, powerful, gravelly; from mere inches away, it thrums in my belly almost like standing too near a speaker at a concert.

"Yeah." I straighten. Look at him. "What do you want?"

He just peers down at me, implacable, unreadable. "Got your breath back?"

I nod. "Yes. I'll repeat, what do you *want*?"

He doesn't answer, just places that hand at my back again—and again, I'm six-three, so in no way am I dainty or small, but when he places that hand at the small of my back, his thumb extends nearly to my bra strap. It's ridiculous, the size of that hand.

I'm propelled into a walk again, and I give a growl of frustration, pull away from his touch, and stamp my cane against the floor. "Stop—for fuck's sake! Where are we going? What do you *want* from me?"

He turns in place, staring at me without expression. "Get you somewhere you can sit down, get a drink, and relax away from the crowd till I'm off. That work for you?"

I narrow my eyes. "Don't need to sit down. I'm fine."

He laughs. "You're gonna stand around until four in the morning just to be stubborn and prove a point?"

I huff. "No, I just meant—"

"I know what you meant." He steps closer, into my space, until I smell him—sweat, an earthy, almost musky scent that's likely his cologne. "What's your name?"

"Annika," I answer—*AH-nick-uh.*

"Last name?"

I lift an eyebrow at him. "What is this, an interview?" When he just stares at me, I snort a laugh. "Scott. My name is Annika Scott."

"Annika Scott." He muses. "Beautiful name."

"Thank you." I gesture at him. "And your last name is? Since we're interviewing each other and all."

"Kapule."

"Chance Kapule." I nod. "It's a good, strong name. What kind of name is that?"

"Hawaiian."

I notice his arms in more detail, now—there are tattoos all over both of them, down to his wrists. Black ink, frequently using blank space to artistic effect, with geometric designs, intricate, wave-like swirls, nearly abstract flower designs. They go up under the tight sleeves of his shirt, making me wonder how far over his chest they go.

"I'm half Hawaiian," he says, after a moment of awkward silence. "My mother was from Mexico, my father from Hawaii."

I notice for both mother and father, he used past tense, but I opt to not ask the obvious question. "Your tattoos—they have meaning?"

He nods. "Yes."

Nothing else.

I gesture at the corridor. "Lead on, Chance Kapule."

The corridor is narrow with high ceilings, racks of paper and plastic goods stocked on large industrial racks, along with cases of beer stacked on the floor three and four high and cases of liquor on yet more racks. A few paces away from the door, the stacks and racks fade and it's just the corridor, dimly lit, our shoes squeaking on the epoxy floor.

A long walk, then—we pass another door which I assume leads out to the club, judging by the bartending supplies around the door. We go by two more of these supply stations; at the last one, there's an exit to the exterior, which is propped open by a box of plastic cocktail straws; I hear low voices, a male and a female, murmuring and laughing, smell cigarettes—employees taking a break.

Chance halts here, shoves open the door. "Don't prop open the door. Use your keycards. That's what they're for."

He takes up the whole doorway, so I only hear the reply: "Yeah, Chance. Got it." He kicks the box inside and back over near the rack, but leaves it on the floor rather than placing it back on the shelf.

At the end of the long, long hallway, we reach a corner. The hallway continues on at a right angle, but an exit sign here indicates a stairwell. He scans his card, the light turns green, and he yanks open the door, gesturing me through. Stairs go up and down.

He pauses beside me. "Alone, or company with a stranger?"

I blink up at him. "What?"

He enunciates overly clearly. "Would you like to be alone, or hang out with someone you don't know?"

"Alone," I answer right away.

He nods, his only reply, and heads down the stairs. They turn at the first landing, with another closed door at the bottom—another card reader.

I stand a couple stairs up from him, watching as he scans his card again. "Serious about security, aren't you?"

He just nods. Steps through the door and holds it for me. I move through: to my right, a serious-as-shit gym, and considering the muscles on Chance, I surmise it's where he works out. I eye the gear with a professional eye: Rogue equipment, mainly, with some other high-end brands here and there. Power racks, barbells, Olympic plates, dumbbells, battle ropes, several assault air-bikes, a heavy bag, a deadlifting platform, and incline/decline benches. An old part of me, which I'd thought long dead, stirs at the sight. It's a beautiful gym, lots of space, brightly lit, with mirrors on the wall, thick mats on the floor. It's neat, clean, and organized. For a moment, I almost want to go in there, slap some chalk onto my hands...

I shake my head and turn away.

Chance doesn't move. "You lift?"

I lift my cane, wiggle it. "Not anymore."

He looks at me, his hard eyes penetrating, assessing, yet giving nothing away. "Not anymore, huh?" The question is there, but I decline to answer it.

I shake my head. "No. Not anymore."

He just nods, seeming to recognize I'm unwilling to discuss it.

Across from the doorway I'm still standing in is another door, closed and locked. To the left, a common area. We move that way, and I take in the common space. On the left, there's a large sectional couch facing a huge TV; another hallway extends directly opposite where I stand, with several closed doors on either side; to the right, two long cafeteria tables separate the common area from the kitchen beyond the tables, and the kitchen is industrial, commercial-grade.

I look at Chance. "So when you said I could live in this club, you weren't joking."

He shakes his head slowly. "No." He moves away from me, into the common area, heading for the kitchen. "What do you want to drink?"

"Just a beer is fine. Anything will do, I'm not particular." I follow him, leaning hard on my cane; my knee hurts again after the stairs.

He goes to a huge refrigerator, pulls out a bottle of Heineken, flicks the top off with a bottle opener. He points at the couch. "Sit."

I do need to sit, so as much as I want to stay on my feet just to spite his order, I cross to the couch and lower myself to it. Toss my cane on the couch beside me, the handle near my hand. Chance brings me the beer, then grabs a stack of remotes, brings them to me, tossing them onto my lap.

"Big one is the TV, cable, and DVD player," he says. "Long thin one is sound. Little one is for the Fire thing."

I blink up at him. "So I'm just going to hang out in your secret lair beneath the club?"

He arches an eyebrow, a corner of his mouth tipping up—almost a grin. "Yeah. Not my secret lair, though. *Ours*."

"Ours? Ours who?" I ask.

"You'll see," is his cryptic response. "Just stay here in this room, on the couch. You want to eat, help yourself to the kitchen."

"Am I allowed to leave?" I ask, my tone bitingly sarcastic.

He snorts. "Yeah, of course." He gestures at the hallway with the doors on either side. "End of that hall is stairs up to the parking lot, side of the club. "You want to leave, leave. Make sure the door closes behind you. Call a cab, get a Lyft or an Uber. Whatever."

I eye him. "Why are you helping me?"

He blinks at me. I can almost see him chewing on what to say. "Lotta reasons."

"Give me one."

"You're the most beautiful woman I've ever seen. Didn't like how that little fucker was treating you." He shakes his head again. "There's more to that situation up there. I know it. More to you. To this." He gestures between himself and me. "For now, I gotta go back to work." He turns and heads back the way we came.

"Chance," I call.

He pauses at the door. "Yeah."

"This, meaning me and you?"

He gives me a grin, then. A real, full smile. And god almighty, it transforms his features—the hardness dissolves, the blank mask fades, and I see humor in him, mischief, something wild, something intense. "Yeah, mama. Like you and me."

I frown. "I don't even know you."

"Gotta start somewhere."

"Maybe I don't want to," I shoot back.

He blinks slowly, that grin still in place. "You do."

I glare at him. "You're sure of that, huh?" I snark, eyebrow lifted. "With your telepathy and all?"

He just nods, as if my statement was not sarcastic. "Pretty much." He steps through the doorway, then pops his head back out. "Annika?"

I lift a hand, palm up. "Haven't gone anywhere in the last five seconds."

"You're safe here." That quiet, gentle voice, those deep dark eyes, those fucking words—shit.

I blink hard and swallow harder. "Right. Thanks."

"I mean it. Whatever the fuck is going on with you, it's not here. You're safe."

"Heard you," I repeat. "Thanks."

He vanishes, and I slump—I've been holding myself tense, upright, not breathing. Not daring to.

Safe.

What a joke.

I wait, half expecting him to return. I wonder what he wants from me.

But hell, it's obvious enough, isn't it? He'll keep me safe here…and I know damn well what he'll expect in return.

I turn on the TV, find a nature documentary to watch as I sip my beer. I'm hungry, but now that I'm on the couch, the thought of getting up and fixing myself food sounds way too hard. So I don't. I sit, I watch the doc, and I sip.

And, at some point, I find myself slumping sideways, fighting to keep my eyes open. I forget how long I've been awake—nearly twenty-four hours, by now.

I fall asleep.

———— ◆ ————

I wake to subdued voices—people speaking and moving around but attempting to be quiet about it.

Where am I? I'm not very coherent when I wake up, at the best of times, and these are far from the best of times.

I blink my eyes open—a TV, unfamiliar, set to the home screen of a streaming service, showing the last thing watched, a documentary. I'm on a couch, covered by a thick, soft blanket, fleece on one side, sherpa-lined on the other.

Where am I? Shit, I don't remember.

I'm stretched out on a comfortable leather couch; I sit up, and my hair feels wild…or, wild*er*. In my face, in my eyes, poofed everywhere. I brush it out of my eyes and look around. An industrial kitchen, fairly high drop-tile ceiling, incandescent can lights rather than fluorescent.

Ah, I remember. Alvin. The club. Being sent to fetch a girl for him—he's got this uncanny ability to spot people who are users, who will want what he's offering and are willing to pay his price. She took one look at him, knew what he was offering and what he wanted, took it and paid his price.

Gross. I shudder in revulsion, remembering all too vividly.

Alvin, tossing me around. Being a dick, but it's not like he has any other setting. He's set to full dick, all the time.

The huge guy, Chance—*Yeah, mama. Like you and me.*

Falling asleep.

I stretch and twist, assessing.

There are people in the kitchen. Men. Two women.

A lot of men—a lot of intensely, bizarrely hot men, hypermasculine, massively muscled beefcake men.

Two blondes, not twins but for sure brothers, both of whom could easily play a Hollywood superhero. A copper-haired man sits with them, with features alike enough to the blondes that he's their brother as well. Put the three together, and a lesser woman might just have spontaneous orgasms just looking at them—the jawlines, the light eyes, the ridiculous musculature...they're shirtless, wearing workout shorts and nothing else, sitting together sipping coffee and looking tired and grumpy and fucking delicious.

Those three are at a table on their own. At the other table, more male hotness, and two beautiful women. The men: one is nearly as tall as Chance, with brown skin and a wide short mohawk, shirtless, with muscles sculpted by the good Lord himself; another man with brown skin, but he's much shorter, perhaps under six feet, but his shoulders are broad and his arms thick, his hair inky black and long and loose, hanging to his shoulders in a glossy raven's-wing sheet, with a long black beard coming to a neat point at his chest and a debonair mustache which curls up at his cheekbones, also shirtless in shorts with his ripped torso on display; a blond man, long hair brushing his shoulders, with a fairly long, bushy blond beard trimmed in a neat U, again bare chested, and he's pure brawn, mountains of muscle piled upon mountains of muscle, veiny, hard, bulging, sculpted; Chance, shirtless as all the others, and his tattoos begin at his shoulders and cover his whole upper body, both arms to his wrists, down to his diaphragm, and not a single image is exactly the same as any other.

Chance, fucking hell, the man is beautiful. He's not ripped, nor is he jacked. He carries a layer of fat over his muscle, but only a blind person could look at him and not see that as the thin layer of padding it is. His hair is loose, his beard thicker than yesterday. He's sipping coffee, looking sleepy and slow-moving, like a bear emerging from hibernation.

One of the women sits on one side of the man with the mohawk. She's leaning against his side, head on his shoulder, sleepily peering into a mug of coffee, and they're having a quietly murmured conversation—she lifts her head, sips, puts it back on his shoulder. He peers down at her, an affectionate smile touching the corners of his mouth. She's blond, stunningly beautiful, wearing a purple tank top, and since she's on the other side of the table I can't see her bottom half.

The other woman is Indian, again remarkably beautiful with fine, regal features, her hair neatly braided back, wearing a plain white V-neck T-shirt. She's sitting close to the huge blond man with the thick beard, also sipping coffee, also having a quiet conversation with him.

The scene is familial. They're all comfortable with each other, at ease in silence as they wake up.

Chance, straddling the bench so he's in profile, one elbow leaning on the table, twists to look at me. "Mornin', Annika." He indicates people as he points at them. "Anjalee and her man Kane. The blond lady is Myka, and that's her man Rev. The man with the fancy mustache is Lash. Me, you know already. At the other table we have the Brothers Antisocial." He laughs. "Really, they're just not morning people. Or afternoon people, or night people." Another snickering laugh. "The one with the scar is Saxon, the other blond is Solomon, and the one that looks like a young but cranky Robert Redford is Silas. Everyone, this is Annika Scott."

"Another stray we're adopting?" This is from the scarred blond, Saxon. "When do I get a hot chick to rescue?"

"Ignore him," Chance says. "We've had a weird few weeks."

I stare. "Is there a bathroom I can use?"

"My room is unlocked. Down the hall, first door on the right."

My knee is always stiff and achy when I first wake up, so I'm less mobile in the mornings—limping, shuffling, leaning heavily on my cane. I feel the eyes on me, the attention, the curiosity, the questions. They keep them to themselves though, and I make my way to Chance's room.

It's small, nothing more than a bedroom with an *en suite* bathroom. Just a large bed, a six-drawer bureau, and a bathroom. Pale gray-blue walls, the same gray epoxy flooring with blue flecks as in the common area. The bureau has a few personal belongings on the top: of primary interest is a framed photograph of a group of soldiers in camouflage gear, carrying big fuck-off guns and wearing bucket hats; some of the men are smiling, others are serious, one has his gun held against his shoulder, showing the camera his middle finger with his free hand; I spot Chance in the photograph—it's easy since he's by far the largest man in the group, although in the photograph he's quite a bit leaner and clean-shaven, with short hair under his bucket hat. Rev, the mohawk man from the common room, is beside him, leaning an elbow on Chance's shoulder with casual, affectionate familiarity, one foot propped on its toe across his other shin. They're in Afghanistan, if I had to guess based on the spiked, serrated ridges in the background.

The only other thing in the room other than the bureau are bookshelves, floor to ceiling, stacked with books two deep and two high—dog-eared and battered paperbacks mostly, with a few hardcovers and trade paperbacks here and there. Two of the floor-to-ceiling bookshelves are across from the bed, with a smaller one in the corner beside the bureau; two nightstands on either side of the bed are also two-shelf bookshelves doubling as nightstands, each overstuffed with books stacked two deep and more stuffed in on their sides. Clearly, the man likes books—unexpected, which is, perhaps, an unfair assumption based solely on the fact that he's huge and brawny and powerful and sexy as hell.

My attention goes back to the photograph, but I feel like I'm prying, looking at it, so I go into the bathroom and do my business.

Back out in the common room, Chance gestures at the kitchen. "Help yourself, mama."

"Don't call me that," I snap. "I'm no one's mother, least of all yours."

"Just a word. Don't mean nothin' by it." He sips his coffee, and then lifts the mug in my direction. "Coffee?"

"Please Jesus," I say, heading for the industrial coffeemaker and pouring myself a mug—there's a whole coffee station on one wall: a rack fixed to the wall with white diner-style mugs hanging on hooks, a small glass-fronted mini-fridge beneath it with cartons of half-and-half and gallons of regular milk as well as creamers in a variety of flavors, as well as a black plastic three-section container with packets of sugar, Sugar in the Raw, and Splenda. I fix my coffee with enough hazelnut creamer to turn it nearly white and take a seat on the bench near Chance… "near" being relative, as I've put at least two feet between us. I hook my cane on the edge of the table and take a sip.

Chance leans over and peers into my mug. "Little bit of coffee with your creamer, huh?"

I glare at him. "Sorry, does my coffee preference not meet your approval?"

He backs away, snickering. "Just teasing, woman. Shit."

I gesture at Rev with my mug. "Tease him. Bet he likes it."

Rev just stares at me, his gaze dark, expression blank. "No."

I blink and turn away. "Okay then. I take that back. Don't tease him."

Chance laughs. "I've known him since I was ten. I know better."

"Chance is a pathological teaser," Rev says. "He nearly got busted down a rank for teasing our X-O. The big dumb fuck just can't help himself."

"I did not almost get busted down a rank, you tool." Chance sips, shrugging, his mug hiding a grin. "I just got KP for, like, a fuckin' month."

I watch them bicker, and drink my coffee, and wait for the questions to start. Eventually, it becomes clear none are forthcoming, which leaves me off-balance.

"Well," Myka says, getting up to rinse her mug out.

"My landlord found someone to take over my lease, so I'm gonna go start packing my clothing."

"Would you care for some assistance?" Anjalee asks. "I am not doing anything else today."

Myka's smile is friendly and welcoming. "Sure. Mom always says many hands make light work."

Rev slugs back his coffee. "I'll find us a storage place for your furniture."

The three brothers all rise from their table, set their mugs in the sink, and wander into the gym, together as one, without a word of communication—Metallica starts up, loudly, and within minutes I hear the distinctive clink of weights being moved.

Lash sets his mug in the sink, and then pauses beside me. "It is a pleasure to meet you, Annika Scott."

"You too, Lash."

He vanishes into one of the rooms, closes the door. Leaving me alone with Chance.

He gets up, refills his mug. Sits closer to me than he was before he got up, close enough his knee nudges my thigh. "So, Annika Scott."

I sigh. "Here we go."

He lifts an eyebrow. "Here we go, what?"

"You helped me out with the situation with Alvin. Albeit, I didn't ask for or need your help, but still, there it is. Now, I assume, we're going to discuss what I owe you."

He stares hard at me for a very long time. "Jesus. That's where your brain goes?"

I stare back. "Am I wrong?"

He nods, sips coffee with a loud slurp. "Yes."

"You handled Alvin like he was nothing," I say, rather than addressing his answer. "You should've dropped him off the side, though. Would've saved yourself trouble. He may be small, he may be dumb, and he may be a sick, twisted pain in the ass, but what he's *not* is forgiving. He's a seriously vengeful little fucker, and you made yourself a very bad enemy."

Chance cackles. "Ain't scared of a little shit like him."

"It's not him you should be scared of, it's the guys he'll hire to murder you. Or, injure you to the point that they can drag you to him so he can do the honor himself."

Chance laughs again. "Also not a worry."

"Well, it should be." I switch my grip on my mug, threading my two middle fingers through the handle. "He's easy to underestimate, trust me on this. One-to-one, he's about as threatening as a newborn kitten. He's dumber than a bag of hammers. But he's street savvy, and he knows very, very bad people, and he's very, very good at getting them to do his dirty work."

He just shrugs. "Oh, I believe you. I'm just not worried. Not about him, and not about the people he knows. He can order as many hits on me as he wants—he has to know how to find me for them to carry out the hits."

"Well, you have to leave this club at some point."

He smirks. "Don't be so sure."

"You never leave?" I eye him skeptically. "Not ever?"

He shakes his head. "Got everything I need, and there's nothing out there I want."

I consider this. "So you work up there, and live down here."

He nods. "Yup."

"What do you do when you're not working?"

"Read," he says, then tips his head to the side. "And lift."

I shake my head. "Yeah, I couldn't do that."

"Do what?" His brown eyes take on a twinkle. "Read?"

I just roll my eyes. "No, asshole—live my entire life in one building and never leave."

His eyes lose the twinkle. "Yeah, well, I have my reasons." He points at me. "What's the deal with you and that guy anyway? You said his name is Alvin?"

I nod. "Yeah, Alvin Robertson." I turn away from him. "And my deal with him is none of your fucking business."

"Owe him money?" He guesses. I don't answer, and he nods. "You owe him money."

"I said it's none of your business."

He just looks at me, humor and teasing gone. "I told you you're safe here."

"Safe is relative. And unlike you, I can't just hide in the basement of a nightclub."

"Oh no? Why not?"

"Because I have a life."

He arches that damn eyebrow again. "A life that includes owing a two-bit sack of shit like that enough money that you're acting like his goddamn servant?"

I feel my mouth tighten, my gut burn. I shoot to my feet, snatching my cane and doing my damndest to make a nice, dramatic, stomping-away exit. "Fuck you. You don't know the first goddamn thing about me."

He makes a rather effective point—waits where he is as I walk away, only to follow me and catch up within a few long strides. He pivots in front of me. Blocks me in.

"Move," I snap. "I'm leaving. I'll take my *chances* out there with fucking Alvin."

"I'm offering you an alternative, Annika." His voice is gentle again.

This cuts me deep, because it almost feels genuine. I know it can't be, I know anything he's offering comes with a catch. There's always a catch.

"Yeah. Owe him, or owe you." I push around him. "Sorry, buddy, but better the devil you know, you know?"

He moves faster than I'd have believed possible—for anyone, let alone a man his size. He's just there in front of me again, and now my free hand is clutched in his paw. His hand is so big he's gripping my closed fist in his hand, engulfing it.

"Not always, no." He lifts my hand in his, touching the underside of my chin until I'm forced to look at him. "You gotta know what's out there for you, Annika. That being not a damn thing. Nothing good, at any rate. Owing that rat fucking bastard. Cowed by him. Doing what he tells you. Taking his shit and eating it." His eyes are hard. "Or worse. Man like that, in the end, only one thing he'll take as payment. You can fetch him drinks all day long and you'll never get free of him."

I lift my chin, jerk it away. "Yeah, I fucking *know*." I hold his gaze. "And what's it to you, huh? *You're* different? You want something else from me, do you? You're gonna help me out of debt to Alvin fucking Robertson out of the goodness of your heart, are you?"

"Yeah, maybe I will."

"Right." I lift an eyebrow back at him. "And I'm Mother Theresa reborn."

"You don't have to leave, Annika."

"I want to leave."

"No, I don't think you do. I think you're scared and going back to what you know."

"Literally, I just said better the devil you know. So

yeah. Except I'm not scared, I just don't know you and I don't trust you—no offense, but I don't trust anyone."

He still has a hold on my hand—with no effort whatsoever, and with a gentility that takes my breath away, he unfolds my hand in his, despite my resistance. "You can trust me. I don't want anything from you that you won't eventually want to give me."

I snort and yank my hand away. "Fuck you. I know *exactly* what *that* means, *ass*hole."

He shakes his head. "Not what you're assuming."

"Not what I'm assuming? I'm assuming you mean eventually you'll decide my debt is due and you'll take it from me one way or another—you'll just tell yourself I wanted it."

He rears back as if struck, and then throws my words back in my face. "You don't know the first fucking thing about me."

"You're a man. That's all I need to know."

"That's pretty damn sexist."

"Oh, boo-hoo. Did I hurt your poor little feelings?" The sarcasm drips from my voice like acid. "I've fucking *learned* time and time again—men, *all* men, want *one* fucking thing from me. And they'll do anything, go to any lengths and do any mental gymnastics to convince themselves *I want it.*"

He puts his face in mine. "Not me."

"Right." I lean close and make my voice breathy, push my chest into him. "I know what you want. You want *this*, don't you?" I writhe against him, knowing I'm baiting a bear, but too pissed off and freaked out to stop myself. "You want *me*, don't you? Wanna tap this ass? Tell all your buddies you tapped the tall gimpy redhead. You *earned* it, right? You *saved* me, after all, right? You deserve a reward."

He doesn't move. Just lets me writhe against him, pushing my crotch against his. Stares down at me with those deep brown eyes—I see compassion in them, understanding, sadness. Eventually, he puts a hand to my belly and presses me backward, taking a step back at the same time.

"Annika…that's *not* what this is." Again, the gentle voice.

"Then what is it?" I demand.

"Help." He closes the distance again. Gentle brown eyes. Gentle voice. His thumb touches my chin beneath my lower lip—gently. "I'm offering you safety."

My lungs squeeze hard, all the oxygen leaking out, and my heart thuds painfully. Panic, panic, panic. "Oh yeah? In exchange for what?"

"Nothing."

"Not what you just said."

"I said nothing you wouldn't eventually want. And by that I mean, nothing you won't eventually offer me yourself."

"I'm gonna end up begging for your dick, you mean."

He shakes his head. "Jesus, you're cynical." He shrugs. "You wanna see it that way, sure." Another shuffled half step closer, so he's in my space, so I'm breathing his air, looking up at him and trying to remember how to make my body cooperate so I can run the fuck away. "How about I make you a promise."

I force oxygen into my lungs. I can't move, I'm still stuck in place. "Fine, I'll play along." My voice is steady, but then, I'm always steady. Even when I'm freaking the hell out. "What promise?"

His eyes touch on mine, roaming my face, my lips, my throat, my cleavage, back up to my eyes. "I will not touch you in a sexual way unless you directly ask me to."

I laugh. "That'll *never* happen."

"So then what do you have to lose?"

"What is it you're asking me to do, exactly?"

"Just stay."

"Stay," I repeat. "Just stay here, in this secret night-club lair with you and your gang of over-testosteroned beefcakes?"

He snorts at that. "You're funny." His thumb slides over my lips. "Yes. I mean you, stay here, in my secret night-club lair with my gang of over-testosteroned beefcakes, and our two kind, amazing, welcoming women."

"*Our* women, huh? You share them?"

He growls. "No. *Our* in the sense that we're protective of them, even if they aren't actually *ours* in that sense." He shakes his head. "You have a way of twisting shit, Annika, you know that?"

No one has ever been protective of me. Wonder how that feels.

"And then what?" I ask. "I stay here, and then what? Or that's it, I just live here in this underground prison and I never leave?"

"And then we sort your shit out."

"We. Meaning you and me?"

"We meaning whoever it takes."

I shake my head. "Sort my shit out. Just like that? Just fix all my problems?"

He shrugs, nods. "Sure. All problems can be solved."

"Not all." I look away from him. "Not mine."

"All." He gets closer yet, towering over me, gazing softly down at me, like he sees something when he looks at me—something other than what I am. "Even yours. No matter what they are."

"Fuck you," I whisper. "You don't know the first fucking thing about me *or* my problems."

He reaches up and curls a springy tendril of my hair around his forefinger—for reasons I'm not entirely certain of, I seem to allow it. "I know you're a fighter—a survivor. I know you're an athlete. Or, you were. I know that vile little shit you came with has you by the balls, metaphorically speaking. I know you know it's only a matter of time before he starts demanding shit you clearly refuse to give." He's not done. "I know you're fucking gorgeous—you took my breath away, literally, the first time I saw you. I know you're scared out of your goddamn mind but too stubborn and too proud to ever admit it, to yourself let alone me."

"Joke's on you—I'm fucking terrified."

"Of what?"

"Alvin." I shake my head. "Not even really him, but what he represents. Who he is and what he does." I swallow hard. "And what my debt to him says about me."

"Addiction," he murmurs. "You're an addict."

I flinch as if struck—because it feels like being struck. "Like I said—not all problems can be solved."

"Look at me, Annika."

I shake my head, stubbornly refusing to do so. "Save your breath, Chance. I'm not looking for some hero to fucking swoop in and fix me."

"Well, that's a good news bad news situation," he says. "Good news is, I'm not trying to be a hero who swoops in and fixes you. Bad news is, I can't fix you. No one can fix you but you."

"Maybe I don't want to be fixed," I lie through my teeth.

He just laughs. "Never bullshit a bullshitter, Annika."

"So you're a bullshitter, then."

"Absolutely. I'm a bullshit artist of the highest caliber." He smirks. "I'm not bullshitting you, now, though."

"How am I supposed to trust you if you're a bullshit artist?"

"Because you and me, we're more alike than I think you'd care to admit."

"Again, you don't know me. You just met me." I look up at him, assessing, searching—unfortunately, I see only truth in him.

He shakes his head. "Listen to me, mama—I want to help you. Yes, I expect to get something out of it—eventually. That's no bullshit. What I expect to get out of it is *you.* The real you."

"What's that supposed to mean, the *real* me?" I demand.

"You're shielding. You've got solid steel walls around the real, genuine core of you a mile fucking thick. No one gets in, nothing gets out." He touches my lips with his thumb again, a soft, brushing touch.

"Stop doing that," I say testily, batting his hand away. "I don't like it."

He does it again. "Then why do your eyes dilate when I do it? Why do you suck in a breath like it's your last one when I do it?" Another swipe of his thumb, ghost-soft, over my lips.

And shit, shit, shit—he's right. He's fucking right. He

does it, and my chest swells with a deep breath I'm helpless to stop.

"I know you're shielding and I know you've got giant-ass fuckin' walls because you and me, mama, we're the same."

"Why do you call me mama?" I ask, my voice quiet.

He shrugs. "Dunno."

"Bullshit." I see the lie in his eyes. And I call him on it. "Never bullshit a bullshitter," I say, my turn to throw his words in his face. "Why do you call me mama, Chance? The truth."

He stares down at me. "Personal reasons."

"So you won't tell me."

"Sure I will."

"So?"

"If you tell me something of equally personal value."

"How am I supposed to know what's equally personal value?"

He grins. "Because if you agree, I'll go first, as a matter of trust."

I stare up at him, and damn him, but I see nothing but truth. "Fuck, fine."

He nods. "And so it begins." He tugs me by the hand. "Come on. Personal conversations like this are best had in private."

He leads me to his room, lies on his bed—I notice he leaves plenty of room beside him. When I stay standing in the doorway, he pats the bed next to him. "Close the door and come sit."

Moving reluctantly, I close his door and move to his bed, perching on the edge—stiffly, awkwardly, with no intention of relaxing.

He laughs. His bed contains at least half a dozen thick, puffy, soft pillows in heather gray jersey pillowcases; he stuffs two behind his back and a third behind his head, scooching down and burrowing back, ankles crossed. "Get comfy, Annika. No sense acting all…" He wiggles a hand at me. "Awkward and shit. I ain't gonna bite."

"I'm fine."

He stares at me, shaking his head in amusement. And then, managing to move both lightning fast and yet still gently, he snags me around the middle and tugs me toward him. Before I understand what's happening, I'm tucked against him, sheltered under the massive weight of his huge arm, his skin soft and warm under my ear and cheek.

"Relax."

"Let *go*," I hiss.

"Do me a favor and take three deep breaths. Close your eyes, take the breaths, and *then* tell me to let go."

"Chance, goddammit—"

"Try it."

Every muscle tensed, not breathing, not daring to so much as blink, I'm trapped inside the curl of his arm, pinned to his side.

Forced snuggles.

If I wasn't so panicked, freaked out, and pissed off, I'd almost find it funny.

I wriggle. "Let go," I snarl. "Get off me."

"I'm not on you, I'm holding you. Humor me for thirty fuckin' seconds, Annika. Close your eyes. Relax. Take three deep breaths. You do that, genuinely, and you still want me to let you go, I will."

"Swear?"

The arm wrapped over me—which seems to weigh

approximately as much as I do—lifts slightly, and his pinky appears, extended toward my hands. "Swear."

I can't help a laugh. "Really? A pinky swear?"

"Sure," he laughs. "Real men pinky swear."

I ignore his hand. "Well real women don't. Or at least this one doesn't." I let out a breath. "Fine, fuck."

Mainly because surging underneath the panic is a strong current of security and enjoyment, I close my eyes and force my muscles to unclench, one by one. Toes. Calves. Thighs. Belly. Arms. Shoulders. Neck. Same way I get to sleep at night—the only way I can. I pull in a long, slow, deep breath through my nose, let it out just as slowly. Again. A third time.

By the end of the third breath, I can't ignore the fact that I feel…safe. That I don't utterly hate, loathe, and despise being held by him like this.

Which, in and of itself is just fucking weird.

Before I can say anything, he speaks. His voice is a quiet rumble, like faraway thunder. "My dad called my mother that—mama. It was his thing. He…he fuckin' loved her so goddamn hard, shit. You don't even know. The shit that man did for her." He's quiet a moment, then lets out a sigh. "That was his…whaddyou call it. His term of endearment for her. Don't know I ever heard him call her by her actual name. Just…mama. I guess I sort of absorbed it."

"So you call all your girlfriends mama, then."

Another pause. "Nope."

"You don't?"

"Nope."

I twist my head to look up at him. "Why not?"

"Well, cause first and foremost, never really had what

you'd consider a girlfriend. And also, the women who *have* been in my life…I wouldn't call 'em that. Callin' a woman mama, for me, is…it's for when it's special."

I choke on my shock. "Wh-what? Why?"

He laughs. "Why? What do you mean, why? I just told you."

"No—me. Why me? Why do you call *me* mama, then? I'm not special to you. You don't even know me."

"You are."

"That's ridiculous."

"Sure is," he agrees.

I cackle. "Oh, great, thanks."

He barks a laugh. "Hey now, you're laying here in my arms, in my bed with me. I'm telling you there's something special about you—and you say it's ridiculous, then get pissy when I agree?"

I decline to answer that. "You've never had a girlfriend?"

"Nope." He moves a heavy shoulder in a shrug. "Like I said, not like you'd consider a girlfriend."

"But there have been women."

"Yes, there have been women."

"But only casual."

He shakes his head. "No. I'm no hookup artist. It's complicated, okay?"

"How complicated can it be?" I ask. "You've been with women, but it's never been a relationship… Therefore, it's always been casual."

"There *are* places in between relationship and casual," he says, sounding defensive.

I shift, resting my head a little further onto his pec than his shoulder. "Oh yeah? Like what? And don't say friends with benefits. That's casual sex, just with the same person instead of randoms."

I'm not letting myself think about how this feels. That I'm doing it at all. It's just conversation. It means nothing.

"Like when shit is complicated." He pats my hip. "Your turn."

"My turn?" Like I don't know what he means.

"Yeah. Your turn. Share something of equally personal value to why I call you mama. It ain't my deepest darkest secret, but it ain't something inane, like my favorite color. Which, by the way, is purple."

I consider. "Fine. I'll give you the obvious—what happened to my knee."

He squeezes my hip. "Nope. Save that."

"Why?"

"Cause that's big. Mine wasn't big. It was personal, but minor. What happened to your knee is personal, and big. Shit like that changes your life. Affects who you are as a person. This ain't that kinda conversation."

I huff. "Fine. I guess I just like to get it out of the way. People are always asking."

He lets out a deep, low hum, the vibration of it rattling through me. "I bet. Notice, not one of those folks out there did?"

"Yeah," I whisper. "I noticed."

"We aren't the prying kind."

"This cane." I have it on the edge of the bed beside me, behind me; I lift it over our heads, twisting it in my fingers. "My grandfather made it for me, after the accident. He was a woodworker—as a hobby, not a profession. He could've made a living at it, he was that good. He carved this by hand, from a piece of Brazilian Ipe wood. From what he told me at the time, Ipe is the hardest of the hardwoods to come out of Brazil. Very desirable kind of wood, but very hard to work with, I guess." I examine the cane, as I have countless times; it's a helix, braided sections twisting upward around each other to the sharp, hooked handle and downward to the tip. A simple style, but fascinating and beautiful. "My grandfather was my favorite human. He, um. He passed away just eight months ago, and this is… to me, this cane is *him*. I miss him every day, every hour. I think about him all the fucking time, and I would give *any*-thing, even my other leg, to have him back."

"Sorry for your loss, Annika."

"Thanks."

"So when you said *all* men….?"

I let out a breath. "Asshole," I mutter, not really meaning it this time. "When Grandpa died, the last truly *good* man on earth died."

"Tell me about him." I feel his fingers in my hair, glance sideways to watch him again twirling a curl around his finger, between finger and thumb, his gaze intent, as if my hair is the most fascinating thing he's ever seen.

I find myself wondering, in turn, if his hair is as silky as it looks.

I clench my hands into fists to stop myself from finding out. "His name was Hezekiah—for real. I called him Grandpa Zeke." I swallow hard. "He was…fuck. He was everything good in the world. I get my height from him, he was six-six, about the same as your friend Rev. I think I get my hair from him, too, or so Gram used to say. He kept his short, being a guy, but I guess it was red like mine and would have been curly if he'd let it grow. I remember when I was a little girl, he seemed like a giant, and like he was just…hewn from granite. Everything about him was just *hard*, like literally, physically hard. His hands were *so* rough, you know? Like, he'd pick me up and it was like his hands were pumice. But he was just…pure light and love. Sweet, gentle, and quiet. I went through a goth phase as a teenager—and yes, it looked every bit as hysterically awful with my hair and coloring as you'd imagine. And Grandpa just…accepted me. When I'd go apeshit and get all angsty and difficult, the only person who could get through to me was him."

"Sounds like an amazing man."

I nod. "He really was. He…" I have to pause, swallow. Fight back the burn. "He's really the only real reason I'm even still here. But that's heavy, and for a different day. Like never."

He doesn't fill the silence, and I appreciate that.

Chance

HER STOMACH GROWLS INTO THE SILENCE, loudly.

I chuckle. "Hungry?"

"I could eat," she mutters.

I twist and sit up, taking her with me to the edge of the bed. "Let's rustle you up some grub, then, huh?"

She plants her cane into the floor, presses hard to assist her in standing up—I watch carefully. When Phil, a squad-mate from the Marines, lost his leg from the knee down, I took him to a bunch of his PT appointments as he learned to walk on the prosthetic. There was a guy there who had a gnarly knee injury that looked a lot like hers does. He was determined to rehab the knee until he was back to as normal as he could be, and last time I saw him, he was sprinting hundreds and doing pretty monster back squats. He still had a hitch in his walk, but he was active, strong, and mobile. So either this injury is recent, or she's quit on the rehab efforts, seeing as she can still barely put weight on it. Or, it's worse than I understand, and I'm full of shit.

She moves to her feet, leans her cane against her thigh,

and rakes her fingers through her hair, shoving it back out of her face.

I can't help but stare. She's wearing a denim skirt with a frayed hem, short, a good three inches above her knee; the skirt cups her ass, molded to each cheek with that slight gap in between where the denim is stretched tight, and as she lifts up on her toes in a stretch, her ass goes taut, tightening as she clenches it through the stretch. Her top is a sheer white tank, worn with a black bra beneath it. Her legs beneath the skirt are a mile long, bare, sleek, almost shiny, with thick, powerful thighs and sculpted calves. She's wearing flat sandals with thin black silver-studded straps that crisscross all the way up her calves, ending just below her knee.

God, fucking gorgeous. And that fucking hair. An explosion of almost crimson curls, fiery red ringlets that bounce and shift with each twitch of her body, long enough to drape around her shoulders.

I'm jonesing to bury my fingers in that wild mass of hair, to get those long, long legs wrapped around my neck as I taste her sweetness....

Fuck.

I push up to my feet and out the door, ripping my eyes off of her tight, curvy body. Head for the kitchen. I hear her cane clicking on the floor—she goes to the coffeemaker and pours another cup, leans a hip against the counter and looks at me.

I glance at her. "You eat eggs?" She just nods, eyes on mine over her mug. "How you like 'em?"

She shrugs. "Scrambled with cheese?"

I snort. "Saying scrambled with cheese is redundant. Who the fuck eats scrambled eggs without cheese?"

"Savages?" she jokes.

"Exactly," I mumble. "Great minds think alike, clearly."

I pull a carton from the fridge, a bowl from a cabinet, and start cracking. Seeing as I can eat at least six scrambled on my own, I just crack the whole dozen, and feel her amused surprise the farther through the carton I get.

"I hope you're hungry because there's no way in hell I'm eating even half that many," she says.

I eye her sideways. "You see me?" I pat my stomach—which isn't flat and doesn't sport anything like definition; my abs are more like a solid steel keg than little individual packages, and that keg is wrapped in a dense layer of cladding...e.g., fat. "You don't get this by eating little portions, mama."

Her eyes flit over me, shoulders, chest, stomach. And unless I miss my guess, she likes what she sees. Which is nice. Being best friends with a man who looks like Rev has its challenges—most female attention is fixed on him, if we're together. I'm just the wingman. Not that I've ever minded, really. But it's nice to have female eyes look at me and seem to enjoy the view.

I scramble the eggs, and in between stirs I gesture at her with a loaf of bread.

She shrugs, nods. "Haven't eaten in...well, I don't know what time it is, but since early the day I met you, which I'm assuming is yesterday."

I frown at her. "Why's that?"

She rolls her eyes. "Alvin."

"Elaborate?"

"He had me make a delivery to Reno. But I had to be back here in Vegas for my shift at work, and work was nuts, and then Alvin showed up at work after my shift and demanded I accompany him here. And there just wasn't time to eat except for the Panera salad I had while driving back here."

"You ate a salad while driving?" I ask.

She snickers. "Yeah, and I do not recommend it, at all. Seriously messy, and very difficult. But it was that or McDonalds, so…"

"Salad it is." I sprinkle cheese, stir, sprinkle, stir, and then when it's melted and gooey, I divide it into two portions and set out a variety of toast toppings—butter, jelly, cream cheese, peanut butter. "What kind of delivery?"

She snorts. "What do you think? Meth."

I put the butter knife down at stare at her. "Aren't you working off a debt?"

"Yes."

"Which I assume you accumulated via addiction."

"Yes." This is quiet, almost inaudible.

"You don't seem like a tweaker. Or in withdrawal."

"I'm clean." Her eyes plead with me to believe her, even as her tone remains almost belligerent.

I scratch my jaw. "So…let me see if I'm putting the pieces together correctly here." I finish putting cream cheese and peanut butter on my toast, watch her do the same with butter and jelly. "You had a habit—emphasis on past tense. This habit landed you seriously in debt to a seriously bad dude, and all jokes and insults aside, your guy Alvin is bad news. You got clean, quit the habit, but you still owe Alvin a few large at minimum. For whatever reason, he's letting you work your debt off but not on your knees…*yet*. And you're clean, but once an addict always an addict—and yet you're working for the dealer…transporting the very drug I assume you were addicted to."

"Yeah, well, gotta do what you gotta do, right?" She's dropped her eyes to her toes, now. "Can't say I like it, but it's better than the alternative."

"Recipe for relapse."

"No shit." She shrugs. "There's a bit of a mitigating factor: it's taped up in boxes so it looks like I'm delivering packages—auto parts, to be specific. So, I'd have to cut open the boxes and then rip open the packaging to get at it, and then the guys I'm dropping it to would obviously know I'd stolen product, and then I'm fish food or whatever. Less of a temptation than you'd think."

I huff a laugh. "Bullshit. Every single moment you're in that car with that shit, you're trying to figure out how you can get some without anyone knowing."

She whips her head up to look at me. "You say that like you know from experience."

"Maybe I am."

She looks away from me, and mumbles under her breath. Hard to hear because it's not meant for me, but it sounds like she's telling herself, "I don't wanna know, I don't wanna know, I *don't* wanna know."

I let her have that play for now, because I don't know if I'm ready to give her that story just yet. "How long have you been clean?"

She swallows hard. Still not looking at me. "Seven months and two weeks."

"You said your grandfather died eight months ago."

She nods. "Yes, I did."

"So…?"

A long, difficult silence. "I had thirty days clean. I was staying with Gram and Grandpa. They knew I was trying to get clean. They supported me. Didn't judge me. Gave me a safe place to detox, made me food, sat with me, held me, helped me take showers, all of it. Grandpa, who could barely operate the TV, was googling how to help someone through detox." She chokes up, controls it, keeps going. "Then he died, a massive heart attack in his sleep. Never woke up. And I...I fucking—he was my best friend. The only father figure I ever had, and I couldn't deal. I relapsed. Missed his funeral because I was tweaked out on a couch somewhere. I was broke—beyond broke. Already owed Alvin a fuckload of money, so I knew I couldn't go to him for more. So I..."

"You don't have to tell me any more, Annika," I say.

She nods. "Yeah, this part is pretty fucking ugly anyway. You don't wanna know."

"That's not it. I'm saying you don't have to tell me. It's not that I don't wanna know. I do." I cup her jaw, far enough away that I'm at full arm extension to reach her. "You share what you feel comfortable sharing."

She looks at me, pain in her eyes, and then pulls her face away from my hand. "I honestly don't know why I'm telling you a goddamn thing."

"Because you can tell that I get it. I *know*. Because I think some part of you recognizes on an intrinsic level that I'm a safe place for you."

"There *is* no safe place for me." Balancing her cane on her forearm, she takes her plate and mug to the sectional.

I sit beside her, and we eat in silence. I finish by the time she's on her fourth bite, earning me an amused smirk from her. I set my plate on the coffee table and lean back, feet up.

"I have nightmares," I say, apropos of nothing. "About combat."

She pauses, looks at me. "You do?"

"Yeah. Not all the time, but yeah."

"Why tell me?"

"Something to share." I shrug. "Most of the time, it's the same thing—my boy Julius getting shot in the throat. After Rev, I was closest to Julius. He was with us from Basic through Recon training, same squad, everything. Took a round to the throat. I held his shit together until the medic showed. He survived, but the trauma to his larynx was... fuck, it was awful. He can still barely manage a whisper. I dream of that moment, him beside me, the bullet hitting him, blood everywhere, coming out through my fingers while he chokes."

She sets her plate and fork down on her thighs. "Jesus, Chance." She looks at me. "Talk about heavy."

"Sorry."

At that moment, Silas, Saxon, and Solomon exit the gym, each of them dripping sweat, panting. They head to their individual rooms without a word to each other or us, without so much as glancing this way. I watch her watch them, then look at me.

"Strong silent types, huh?" she says, cracking a grin.

I laugh. "You could say that, yeah."

She finishes her food, sets her plate on mine and kicks back with me, bad leg resting over her good. "Thanks for breakfast."

"Yup."

Silence.

"I can't stay down here forever." She says this quietly.

"Why not?" I ask.

"Just can't. I'll go nuts. I have a job. And no matter

how long I stay, Alvin will still be out there, and I guarantee you he won't forget."

"I'm not saying stay down here forever."

"What are you saying, then?"

I shrug. "I dunno. Just stay, for now. We'll figure out the rest."

"We will, huh?" She looks at me. "You gonna pay my debt for me?"

"Maybe."

"Bullshit." She snaps this. "*Bull*shit. I owe twenty-five grand. You got that much?"

I lift an eyebrow at her. "Good lord, woman."

"Oh fuck off." She hangs her head, shaking it, and then lifts it and looks at me. "Wasn't just meth. Painkillers, too. You wanna be technical about it, it was painkillers first, and then when I tried to quit those, I ended up on meth."

"Frying pan into the fucking volcano, Jesus." I wipe my face. "You don't do things in half measures, do you?"

She snorts a laugh. "No, I do not."

"Tell me something you're proud of."

"What are you, my fucking therapist?" she snaps, but it's with a suppressed half grin.

"Yeah, maybe I am," I shoot back. "There's a surprising amount of downtime in the military, and they provide a shitload of online options for continuing education. I have a degree in psychology." I lean toward her, stage whispering. "Don't tell anyone."

She blinks at me. "No shit?"

"No shit."

"Well aren't you full of surprises." She flips her cane, holding it by the bottom tip, and uses the sharp hooked end to scratch her calf. "Something I'm proud of? Making the US Women's Olympic Beach Volleyball team."

My eyes widen. "No shit?"

She nods. "No shit." She pulls her mane of red ringlets back from her face, holds it with both hands behind her head for a moment, and then releases the hair to fall around her face and shoulders. "I'm from LA originally. Grew up playing beach volleyball. Played indoor varsity in high school, as well as beach ball competitively. Once I graduated high school, I competed professionally. I had endorsements, the whole shebang. I was on track to be one of the best."

I wait. She says nothing else, so I fill in. "And then the accident happened."

She nods, not looking at me again. She uses the hooked handle of her cane to scratch and probe at her bad knee. "And then the accident happened." She looks at me. "It was a freak accident. At the quals. Kelly and I had made it through, and we were celebrating. We'd gone out to eat, had a few drinks—there was a group of us. Me, my teammate Kelly, a couple girls from Ireland, a couple from Sweden. We'd all made it. After eating, we were heading…somewhere else. I don't remember. A bar, maybe? Regardless, we were on the sidewalk, walking together, the group of us. There was a car accident." She sets her cane on the floor, spins it between her fingers, watching the helix move in a twisting spiral. "In my memory, it happens in slow motion, mainly I think because it felt like it was happening in slow-mo at the time. I heard it first—the squealing tires, the horn, the smash. I looked, and I saw the car heading for us. It was a not-quite head-on collision, so one of the cars bounced off the other and was barreling right towards us. I was on the outside, a little ahead of the group, and Kelly was just ahead of me. And I just…I knew the car was gonna hit her. It wasn't a conscious thought, I just…reacted, before my brain even knew what was going on. I pushed her out of the way and then I got hit. The bumper hit my knee and pinned it to the wall. It just…it fucking *demolished* my knee. I don't remember pain, don't remember much of anything, just being pinned, not able to move, laying on my back on the hood, one leg free, the other pinned between the car and the wall."

"Jesus." I shake my head, sighing. "The day you make the Olympics."

"Literally two hours after qualifying."

"Good fucking lord, Annika. I'm sorry."

She nods. "Me too. But thanks. I almost lost it. The leg, I mean. It was so mangled, so fucking shattered that it wasn't clear a reconstruction would even work. It was that or lose it and get a prosthetic. They told me there was a *chance* I'd get normal movement back. Not a good one, but a chance. *If* I worked *really* fucking hard." She laughs bitterly. "It quickly became obvious that wasn't happening. And I…" she shakes her head. "I did not handle it well at all." She barks a bitter, sarcastic laugh, making the comment an understatement.

"I guess that's understandable," I say. "A hell of a traumatic, life-changing event."

She laughs again. "It's *understandable*? Then you're far too understanding."

"Or you're not understanding enough."

"Nah, you're too understanding." She rests her head on the back of the couch, stares upward. "It took several surgeries and months of physical therapy just to be able to walk again. And I swear I fucking worked at it. For *months*. Just to *walk*. I used to be one of the top athletes in the world, and I was in tears just trying to take ten goddamn steps. My career was over. Gone. Done. Even if I did everything right and kept at it and fought like hell, I'll never play competitively again."

"Annika," I start, but she cuts over me, keeps going.

"I didn't see the point. I was too depressed. It hurt all the time. I got hooked on the fucking opiates they gave me to help with the pain. Fought that shit, quit cold turkey. But the pain was…you can't imagine, unless you know from experience. Then I went to a party." She thunks herself in the forehead with her cane. Not hard, just a gesture of frustration and recrimination. "I was out of my mind with pain, angry at myself, at life, at the world. Someone at the party handed me a pipe and told me to take a hit. I didn't think twice. Just said fuck it, why not, and took a hit. Boom. Hooked. That turned into a fun little game where I'd try to quit the pills and end up on meth, then try to quit meth and end up on pills again. Around and around I went, for over a year. Blew through my endorsement money and became increasingly desperate as I ran out of money and got more and more hooked. Started doing unbelievably despicable shit just to get money for a hit. Wasn't long before I alienated my mom and sister, alienated Kelly and everyone I knew from the volleyball world. Everyone. Except Gram and Grandpa. No matter what I did, they let me back in. And they're the only ones I never stole from to feed my habit. I couldn't. Not from them. I almost did. I stole some of Gram's jewelry and was in the parking lot of a pawn shop. But I couldn't do it. And she…she knew. She watched me walk back in, followed me to her room, watched me dump the shit I stole back in her box. And she gave me fucking hug and told me she loved me." This is followed by a sniffle.

I shift closer. "Annika."

"If you try and hug me right now, I swear I'll hit you with my cane." She says this in a small, tight, bitter voice that makes me keep my hands to myself.

"Maybe we put a little pause on the life story," I say.

She lets out a slow breath. "No. It's your turn. What are you proud of?"

"That psychology degree," I say immediately. "Because in order to get it, I first had to catch up because my education stopped at whatever grade you'd be in when you're eight."

"Third," she answers. "Why did your education stop there?"

"Because my parents were murdered when I was eight," I answer.

She swivels her head on the couch, looks at me sideways. "No shit?"

"No shit." I shrug. "Spent a few months in the foster system, but that shit was *not* it, so I ran away. That's when I met Rev, who was an orphan like me, except he always had been. I had parents, I just lost 'em."

"Both at the same time?"

I nod. "Yeah, mama. Both at once."

She closes her eyes. "At *eight*."

"Yeah."

"We're quite a pair, aren't we?" She rolls her head back to stare up at the ceiling again. "What is it about you, though, for real? I can't seem to shut up about shit I *never* talk about. I just met you and here I am dumping my darkest secrets on you."

"It's the psychology degree, probably," I joke, and this gets a snicker from her. "You wanna know how I lost them?" I ask her.

She shakes her head. "Honestly, no. Not because I don't want to know, I just think I need a break from the heavy."

"Fair enough," I say. I grab the remotes and hand them to her. "Entertain us."

———— ◆ ————

Two a.m. Night's almost over. It's been largely uneventful, only a few too-drunk patrons causing the usual ruckus—those kinds of things are almost always solved quickly and quietly, with one look at Rev or me.

Then my earpiece crackles. "Chance, you are needed in Hel, please. There is quite a major disturbance occurring." Anjalee, monitoring the security camera feeds.

"Headed down," I say, turning away from my view of the club from the second-level railing.

I head for the nearest door to the service corridors and then jog to the secure, private stairs leading down to Hel, accessible from both levels. The stairs let out at a hidden door in an intentionally shadowed corner—you'd have to know it was there to know it's there.

Immediately, I see and hear the disturbance. Voices, raised and shouting, a woman screaming. I round the corner into the hallway where the girls have their rooms. A patron has Brie front of him, fist in her hair, a knife to her throat. He's huge, sweaty, overweight, and visibly wigged out on some drug or other.

He's shouting incoherently in a language I don't recognize, threatening Brie with the knife, threatening the small crowd gathered around him. The crowd includes Danni the bartender, topless as always, wearing knee-high platform lace-up boots and skin-tight denim Daisy Dukes, glitter sprinkled on her bare, massive rack. She's closest to him, trying to talk him down in a soothing voice, while others—Candi, Abby, and Tamra—are just being loud and panicky. Toro is there, calm and silent, watching, edging along the wall, hand in his pocket. I catch his eye and give him a hold sign.

He nods, an almost imperceptible lift of his chin, and holds where he is.

I slip my hand in my pocket and grab the roll of quarters I keep there—gripping it in my fist adds weight and solidity to my punch, making my already prodigious punching power damn near deadly. I carry the quarters but rarely need to use them. My mere size is intimidating enough for most people, and if it's not, my unaided punch tends to do the job. But when some asshole has a knife to one of my girls, I'm not taking any chances.

"Girls," I say, "let me handle it. Go entertain the clients."

Tamra, Candi, and Abby vanish, leaving Toro and Danni.

"Dan, I got it." I put a hand on her shoulder. "I'll handle it."

She looks up at me, lifts her chin, and clomps away without a word.

Toro, me, the patron, and Brie. A new girl. Just signed her contract a couple months ago, but already a favorite, especially among the younger guys. She's got a girl next door vibe, with blond hair, blue eyes, big tits on a small frame, and a soft voice. She's a sweet girl, too sweet for the work she's doing, I sometimes think. Inez does the vetting and says Brie can handle it. I got no choice but to trust Inez, but I do worry about Brie.

Seems I was right.

She's keeping it together, but barely. Tears shine in her eyes, but don't fall. She's wearing a white silk kimono with pink flowers on it, mostly opened, revealing a three-inch wide slice of her naked body beneath it. Her left eye is already bruising, and she's got a nasty-looking cut on her cheek opposite her blackening eye.

Rage boils through me.

"Brie, talk to me, babe. What's going on?"

She swallows. "I don't know. I don't know. He paid for an hour, cash. He wanted oral, so I started giving it to him. I didn't—I swear, I didn't do anything. I didn't bite him, nothing. He just went nuts."

The man screams something, gesturing at me, jabbering. The language is European, I think, Slavic or something. He's naked, and red-faced with rage, spittle on his lips, thinning hair sticking to his forehead.

"Hey, man," I murmur, one empty hand out. "Just calm down. English?"

"*Fuck* you, American."

Clear enough, I suppose. "Let her go."

More shouted babbling.

"I don't understand you," I say. "You gotta calm down and speak English. We can't solve this if you're screaming like that, man."

I edge closer.

He shakes Brie by the hair, causing her to shriek, then gestures at her throat with the knife. The threat is clear enough.

I look at him, make a calm-down gesture. "You don't wanna do that, man. You hurt her, you're not walking out of here."

His eyes dart from me to Toro, then behind me. I don't have to look to know it's Rev. The guy understands the stakes; the question is if he's willing to back down or if he's too far gone for that.

I edge closer again. He releases her hair, but grabs her by the chin, lifting, touching the knife to her throat.

"Hey, hey, okay, okay." I back up a step, hand out still. "Just relax. Why don't you put down the knife, huh? Talk to me."

"No talk."

"Then what do you want?"

"She touch!" He switches to whatever language he speaks and gestures at his crotch, angrily.

"You wanted a blowjob, man. She can't do that and not touch you. Sorta the point, my guy." I look at Brie. "How much he pay you?"

"Seven-fifty."

I turn and look at Toro. "Get me seven-fifty from Danni."

He nods, jogs off. Comes back in a minute with a stack of cash, hands it to me.

I extend it to him. "Money back, man. Let her go."

He eyes me, suspicious. "You give."

"Toss the knife and let her go, it's yours. Promise."

He looks at me, still suspicious. Then, with a violent shove, he sends Brie flying. She hits the floor, rolls, her robe coming open completely, and goes still, shoulders shaking as she sobs, curled into a ball.

The moment she's clear, I'm in motion.

His eyes are on the money, first, and then Brie, second—she's on her side, facing us, robe open. Thus, he misses my charge. Or, the start of it. By the time he realizes I'm in motion, it's too late. My fist with the quarters cracks across his jaw, and I feel it give. Teeth go loose. The lower mandible is dislocated.

He screams.

I dance back, slap his knife hand away and slug him hard as fuck in the diaphragm. To his credit, he's still standing. And his eyes are now full of fury.

Unbelievably, he comes at me.

Fucking drugs, man. Not even once.

He slashes at me with the knife, and I dance back, dance back again at another wild slash, watching his hand, his eyes, the angle of his hips. He darts at me, and I'm just barely too slow in dodging—a hot line of pain carves across my bicep and chest, above my nipple. That's his mistake, though—letting me close in. I clench my arm over his, bend it the wrong direction, step out and pivot, slam my palm into the back of his elbow, turning it inside out with a sickening *crunch*. The knife clatters to the floor, and I step in front of him, grab a fistful of his hair.

"Fucking motherfucker," I growl. "Hit one of my girls, cut her, scare her, and then you cut *me*?"

He begs in his language. Don't need to know the words to know begging. Or, well, he's begging as best he can with a broken jaw and missing molars.

"Toro. You and Fonz take this fucker and dump him on the Strip. You know the drill."

"*Sí, señor.*" Toro grabs the man by the hair and drags him away, the naked, broken piece of shit scrambling to find his feet, arm dangling uselessly, drooling blood all over the floor.

Once he's out of sight, I turn to Brie, who's still on the floor. I crouch beside her, lift her up to a sitting position. "Up you go, darlin'." I close the edges of her robe. "Hurt?"

She shakes her head. "No, I'm okay. Just shaken up."

"It was him, you know, not you. He was tweakin' or something."

She nods. "I know." She points at me. "You're bleeding pretty bad. You need stitches."

I look down and realize she's right—my shirt is sliced open across the chest, a good six or eight inches, with another short but deep cut on my bicep. "Oh, shit. Fucker got me good." I peel my shirt off and examine the cuts, peeling the edges open to see how deep they are—it's not good. "Yeah, that's some stitches."

Rev comes up beside me. "You need to get that seen to."

I move away, for the hidden doorway. "Brie, take some time. Got me?"

She nods. "Got you. I'm good, though, promise."

I swipe my card against the reader and shove through. Rev is there with me, doing what I did—pulling at the edges of the cuts gingerly, assessing with a practiced eye. "Deep. You need a doctor, Chance, and I don't mean Doc Adnan."

"I'm not leaving, Rev."

He holds my eyes. "You fuckin' are. This shit's into the muscle."

"What's wrong with Adnan?" I demand.

"Nothing. He's a good doc for the little shit you get in a cage fight. That shit there, it's *deep.*"

I lean back against the wall beside the door, one foot up on a step. "It fuckin' hurts like a bitch all of a sudden."

"Thus, you need to go to the ER." He presses my shirt against my chest. "You're bleeding a lot, brother. You know I'm every bit as much of a hard-ass motherfucker as you, and I'm *tellin'* you, *go* to the ER."

"Club's still open."

He laughs. "We got it, man. We can cover you for a couple hours." He grins at me. "Have your new friend Annika go with you. Better yet, have her drive you."

I shove past him. "Shut the fuck up. I'm not letting her drive."

"When was the last time you operated a motor vehicle, man? Even in the Corps, you never drove. Shit, I'm not sure you even *can* drive."

I bark a laugh. "Fuck you. I can drive."

We're on the way back to the main level service corridor. There are only two ways into our quarters under the building: from the back corner employee stairs, or the side entrance.

Rev halts with me at the door to the stairs. "You're going to the ER?"

"Yes, Mommy, I'm going." I shove him playfully, and he rocks back a few steps.

"Don't fuck around driving with blood loss."

"I'm barely bleeding," I argue.

He cocks an eyebrow at me, and I look down—my shirt is soaked, my belly reddening, the waistband of my pants and underwear going sodden. "Quit being a stubborn little bitch, Chance." He shoves me at the stairs. "Come on."

As we're on the way down, I hear Inez in my ear. "Sit-rep."

"Threat is neutralized. Toro is escorting him off premises," I answer. "Brie is okay. A little shaken but refusing to leave."

Rev chimes in. "Chance is cut pretty badly. He needs medical attention off-site."

"Chance, see to yourself. That's an order."

I shoot Rev a dirty look. "Fuckin' snitch."

He just laughs. "You're too damn stubborn for your own good. Like when you stepped on a nail and did a twenty-mile ruck with your boot full of blood."

"What was I supposed to do, asshole? We were in the middle of fuckin' nowhere. I was gonna, what? Cry about it? Beg X-O for a little break and a Band-Aid?"

"Or a fuckin' bandage, yeah!" He shoots back. "It's called *not bleeding to death*, you dumbfuck."

We shove through the door and the common area, still bickering.

"I didn't bleed to death, though, did I? And I seem to remember being point on the way back."

"Again, because you're the most stupid, stubborn son of a bitch I've ever met."

"You know, I think I liked you better when you barely spoke." I sag against the counter, tossing my sodden shirt into the sink and ripping a long sheaf of paper towel off the roll, pressing it against my chest.

"Chance, brother." He's not joking, now. "Just go. There and back. You can do it."

I hold his eyes. "I can't."

Annika appears, sleepy-eyed. "What's going—HOLYSHITYOU'REBLEEDING."

"I'm good, I'm fine." I try to grin, but it fucking hurts and it comes across as a feral grimace.

Rev glances at her. "He needs to go to the ER. He's being stubborn."

"Stubborn? You're covered in blood, Chance, Jesus." She holds up a finger. "Hold on, let me get my sandals. I'll take you."

She's gone a matter of seconds, dancing toward me as she tries to tie the straps around her calves while walking. She has a small black Patagonia bag slung across her torso.

"Slow down, mama, I'm not gonna bleed out," I say, laughing.

Her eyes blaze. "You damn well could! Look at all that blood!"

"Looks worse than it is," I argue.

"Bullshit," Rev says. "It's as bad as it looks."

I glare at him. "You're not helping, Rev. Fuck off."

He just crosses his arms over his chest. "I'm helping you how you *need* to be helped, not just how you *want* to be helped." He looks at Annika. "There are company cars out in the lot. He can get the key for you. You drive. Closest ER." He gets closer to her, lowering his voice. "Stay with him at all times, yeah?"

"Rev," I call, my voice low and hard. "Don't. Do fucking *not*."

Rev ignores me and my warning. "I'm dead fuckin' serious, Annika. You are at his side every goddamn second. Yeah?"

She peers up at him. "Is there something I need to know?"

"You *get* me?"

She nods. "I get you. I won't leave his side for anything. But what's going on? What am I missing?"

Rev looks at me while speaking to her. "Not mine to say. But it's important."

He rummages in a drawer, comes up with a roll of duct tape, taping the thick wad of paper towel in place over my chest.

As he does this, Annika looks at me, at Rev for a long moment, then back to me. Nods. "Let's go." When I hesitate, she wraps a soft, strong hand around my forearm and pulls me. "Chance, come on."

I grit my molars and let out a rough sigh. "Fuck. Fine." I pull back on her grip. "Gimme thirty seconds to change out of these clothes."

She follows me to my room, watching as I sit on the bed, unlace my boots and toss them aside, then shuck my pants and socks. I glance at her. "Changing my drawers too," I tell her, grinning. "Welcome to watch, if you want."

She reddens and spins on her heel, facing away. I toss my boxers aside, grab a clean pair, step into a pair of shorts, slip my bare feet into my slides. Phone and wallet in my pockets, yank my hair free from the ponytail holder, which I slide up onto my right wrist.

"Ready," I say.

She turns around again, and I'm pleased when her eyes spend a long moment looking me over, head to toe, slowly—appreciation is rife and apparent. She likes what she sees. A lot.

Her appreciation is a momentary distraction.

"Let's go," she says, turning and marching out.

Reluctantly, I follow.

I do so feeling a sensation I'm largely unfamiliar with and mostly immune to: fear.

3

STITCHES, GUNSHOTS, AND CAR CHASES, OH MY

Annika

THERE'S AN OFFICE ON THE THIRD FLOOR OF THE building, down the hall from a command center where the security cameras feed into, monitored, I'm told, by Anjalee. The office is fairly large, an interior room with no view of the outside. There's a large desk littered with paper and folders and clipboards and a computer monitor. On one wall, near the desk is a small cabinet, inside of which are hooks with identical key fobs, each one with the distinctive Mercedes-Benz logo. He takes one. Hanging from a nail in the wall next to the cabinet is a clipboard with a plain sheet of printer paper, on which are scrawled dates, times, and initials—a sign-in-sign-out sheet for company vehicles. Chance scrawls the date and time, glances at the back of the key fob—there's a sticker with a numeral 4 on it, which he adds to the sheet beside the date, along with his initials.

"All right, let's go." He hands me the key fob and leads me back down and through the service corridors to an exit that opens to the side of the club. A wide tarmac separates the building from a row of identical boxy Mercedes-Benz SUVs. There's also a vintage motorcycle parked with them, as well as an older model Wrangler with a lift kit and large tires.

I blip the lock button on the key fob, and one of the SUVs, four in from the left, flashes its lights with a blip of a horn. I climb into the driver's side, realizing this is no normal, off-the-lot Mercedes. Even for the luxury brand, the seat leather is seriously upscale, quilted black leather with red contrast stitching. When I press the pedal and hit the start button, the aggressive snarl of the engine which greets my ears tells me what's under the hood is far from stock as well.

Chance settles into the passenger seat, levering his seat backward to accommodate his muscular bulk as well as his height, and even so his head nearly brushes the ceiling. "They don't make cars for men like me," he grumbles.

"Seat belt," I say, clicking mine into place, and then tossing my cane and Patagonia on the rear bench.

He eyes me, but tugs the belt across his torso and clicks it in, tugging the strap once more to keep it loose, holding it away from the duct taped-in-place makeshift bandage. His jaw is tight, his body posture tense.

I pull back out of the spot and angle for the parking lot exit. I drove Alvin's truck here, so I remember where I'm going. Once we're on the main road with the bright lights of Vegas ahead of us, I glance at him. "You okay?"

"Fine." His voice is hard, quiet, low.

"You wouldn't lie to me, would you?" I try to make it light.

"Just get to the hospital." Not looking at me.

Not looking at anything. Staring into space, jaw clenching spastically—I catch this in the occasional pool of light as we pass under streetlights.

"Chance." I look at him. "What's going on?"

"Nothing."

"Then why do I have to stay near you at all times?"

No answer.

I suspect I know the answer, though. Do I dare voice my suspicion? It's inviting deeper questioning in return, inviting more conversation. And I've proven I have verbal diarrhea around this man, which is a bad thing. I feel safe with him, which should be good, but is actually bad, because *feeling* safe doesn't mean I *am* safe with him. I've learned that the hard way.

I'm torn. Ripped apart, really. I'm attracted to him in a major, major way. Physically, even mentally. He's easy to talk to. He's a good listener. He has a way of pulling things out of me without even trying, and I feel like if anyone could "get" me, it's him. I sense it, his deep understanding of me.

But I'm broken.

Emotionally, I'm a fucking train wreck. I don't know how to trust him. How to trust anyone. I trusted Grandpa, and that was it. Now he's gone and there's no one.

Telling Chance my history wasn't an act of trust. It's just information. Just facts. You take one look at me, the story is there. The knee, especially. Fortunately and through what feels like, most days, a lot of pure luck, I got clean of the meth before it had a chance to really fuck up my appearance—the teeth, the skin sores, all that shit. I was going down that path, though. And I know with a certainty as rock solid as I know my own reflection that if I go back to it, I'll never, ever get clean again.

And Chance was a hundred percent right when he said the deliveries are a fucking nightmare of temptation.

And honestly, only the fact that I haven't figured out a way of stealing any without getting caught has kept me clean so far. I live in terror every single goddamn second of every single goddamn day that I'll relapse. And being in a car with that fucking satanic shit? It's pure hell.

I look at Chance, and he's scratching at a spot on his jaw, under his beard. I know the look on his face, visible in snatches and glimpses. I know the way he's idly scratching, even now, clearly years past the physical addiction and recovery.

"Stop." I reach out, grab his wrist, pull it away.

He looks at me, and his face is a hard, blank mask. Looks away. "Fuckin' Rev and his big fat fuckin' mouth. Seriously liked him better when he barely put two words together all fuckin' day."

"Didn't need what he said to figure it out, Chance. Like recognizes like." I still have his wrist, and he's letting me hold on to it. "I knew already. Or, strongly suspected."

"Bullshit. He gave out shit that wasn't his to give." His voice is that low rumble again, quiet but vibrating with power, with deep emotion.

"He didn't," I insist, glancing at him and then back at the road. "And he didn't give away anything I didn't already suspect from our conversation."

No answer.

"Chance, talk to me."

"Why?"

I frown in his direction. "What do you mean, *why*? I told you, like, eighty percent of the worst shit about me within hours of meeting you. Now you're gonna clam up on me?"

He stares out the window.

"Okay, well I get it. You want *me* to share, but will *you*? Of course not." I let go of his wrist and hold the wheel with both hands.

He looks in my direction—I feel his gaze more than I'm able to actually see his eyes. "My mother was an addict."

I reach out again, touch his wrist, just my fingertips on his skin. Say nothing. Just wait.

"She was an immigrant—illegal, I'm pretty sure. I dunno how, but she got hooked on tweak. Met my dad during one of her clean spells, and they fell in love. What I figure is, she didn't bother to inform my dad of her addiction. Thought she had it beat, so she just kept that little tidbit to herself. Only clean didn't take for her. She got pregnant with me, used while she was pregnant. I was born hooked."

"My god, Chance."

"She used on and off, my whole childhood. I remember it. I remember wakin' up, my dad would be at work, and Mom would fuckin' vanish, leave me with my cartoons and come back hours later, fucked up. I was, shit, like, three, four? You know how fucked up you have to be for a four-year-old to understand you're fucked up and remember that *decades* later?" He shakes his head. "She'd go on days-long benders, drinking, tweaking, doing blow. Doing whatever it took to get either cash for a hit or just the hit itself. Dad would find her and bring her back. I remember the arguments. Him yellin' in her face about how he found her in some meth den, blowing a dealer for a hit. Still he took her back. He always brought her back."

I hear the pain in his voice. Wrap my fingers around his wrist, hold tight. "Chance," I murmur. "I'm so sorry."

"He...fuck, I don't know why he stuck with her. Why

he didn't just take me and…go. Get me somewhere safe. Any-fuckin'-thing woulda been better than just sticking it out like he did. I mean, look, I'm all about loyalty. I get he loved her. And I even can believe she loved him, and me. When she wasn't high or off chasin' the high, she was a hell of a mom. Cooked some bomb-ass food, played with me, took me to the park and shit. But the problem was, her addiction was stronger than her love—for me *or* for Dad."

"That's a shitty thing to know about your own mother."

"Yeah," he agrees, "it sure as hell is."

"You're afraid you're like her."

"Fuck that. I *know* I am." He says this in a voice that's hard and angry and tight.

"You abandoned a child to chase a high?"

"No, Annika," he snaps, "I don't have a kid. I just know I'm that fuckin' weak."

"You think *I'm* weak?" I ask, looking at him. "For getting hooked? For all the shit I told you? And you gotta know there's shit I haven't told you. I haven't told you the worst of it."

He glances at me, head tilted, angled slightly toward me. "You're clean. You ain't weak."

"You're clean, so same for you."

"Because I live in a fucking basement. I never leave that building, Annika. Legit, I've left it *once* in the past two and a half years. That one time, I was with Rev and Kane the whole time, and I was freaking the fuck out on the inside. And I wouldn't have left in the first place if it hadn't been a matter of life or death."

"What happened?"

"Myka got kidnapped by some assholes from Rev's past. Some seriously shitty, not-good assholes working on the orders of a fucked-up, jealous piece of shit cartel boss. They took Myka to try and rile up Rev. Which worked, but not in their favor."

I laugh. "I don't know the man at all, but it doesn't strike me as a good idea to piss off a man like him. He just seems like he's good at doing violent things."

He laughs. "You could say that. We both are. But Rev…he's not just *good* at it—he's *freakishly* good at it. Always has been. Even before we joined the Marines, we were…our lives were not safe or good or peaceful. We were in a gang, if you want the truth. It was a lifestyle that kept us alive, kept us fed, gave us somewhere to live, a group of people to be with. Came with a lot of shit I regret doing, but it was sorta the only choice we had at the time."

I wait, and drive. The hospital is ahead—I see the bulk of it, the lights, the signs.

"You were an orphan, and homeless."

"Rev and me, we were just kids. Little fuckin' kids tryin' to survive on the streets of New Orleans on our own. The guys in our gang, they took us in, adopted us, so to speak. We never fully accepted some of the shit the gang was into, I dunno why. Seems like we both just have a bit of a stronger moral compass, I guess. We had no problem scrappin' for territory with other gangs. That shit was… equal, if you get what I mean: they wanted our patch, we wanted theirs. We all knew the score. We'd move drugs, sell 'em, lean on people who didn't pay, shit like that. But Rev and I never felt comfortable knocking over stores or gettin' in on drive-bys or any of that kinda shit. They also started to get into moving girls. Pimping, transporting, outright selling. That shit wasn't cool with us, and it's why we ended up in the Marines. We were forced to make a choice between letting shit go down that we were not in any way, shape, or form okay with, or do something about it and go against the gang that had taken us in and given us a life."

"You chose door number two," I state.

He nods. "Yeah. Sucked, hard. But we did it."

"I can't imagine." I look at him. "And that's not weak either."

"I want it, Annika. Tweak. Right now, I want a bowl. Mentally, I fuckin' *want* it. I don't think I'll never *not* want it. In equal measure, I'm fuckin' scared out of my goddamn mind of it. Because I know—I fuckin' *know* that shit will…"

"It'll win," I fill in for him, when he trails off. "It always wins. It demands all or nothing. There's no once in a while, no just a little bit. We've got a choice: use and die or stay clean."

He nods. "Yeah."

"I get it, Chance. And it's not weak. Addiction like that is no fucking joke. And it's not weakness."

"If I had it in front of me right now, I can't guarantee I wouldn't use." His voice is ragged.

"Same."

"You drove a car full of it."

"And the only thing stopping me was knowing I'd get caught, and if I get caught, I'll get killed. And knowing the guys Alvin deals with, getting shot in the face will only happen *after* a bunch of other horrible stuff. I guess for now, the fear of getting gang-raped and shot is stronger than the need for a hit. Also, I'm every bit as terrified as you are of what I'll become if I go back to that shit."

"I guess that's fair," he says, a note of bitter humor in his voice.

"You said you were born addicted…" I say, leading.

He points at the hospital, ahead of us. "We're here. We can continue this later."

"Will you, though?"

He just looks at me as I pull to a stop in a parking space in the ER lot. "Probably."

"Let's go get you some stitches," I say, sliding out of the expensive SUV.

I close the driver's door, shuffle to the back door, hold on to the car for balance, grab my bag and my cane, then blip the locks. Chance has waited for me, standing by the front right quarter panel. He's still shirtless, the thick pad of paper towel duct taped around his shoulder and back— the wad is more red than white now. The cut on his arm is seeping as well, but not as badly as the one on his chest.

"You're still bleeding, Chance."

He nods. "Yeah, it's a pretty bad cut. Let's get in there and get this shit done."

The ER is busy, some of the folks with worse injuries than Chance's, others less so. He's taken to triage in fairly short order when they see the amount of blood he's still losing.

I sit in the visitor chair in the room with him—he looks comically huge on the paper-lined table, his feet flat on the floor. Only a slight crinkling hardness at the corners of his eyes and a tightening of his mouth shows that he's feeling anything at all.

"You're surprisingly calm," I tell him.

He shrugs. "Been hurt worse. Doesn't exactly tickle, but it's better than gettin' shot."

I look at him, eyes wide. "You've been shot before?"

He snorts. "Hell yeah. More than once. Ran in a notoriously violent street gang, and then I was an infantry soldier in the Marines and *then* I was a Special Forces operator. Rev and I fought in some of the worst battles in Iraq, and that was *before* we made Force Recon. You don't see as much combat as I have and not get injured at fuckin' all."

"Oh, I guess that makes sense. I suppose I sort of assumed if you got shot, you got out."

He shrugs. "Nope. Only if the injury makes it so you can't go back to work, basically." He looks at me, smirking. "You wanna know, don't you?"

I shrug. "Not if talking about it is going to bring up bad memories."

"Nah," he says. "First time I got hit, I was…fifteen? Sixteen? Just a minor graze, really. Ricochet hit my arm during a dumbfuck shoot-out with some dicks from a rival gang. I didn't even have a gun at the time." He shows me his bicep, the uninjured one, and I can see a faint white line under the ink of the tattoo. "First tour in Iraq, took a glancing round across the thigh. That one wasn't fun. We were cut off from our transport, pinned down—a bad situation. Some asshole just got an angle on me. Bled like a motherfucker and hurt like a motherfucker, but wasn't actually all that bad. Worst one was when I was a Recon. Took a round right to the shoulder." He snorts. "In the movies, they make that seem like the quote-unquote *best* place to get shot, like you get shot in the shoulder, oh well, I'm a tough badass, I can still run around and shoot assault rifles one-handed from the hip and pull myself up the side of a flying helicopter and it'll just look all bloody and cool but really, it's fine."

I laugh. "I'm guessing it's not like that."

He snorts. "Yeah, no. You know what's in the shoulder? Muscle. You know what happens when you get a hole in your muscle? It doesn't fuckin' work. You take a round to the shoulder, that shoulder, shit, that whole arm is fucked. Useless. No matter how fuckin' tough you are, you ain't doin' a goddamn pull-up. Not for weeks, at least. Here's the thing—there is no *good* place to get shot. The whole body is made up of vital, important shit, and if you get shot, it's gonna hurt and that part is not gonna work right until it heals. And even then, after it's healed, it may not be exactly the same. My shoulder wound was pretty bad, because the round hit bone, which meant I needed surgery, and I was out of commission for a couple months. I like Vegas because it doesn't rain here much, and when there's rain, that bone fuckin' hurts." He shrugs. "That said, when you're on an op and people are depending on you, you do what you gotta do, even if it hurts like a fuckin' abomination. You suck it up and you get the job done."

A doctor comes in, then. She's young, pretty, soft-spoken, and seems a little unnerved by Chance. She applies a local anesthetic and sews him up in short order, gives him basic care instructions, and we're on our way.

Halfway across the parking lot, I notice a change in Chance. He slows, his brow furrowing, and he starts scanning the parking lot around us.

I follow his gaze. "What?"

He halts a few feet away from our SUV, pivoting, scanning. "Dunno. Bad feeling." He glances at me. "Unlock the doors for me."

I do so, the light flashing briefly, the horn blipping.

Immediately, there's a squealing of tires from behind us, and Chance shoves me at the SUV, pushing me into a hobbling jog, his body behind me—sheltering me. "RUN!"

I do my best, which is more of a hopping and skipping

motion than a real run, but it covers more distance faster than just hobbling.

POP-POP-POP!

Something buzzes past me with the sound of an angry bee inside my ear, and then the back windshield of the car to my left explodes in a spiderweb of shattering glass, a single round hole at the center of the spiderwebbing, and then the rear left quarter panel of our SUV is dented with another pocked almost-hole.

Chance yanks open the nearest door, the back left, and bodily hurls me in and onto the bench. I land on my belly, my cane thumping to the footwell. Before I'm even fully prone, Chance is in the driver's seat, the engine roaring to life, and we're in motion. My door isn't even closed—I scramble in, twist on the seat, and slam the door closed. There's a loud *thunk*, and the rear glass is pocked by a bullet, but it doesn't even spiderweb, much less shatter. Another round impacts, a third, but the glass only receives two more pocks.

"Bulletproof glass?" I ask.

"And armored panels," he responds.

"No shit." I scramble, with supremely awkward difficulty, into the front passenger seat. "Fancy. So, who's shooting at us?"

He snorts. "The Pope, Annika. Who you think?"

I feel surprisingly calm, considering we were just shot at. "I think I was nearly hit," I tell him.

"What'd it sound like?" he asks, slamming the brakes and hauling the wheel around for a hard right, then gunning it—the back end slides too far, skidding and stuttering in an arc before he rights it.

"What'd what sound like?" I click my seat belt into

place and grab the oh-shit handle as he yanks us around another hard turn, this one a left followed by a pedal-to-the-metal straightaway into another hard right.

"The round when it went past you. You said you thought you almost got hit."

"Like a really big, really pissed-off hornet," I answer.

He cranks us around another turn. "Yeah, that was pretty close, then."

"It sounds different?"

"Yeah," he says. "If it sounds like a snap, it's not too close, but if it's a hum, like a big-ass hornet, yeah, that's close."

He checks the rearview mirror, sucks his teeth in irritation, which I assume means they're still behind us; I glance back and see an older model pickup a car length or so behind us. It's a truck I recognize as belonging to Alvin.

"Yeah, that's Alvin all right," I say. "I'd recognize his truck anywhere."

Chance doesn't answer immediately, instead focuses on another series of turns, each taken too hard, too fast, often skidding too far around and overcorrecting before righting it. "Fucker can drive, I'll give him that. Wouldn't think that truck could move that well."

I sigh. "Yeah, it's his baby. He's always working on it. The engine is souped up, and he's always bragging about some fancy suspension system he's got on it."

"Well, hate to give that shit-stain any kind of credit for anything, but clearly whatever he's done to it worked because this Benz we're in is a souped-up monster and he's having no trouble keeping up."

"He's damn good with cars." I glance in the rearview

mirror, and then at Chance. "Not sure outrunning him is working, Chance."

He huffs. "No shit. I just don't know how else to handle this fucker."

I eye him. "Can't you do some commando shit? Shoot out his tires or something?"

He laughs. "Few problems with that suggestion, mama. One, I don't have a gun, and it's hard to shoot out tires without a gun. Number two, shooting out tires isn't really a commando thing, since we don't really get into car chase shoot-outs, as a general rule. Number three, I've sworn a vow not to take another human life again, under any circumstances." He moves his arm to show me the inside of his bicep—he drives with his knee for a moment, touching a particular tattoo somewhat hidden amid the others, a simple, stylized arrow broken in half, the halves at angles to each other. "Swore an oath and got a branded tattoo to memorialize it. Terms and conditions of my residence at the Broken Arrow compound."

I frown at him. "So you're a Special Forces commando who can't kill?"

"Not can't—won't. And *former* commando. Once a Marine, always a Marine and all that, but I'm officially honorably discharged." He grins at me. "And I swore an oath not to *kill*. Nothing in that oath says I can't really hurt a motherfucker, if needed. And this Alvin punk is getting on my damn nerves."

I glance behind us again, and note that Alvin is still back there, a car length or so behind us. "He's great at getting on your nerves. It's his biggest specialty."

"No kidding." He glances in the mirror again, and growls—a sound of indignant resignation. "Fine, fuck.

Gotta play this the hard way, then." He grips the wheel in both hands. "Hold on tight, mama, this is gonna get gnarly." A pause, a snort. "Especially since I've got zero evasive driving training."

I tighten the belt, grip the oh-shit handle with both hands, and brace my feet against the footwell. Chance slews the wheel over and jams down hard on the brakes— we twist into a fishtailing slide. I suppose it's fortunate all around that it's the middle of the night and we're far from the always-busy downtown area by now. Alvin's truck rockets past us, brake lights bright red, tires locked and screaming as he skids, fishtails, and then the tires spin and smoke as he peels around.

I see Chance's gambit, then—he floors the gas pedal and we bolt forward. The front left corner of our vehicle smashes into the side of the hood, buckling the metal inward. Smoke plumes from the engine compartment of Alvin's truck. Our front left quarter panel is crumpled, the headlight smashed, but otherwise our vehicle is fine. Chance shoves the shifter into reverse, guns it hard, spins the wheel, slams it into neutral as we haul around in a half circle, and then jerks it again into drive, flooring the gas once more.

"Oooh, man," I crow, "if Alvin didn't already hate you, he does now. You just smashed up his baby."

"Not all I'm gonna smash up before this is over," he mutters. Glancing at me briefly, he pulls us away from the still-smoking hulk of Alvin's beloved truck. "Question for you, mama."

"Hit me with it," I say.

"How much weight this guy pull?"

"Meaning what?"

"Meaning, is he a real player? Can he mobilize people to look for us? Or is he a bit player with more swagger than sense?"

"Honestly," I say, "as much as I love to hate him, he's a pretty big player, from what I understand. He's got a corner on the low-life junkie market. He knows the turf he can't get near—he won't fuck with the cartels or the gangs. I've heard him talking about this on any number of occasions."

I brace again as he takes another hard turn, followed immediately by another into a subdivision, where he turns at random until he finds a kids' play park—he squeals us to a stop in a corner, shuts the headlights off.

Chance tugs the seat belt away from his chest, wincing subtly. "So, my question is, if he's determined to get revenge on me and get his money owed out of you, what kind of forces can he muster to find us?"

I lift a shoulder. "Unfortunately, I suspect if he's determined enough, he can get a lot of bodies to do his bidding. Now, the caveat here is that the bodies he gets aren't gonna be the cream of the crop—they'll be people desperate enough to do anything he asks…either for another hit, or to get out of debt."

"In a way, that's worse. In the criminal world, like anything else, there are professionals and there are amateurs. Both are dangerous in different ways. In this, the people you're saying your buddy Alvin can field are gonna be not just amateurs but desperate junkies, and those motherfuckers, as we both know from personal experience, are seriously dangerous." He shrugs. "I'd honestly rather the pros were after us. Desperation is unpredictable."

"So, what now?" I ask.

He lets out a slow breath. "Tryin' to figure that out,

mama. I don't feel good going back to Sin. Obviously, they were watching us there, and I figure they'll still be watching. As long as they're following us, they're not gonna fuck with the others."

"But if they want me, and now you, why would they fuck with anyone else?" I ask.

He shrugs. "I dunno that they would, but you wanna take that chance?"

I sigh. "No, you're right, I don't." I look at him. "But what do we do, then? Where do we go? You're injured, and we can't just…fight our way through all of Alvin's minions. Especially since you're sworn against killing. And knowing Alvin and the assholes he's capable of deputizing, they're not gonna stop just because you clock 'em a couple times. It very well could get seriously violent."

He reaches out and taps the glass where it's pocked by a bullet. "I'd say it already is." He stares through the windshield. "They'll find us here. They know we came into this sub, so it's only a matter of time. So we gotta get back into motion. Put some miles between where we are and where they think we are. A motel, maybe. Somewhere with a back parking lot where we can stash the Benz so it can't be seen from the road."

I roll my eyes. "Yeah, unfortunately I know just the spot." I shove open my door. "I'll drive."

4

CONFESSIONS AND KISSES

Chance

I T'S EXACTLY WHAT I ASKED FOR: A CHEAP, SHITTY, run-down no-tell motel, with a parking lot bathed in shadows. Annika's got cash and I don't, so she pays for the room for the night, with a little extra for the clerk to deny having seen her. I wait in the car while she gets our key. The room is ground floor, a corner room where the L-shaped building angles away from the office.

Inside, the room is what you'd expect: a single queen bed, a thin springy mattress on a cheap frame and box spring, cheap bedding; a TV that was cheap and shitty twenty years ago, with exorbitant rates for pay-per-view porn posted under laminate on the wall; the TV is chained to the pressboard bureau, as is the cable box; the carpet is slightly squishy, for some reason, which makes my stomach turn; there are dead flies in the bottom of the tub, and the toilet is truly and unspeakably vile.

I slump onto the bed after inspecting our room. "Well. This is romantic."

This gets me a snort from Annika. "Only the best for you, dear." She looks at me. "Brave of you, putting your ass on that bed."

I groan, stuffing a pillow behind my head and lounging. "Yeah, well, what are you gonna do? Stand there all night?"

She sighs, and settles herself onto the bed beside me, leaving as much room between us as possible without falling over the side. "Sure as hell not getting under the covers, though."

I close my eyes and let myself settle. "How do you know about this place?"

She doesn't answer for a while. "You need to ask?"

"Guess not." I look at her; she's staring up at the ceiling, features pinched, unhappy. "Not good memories, I take it."

"No," she says, with a soft, sarcastic snort. "Not quite."

It's kind of awkward between us. Stiff. Tense. We don't really know each other, but we share a common bond, and now we're stuck in this situation together. Plus, speaking for myself, I'm insanely attracted to her, physically. I feel like she reciprocates, but it's hard to tell. She plays her cards close to the vest.

"Nope." She says this without looking at me.

I snicker. "Nope what?"

"Don't look at me like that." She laces her fingers behind her head. "That thing you did, back in your room? Not happening again. I was disoriented and freaked out. Don't get any ideas."

"Wasn't looking at you any kind of way."

"You were."

"How was I looking at you, then?"

She moves her bad knee, bending it, straightening it. "Don't play games, Chance."

"What thing I did back in my room?"

She sighs, as if in long-suffering annoyance. "Where you grabbed me and force-cuddled me."

I can't help a burst of laughter. "You say it like I assaulted you with snuggles."

"You did!" She can't quite stifle a giggle. "It was snuggle assault."

"You weren't arguing then."

"I was…taken by surprise."

"You could have gotten up at any time. I asked you to give it thirty seconds, and you did, and you stayed your ass in my arms." I roll to face her, head pillowed on the crook of my arm, bent beneath the pillow.

"Call it a moment of weakness." She remains on her back, eyes on the ceiling.

"Could you rehab your knee more, if you worked at it?"

This gets me a look, and a dirty one. "Sure, to a degree, I guess. I dunno. Believe it or not, it's taken a shitload of work just to get the degree of mobility I have now. But staying clean and trying to get clear of Alvin has sort of taken all my time and attention." She shrugs. "So, yeah, maybe if I train like I'm trying out for the Olympics again, I might get it to a point where I don't need the cane. Or, maybe I'll do all that work and only get marginally more mobility. I dunno. Would it be worth it to half kill myself only to end up still needing the cane still anyway?"

I reach out and pluck at a loose tendril of her hair, twirling the red ringlet around my finger. "Alternate question: would it be worth it to half kill yourself and get at least some degree of your athleticism back?"

"I'll never compete again, Chance." She finally rolls to

face me, not pulling her hair out of my touch. "So what's the point?"

"The point is you're an athlete. I can see it written in every line of your goddamn incredible body. You can get it back. Sure, maybe you won't be an Olympic athlete again. But there's other things to do in life with athletic ability."

She closes her eyes, shakes her head. "Maybe if I'd capitalized on it right after the accident—it was a pretty well-publicized thing." She moves her hand over her face, in a miming gesture of reading newspaper headlines. "'Star athlete's Olympic dreams crushed in tragic car accident.'" Another shake of her head. "If I'd stayed clean I could have translated that publicity into, like, a coaching career or something. Now? No way. I fucked it all up. Kelly, my partner, cut me out of her life. Won't take my calls, won't answer texts, won't respond to DM's on social media. Even after getting clean and staying clean for six months and trying to make amends and all that…nothing. No response. Not one person from the whole goddamn volleyball world wants anything to do with me now that I'm a half-crippled junkie. Or, former, recovering junkie. And yeah, I get that it's the junkie part that has them cutting me off, not the half-crippled part. But I'm still a washed-up junkie who once had a lot of potential."

"I think you're selling yourself short, mama."

She opens her eyes, fixes them on me—endlessly green, fathomless and deep as the ocean. "Wish I was, Chance. But I'm not."

I let go of her hair and brush my thumb over her lips. "You are."

She twitches away, brow furrowing in a frown. "Don't—don't touch me like that."

"Why not?"

"I don't like it." Her hands tighten into fists beneath her chin.

"Liar." I whisper it. "You do like it."

"This the psychology degree speaking again?"

"Yep. I aced the course on how to spot a liar." I trace my fingertips over her cheekbone, brushing locks of hair behind her ear; her jaw flexes, hardens.

She pulls away again. "Quit fucking *touching* me, Chance." She glares at me, sharp anger blazing from her eyes. "Just because we're sharing a bed and a room doesn't mean I'm gonna hop onto your dick."

"Who said anything about that?"

She narrows her eyes at me. "Ah. Right. I'm supposed to believe you're just being all sweet and gentle for the fun of it. Because you're *just that nice*, right?" A quirked eyebrow. "No ulterior motives at all?"

"You remember the promise I made?" I ask her.

She rolls her eyes. "Yeah, you said you wouldn't touch me unless I asked you to. Which clearly went right out the window seeing as you're touching me even after I've told you not to."

"Actually, I promised I wouldn't touch you *sexually*." I touch her chin, just below her lip, tugging her mouth open slightly. "This isn't sexual."

She again jerks her head away. "Stop," she hisses. "Seriously."

I drop my hand. Hold her eyes. "Tell me about your childhood."

"Why?"

I laugh. "Because I wanna know."

"Know what?" she asks. "It was nothing special,

mostly. Grew up in Santa Monica. Mom's a teacher—when I was young she taught high school science. Then once my sister Erin and I were in high school and could mostly take care ourselves, she went back to school, got her masters, and got a job at a community college. We were never hard up to the point of feeling poor, but we weren't rolling in it, either. Lower end of middle class, I guess. I had nice enough clothes, but never the name-brand stuff my friends all had. My sister was the popular one. The pretty one. The funny one. I was Erin's sister, not Annika. 'Hey, you're Erin's sister, right?' Hated that shit with a *passion*." She shakes her head, snorting. "To make it worse, I was freakishly tall, and before I grew into my build, I was awkward, gangly, knock-kneed, and clumsy. I was at least eighty-seven percent leg, and I couldn't make those legs work right, so I was always tripping over my feet and bumping into things. Plus, I have this mop of crazy-ass bright red hair. And let me tell you, it takes a lot of learning to figure out how to make this shit look halfway decent." She grabs a handful of fiery curls and shakes. "Unruly and impossible isn't even halfway accurate, so it was always tangled and frizzy, it would never stay in a ponytail, and I can't braid it for shit on my own. Basically, I was a baby giraffe with wild-ass red hair. Imagine the bullying, if you can."

I laugh. "Oh, I can imagine. Try being six foot tall by ten years old, but so fuckin' skinny you could see my ribs."

She frowns at me. "I guess I kinda assumed you'd have struggled with the opposite issue." Her frown deepens. "No offense."

I snort. "I can see, looking at me now, how you'd come to that assumption. And if I'd had a home and access to regular meals, you'd probably have been right. But I was a street rat. Rev and I were begging and stealing just to eat scraps most of the time, at least until we clicked in with the gang. And even then, food wasn't plentiful or good. It wasn't until we joined the military that I had access to regular meals of decent food and not just junk food from a convenience store." I laugh again. "Point is, I get not fitting in, and I sure as hell understand not really having grown into your body. I was fucking twenty before I felt totally in control of my body, like I'd really grown into the way I was built."

She sighs, smiles. "I had moments of brilliance in high school, I have to admit. By the time I was a senior, I'd mostly figured it out. Because I was always the tallest girl on my team, I played middle blocker, but by senior year I was discovering I was actually more suited for opposite hitter." She smirks at me. "You probably have no clue what those terms mean. Opposite hitter needs to be equally good at both offense and defense, hitting, blocking, receiving serves. It took a lot of convincing for me to get my high school varsity coach to give up her over-six-foot-tall middle blocker to be an outside hitter—mainly because I was really, *really* fucking good as a middle blocker. I just turned out to be even better as an opposite hitter."

"How'd you go from indoor six-person ball to two-person beach ball?" I ask.

She rolls a shoulder. "When I was a freshman, I was at the beach, and I was watching some older girls play. One of the girls had to leave unexpectedly, and they saw me watching and asked me to play with them. I was hooked instantly. It was so intense, so fast-paced, and the teamwork required to be effective with just one other person instead of five other girls is totally different. By then, I'd been playing indoor since sixth grade. So I knew volleyball and I was decent at it. But beach ball was just...different. I would ride my bike to the beach in the morning and meet my friends, and we'd play all day, every day, all summer. Then, summer of sophomore year, a coach for a club in Santa Monica saw me playing, invited me to try out, and that was that. Beach ball was it for me. I stuck with indoor varsity because I'd made varsity as a freshman and we had the chops to make states—which we did, all four years I played. We actually won states senior year. But I played with the beach volleyball club team every spare moment and the coach understood I couldn't commit full-time until I graduated, so that was cool."

"Did you think about college? Or was it professional beach volleyball and that was it?"

She sighs. "God, you ask hard questions. Of course I thought about college. I got offers from a shit-ton of universities. Full-rides, to boot. I got offers from Stanford, USC, FSU. Not all full-rides—if I'd gotten a full-ride offer from Stanford I *might* have thought about it. But my coach on the beach team made it clear she thought I had the potential for far more than just playing college ball. Even then, she had her eye on the Olympics. And I wanted to play volleyball, not do fucking homework." She laughs. "I was a terrible student. I hated school, hated every single subject, hated teachers, hated authority. I hated everything to do with school, so the thought of going to school after I'd just finished twelve years of that bullshit? Hell no. College was a hard no."

I smirk. "So, wait—the attitude isn't new?"

"Shut up."

"I see." I test her mood again—trace the shell of her

ear, then behind her ear, down the line of her jaw to her chin.

She lifts an eyebrow at me. "You just can't help yourself, can you?"

"Nope." I grin. "Other places I'd much rather touch, but I made a promise and I'm gonna keep it."

"Well, don't hold your breath. I won't be begging you to touch me sexually any time soon."

I watch her carefully as she says this—her nostrils flare, her eyes flit away from mine, and there's something indefinable in the way she goes still as she says that which gives her away.

"Liar." I touch her lips again, my thumb brushing across them…for a split second, they part, her eyes going soft, warm, and inviting.

And then, bam—the gates slam down. She tugs her face away from my touch. "I'm not lying."

I wriggle closer. She goes still as a statue, watching me like a rabbit would watch a fox crouched in the grass a few feet away. "You're lying through your teeth. The only question is if you're lying to yourself, to me, or both of us."

"There's that psychology degree at work again," she quips, "or so you think. You don't know me well enough to know when I'm lying or not."

"I do know. I know for a fact you're lying. You want me. You want to know what I can do. How I can make you feel."

"Do not." She snaps this. Brows furrowed. Jaw hard. Eyes harder.

"Do too." I wriggle closer yet, and she moves away, but there's nowhere to go except off the bed. "You want to feel good. You've had nothing but shit. No one taking care of you. No one to give one single solitary flying fuck what happens to you or how you feel. You're tough. You're strong. You're independent. You take care of yourself. You've been through hell and back, and you're still on your feet."

"Shut up, Chance. You don't fucking know me."

"'The lady doth protest too much, methinks.'"

"So now you're gonna quote Macbeth at me?"

"Hamlet, actually. Act three, scene two." I grin. "I almost majored in literature, but I figured psychology might end up having more long-term value. Plus, I love reading and I didn't want to risk having my love for it ruined by overstudying shit. So now, I just read for fun." I touch the tip of her nose. "You probably were thrown for a loop when you saw my bookshelves. Made some more understandable assumptions."

She looks away. "Maybe."

"It's okay. I forgive you. I know I don't look like your stereotypical bookworm."

"I guess also from what you've told me, I'm not sure when in your life you'd have gotten into reading."

I nod. "A good question. Rev and me, when we were homeless, one of the few places we could go when it was cold or raining or whatever was the library. The librarian there sorta took a liking to me, I guess. Rev tended to stick to the magazines and the computers, but I was interested in the books. See, we had to act like we were there for a reason, or they'd kick us out. If we were just loitering— well, two big dirty brown kids scaring off the patrons? Nah. But if we kept quiet and kept busy, the librarian let us stay all day long. She knew what was up with us. She'd make a point of corralling us at a table in the back, and she'd bring little snacks for us. Can't eat or drink in the library, but she knew we were hungry homeless kids, so she was sneaky about it. Didn't make a big deal out of it, for the sake of our egos. She'd bring me books. It was obvious I wasn't in school, and my reading ability was...not great. But between helping other people, she'd spend a few minutes with me here and there, helping me read." I swallow hard. "Her name was Ms. Jones. Pretty, fairly young, quiet, kinda shy, super sweet. She got me a library card, and I stole a backpack, and I'd keep my books in it. I always had that backpack with me. Never let anyone but Rev see me reading, but no matter what was going on with the gang, I always had books. I always went back to see Ms. Jones. Talk to her, get book recommendations. She was the only adult I knew, liked, or trusted. And I mainly trusted her simply because she never tried to...butt in, I guess. She knew the score—knew she couldn't get us homes or back in school or feed us or any of that shit. She did give me a big hoodie once, that was cool. But she just...she was kind and gave her time to a homeless kid. I didn't always smell good, and as I got older, I was big, I was scary, and I was a thug. She never acted scared of me. Just talked to me. Recommended books. She only ever gave me the one thing she could give me, and that was her time and her sweetness, and it's something I've never forgotten."

"You ever go back to see her?" she asks.

I nod. "Yeah. On leave. She didn't work at that library anymore and no one knew where she was."

"Sucks." She says this with a deep frown.

I nod. "It does. I've looked around online but haven't been able to find her." I scooch closer yet, so mere inches separate us.

"Why do you keep doing that?" she demands.

"Doing what?"

"Getting closer. You're all over the place, dude. One second you're talking about how you want to make me feel and then you're talking about a librarian who was nice to you. I can't keep up with you."

I grin. "All part of my nefarious plan, mama. Keep you guessin'." I hold her eyes, assessing her reaction as I trace my index finger lightly over her skin—earlobe, jaw, down the side of her neck, over her shoulder to her bicep, jumping to her ribcage and down her side, until my hand comes to rest on her hip.

"Well I am guessing, but I'm trying to figure out why you keep touching me when I've told you to stop."

"'Cause you don't really want me to."

"Sounds sketchy as hell. You know where else I've heard that? *You know you want it, baby.*"

I feel my eyes narrow, harden, and turn angry. "You think that's what I mean? You think I'm like that?"

She frowns. "Well, no. But it's sketchy, Chance. I've told you to stop."

"You're still in bed with me." I cup her hip. "You're not angry. You're not jumping outta bed, running away from me. You're still here, still talking to me, still listening to me tellin' you shit I don't ever fuckin' talk about. And you're also tellin' me shit I'm guessing you don't talk about much either. So like I said, the lady doth protest too much, methinks."

"You think I'm telling you not to touch me because I actually like it, I'm just playing games? Like hard to get or some bullshit like that?"

I shake my head. My hand still rests on her hip, and I

have no intention of pushing it when I've gotten that win. "No. You're not playing games. I don't think you have it in you to play hard to get. Fact is, you're not playing hard to get because you don't have to play at it. You just are."

"Because I don't wanna be gotten." She looks at me, deep into my eyes, and I see her truth there. "So I'm not playing, and I'm not protesting too much or whatever. I'm telling you, I don't want you that way."

I press my thumb into the denim of her skirt, rub, massage. "There's the lie you're telling the both of us."

"It's *not* a lie." She says this like she's trying to snap it, but can't.

"When was the last time you had an orgasm you didn't give to yourself, Annika?" I ask, my voice pitched low.

"None of your goddamn business." She does snap this, venomously.

"Been a while, I'm guessing."

"I get plenty of action."

"Sexy, badass mama like you? I'm sure you do." I slip my hand a little lower. Closer to the hem of her skirt—her teeth sink into her plump lower lip. "Not what I asked."

"And I said it's not any of your goddamn business when I had an orgasm or who gave it to me." She rolls her eyes, shakes her head. "I know your game, Chance. You think you're gonna be the guy who fixes everything for me, including your perceived notion that all I really need to get over the shittiness of my life is a good orgasm given to me by you."

"I don't think I can fix shit, mama. I know better than that. Nothing like being a helpless fuckin' addict to teach you real fuckin' good that no one can do *shit* to fix a goddamn thing about you, except you. So no, I ain't gonna fix shit. You got shit in your life to fix, *you* gotta fix it. Doesn't mean you can't get help along the way. I had help. I wouldn't be here but for that help—I'd be dead in a ditch in Hawaii. And yeah, I'll give you that story someday, if you want it. But that shit ain't free. Just like the shit you referenced, the worst part, the darkest part. I know that shit ain't free. You ain't gonna just give me that story, I gotta earn it."

"You don't want that, Chance. Trust me. Seriously listen to me and trust me when I say you *do not* want to hear that garbage. And I sure as fuck don't want to tell it."

"Funny, I feel the same way about my addiction and where it led me. But that's the shit that really matters, mama. The deepest darkest shit. When you find someone you can give that to, that's when you know it's real. That *they're* real."

"And you know this how?"

"Watched it happen twice in a row, in a matter of weeks. First Rev and Myka—she showed him a kind of sweetness he never knew existed. She chose to see past the big tough badass exterior he puts on and pulled out the man beneath it. Not that he's not a badass down to his bones—he fuckin' is. But he's more—she *saw* it. He gave her the worst of him. And when that worst got her kidnapped, she didn't hold it against him. She used it to give him even more of that sweetness."

She shakes her head. "I don't have that kinda sweetness to give, Chance. So if you think you're ever gonna get that outta me, I hate to disappoint you but *you—will—not*. You won't get it from me because it doesn't exist. It never did. I'm not that woman."

I smile at her. "I disagree. But that's not for now. That's for later."

She rolls her eyes. "Yeah, okay. So the second time was Kane and Anjalee, am I right?"

"You are. He had some shit in his past that's every bit as dark as yours and mine. He was running from it, hiding from it."

"That doesn't work," Annika says. "Demons follow you wherever you go."

"Yeah, well, you and I also know that even if you know the demons follow you, we also can't help trying to run and hide anyway."

A sigh through pursed lips. "That's the truth."

"She showed him another way. Face it, deal with it, and let it go. Forgive yourself and choose to be better."

"Wish it was that easy."

"Simple, yes. Easy, no."

She quirks her eyebrow, full of sarcasm. "And let me guess, she showed him the sweetness he needed to face his demons and overcome them, and now the beauty and the beast live happily ever after, the end."

I snort. "Pretty much."

"Nice for them. Really. But not everyone gets that ending."

"You're not even interested in trying for it?"

She frowns at me. "You're offering?"

"Would you accept, if I was?"

"You can't offer that to me." She shakes her head. "You're deluding yourself if you think you can."

"I could try. I can't guarantee anything. But I could sure as fuck try." I slip my hand down the denim until I touch skin—smooth, warm, soft. "And I would promise to do my best to give it to you. Everyone deserves a shot at happy, mama."

"Not me," she whispers.

"Why not?" I cup her thigh, the back of it, just above the crease of her knee. "You murder a nun or something?"

A snort of laughter rips from her. "God, Chance. No. I just…don't."

"Because you got hooked on some of the most addictive, destructive shit on the planet?"

"Partially."

"That doesn't mean you don't deserve good, Annika," I say. "You got clean. You're still clean. You're gonna stay clean." I squeeze. "You *fought* for it, mama. And now you're clean, you're alive, and you're on your way to good. Why can't I be part of that path?"

"Why would you want to be?" she whispers. "You barely know me. Just met me."

"Maybe something in my soul recognizes something in yours."

"I did bad shit when I was tweaking, Chance. I did bad shit to get another hit. I've done bad shit so I don't have to pay Alvin back on my knees." She swallows hard. "I *really* don't wanna have to pay Alvin back on my knees, Chance."

"You won't, Annika."

"You don't know that." Her eyes drop, lids sliding closed.

I cup her jaw. "Look at me."

She shakes her head. "No."

"Annika, look at me." She shakes her head, eyes closed tight; I lift her chin, rub my thumb over her lips. "Look at me, mama. Please."

Her eyes open, not wet exactly, but sort of shimmery,

fighting it and losing. "*What*, Chance? You're gonna save me? You're gonna break your vow and kill Alvin for me? Because that's what it will take. He *wants* me. He *wants* me to owe him because he knows eventually I'll get desperate enough that I'll have no choice but to pay him that way. He knows it. He fucking *knows* I will, because I fucking *have*!" Her voice cracks, but it's thin as a razor and sharp as one. "That what you want to know, *Chance*? That I sucked dick to get a hit? That I was exactly that *fucking* desperate?"

I allow no reaction on my features. Not shock—which I do not feel—nor disgust, which I do not feel either. Nor pity. Nothing but, I hope, compassion. "I know perfectly goddamn well what that fucking drug will do. Where it'll take you. What it'll make you do."

"No fucking way you know where it took me, Chance. You're a man. A dealer takes one look at me and assumes if I need a hit, he stands a damn good chance of getting me to blow him for a baggie. He *assumes* it."

"You think I didn't do godawful shit when I was a tweaker? Look at me, mama. People get scared of me when I walk into a room, even if I don't say or do a goddamn thing except exist. People assume shit about me, too. Different than what they assume about you, but they still assume. Need a hit? Guess what, big man, I need a favor. You put the hurt on this dude who owes me a G, I'll give you dime. And guess what? I did it. I kicked a man's door in and beat him fuckin' senseless, right in front of his woman and his kid. All because he owed a dealer a fuckin' measly ass grand, and I needed a fuckin' hit." I hold her eyes. "You think that's any better or easier to live with than what you did, it's you who better think a-fuckin'-gain."

She swallows hard. "You did that?"

"And worse."

"Worse?"

I nod. "I was *gone*, Annika. Man I was *Gone*. I was fully in the grip of some serious PTSD, plus I was drinking like a fish and smoking all the meth I could get my hands on. And the only dealer who would get anywhere near me because I was such a big sloppy mess *used* me. Used my skills at violence. Used my desperation. Turned me on myself. Kept me hooked. Shit, I can't blame it on him, I did that shit to myself. So yeah, I did some evil-ass shit, Annika."

"You're clean now," she whispers. "That's not you anymore."

I smile. "It's not me anymore. I left that sorry piece of shit back in Hawaii. But you take my point, yeah? You gonna hold that against me, Annika? I hurt people. I was an addict, and I needed my drug, and I hurt people to get it. Actually, physically hurt, I'm not talking I stole from them or alienated them because of my addiction. I mean I literally hurt them. Put people in the hospital. Know for a fact I crippled one dude for fuckin' *life*."

"It's not the same."

I snort. "Oh come the fuck on, Annika. Jesus. It's worse!"

She doesn't answer. I palm her jaw, her cheek. Her eyes are closed, wet. "I won't do it again, Chance. I *will not*."

"No, you won't." I brush my thumb over her eye. "Your days of dealing with Alvin on your own are over." Thumb to her lips again. "I've *got* you, Annika."

"You don't have shit."

"I took care of you in the club, didn't I?"

"That was your job."

"Taking you down to my room and introducing you to my people wasn't my job."

Her eyes open, again fiery and stubborn. "You just want in my pants."

I grin. "Damn right I do. Never wanted anything as bad as I want you, naked, riding my cock." I feel her shock, feel her jerk her head back, watch her brow furrow, her jaw drop open. "But that's not why I did that. It's not why I've done anything."

"No?"

"Nope."

"It's altruism, I bet." Sarcasm drips from her words.

"Nope. It's the long game. I could probably get you to fuck me. But I want more than just a one-time fuck with you, so I'm playing the long game. Waiting on getting into your pants because I want more than that. As much as I want to watch your beautiful face as you come for me, I want more than *just* that."

"And what's that?" She rolls her eyes. "Wait no, don't tell me. You want my heart. You want that sweetness Rev and Kane have."

"Damn right."

"Told you," she says, grabbing my wrist and pulling my hand away from her face. "You're looking in the wrong place. I don't have that to give. I'm not *sweet*, Chance."

"And I think you could be. You just need a reason, and the right man to give it to."

"And you're him?"

"Could be. Want to be."

"Why?"

I just look at her—green eyes, fair skin, freckles, explosion of red ringlets. Pure beauty. "Because."

This gets me a snort. "Ah, yes, that romantic reason. *Because.*" Another snort. "What are you, five?"

"Because you're the most beautiful woman I've ever met, Annika, that's why," I say, snapping with impatience. "Because I bet I could kiss you standing up and not have to bend double to do it. Because you fuckin' *get* it—where I've been, what it means, and you wouldn't hold it against me. And you'd know what to look for, if I ever started slipping. Because you're strong. Because I have a feeling once you learn how to trust in what we'd have, you'd have a whole fuckin' *universe* of sweet to give me, and you'd have that to give because you'd be getting that from me—all you need and want and more."

She rolls away, at this. Rocks to her feet, limping away, raking her hands through her hair. "Shut *up*, Chance."

I follow her. She halts halfway across the tiny room, and I only need one long step to reach her. Stand behind her. "Not gonna shut up, Annika."

"I don't have a universe of sweet to give you, and no matter how much you think you could give me, you'd be pouring it down a black hole."

"That'd be my problem to worry about, not yours."

"Why are we even having this fucking discussion, Chance? You don't know me. I don't know you. We just met. This isn't the start of something between us." She shakes her head, ringlets bouncing. Shoulders are tense and tight. Her posture is standoffish. "It's nothing—*we're* nothing. There *is no* we. I'm not fucking you and I'm sure as hell not falling in love with you."

"You want the first and you're just scared the second will happen if we do the first."

She whirls, green eyes spitting sparks. "You've got an answer for everything, don't you?"

I know I shouldn't. It's too soon. She's not ready. But I can't help it.

I kiss her.

It's a surprise to me as much as it is her, that I suddenly have her yanked up against me, my hand snarled into her mass of red curls, the other wrapped around her back, a few inches up from her ass. I'm as shocked as she is when my mouth slams down on hers.

What truly shocks me, though, is when her tongue is the first to taste my lips, the first to demand I open for her. I do, eagerly, and I taste her, feel her lips on mine and her taste her tongue, her breath.

The match is lit, then. Lit, and tossed onto the pile of dynamite that is the sexual and emotional tension conflagrating between us ever since we met.

It's a wild kiss. All teeth and tongues. Her arms are crushed and trapped between us, caught there in the surprise attack of my kiss. Yet, when she twists them out from between us, it's not to push me away. It's to reach up, wrap them around my neck, and pull me down. Kiss me harder. Opening her mouth to mine, she demands more. Her fingers knot in my hair, then release and clasp at my head, my neck. My shoulders—I'm shirtless, as I always tend to be when I'm not on duty in the club. Her palms roam my shoulders, my back, my arms. She lifts up on her toes, pressing her body against mine—sweet soft curves squishing beautifully into me.

My cock rages, hard as a steel I-beam.

I long to fill my hands with her body, but I don't.

I made a promise, and I intend to keep it.

Instead, I take her tongue and I kiss her all the harder.

5

I KNOW YOUR SOUL

Annika

GOD, HIS MOUTH. IT'S FUCKING MAGICAL.

It erases *everything*. The present, the future, and even the past. I always kinda thought nothing could ever erase the stain of filth from my past, but somehow, his kiss manages to do just that.

I've had plenty of partners. A few lovers. A lot of hookups. And there's been a few men who can claim to have gotten there with me only through what I might call coercion—and that's putting it far too nicely.

But none of them have ever kissed me like Chance is kissing me.

He manages to communicate via his mouth, but without words. His kiss speaks to me. It whispers to me. Sings to me. What does it say?

I need you.

I want you.

Kiss me back, Annika.

Yeah, mama, kiss me just like that.

Feel this, mama? There's more where that came from.

I hear it in his voice. But it's wordless. It's in the way he slants his mouth, the way he pulls back and ghosts back in for a new angle, the way his tongue sweeps across my lips, nudges against my tongue. It's in the way his hand tightens in my hair and pulls me up against his mouth, as if I was trying to get away. If anything, I'm seconds from begging him for more.

I feel myself pressing up against him. On my toes, arms around his massive shoulders—I have to reach *up*, and *around*. He's so fucking huge holding on to him is like trying to put my arms around a refrigerator—albeit, a warm, soft-skinned, hard-muscled one.

I want more.

Goddammit, I do.

And I understand now why he made the promise he did—he must know damn well how good a kisser he is. Because I want him. I want to kiss him and I want to feel his hands on my body.

He's got my number, goddammit, and I'm woman enough to admit—to myself, at the very least—that he knows damn well I'm lying when I say I don't want him to touch me.

I do.

I want his hands on my skin. I want him above me. I want him beneath me. I want him inside me. I want to lose myself in him. Right now, I *want* it.

All from a kiss.

He's awakening something inside me that I thought was, at minimum, in a coma, if not outright dead—that being my libido.

That was taken away from me along with everything else good in my life. I haven't *wanted* anyone in a long, *long* damn time. Fact is, I don't remember the last man I felt anything for at all—attraction, lust, or anything other than revulsion, really.

Mostly because for a long time, the only men in my life have been men like Alvin and his ilk.

Chance is different.

In every way there is.

And I fucking know it.

Chance breaks the kiss—pulls away, touches his forehead to mine. "Jesus, Annika."

I'm gasping, breathless, chest swelling against his with my rapid breaths. "You stopped."

"Yeah."

"Why?"

He does it again—his big, rough-padded thumb grazing softly over my lips. "You want more, mama?"

"I—I just—" I have no idea what I'm struggling and failing to say.

Yes, I want more. Am I willing to admit that to him when I've made such a show of pushing him away? No.

He huffs a laugh. "Not there yet, huh?"

He slides his hand from one hip to the other—around my back, low, teasingly low, to the opposite hip so I'm wrapped in his arm. Pulls tight, my body flush against his. I feel his reaction to the kiss—thick, hard, promising. My own reaction is surely just as noticeable—hard nipples, wetness between my thighs, shaky legs. I don't have to shift my weight to spare my bad knee, because he's supporting my weight easily. Just holding me one-handed, his other palm on my cheek, huge against my face—just his palm alone covers my entire cheek, his fingers splayed across my temple, into my hair, behind my ear, and down to my nape. Huge, powerful, yet still gentle.

"No," he whispers. "Not yet."

"Chance," I murmur, but I have no idea what else to say.

He drifts his mouth across mine in a phantom kiss, a tease, a promise. "Not yet, mama. That was a damn good start, though." He dips, bends, and scoops me up in his arms, one behind my shoulders and the other beneath my knees. Carrying my not-insignificant weight as easily as if I weighed no more than a puppy, he strides to the bed and climbs onto it. Keeping me tucked against his chest, he leans forward, nabs a pillow and shoves it behind his head, shifting downward until he's lying with me fully on him, my head on his chest just beneath his chin. A matter of instinct has me twisting to my belly—I'm a belly sleeper anyway.

Fuck me if this isn't the most comfortable I've ever been. He's a firm, warm, solid presence beneath me. His arms are like twin weighted blankets banded around me, one at my shoulders and the other at my waist. He's just holding me.

For a long time, I'm fighting myself. I'm tensed, waiting for his hands to drift, to grope.

They don't.

He just holds me.

I don't know what to do with it. I don't know how to feel. I'm comfortable because I feel *safe*. For the first time in a very, very long time, I feel safe. Which is weird because I know Alvin is looking for us, and he tends to find people when he's looking for them. And now we've pissed him off, ruining his beloved truck. He wants Chance dead—after torture, no doubt. And me? After this, he's probably done fucking around. He gets ahold of me, I don't see good things in my future. No more mule errands, no more playing escort. I'll be, for all intents and purposes, a sex slave; deny, I die. Perform as expected, I live.

Yet, despite the reality and gravity of the situation, I somehow feel safe, simply because I'm in his arms.

Also, he's warm. He radiates heat. His skin is smooth and soft under my cheek. I can hear his heartbeat.

Fuck.

I really, really like this. I don't want to like it. I want to dislike it. I want to dislike him.

I don't.

In the end, I find myself slowly fading into sleep. I can't help it—I'm warm, I'm safe.

———— ◆ ————

I'm woken abruptly and violently—iron-band arms clenching tight around me so hard I yelp in surprised pain, and then an instant of weightlessness and I hit the floor. The impact is cushioned by Chance's arms, and his weight is on me, above me, sheltering me.

And then the world explodes into gunfire. Automatic weapons-fire cracks and barks, and I hear glass shattering, wood splintering, drywall pitting. It goes on forever, it feels like. Softer thuds of bullets hitting the bed where we were moments before.

I hear Chance grunt in my ear.

I'm not breathing, not at all. My lungs burn but I can't manage to suck in a breath—fear has them frozen.

A moment of silence.

I'm airborne, in Chance's arms, moving. Deposited swiftly but gently in the tub; I scramble to my feet, or try to. "Lay the fuck down," he snaps, and I lie down. "Do *not* leave that spot until I say the word 'clear.' If I say 'you can come out now,' you stay the fuck down. If I say *anything* at fucking all other than that one word—clear—you stay the fuck down. Got me?"

I nod once.

"Good."

He's gone.

I hear a loud cracking, splintering noise, of a door being kicked open. There's a gunshot. A *thwack*, a grunt, a cry of pain… *thud*. Another gunshot. Several more grunts with accompanying sounds of fists or feet on flesh. A loud crack, a louder cry of agony.

"Stay the fuck down, bitch," I hear Chance growl. Pause. "Dumbfuck." Another crack, a weaker cry of pain.

More silence.

"Annika—clear." His voice is strong, calm. "You can come out here now, but if you've got a squeamish stomach, you may not want to."

I clamber to my feet awkwardly, hobble out of the tub, and limp out of the bathroom. I halt abruptly just beyond the doorway, lean against the frame, hand covering my mouth.

Chance stands at the center of a pile of moaning, writhing bodies, his massive bare torso heaving deep breaths, hands clenched in loose fists at his sides, hair loose and wild. He looks like a primal warrior god, especially with the spray of blood dotting his chest and face.

One of the bodies has an arm bent *way* the wrong way. Another of the downed attackers looks like he's had his knee kicked in backward. Guns litter the floor. The whole front wall, facing the parking lot, is dotted with holes streaming bright holes of daylight.

Chance's eyes find me. "You good?"

"I'm unhurt, yes." I limp toward him. "You?"

He glances down at himself, shrugs, looks back at me. "Fine. These clumsy dimwits couldn't hit the broad side of a barn with a shotgun."

"That's not your blood, I take it." I twist, snag a towel from the rack just inside the bathroom, toss it to him.

He catches it, wiping at his chest and belly. "Nah." He scans his arms, shoulders, belly again, then chucks a pink-stained towel onto the floor, grabs my cane from the bed and brings it to me. "Come on, mama. Time to make ourselves scarce."

I move toward him, stepping over and around moving, writhing, groaning men. They're street thugs, this much obvious from their attire—sagged jeans, too-big T-shirts, boots, bandanas, backward hats. Definitely the kind of assholes Alvin would recruit for a job like this, telling them it's simple and easy, just drive by, shoot up a motel room, go in make sure they're dead.

They clearly didn't take into account the kind of man Chance is.

He takes my free hand and helps me over the last of the thugs, kicking aside what looks like an AK-47. The door hangs off its hinges, the latch and frame splintered. The sheer number of bullet holes is mind-boggling.

"How did they not hit us?" I ask, as we emerge in early morning daylight.

"Aimed high. Basically, they were just spraying and praying." He mimes holding a gun at waist height and moving it side to side. "One bullet hit the bed, and none came even close to the floor."

I frown. "I mean, I don't know the first thing about shooting people or whatever, but it seems logical enough that if someone hears gunfire, they're going to hit the floor. So if I was trying to kill them, I'd aim low."

He nods. "No shit. These dudes aren't working with a full deck, obviously. I mean, if you want to make sure your target is dead, you can't spray and pray."

"Do you, um, want a gun?" I ask.

He pauses, glances back into the room. "Want? No. Need? Probably."

He shuffles back into the room, kicks aside another AK-47, bends to grab a handgun. He then shoves the near-est attacker over to his back, rifling through his pockets until he finds a magazine. On the way back to me, he ejects the magazine from the handle of the gun, glances at it, and replaces it with a speed and efficiency which speaks of long practice. The pistol goes into his waistband at the small of his back, and the spare magazine in his hip pocket.

"You don't want the AK-47?" I ask as he rejoins me outside in the parking lot. "Seems like you would."

He shakes his head. "Too big, too hard to conceal, too many questions if we're seen with it. Not enough rea-son to carry it, either. I'm not looking to kill anyone, much less a lot of people, and assault rifles are built for one thing and one thing only—killing a lot of people very quickly. A handgun, I can conceal it. I can threaten someone with it. I can toss the components in various places across the city when I'm done with it and no one will ever be able to match the pieces to me."

"I…" trailing off, I stare at him. "Oh."

He turns away from me, looking toward the Benz. "Well fuck."

All four tires have been shot out. The glass has been riddled with bullets on all sides, as has the hood.

"Well that's unhelpful," I say.

"Very." He scratches his jaw, shakes his head. "Stupid. What's the point? They were sent to kill us. So if we're dead, why wouldn't you want to take the truck? Even assuming they have no way of knowing it's a Brabus armored G-Wagen, it's still a fucking G-Wagen worth, base trim, at least a hundred grand. Why shoot it to hell? Dumbass fucking turd-lickers, I swear to fuck."

"It's a what?" I ask.

"Brabus. A tuner company based in Germany. They take stock Mercedes-Benzes and tune shit out of the engines so they're stupid powerful, fix up the interior so they're even more lux, and in this case, they kitted it out with armor." He gestures. "They dumped entire magazines at that thing, and the glass is intact. If we'd been in there, we'd be fine. As is, it probably still runs. We just couldn't see shit, and the tires are flat." He shakes his head again.

"So…now what?"

He scans the parking lot—it's obvious which car the attackers came in. It's an older model Tahoe, lowered so it's only an inch or two off the ground, with giant thin tires and brilliant chrome rims. It's still running.

"Jesus shits," he murmurs, sighing in disgust. "Why slam a Tahoe? Defeats the entire purpose of owning a fucking SUV."

"Slam?" I ask.

He gestures at the vehicle. "Lower it like that." He shakes his head. "A muscle car, or a badass old boat like a vintage Cadillac, I can get it. This is an early two-thou-sands fucking Tahoe. Stupid." He sighs again. "Probably too much to hope that it's bagged instead of just slammed." He looks at me, grins, answering my question before I can ask it. "Bagged meaning air bag suspension. Which has an actual purpose, function, and utility." He opens the driv-er's side door, glances in, hisses. "Nope. Slammed. Shit." He shoves the seat as far back as it will go, slides in, leans the seat way back. "Let's go, mama. Time to get scarce be-fore cops come investigate the automatic weapons fire."

I move to the passenger side, shove my cane in first and use the oh-shit bar to haul myself in. "Well, you may not appreciate it, but I do. It's a hell of a lot easier for me to get into than something lifted way up."

"Wait till we hit a bump, honey. You'll be singing a different tune." He waits till I'm buckled in to shove the shifter into gear.

And, indeed, as we exit the hotel parking lot, we go down a slight curb from parking lot to road, and the jolt is shocking and loud.

"Oh, I see what you mean," I say with a laugh.

"Right. Why? Just why?" He digs in his pocket and comes up with a cell phone. As we stop at a light, he hits a speed dial, puts it to his ear. "Hey, Inez. Yeah, so we've run into some issues. No, we're both fine, but Annika and I are dealing with a real bastard named Alvin, a drug dealer with a vindictive streak. He's a loose cannon so we're gonna avoid the club until I figure out how to deal with his punk ass." He listens. "Yeah, Inez, I'm good, I swear. Annika and I actually have that problem in common, so we'll keep each other on the wagon." More listening. "So, one further, minor issue. We were holed up in a shitty no-tell motel in a not-great section of town, and there was a little bit of a drive-by—no, I told you, we're good, we're safe, I dealt with them and yes, I kept my vow. But the problem is they shot up the Benz…eh, it can probably be salvaged, but it'll be expensive as fuck…no, the fuckers emptied into it, shot out the tires, riddled it with holes, shot up the windows. Yeah, I've got wheels. Shitty wheels, but wheels…" More listening. "Yeah, I'll call in if I need anything. Yeah, if you can find me leverage on this fucker, info, anything, I'd be grateful." He listens again, turns to me. "Last name?"

"Robertson," I say. "His name is Alvin Robertson. And I actually do happen to know where he lives."

His eyes cut from the road to mine, narrowing. "Well shit, woman, share the info. We can pay his ass a visit." He turns his attention back to the road, and the phone at his ear. "Yeah, okay, cool. Thanks, Inez. Let the guys know I'm all good and I'll check in…yeah, if I need backup, I'll let ya'll know. All right. Bye." He hangs up the phone, looks at me again. "Address?"

I relay it to him, and he puts it into a navigation app on his phone. Conveniently enough, there's a phone holder attached to the dashboard next to the steering wheel, and he slots his phone into it.

"What are we going to do when we get to Alvin's house?" I ask.

He eyes me, eyebrow quirked, amusement on his face. "I'm gonna tickle him, Annika. What do you think?"

"Talk to him?"

"Talking is for people with common sense. He hired a bunch of goons to shoot up a motel. Motherfucker clearly ain't got a lick of sense. What I'm gonna do is put the un-holy fear of god in him, in this case god being me. He doesn't have that first fuckin' clue who he fucked with." His jaw goes hard and tight, his eyes cold. "You shoot at me, you best hit me and you best kill me. He didn't. He's gonna regret it."

I shift in my seat, becoming increasingly uncomfortable as we enter Alvin's neighborhood on the west side—a rough, dangerous area. We turn onto his street, and I feel my anxiety spiking.

I point out a car as we approach it. "That's one of his lookouts."

He slams on the brakes and pulls over. "Wait here."

"Um…"

He shoves the shifter into park, exits the Tahoe, and swaggers toward the car I'd tagged as a lookout. His gait is loose, slow, easy—not lumbering, not heavy-footed. He moves far more easily and lithely than a man his size has any right to do. He walks right up to the driver's side, yanks open the door and reaches in, all in one movement, hauling out a young white male dressed in baggy khaki shorts, a tight white tank top, and high-top sneakers with white socks pulled up nearly to his knees. Using both hands, Chance pins him up off the ground against the side of the car, bending his torso backward over the roof. One-handed, then, Chance rifles in the lookout's pockets, withdrawing a cell phone which he drops to the ground and stomps on, then comes back up with a handgun, which he stuffs behind his waistband next to the other one, shaking the thug, threat written in every pore. Chance drops him and steps back. Allows the lookout to get into his car—with a squeal of tires, the lookout hauls ass out of the neighborhood, taking a turn on two wheels.

He eyes the house three doors down from our

location. "Yellow house, white porch, barred windows. Yeah?"

I nod, swallowing. "Yeah, that's him."

His eyes search me. "You good?"

I shake my head. "Nope."

"Talk to me, Annika."

I pause a beat, roll a shoulder. "I don't like being here. Every time I've ever been here, it's been to beg Alvin for a hit. Or to beg him to give me more time to pay him back. I just...I'm freaking out a little." I swallow hard. "Or a lot."

He reaches out and grabs my hand. "It's a new day, mama. Today, you're here to scrape Alvin off for good."

"Just like that?"

He nods. "You got me, now. Nobody's ever gonna fuck with you again, promise."

"You don't know Alvin."

He grins, and it's not a nice, happy grin. "Alvin don't know me." The eyebrow goes up, the grin widening, amused, arrogant. "Trust me, mama. Stick with me, Alvin'll be history. So will your debt."

I swallow hard, hold his eyes. "I want to believe you."

He puts the Tahoe in gear and pulls down the street to Alvin's driveway. There's a Challenger in the driveway, an older model but shiny and clean, still with the tags and stickers from a used car dealership. Parking at the curb in front of the house, he parks the Tahoe and turns it off. Hands me the spare pistol.

He looks at me, gaze hard, serious. "You're outside. Back to the Tahoe, eyes peeled. Anyone fucks with you, pop 'em. Aim center mass. Don't hesitate. I'll be out in a few minutes."

"You mean *shoot* them?"

"If they're a threat, yes." He gestures at the house. "Unless you want to come in and watch me deal with Alvin."

"Actually, I would rather go with you. I don't know if I could shoot anyone."

He nods. "Fair enough." He points at the gun. "Hold on to that anyway. I tell you to use it, you do as I say, no questions. Got me?"

I nod. "Got you."

"Stay behind me. Don't talk. Don't interfere. Just watch, no matter what happens."

"Understood."

He shows me how to use the pistol—how to engage and disengage the safety, how to eject the magazine, and then hands it to me with a stern, serious glare.

"Never draw a weapon on someone unless you're ready to use it to kill them. And if you're not ready to shoot to kill, the safety is on. Got it?"

I nod again. "Got it." I press the safety so it's on and shove it behind the waist of my skirt at the small of my back. Drape my shirt over it. "This is way more uncomfortable than they make it look in the movies," I say, wriggling my spine side to side.

He laughs. "Yeah, well, movies get a lot of shit wrong, especially where firearms are concerned." He exits the Tahoe, pocketing the keys. "Let's go, mama. Remember, stay behind me."

We approach the front door, right up the front walk. Pistol at his back, hands empty, Chance gestures for me to stand behind him and to the side. Then, taking a step back, he lunges forward and plants a kick to the door, just left of the knob. The door frame splinters into shredded shards of wood, the door itself rocketing inward and hanging from the topmost hinge. Immediately, shouts arise. Chance stomps in, and I watch from my place on the porch.

There are four men in the living room—two on a couch, one on a love seat, and Alvin in his customary place in his easy chair, facing the door. There are drugs and drug paraphernalia on the low coffee table—baggies, pipes, bongs, ashtrays, lighters—as well as bottles of liquor and cans of beer and packs of cigarettes.

Alvin is reaching down to the floor left of his chair— he keeps a sawed-off shotgun there, I know. I should've warned Chance, probably. But Chance is there, too fast for Alvin to make the grab. With one hand, Chance yanks Alvin out of his chair and flings him across the room to slam into the two men on the couch. Bending, unhurried, Chance snags the shotgun, a single-barrel, pump-action shotgun with a shortened barrel. He racks the pump with one hand, then tosses it up and catches it, angling it at the tangle on the couch.

"Stay still, fuckwads." Chance steps closer, presses the barrel to Alvin's nose. "Sit. Hands on your head."

Moving slowly, dazed, Alvin wiggles to his ass on the couch.

"Annika, in here. At my side." Chance barks the order.

I move in and stand at his side, slightly behind him.

Alvin glares at me, at Chance. "You're makin' a big fuckin mistake, big man."

Chance grins. "Motherfucker, you don't know shit." He eyes the men on the couch, the other on the love seat. "Empty your pockets. Slowly. I'll shoot your goddamn heads off if you so much as twitch in a way I don't fuckin' like."

The men comply, dumping out packets of smokes, baggies, change, wallets, phones.

"Weapons," Chance snarls.

"We ain't strapped," one of them whines. "Can't come to Alvin's strapped. Everyone knows that."

Chance jerks his head at them. "Pat 'em down, mama." To them, then. "Up. On your feet. Hands laced on your heads. Move slow."

I do as I'm told, patting their waists, pockets, pant legs, ankles. "Clean," I say, and move back to his side.

"Fuck off. And I mean fuckin' *run*." Chance gestures with the shotgun.

The men run, sprinting out the door, leaving their belongings on the coffee table.

Alvin leans back on the couch, arms stretched out, casual. "Now what, bitch? Gonna shoot me?"

"Did I say you could move?" Chance snaps. "Hands on your head. You don't even fuckin' blink unless I say so."

Alvin just lifts his chin, defiant. Stupid.

There's no warning, no wind up—Chance's foot lashes out in a scything sideways arc, smashing against Alvin's cheek. Finishing with a lithe spin, Chance comes back to a wide stance, shotgun back in Alvin's face—from which he's now bleeding, cheek split open, blood seeping from loosened teeth. I'm pretty sure teeth are missing, or a cheekbone is broken, or both.

"Hands…on…your…*head*." Chance bites out each word.

Immediately, Alvin sits upright, hands laced on his head, drooling blood from a jaw that won't close properly.

I wince, watching him bleed. And I realize that Chance doesn't need the guns…they're for show, for intimidation value. He's got no intention of using them unless absolutely necessary.

He *is* the weapon.

He's a badass. And I have to admit, part of me likes watching Alvin get some of his due.

His eyes cutting to me, Chance points with the shotgun at the product on the table. "Dump it in the toilet and flush it all, mama."

"Fuck, no," Alvin moans. "Don't do that. Please."

I scoop up the bags of meth, hands shaking, gut sour, heart pounding. I've not held meth like this—unpackaged, open, visible, tempting—since I got clean. I stare at the baggie of whitish crystals, sucking in harsh, shaky breaths.

"Annika?" His voice cuts through the haze of need, fear, and anxiety. "Dump it. Flush it."

I nod jerkily and move to comply. His bathroom is tiny, dirty, cramped. The mirror is filmed so badly I can't see my reflection in it. The toilet is vile, crusted and stained and unflushed. One after another, I dump the bags into the toilet. Flush. No hesitation. Glee burns in my chest as the water swirls and the poison vanishes, and I feel a weight lift off my chest. Like I can breathe again. Like I've got a piece of my old self back.

I toss the empty baggies into the sink and go back to Chance. "That felt good."

Chance grins at me. "See? You've got the power back, mama. You're in control, not it. Yeah?"

I swallow hard, eyes burning. "Yeah, Chance."

His eyes go back to Alvin, going hard, losing the soft and warm they have when they're on me. "You, motherfucker. I'm gonna make you a real sweet deal, ready?"

Alvin spits blood. "Fuck you."

"You haven't learned?" Chance tisks his tongue.

Tossing the shotgun onto the coffee table, he grabs Alvin and hurls him across the room again, this time with both hands, hard, into the kitchen, where he crashes into a cabinet over the stove. The cheap cabinet crumples under the impact, glassware shattering, and Alvin slams down onto the counter. Chance is there, hand around Alvin's throat, lifting him one-handed away from the counter, feet dangling six inches off the floor.

"You ain't shit, *Alvin*," Chance snarls. "You think I'd give it a second thought to snap this puny little neck of yours?" He squeezes, and Alvin's feet kick, fingers scrabbling at Chance's hand. "Now. You ready to listen?"

Alvin attempts a nod. "Y-yeah," he scrapes. "Listen. Pl—please. Listen."

Chance drops him to the floor, squatting over him. Draws his pistol and jams the barrel into Alvin's mouth. "Now. Listen up, dumbfuck." He waits. Cocks his head. "You listenin' *real* fuckin' hard, dumbfuck?"

Alvin nods, eyes wide. Grunts an affirmative, the sound muffled by the gun barrel.

"Consider this your one and only warning. Annika no longer exists for you. You forget her name. You forget what she looks like. What she smells like, where she lives, who she knows." He shoves the gun deeper into Alvin's mouth, prompting a whimpering gag. "Most of all, you forget she owes you. This is it, Alvin. That's done. She don't owe you shit. Now, I'm gonna pull this gun out of your mouth and I'm gonna ask you some questions, and you're going to answer. If you don't answer in a way I like, I'm gonna drill a round through your balls. Got it?"

Alvin grunts an affirmative.

Chance draws the gun out and jams it, none too gently, into Alvin's crotch. Jerks his head toward me. "Who's that?"

Alvin spits blood, the reddish saliva dribbling down his chin. "I...I don't know." His words are garbled, slurred.

"Good answer." He tilts his head to the side. "She owe you money?"

"N-n-no."

"She ever, ever, fuckin' *ever* gonna so much as catch a whiff of your sorry carcass for the rest of her life?"

"No."

Chance nods slowly. "All right then." He stands up, keeping the pistol trained on him. "That your Challenger out there?"

"Y-yeah."

"Keys."

Alvin digs them from his pocket, tosses them to Chance. "You already trashed one ride, man. Come on. Cut me a break." He spits blood, and I see pieces of tooth in the blood.

"Like you cut her a break?" Chance barks a laugh. "Bitch, please." He turns away, and then pauses, turning back. "Oh yeah. And if you send anyone else after us, I'll find you. Promise. I'll deal with anyone you send my way like I dealt with those wannabe fuckin' punks back at the motel, and then I'll find you, and then I'll break every bone in your goddamn pathetic body. You with me, *Alvin*?"

Alvin nods. "Yeah, yeah. I'm with you."

Chance stares at him. "I don't know that I believe you, shitstain. I kinda worry that you're too stupid to know any better."

"Swear," Alvin pleads. "I'm done. Just…go. Just leave me alone. Please."

"Well…" he sighs, as if coming to a decision. "Fine. But I feel like I gotta make my point crystal fuckin' clear."

"It's clear, I fuckin' swear, bro!"

Too late.

BANG!

Alvin's left kneecap dissolves into red, and he screams. Chance shoves the gun away. "Think I've made my point, now." He looks at me—I'm shaken by the gunshot. "Let's go, mama."

I hurry toward the front door, stomach writhing.

"I see you, I see anyone I think could've been sent by you, Alvin, I'll be back. And no matter where you go, I'll find you and I'll hurt you. I won't kill you, because that'd be too quick. I'll just make you wish I would." I hear Chance's voice, but I need the fresh air, need out of the house. "Best plan for you is to leave Vegas. Go peddle your poison somewhere else. Better yet, get out of the drug game. You got skill with cars, I hear. That's some free advice for you, buddy, take it or leave it."

I feel him approach, a few moments later. "You shot him." I look at him as he steps onto the porch.

He nods, seeming unconcerned. "Yep."

"Why?"

"I could tell he wasn't getting it. I could see it in his eyes. The second we left, he was gonna try some shit."

"You don't know that," I say.

He looks down at me. "Mama—I *do*." His eyes are hard, cold. "I lived that life, remember?" He gestures at the house. "I dealt with dudes like him every goddamn day. I *know* his kind. The lesson has to be harsh as hell or he won't learn it."

"His knee…it'll never—"

He interrupts me. "You gonna lose sleep over a guy like him, Annika?"

I swallow. "No."

"It was a shock, I know." He cups my jaw, and it's a marvel to me that his hand, so large, so powerful, capable of such violence and destruction, can be so gentle. "Now it's done. Alvin is out of your life, for good."

I look through the broken-open door to where Alvin is visible on the floor, writhing and moaning. Then back to Chance. "It's really over?"

His thumb traces my lips. "It's over, Annika. He's not gonna bother you again."

I sag against the porch support. "It's over."

"Your debt is gone. Cleared. Take a breath, mama, and feel the freedom."

"Just like that?"

"Just like that."

"You did that for me." My words are faint, shaky.

"Well, his ass was comin' for me too," he buries his fingers in my hair, his eyes impossibly gentle, "but yeah, Annika, I did that for you. You gotta be free. Now you are."

I look back inside. I see the pipes, the bongs, the empty baggies. I held the poison in my hand, and I flushed it away. Because I wanted to. Because I could.

"I flushed it all away, Chance," I whisper.

"You did."

"I didn't want it. I *wanted* to flush it."

His smile is one of empathetic joy, and I feel it in my bones. "How's it feel to be free and clean, mama?"

I swallow, eyes burning. "I can't even tell you." I look back at Alvin once more. "You don't think he'll recover and still try something?"

"I mean, he's dumb enough it's a possibility. But ain't a damn thing he can do to you, now, Annika. Now, you got somethin' in your life you were missin' before."

I can't help a laugh, an eye roll, and a sigh. "Let me guess…you."

"Damn right, baby." He pulls me up to him, bending to meet me, and his lips slant across mine, pressing hard, his tongue swiping across the seam of my closed mouth, demanding entry, which I give him—his kiss is potent, disorienting and wild and heart-palpitating. "*Nobody* and *nothing* will ever touch you again, beautiful. You got my vow."

I shake my head. "Chance, you barely know me."

"I know you, woman. Have we been acquainted for a long time? No. That shit don't matter. The heart recognizes kindred souls, darlin'. And you and me are that. We're connected. I fuckin' *know* you. I know your soul. I understand the demon that lives in here." He slams his fist over his chest, hard, twice—*thump-thump*. "I know what that motherfucker will tell you to do just to get another fuckin' hit. I know *exactly* how it feels to burn inside and out with the need for that poison. Just like you, I've laid on the bathroom floor, puking my guts out, shaking like a leaf, sweating like a pig, detoxing and hating every single goddamn second of being alive." He touches his forehead to mine, his voice a low, intense whisper. "I *know* you. I don't need to have known you for a long time to know we are fuckin' destined for each other. I knew that in my balls and in my bones and in my blood the moment I saw you. How, why,

I don't know, but I ain't fightin' it, honey. You're fighting it, and I get it. But I'll be here on the other side, ready for you when you finally give up and accept it."

I just breathe, and fight the burn in my chest and my eyes. "Let's get out of here," I whisper, my voice hoarse.

I can't handle him. I can't handle his intensity, his brutal honesty. It's too much. I never wanted a fucking soul mate or kindred spirit or whatever. I only ever wanted to play volleyball, to make the Olympics. And then I just wanted to not end up dead in a drug den somewhere. Then I just wanted to not end up sucking Alvin's dick to pay off my debt to him.

I don't even know what I want anymore.

I can't deal with Chance and his *I know you, woman* bullshit. Maybe it's not bullshit, but it's too much. Especially for right this moment. Right now, I just want to focus on enjoying being free of Alvin and free of the pull of the meth. I know better than to think I can let my guard down, but it's almost as major a step as getting clean in the first place.

He takes my hand and leads me to the Challenger, waits till I have my cane settled before closing the door.

We drive away from Alvin's neighborhood, and I don't know that I've ever been so glad to leave somewhere.

I close my eyes, and I just float and trust Chance to take us wherever he wants to go. I don't care.

For the first time in years, I'm truly free.

6

AN ADDICTION ORIGIN STORY

Chance

I WANTED IT.

I could almost fucking taste it. It was *right there*, baggies and baggies of that shit, plus pipes and lighters and shit. I coulda taken it and there wouldn't have been shit those punk-ass motherfuckers could've done about it.

I watched Annika flush it, and even though I didn't do the flushing myself, I felt a sense of pride. Freedom. There's something in that act, flushing the poison, that makes you feel liberated from the hold it has on you.

I don't have a clue where we're going, I'm just driving west, out of Vegas, away from it all. Annika is lost in her head, staring out the window, silent. I give her that space. God knows I need it myself, to work through my own shit.

Such as, my fear of leaving the club—meaning, my fear that if I leave and go out into the world and live life outside of the safe confines of the club, I'll relapse. Have I been limiting myself, all this time? I don't think so. I wouldn't have had the courage to leave, on my own. I didn't even do it for myself, I did it for Annika.

I have a complex, you see. Because I'm so huge and so strong, I've always felt the compulsion to do more, be more, take on more, simply because I can. I was homeless and starving when I came across Rev, a sad, scared, angry, lost kid, and I helped him. Taught him what little I knew about surviving on the streets. It was the blind leading the blind, but I still felt compelled to help. To be fair, he ended up saving my ass as much as I did his, but still. As a Marine, I always volunteered for the hardest and most dangerous shit. It's a savior complex. I always feel like I gotta save everyone else.

The meth took that right outta me. Made me as pathetic and helpless as someone a quarter of my size. Because with that shit, size means nothing. Strength means nothing. It wins, you die, and you fuck up your whole life on the way to an early grave. And probably fuck up life for a lot of other folks in the process.

Or you get clean.

I never had the balls to get clean on my own. Not like Annika. She chose life, she chose sobriety. She did it. Stuck it out.

Me? I was rescued.

"Penny for your thoughts?" Annika's voice is quiet, cutting through my thoughts with its dulcet softness.

"I didn't choose sobriety." I clench the wheel in a white-knuckle grip. "The man I work for—I don't even know his name. I've never met him. I never will meet him, most likely. I just know him as The Boss. Inez, our direct superior, calls him 'your employer.' He found me mostly dead in a ditch in Hawaii, and basically had me kidnapped. I don't know if he just…saw me and figured he'd do something about me or if he knew who I was and was looking for me, I don't fuckin' know." I swallow hard, thinking back. "I remember trying to get clean. I'd gotten off the junk for about a week. Avoided my usual hangouts, the people and places I knew I'd find meth or be tempted to get it. I made it...two weeks, I think. I pussed out. Weak. Couldn't hack it."

"Chance..."

I shake my head. Keep talking. "You asked, I'm answering." We're in the desert, hauling ass down the black ribbon toward LA. "I owed my dealer several grand, and he wasn't about to hand me anymore without getting paid. But I fuckin'...I *needed* it. I beat him nearly to fuckin' death with my bare hands, Annika. Left his ass in a puddle of blood in his living room, took his whole fuckin' stash, and skipped islands. Hiked out into the jungle and smoked all of it. I think I was trying to OD. Inez told me later that they found me tweaked out of my fucking mind, having smoked enough meth to kill three grown men. Somehow, I didn't fuckin' die. I don't know why I didn't, don't know how I survived when by all accounts I damn well should have. I have no memory of any of it, but Inez says they somehow got my tweaker ass on a cargo freighter.

"That ride was the most pure hell of my life, and I've been through some serious shit. I was literally locked in a room, essentially a prisoner, given food and water, with basic sanitation facilities, and left to ride out the detox, or die in the process. No weaning, no therapy, no chemical assistance. Just me, my addiction, the withdrawal, and that fucking room for *weeks*. My food was brought to me three times a day, simple but good food and clean water to drink. I had magazines and books. No electronics. No human interaction."

I feel Annika's eyes. Feel her sorrow—horror? Something deep, intense. "My god, Chance."

"I went nuts. Raged, screamed, threw myself against the walls. Tore my fingernails out, broke my knuckles pounding on the door, screamed my throat bloody. Thought about suicide, it was that brutal. There wasn't anything I could use to off myself, though, because they'd thought of that too." I laugh. "I've never laid eyes on The Boss—only Inez actually knows the man personally. But yet, I owe that motherfucker my life. I also hate him in equal measure for putting me through that."

"You're still clean, Chance. And that's still something to be proud of."

I shake my head. "It was forced on me. Not like you— you chose it. You lived it. I fuckin' hid in a basement. And I was too fuckin' scared of relapsing to leave."

She reaches out, curls a small soft hand around my forearm where it rests on the manual shifter. "Chance. You were in that house, same as me. You had every opportunity. You felt the temptation, same as me." She squeezes my forearm hard, fingernails digging into flesh and muscle. "You stayed strong. We flushed it down the toilet. It's gone. *We* did that, Chance. Together. So quit selling yourself short, okay?"

I shake my head. "I just…it feels like I cheated."

She laughs at that, and it's not exactly kind. It's overtly sarcastic. "That's bullshit, Chance. There *is* no cheating. We all suffer the same way. You, me, everyone who's ever been addicted to that fucking evil poison. There's no such thing as cheating. However it takes, if you get clean and you stay clean, that's winning. *You* did that. And I almost wish I'd been locked away like you were. Maybe…maybe if I had been, I'd have stayed clean, and I'd have been to Grandpa's funeral."

I hold on to the thought, but I can't stop myself from asking it. "Your gram…"

She swallows hard. "I haven't seen her or spoken to her since I relapsed after Grandpa's death. I…I have an acquaintance. Not a friend. Just someone I know who lives in town near Gram. I call once a month, have her check on Gram. I pay her to check on Gram, make sure she has groceries, a clean house, all that. I…can't bring myself to…to…"

I look at Annika—her green eyes are wet. "Where does she live?"

She shakes her head. "I can't."

I take her hand in mine, tangle our fingers. "Annika—address."

She whispers it to me. "But, Chance, I don't know if I can—"

"You can."

"I abandoned her. She lost her husband of sixty years and I fucking abandoned her to get high."

"I don't know her, so I got no way of knowing how she'll react to seeing you. But I do know you gotta make the effort." I squeeze her hand and glance at her. "You gotta stop leaving messages and sending texts and just show up in front of them. Look 'em in the eye and ask them for forgiveness. Tell 'em you're almost a year clean, and you don't expect them to let you back in their lives but… you want them to know you're trying."

"Have you done that?" she asks.

I laugh. "Got no one in my life to talk to. There was no one for me to alienate. Rev was, at the time, working for a South American drug lord and we didn't reconnect till we were both brought into Sin. Two years, we spent apart. We'd been together every single fuckin' day since we were ten, and those two years were fucking absolute hell without my brother." I laugh again, shake my head. "I'm thankful, though, that he wasn't around for that shit. To see me like that. For me to fuck over. I'm damn grateful." I shrug. "Other than Rev, though, there wasn't anyone in my life. No family, no other friends."

"I thought you were in Hawaii to reconnect with your dad's family?" she asks.

"I was. Who do you think got me on meth? My cousins." I shake my head, huffing a growl.

"No kidding?"

"I wish I was. I tracked 'em down, reconnected. It was cool at first. They seemed like decent dudes. We partied, surfed, hung out. Drinking, sitting around bonfires. They told me about my dad and my uncle, who'd passed in a car accident a few years before I left the Marines. Then one day, they came home with a baggie of some shit, and I was drunk. Hammered off my ass. Wasn't thinking. Figured, fuck it, I know what I can handle. I could always handle my liquor, right? Got nine kinds of fucked up that night, and when I woke up like three days later, I knew I was fuckin' hooked. And my dumbfuck cousins enabled that shit, seein' as they were just as hooked as me."

"God, Chance, I'm sorry."

I nod. "Me too. So, for them, no, there's no going back and making amends. They gave me that shit. I hold myself responsible, because I was the one to take the pipe. No one made me do it. I did it. But they brought it into my life. So I can't face 'em. I can't forgive 'em. I can't and I won't."

She rubs her thumb on my knuckles. "I get it." She nods. "It's different."

"It's different," I agree.

Her grandmother lives in LA, or outside of it, south of it, in Irvine. We stop for gas and to clean up, and for a bite to eat. And for Annika to regroup before we go to her gram's house. But once we're cleaned up and refueled, there's nothing for it but to go. So I go.

It's a tiny ranch-style house in a middling neighborhood. Not great, not awful. Postage stamp lawn needs to be mowed. Driveway is cracked and uneven. Faded blue-gray siding, picture window, some flower beds on either side of the porch with some drooping flowers.

I shut off the engine and sit, watching Annika stare out the window.

"Last time she saw me, I was high off my ass, weighed about thirty pounds less and not in a good way, my hair was tangled and ratted and matted. I had scabs and sores all over my face and arms..." She bites her lip, shakes her head. "She could barely stand to look at me. She closed the door in my face, because she knew she couldn't help me."

"You're not that woman anymore, Annika."

"Gram closing the door in my face hurt almost as much as Grandpa dying."

"She won't close it in your face, now, mama."

"You don't know that."

"No," I admit. "I don't. But it's obvious you're clean. And we're here, so you gotta try."

Her eyes shimmer, wet again. "I don't know if I can," she whispers. "I'm too scared."

I tug the keys free of the ignition and swing out of the car. Round the hood. Open her door and reach a hand down to her. "Come on, mama. You got this. You and me, okay?"

She closes her eyes, then squeezes them tight, a single tear sliding down, and then she nods. Takes my hand and swings her feet out, plants her cane on the concrete, and stands up. Nods again. Sighs with slumped shoulders, and then squares them, head up, tossing her hair with a little shake of her head.

I notice the curtains across the picture window are parted, where they were closed before. It's early evening, sun shining golden and bright.

I hold Annika's free hand as we ascend the curb and make our way up the short walk to the front door. There's no screen or storm door, just the wooden front door, three diamond-shaped windows in the peeling white paint, descending diagonally left to right.

Annika lifts her fist, hesitates, knuckles an inch from the door—she's nearly hyperventilating.

"You can do it, mama," I whisper.

She nods, letting out a shaky breath, and then raps twice on the door.

There's a pause. Locks unlatching. Another pause. And then the door opens, very slowly, revealing a small old woman with pure white hair cut horizontally at her chin. Annika's got her eyes—deep, green, kind, warm. She's hunched, frail, with purple-blue veins popping out of her skin.

"Annika?" Her voice is a low whisper.

"Gram." Annika's is barely audible. More of a gulp and a whimper around a stifled sob.

The little old woman peers up at Annika, eyes sharp, piercing, assessing, intelligent. "Is it...is it really you?"

Annika shuffles forward half a step. "It's really me, Gram."

Her grandmother reaches out and takes Annika's hand,

looking at her arm. Peering up into her face. Hope is bloom-
ing. "You look...well."

"I'm clean, Gram," Annika whispers. "I've been clean
for seven months."

Another long, piercing, assessing look, scanning from
head to toe. "This is the truth?"

Annika nods. "Yes. Seven months, two weeks, and
four days." Annika grabs her grandmother's hands. "Gram,
I...I'm sorry."

A shake of her old, wrinkled head. "Long, long forgiven, my love."

Annika chokes, gasps for air. Drops to a knee, her
good one pressing into the threshold of the doorway. "I'm
sorry. I'm so sorry."

Small, veined hands wrap around Annika's face, pull
her closer, face to belly. Pet her hair, soothing. She clucks,
whispers, shushes. "All done now, dearest. All over. I'm
here, my love. It's all right now."

Sobs. For a long time.

Eventually, her old green eyes come up to mine over
the top off Annika's head. "And you are?"

I offer a smile. "I'm Chance."

"I'm Mary. But you can call me Gram, if you like."
She smiles, then pats Annika on the cheek. "Come now,
darling. Up you go."

Annika reaches for my hand, and I give it to her, help
her up. Annika wipes her eyes, rubs a wrist across her nose.
Lets out a shuddery sigh, and leans against me for a moment. And then she accepts Gram's hand and lets her lead
her into the house.

The interior decoration hasn't been updated in decades, so there's faded wallpaper, threadbare carpet, heavy

oak side tables and a coffee table, a plush maroon couch. A framed painting of Jesus with a rosary hanging beneath it. Rows of framed photos on another wall acting as a timeline of life—Mary and her husband at various ages, as youths in young love, then with a baby, then with the child as a toddler, as an elementary-age child, as a teenager and then an adult—then as a lovely young woman with a handsome young man who I assume must be Annika's father. The next photo in line is not, unlike the previous ones, a studio portrait, but rather a posed family photograph using a timer, in this very room, in front of a Christmas tree; Mary, Zeke, and Annika's mother with two little girls, who I assume are Erin and Annika, at ages perhaps six and eight; Annika's father is absent. The photographic timeline continues, with Erin and Annika aging into teenagers, and her mother and grandparents aging as well. The timeline stops a couple years ago, with the entire family present—this must be not long before the accident; Annika is tall and beautiful, bright-eyed, happy, one arm around her grandfather's waist, the other around her mother's shoulders. A happy family.

Annika's eyes are scanning the photographs as well, and land, as mine do, on the last one. "That was the last time I was happy," she says, her voice quiet but bitter.

Gram clings to Annika's arm, rests her head against Annika's shoulder. "I know, darling. But you'll be happy again." For some reason, she looks at me when she says this, with a knowing smile. "An old woman knows these things."

Annika looks at her grandmother, catches the look at me, the smile. "Gram, really?"

A wink at me, then she tugs Annika through the living room to the kitchen—yellow walls, laminate counters and flooring, appliances as old as the rest of the house. "Come, sit, sit." There's a round white table with four matching chairs in a corner, near a tall, glass-front hutch containing fine china dinnerware. There's a red tea kettle on the stove, steam escaping the lid but not whistling yet.

I sit, cautiously—the chairs look old and delicate, and I'm not exactly a featherweight. The chair creaks under my bulk, but holds.

I see Gram eying me—my stitches, my tats. "Should I ask why you aren't wearing a shirt, young man?"

I snicker a laugh. "Well, nothing to tell, really. I produce a hell of a lot of body heat, so I'm generally more comfortable without one."

The kettle begins whistling at that moment, and she turns off the heat, her eyes going to my shoulder again, the obviously recent stitches. "I thought perhaps it had to do with those stitches." She meets my eyes. "It looks like it was quite the ordeal."

"I'm a bouncer at a club, ma'am. There was a situation, which I handled. It did mean the stitches, but the truth is I generally don't wear a shirt in most circumstances, if I can help it."

She nods. "I see." She looks at Annika. "Mint tea, my lovely?"

Annika smiles. "That sounds great, Gram, thank you."

To me, then. "And you, dear?"

I've never been a tea person, but I shrug. "Sure, thank you."

Three matching mugs, three bags of tea, three careful pours, and then she sits with us, dipping the teabag into the steaming water via the tag and string. Her eyes go to Annika. "So, my dear. Talk to me."

Annika rolls a shoulder. "What do you want to know?"

"Oh, well…everything." A tender smile. "Where you've been, and why it took you so long to come see your grandmother."

Annika swallows hard. "I've…after…" She stares into her tea, dragging the bag around in the mug. "The last time I saw you, when you wouldn't talk to me." Gram opens her mouth to speak, but Annika holds up her hands to forestall it, speaks over her. "It was the right thing to do, Gram. The *only* thing you could do. I'm not gonna lie, it…it fucking hurt, *so* bad. I was strung out, broke, hungry, and alone… but all I could think about was needing a hit. If you'd let me in, there's no telling what I would've done. I'm glad you didn't, now."

"That was the hardest thing I've ever done in my life, next to burying my Zeke." She blinks hard, wipes at her eyes with shaking, curled, arthritic middle fingers.

Annika closes her eyes a moment. "Honestly, Gram, you closing the door in my face is what helped me get clean. I knew if even *you* wouldn't look at me, much less talk to me or let me inside, that I was totally gone. And then one day, about a week later, I woke up and had no idea where I was." She shakes her head, eyes clenching shut, leaking tears. "I don't think I can say it. I can't tell you this."

Gram grabs her hands and squeezes hard. "People think of us older folks as cute and innocent. But you young folks tend to forget that because we're old, we've been around. We've seen a lot. So, Annika dearest, don't think you can shock me. I know exactly what goes on in those drug dens."

Annika looks at me, then at Gram. "I woke up and I had no idea where I was." Her eyes close and I know she's remembering, relating as she recalls it. "It was filthy. The first thing I saw when I woke up was a water-stained ceiling. Like, it was sagging, peeling, about to collapse in on me any second. The walls had once had wallpaper, but it was peeling off in chunks, and the wall beneath it was just…rotting, water stained, god knows what. There was a window, so dirty you couldn't see out of it. Dead insects on the windowsill." A shake of her head. "I remember it all, *so* vividly."

A long pause. Eyes still closed. Disgust and revulsion carve her features into a twisted rictus.

"I was in so much pain. Everything hurt. It was like the worst hangover ever, times a thousand. The floor was… so nasty. Dead bugs. Rat shit. Ants and roaches just out in the open, crawling around. They were in the fucking *bed* with me. I was naked. I…I couldn't—I still *can't*—remember anything. Not for days back. I remember you closing the door. I don't remember where I went, how I got meth, what I paid for it, who I got it from. I had no idea where I was." She shakes her head. Tears leak. "It was obvious I'd been…used. Passed around. There were used condoms all over the floor. Dried…stuff…all over me. All over the bed. In my hair." Her hands clench into fists and press into her eyes, hard. She's shaking, barely able to manage a whisper. "Alvin came in, while I was trying to figure out where the fuck I was, what had happened. He explained to me that I'd offered myself in exchange for drugs. So he invited his friends over and…let his friends do what they wanted to me, in exchange for getting me high. He said I'd been there, doing that, for almost two days."

Gram sucks in a sharp, shaky breath. "Ohhh, honey. Ohhhh, my god. Nikki, my love." She leaves her chair, moves behind Annika and wraps her arm around her from behind, kisses the top of her head. "I'm so sorry, my love. I'm so sorry."

Annika makes a low, high-pitched keening noise, an almost feral growl of raw pain. "You're *sorry*? *I* did that, Gram. I *did* that. Thank fucking *god* I don't remember. Thank god." She covers her face with both hands, rocking back and forth. "I swore, right then, no more. Never again."

"It's over now, my love." Gram kisses her crown again, clinging tightly. "All done. It's all done, my love."

"They'd stolen my fucking clothes. As souvenirs, I guess, I don't know. I begged for an old T-shirt and some shorts of Alvin's just so I could leave that fucking hellhole. I walked…so many miles. Bare feet. Starving. Everything hurt. My soul hurt. My body was…" She trails off, shaking her head. "I went to a homeless shelter at a church. They let me take a shower and gave me clothes. They fed me. They gave me a bed and I just laid there, detoxing. I don't remember much after that, other than agony. Mental, emotional, physical, everything…it was just pure unadulterated hell. I wanted to die. I thought I was going to die. And more than once, I lay there and welcomed it, begged God to just let me die, rather than live with knowing what I'd become."

I slide my hand, palm down, across the table toward her. She peeks through her fingers, looks at my hand, at me, and then extends her hand to me. I wrap her small, delicate hand in mine. "Get it all out, mama."

"If I ever felt like I wanted a hit, whenever the cravings hit, which was oh, every other minute, for days on end, all night and all day—I'd think about waking up in that vile, roach-infested hellhole, covered in semen, used by who knows how many men, just so I could get high. I'd think about that. Remind myself of it. I'd tell myself I'd *whored* myself out for *meth*. And that knowledge? It was horrible enough that it helped me beat the cravings." She moves her hand in mine, tangling our fingers together. "Alvin found me in that shelter. Showed me he had a gun hidden in his waistband, and reminded me that he could find me, he'd always find me, that I owed him. What I'd done in that hellhole hadn't paid any of my debt, it just hadn't added to it. He reminded me I owed him twenty-five thousand dollars and told me I either had to pay him or work for him. Or he'd take what I owed him however he felt like taking it. And we both knew what that meant."

Gram takes her seat, her eyes lingering on Annika's and my joined hands. "You owe someone *twenty-five thousand* dollars, Annika?" Her voice is quiet, but alarmed.

Annika looks to me. I look to Gram. "I took care of that for her."

Gram's eyes cut from Annika to me. "Do I want to know what that means?"

I smile, hoping it doesn't look too frightening. "Probably not. Let's just say I...convinced him...to relinquish his claim."

Gram's kind green eyes contain a surprising note of hardness. "It seems like a big brute like you would be rather convincing."

I let some of my innate primal fury shine through. "You might say it's what I do best."

She nods at me, then takes a tentative sip of tea. "Well then, I'm glad my Nikki found you, Chance."

"I am too." Her lower lip trembles, just slightly, just for a moment.

"We have some very important things in common,"

I say, holding Annika's eyes. "In helping her, I discovered I was helping myself."

Gram's eyes settle on me, then. "You were an addict, too, then." It's a statement.

I nod. "I am. Recovered, and clean, but…once an addict, always an addict. The only question is if you're still a user or if you're clean."

She nods. "My Zeke, he had problems with the drink. It nearly drove me away from him before he gave it up."

Annika sets her tea down with a shocked thud, liquid sloshing over. "Gram—*what*? I had no idea!"

Gram tilts her head to one side, with a shrug of a shoulder. "He kept it to himself, and I respected that wish. It was no one's business but his and mine. It was well before you were ever born, anyway, my dear. In fact, I doubt even your mother remembers him having been a drinker. He went through AA when your mother was…ohhh, four or five? By the time you and your sister came along, he'd been sober for thirty years." She smiles at Annika. "My point in sharing this is that I do understand the power of addiction. He couldn't do it for me. He could only do it for himself. The motivation and the strength to find sobriety, no matter the substance, must come from within. No one can make you do it or make you want to. And this is something I understand. Even thirty, forty years later, Zeke confided in me that being around someone who was drunk made him uncomfortable. Because a part of him still craved it, even all that time later."

Annika looks at her grandmother for a long, long time. "So that's how you knew you had to…" she trails off, swallows hard. "Let me go."

Gram nods. "That's how I knew, my love. Because I'd

been there with your grandfather. He would come home at all hours, barely able to keep himself upright, having driven our vehicle in that state. He was never violent with me, but he…" She inhales a soft, short breath, lets it out with a shudder and a shuttering of her eyes before continuing. "The things he would say. I knew it wasn't him—it was the drink. But the heart doesn't know that even if the mind does." She's quiet a moment. "I…I told him that I'd always love him, always, no matter what. But he was going to have to choose between alcohol and his family. Because I just couldn't keep allowing that awful spirit the alcohol put into him in our house."

"What was it that made him get sober?" Annika asked.

Gram doesn't answer for a while. "He's passed now, so I suppose it's all right to tell you." Another moment or two of thoughtful silence. "He didn't come home one night. He went drinking after work, and he just never came home. I waited up all night. I called the police, the hospitals, but there was no sign of him. So when morning came, I packed up your mother and your aunt and your uncle and I went to my parents' house in Arizona. He had our only vehicle, so I had to take all three of our children, who were all under seven years old at that point, by myself, on a bus from Los Angeles to Flagstaff." She sighs. "He showed up more than a month later, hat in hand, begging me to come home."

"What happened? Where had he been?"

Gram shrugs. "Oh, he'd pulled his usual stunt, got drunk after work and tried to drive home. But he got lost, drove off the road into a ditch or something, and woke up some time past midday, alone and hungover in a wrecked car. By the time he got the car towed out of the ditch, got it running, and got home, the kids and I were long gone.

And he knew where I'd gone. I'd told him, if he didn't get sober I'd take the kids to my parents' house. So he knew that's where we were."

"Why'd it take him a month to go find you?" Annika asks.

"Because he knew I wouldn't even look at him if he hadn't sorted himself out. So he checked himself into a treatment center. He went through a thirty-day program, and then he came to get us."

Annika sips tea. "And you went home with him?"

Gram holds her mug in both hands. "Yes, I did. I was scared. I was worried it was…not faked, but…I suppose I was worried it wouldn't last. But it did." She smiles down at her mug, but it's a slow, sad smile. "He says when he came home to an empty house, all of our clothing packed up, everyone gone, it just…shook him to his core. He knew, in that moment, he was done. He'd never touch alcohol again. And he didn't. Not till his dying day."

"My god, Gram, I had no idea." Annika lets go of my hand and rests hers on Gram's hand. "Not even the slightest clue."

"I'm not surprised, my dear. He was very private about it."

Annika nods, looking into middle distance, thinking. "I guess I just never really thought about the fact that there was never alcohol in this house." She looks at Gram. "Did you give it up because he did?"

A shake of her head, bobbed white hair shaking. "No, dear. I never took it up. I'd watched it take my uncle and my older brother, as well as a very good friend of mine. I knew what it could do, and I never touched it. Zeke didn't take up drinking until after we were married, or I would never have married him. I've always felt very strongly about it, and my history with alcoholism made it even harder to watch him fall into it. I was very close with my uncle, and I never really knew my older brother because by the time I was old enough to understand these things, he was already fully in the clutches of the bottle."

"So you've *never* drank?"

Another shake of her head. "No, dear. It just never appealed to me."

Annika lets out a breath. "Wow, Gram. It feels weird to me that I never knew this stuff."

"Part of growing up is seeing your parents, and I suppose in this case, grandparents, as *people* and not just as your parents or parental figures. Your grandfather didn't want you to know. He was embarrassed, later in life, that he'd ever let it get as bad as it did, and wished to simply let it be in the past. His addiction is also a large part of why he was always so understanding and compassionate toward you when you were using." She sighs. "And why it was so hard for him to watch you go through what you did."

Annika swallows. "I just…I wish he could see me now. Sober. Clean. Looking forward to…" She shakes her head, shrugs. "Figuring out what I want to do with my life, I guess, now that I feel like I've got it back."

"He would be extraordinarily proud of you, my darling girl." Gram pats Annika's hand where it rests on hers. "He would be *so* proud."

Annika blinks hard again, heaves a sigh. "Thank you, Gram."

7

REUNITED

Annika

THERE'S A KNOCK AT THE DOOR, AND GRAM glances over her shoulder at the green numerals of the clock in the range. "Oh, my goodness. In the excitement of seeing you, I'd almost forgotten they were coming over this evening!"

The knock is followed by a voice. "Mom? Whose car is that out front?"

My mother.

I feel the blood drain from my face. "No, no, no." I clutch the mug in my hands, my whole body going so tight and tense it hurts. "I'm not ready—I'm not ready!"

Gram twists her hand so she can clutch mine. "Steady now, sweetheart. It's for the best." She smiles at me, reassuring and calm. "This was entirely unplanned, of course, since I couldn't have known you would be coming today, but it really is propitious timing." Louder, then. "In here, Emily!"

I'm not breathing; I can't. The last time I saw Mom, I'd stolen three hundred dollars from her and smoked it all, and then stole her car and was caught and arrested for trying to trade it for drugs. She hadn't pressed charges and she'd gotten her car back intact, but she'd stood in front of me in the police station and told me, tears in her eyes, that she never wanted to see me again.

Erin had held out a bit longer. Continued to take my calls, continued to try to reach me, begging me to get help. It wasn't until she caught me trying to steal her ATM card—for which I knew the PIN—that she realized how far beyond help I was. She'd ghosted me, then. Refused to speak to me or see me.

After I'd gotten sober, and had six months clean, I'd tried to contact them. I'd left messages saying I was clean, and that I wanted to apologize in person. I'd gotten no response. Still haven't. And that was over a month ago, almost two months ago, now.

Mom enters the kitchen and stops in the doorway when she sees me, pain flashing in her eyes before they shutter. "Dammit, Mom." Her voice is cold and angry. "I thought I made it clear—"

Erin catches up behind Mom and moves beside her in the doorway—her hands go to her mouth and her eyes immediately fill with tears. "Nik?" Her choked gasp of my name cuts off Mom.

Gram looks at Mom and lifts her chin. "Come in, my dears."

"I don't think so." Mom begins to turn, not giving me another glance; my heart aches, and my eyes sting as I understand the reconciliation I was hoping for doesn't seem likely. "Let's go, Erin."

Erin ignores Mom. "Nik, honey, are you..." She squeezes past Mom and dodges Mom's attempt to catch her arm, coming straight to me, sinking to her knees in front of me, hands on my thighs. "Nik. God, Nik. You... you look..."

I nod, tears clogging my throat and blocking my voice; I tangle my fingers together in an anxious knot of white knuckles. "I'm clean, Erin," I whisper. "Almost eight months."

"Erin," Mom snaps, "come. *Now*."

Erin looks over her shoulder at Mom. "*Look* at her, Mom!" This is snapped, angry. "I told you when she called that we should—"

Mom's eyes waver. Her chin wobbles. "She made promises before, Erin. She promised she'd get clean. She *tried* to get clean. And she still lied and stole, and—"

Erin shoots to her feet and stomps over to Mom, gesturing at me as she shouts. "She never made it a fucking *week* before, though, did she? Look at her, Mom! *Look* at her! She's clean. She's healthy. She's here with Gram, and you know Gram wouldn't—"

"Annika didn't betray her like she did me," Mom says, her eyes going to me, finally.

I look like Mom. Mom is tall—not quite as tall as me at just under six feet, but still taller than average—with my wild, curly hair and a lot of curves. Her hair is brown, but otherwise, I'm damn near a spitting image of her. The red, I've been told, is a recessive genetic trait inherited from Gram's side of the family.

Erin missed the height and the curls, being on the taller end of average at five-eight, but she shares our eyes and our tendency to bottom-heavy curviness. Erin is beautiful, with brown hair that hangs pin-straight and thick, with delicate features and a sweet, calm disposition. Unless riled, like she is now.

"She's your *daughter*," Erin snaps. "She's my sister. I won't turn my back on her. Not if she's clean." She turns and addresses me. "If you relapse, I can't—I won't…" She shuts her eyes, shaking her head a few times, and then again meeting my gaze again. "But if you're really, truly sober…"

"I am, Erin. I swear I am. I'm sober for good. Forever. No matter what. I won't relapse." I stand up, move cautiously toward her and Mom. I look at Mom. Not daring to breathe, to hope. "Mom, just…give me a chance. Please."

"I gave you *so many* chances, Annika," Mom says, voice thin and trembling. "Again and again. I let you back in my house, back into my life. I dragged you out of crack houses. I picked you up from alleys. I fed you. I bathed you. I gave you money. Even when you started stealing from me, I'd forgive you and let you back in time and again. But you kept going right back to the drugs."

"I *know*, Mom," I whisper. "I understand if you can't… if I can't have you in my life. I get it. I ruined…everything…and I get that. But I…all I want is to be able to look you in the eyes, just one time, and tell you I'm sorry. I'm so, *so* sorry, Mom. I don't even expect you to forgive me. I know you can't. I know I can't ever pay back what I took from you. I can't fix it. I can't make it better." I lose the ability to speak for a moment, crying too hard—I drop my chin to my chest and squeeze my eyes shut as burning tears stain my lips and drip from my chin.

I look up, finally, as Mom just looks on, eyes wet but her expression otherwise unreadable. "I love you, Mom. And I'm sorry."

Mom shakes her head. "I *want* to believe you." She shakes her head again. "But just because you're clean and don't *look* like you're on drugs doesn't mean I can—"

Chance speaks up, then, his voice quiet—but even quiet, it's still a deep, gravelly, booming sound. "She faced her former dealer. She faced him and she flushed his drugs down the toilet. I watched her do it."

Mom looks at him. "Who are you?"

"My name is Chance. I'm…a friend. Of Annika's."

"What kind of *friend*?" Mom asks, suspicious, alert.

"The kind who knows exactly what Annika's going through, except I don't have any family to make amends with." He holds Mom's eyes. "You only get one family. And what you may not understand is that her addiction and recovery was impossibly more painful and difficult for her than it was for you. Not minimizing what you went through, because I know damn well how that shit makes you act and how it affects the people around you. But what I also know is that family is a precious thing. She's *here*. She's *trying*. She's your daughter, and you're gonna keep punishing her? Because I know for a *fact* she's punished herself far worse than anything you could do or say. Except to not forgive her, one more time. That's probably the cruelest thing you could do."

I look at him. "Chance, enough. It's okay. I get it. I haven't…I never told you all the shit I did to Mom and Erin." I move away from my mother and rest my hand on his shoulder. "It's fine. I said what I needed to say. We can just go." I bend over Gram and rest my face on her head, inhale her scent, kiss her hair. "I love you, Gram, so much. Thank you for…well, letting me in, and listening to me, and most of all for forgiving me."

Chance rises to his feet, and I see Mom's eyes widen as he reaches his full height, taking in the impossible breadth of his shoulders, the mammoth wall of his enormous chest, his long hair loose around his shoulders, his tattoos, his huge, dense arms and treelike thighs. Erin is frozen, staring up at him in something like a mixture of awe and fear.

Which I get. Boy, do I get it.

Chance moves for the doorway, and Mom scuttles into the kitchen and out of his way, as if he is threatening her merely by being close to her. He stops, looks way down at her. He says nothing, but reproach radiates from him.

I press up against his back, press my palm between his shoulder blades. "Chance," I whisper. "It's okay. It really is."

He shakes his head. "I'd do anything to have my parents back." He stares down at Mom even as he speaks to me. "I'd stop at nothing to get even five minutes with them."

I choke. "Chance. This is different, honey."

He tenses when I use that word. I don't even know where it came from. His head pivots and he twists until he can look me in the eye. I see a hint of a smile, a glimmer in his eyes. "It's not. It's easy to hold on to shit when you know they're still out there. Easy to hold on to grudges and shit." He looks back to Mom. "You got a shot at having your girl back, Emily. She's here. Fuckin' *look* at her, and I mean *really* look at her, goddammit. You'll *see* it. You'll see that your girl's back, for real, and for good. All you gotta do is grab on and say three little words."

Mom peers past him, at me. Finally, for the first time since arriving, she really and truly looks at me, and not just *at* me, but *into* me. I let her look. Let it all hang out in my gaze—sorrow, regret, fear, love, hope.

And then...

Mom crumples, sobbing.

Chance catches her, holds her up, turns her to me, and my arms go around her middle. Mom finds her feet and latches onto me. Her arms go around my neck and her face goes into my cheek. For several moments, we just cling to each other.

"My girl, my baby." It's barely intelligible. "It's really you."

"It's me, Mom. I'm here." I cup her face. "Look at me. I'm healthy. I'm *okay*."

Mom's fingers touch my face, my cheeks and my chin and my jaw—touching places where I once had sores and scabs from scratching—feather through my hair, which is now clean and cared for, rather than tangled and matted and filthy. She runs her hands over my forearms, also healed and sore-free. Finally, she just rests a hand on my face and looks into my eyes for a long, long time. I let her.

"My girl." She reaches out for Erin, who moves in and we hug.

The three of us, all together, hugging all at once like we used to.

Mom pulls back. "I love you."

Chance laughs. "I meant, 'I forgive you,' but that'll work too."

————◆————

It's late. Or, early. I'm not sure what time it is, only that Gram, Mom, Erin, Chance, and I spent hours in Gram's kitchen, talking. Gram made dinner, and then we had ice cream for dessert. Chance related some of his story. Mom informed me that she'd sold the house I'd grown up in and now lived by herself in a one-bedroom condo not far from here and was about to finish her doctorate—with plans of moving up to the university level as a professor, after a decade of lower-level teaching at the community college.

Erin was engaged, I learned, to a man who worked in her office building. They've been living together for a year—I remember him, an attractive, kind, quiet man a few years older than Erin, a perfect match for her. He'd only proposed a few weeks before, and I oohed and ahhhhed over her ring, a beautiful princess cut single-carat.

Finally, well past midnight, Mom had to leave, since she had a nine a.m. class to teach. Erin left with her, having ridden to Gram's with Mom. Gram had gone to bed shortly thereafter, with hugs and kisses for me, and a smile for Chance, with a reach-up to pat his bearded cheek, and then instructions for us to use her spare bedroom.

That left Chance and me alone in Gram's kitchen.

Silence hung between us for a long while.

Chance, toying with a spoon, looks at me. "So." He looks at me. "Better?"

I nod, fighting emotions. "Yes." I'm sitting kitty-corner from him at Gram's table. "I can't even tell you."

He nods. "Good." He tosses the spoon back into the empty bowl and leans onto the table, toward me. "Alvin's dealt with and you're reunited with your family. What's next?"

I shake my head. "No clue." A tilt to the side. "Well, that's not true. There's one more person I need to see. Or at least try to."

"Your partner?"

I nod. "Kelly."

"She live in LA?"

I shake my head. "Not anymore. San Diego."

"You want to stay and visit with your gram, or head down to see if you can connect with Kelly?"

I swallow hard. "I don't know," I whisper.

He lets out a breath. "I think you've had enough for one day, mama."

I nod, holding my breath, eyes closed. "I'm…" I swallow again. "I'm really overwhelmed by today, Chance."

He stands up, extends his hand to me. "Come on. Let's crash, yeah?"

I nod. I've been sitting for a few hours so my knee is stiff and sore—I have to lean hard on my cane as well as pulling hard on Chance's hand. Once vertical, I keep hold of his hand for balance and stretch my knee to loosen it. Then, I lead him to the guest room—it's across from Gram's room. It's been the same for as long as I've been alive: a queen bed with a handmade flannel quilt over a thick wool blanket, a pale pink floral sheet set with four thick pillows. White, lacy curtains over the window. Next to the door, a white bureau with fancy scrollwork at the feet and corners, a porcelain dish of potpourri on top. A painting of a pastoral scene over the bed, a classic red barn with pine trees in the background and chickens in the foreground.

Chance turns back the covers, kicks off his slides, and slings a hip onto the bed, reclining half on the bed, one leg trailing on the floor. He's watching me. I don't know what to do with myself.

"Lay down, mama."

I look at him. Shirtless, massive, beautiful. Comfortable. At ease despite the unfamiliar surroundings and the intensity of the day. "I…" Another hard swallow, my throat thick, my tumultuous emotions roiling just beneath the surface, a confusing, churning welter of too much.

He sighs. Moves to his feet and stands in my space,

touches my chin to tilt my face up. "Annika, babe. You've had a hell of a day." He rests his hands on my shoulders, tugs me closer. "Take a deep breath for me."

I suck in a deep breath, hold it, let it out slowly. And again. And again. On the third breath, I find myself falling forward until my forehead meets his breastbone. Which is, in itself, a surreal feeling for me. I've never been with a man I fit with like this. But then, I never knew a man like Chance existed, either. Yet, here he is, and here I am. His arms circle me, gather me closer. I shuffle a half step, and his hips are there against mine, his belly against mine, his chest against mine. His arm cradles me close. His breath is slow and steady and even.

He holds me like that for an amount of time I couldn't begin to measure. Then, he pulls back. "Shoes off, mama."

I comply, lifting one foot and removing my sandal without looking, then the other, tossing them with a soft thump to the rug near the foot of the bed.

"Skirt."

"Chance—"

"Just gettin' comfortable, that's all." He brushes a thumb over my lips. "This ain't the time, and this ain't the place, okay? Not for that. Not what you're afraid of."

I narrow my eyes at him. "I'm not *afraid* of that, Chance."

He just grins, lazy, cocky, and teasing. "Yeah, you are. But that's for later, not for now." He bends and touches his lips to mine, a ghost of a kiss. "Skirt."

Swallowing hard, I unzip and unbutton my skirt, then I have to shimmy my hips and tug the hem to get the skirt past my hips. A few dancing tugs, and the denim slips down my legs to the floor. His eyes remain on mine. "Arms out. Do the bra thing."

I smirk. "The bra thing?"

He shrugs. "You know. Arms inside the shirt, and then voila, there's the bra."

I laugh. "Oh. That."

I do as he suggested—ordered?—arms inside my shirt, unhook it, slip off the bra, arms through sleeves, and then hang the bra off the corner post at the foot of the bed. Shrug my shoulder with my hands lifting palms up. "And now?"

He bends, scoops me up, slips onto the bed and tosses the covers over us. He scoots down, scrunching the pillows under his head. My face is nestled on his chest, my body resting entirely on his. It's becoming familiar, at this point. Comfortable—and comforting.

His hands rest on the small of my back, in the thin slice of bare skin between my thong and sheer white T-shirt. Roam up. Under the tee, skating over bare skin, exploring my back—scratching up and down, smoothing his palms in circles over my skin.

Comforting.

Tender.

"Chance—"

"Shush, Nik." His voice is a breath in my ear. "Relax. I got you."

Nik.

No one's called me that in so long. Only Mom, Gram, and Erin ever used that diminutive as a nickname for me. I missed it. And I really like it from him.

I don't have the energy to fight it.

To fight him.

To fight how comforting and soothing he is, how safe and sheltered I feel. He stood with me. Protected me. Went to bat for me, spilled blood for me. Brought me back to my family.

How do I stay above that? How do I avoid feeling things for him when he does things like that for me?

I don't.

"You scare me," I admit, the words whispered to the soft warm firmness of his chest.

"I'll never hurt you, Annika."

"I know. I don't mean like that."

"You mean you're feelin' shit, and *that* scares you."

I nod. It's the most of an admission I'm capable of, at the moment.

"I told you, babe. I *got* you."

"You're not scared?"

He lets out a breath. "Sure I am. I saw how Dad was. He loved my ma so much, it drove him to stick with her when it was the worst thing for everyone. He loved her so much, it got him killed and left me an orphan. Objectively, he ought to have let her go, let her have the drugs. Let the drugs have her, more like—right? Shit. Maybe I'd have had a dad if he'd have done that. So yeah, mama, I'm scared fuckin' stupid of loving someone like he loved my ma. Scared it'll make me as stupid and blind as it made him."

"Then how can you say you've got me, if you're as scared of this thing between us as I am?" I lift up and look at him.

"So you admit there *is* something between us." His eyes, so brown they're almost black, hold mine.

I nod. "Yes, Chance. I can't deny it at this point. Doesn't mean I like it, doesn't mean I want it, doesn't mean

I have the first fucking clue what to do with it. I'm scared absolutely shitless of it. But it's there, and I can't deny that much. Not after today."

He gives me the thumb brush over my lips again. "You know what courage is, mama?"

I shrug. "Not being afraid."

He shakes his head. "Flat wrong. Courage isn't not being afraid. It's being afraid and doing what's right, what you know you gotta do even though you're pissin' your pants." He wraps a tendril of my hair around his finger. "I was scared shitless every time I went into combat, Annika. Every damn time. Scared I'd catch a bullet with my name on it. Scared I'd step on an IED and end up legless. Scared Rev would catch one and I'd watch him die. I was always scared, Annika. I just learned how to do the damn thing anyway." He smiles at me. "No different with you. Yeah, I'm scared I'm falling for you, and you won't feel the same. Or you won't want me back. I'm scared I'll go all in for you, like I always do—one hundred and fifty fuckin' percent, all the way in, nothin' held back, and you'll just be like, 'nah, not worth it. Too scared. Can't do it. Sorry, big man.'"

"Chance…shit. I—"

"I'm scared as hell." He continues over me. "You decide you can't or won't do this thing with me, it'll…" He lets out a breath, eyes closing briefly before fixing on mine—open, full of emotion, deep and dark and wild. "It'd break something in me, babe. Not gonna bullshit you. But I'll survive that too. And lookin' at you, holdin' you, kissing you…it's obvious to me the possibility of you—the *potential* of you is worth the risk of heartbreak."

The potential of me is worth the risk of heartbreak.

That's too much to process.

So, I don't. I lay my head on his warm, soft chest and I feel his heartbeat, hear it faintly, and I push everything else away.

Eventually, with his large strong gentle hands scratching and soothing over my back, I fall asleep.

Dreamless and deep.

———— ◆ ————

I wake up gradually, drowsy and warm and comfortable. The first thing I'm aware of is that I'm still lying on top of Chance. I don't have to open my eyes to know that he's asleep—I feel it, sense it, hear it. His breathing is slow and even, drawing in long slow breaths and letting them out even longer and slower.

I feel more rested than I have in years—in fact, every time I sleep in Chance's embrace, I sleep better. Not sure that bears thinking about, just yet.

The next thing I'm aware of—and I become aware of it immediately and acutely—is the placement of his hands.

On my ass.

Cupping possessively, resting, fingers naturally curled. I'm wearing a thong, a skimpy piece of fabric over my yoo-hoo, and a string around my hips, and not much else. Meaning, my ass cheeks are totally bare. I was too tired and overwhelmed and emotional to care about this last night. But now, with his hands on me, I'm very, very aware of it.

I swallow hard. Mainly because…I like it. His hands feel good. Right. Natural. Each of my cheeks fill one of his big hands, and let's just say I've got a lot of butt—more so now, since getting off drugs and getting back into regular, and probably more than regular, meals—which means his hands are *big*.

I've always felt…too large. Too tall. Too much. When I was an athlete, especially, I was in peak physical condition. I lifted weights, I ran, I did conditioning drills, I practiced, I competed. I had washboard abs, I had thick, powerful thighs and a tight, toned ass and lean, strong arms. I could deadlift a hundred and fifty percent of my own body weight.

I was a powerhouse athlete. I was quick on my feet, with killer reflexes. I had a serve my opponents feared, it was so hard, so fast, and so accurate. I could dig, set, and hit like fucking no one.

But all this, on top of being six-foot-freaking-three, meant I intimidated men. I mean, I also had a mirror, so I knew I wasn't exactly hard on the eyes in the face, either. Professional athlete, taller than most men, in way better shape than most men, good-looking, successful…it felt good, but it was lonely.

I could score a hookup easily enough. But getting a guy to like me for me, a guy that wasn't intimidated by me? By my size, my conditioning, my success, my looks? Shit, forget it. And let me just tell you, men who are intimidated by you are *not* nice. Most are downright assholes of the worst variety.

And then there's Chance.

No other man has ever been able to pick me up, like at all, let alone make me feel…almost dainty. I mean, sure, I've even gone out with big monster bodybuilder, powerlifter types, back in my athlete days. But those guys? The ones I dated, at least? They were as dedicated to their thing as I was mine, and that generally meant we weren't compatible—we just didn't have the time for each other. Not to mention, I never was able to find one that had the size and strength to handle me like I wanted to be handled *plus* having the intelligence, wit, and emotional maturity to make a real relationship worthwhile. Not saying that man doesn't exist, I just never found him.

Until Chance.

He's so insanely strong he can pick me up like I'm a doll, and he's tall and broad enough that I feel downright small around him—which *no one* has ever made me feel. Plus, he's smart. He's kind. He's wise. He's a protector.

And…he understands who I am. He understands the demon of addiction that lives inside me, and the darkness that comes with it. The things I've done. He doesn't look at me differently because of it.

Anyone else would. *Of course* they would—how could they not? And I certainly wouldn't blame them. But Chance *gets* it.

"Thinking deep thoughts, huh, mama?" His voice is a sleepy, lazy rumble.

"Mmm."

I hadn't even noticed he was awake.

His hands are still on my backside, and I'm tensed. He nuzzles the top of my head. "Hey."

"What?" I whisper.

He squeezes my ass gently, and then sets about really exploring it. Paying attention to it. Caressing the curves of each globe, kneading, dimpling with his fingertips. Squeezing as if testing the heft. Cupping, as if merely appreciating. Tracing the seam with a gentle finger.

"Chance…" I breathe.

"Quiet," he murmurs.

I blink. He just…did he just tell me to be quiet? I lift my head off his chest and meet his eyes—and I see the merry glint there, and realize he knows exactly how I'd react to being told to be quiet.

"Chance," I say, my tone containing a sharp note of warning.

His thumb touches my lips, this time to cover, pressing. "I said *quiet*, mama. I got a beautiful piece of you in my hands, and I'm enjoying it. Been admiring this," he gives one cheek a soft tap of his palm—not even a spank, just a gentle tap, "since the first time I saw you. Finally got my hands on it, and I'm damn well gonna take my time with it."

I arch my eyebrow at him. "Is that so?"

He nods, smiles at me like it ain't no thing, and then… the gall of the man…he closes his eyes, settles his head back into the pillows, and resumes his tactile exploration of my ass. A huge, pleased, relaxed, appreciative smile is fixed on his face.

And I…let him.

I lie on top of him and I feel his hands scouring every inch of my butt, down to where it folds into my thighs, up to the dimples above at the very base of my back. Over, around, under. Touching. Squeezing. Caressing. Just… playing with and enjoying my butt.

Weirdly, it feels like…it's not a sexual thing. He's not trying to start something. He's not making a move. He's just…enjoying me.

And I like it.

He appreciates my body, clearly, and he's showing me. And, I understand, he's doing so without exactly breaking the vow he made to me.

I might as well have some enjoyment, too. I examine

his face. Memorize the angles and planes. The curve of his nose. The heavy bridge. His hard jaw beneath the thick black beard. The column of his throat. Looking leads to touching—he doesn't seem surprised when my fingers graze his cheekbones, his eyebrows, his jaw. He opens his eyes, meets mine with that smile on his face, and then closes them again. Continues his touching, and allows me mine. It's just tracing, feeling. Learning the feel of him.

After a while, his eyes open. Find mine. "You're beautiful, Nik."

I swallow, eyes inexplicably burning *again*. "Been a long, long time since I felt that way."

His thumb grazes my cheekbone just below my eyelid. "You are. You're the most beautiful woman I've ever known."

"I'm not gonna fuck you in my grandmother's guest bedroom, Chance," I say, my tone wry.

He snorts. "Is that all you ever think about, woman?" He shakes his head, his eyes scolding and teasing. "It ain't about that."

"You've got your hands all over my ass," I point out.

"You understood exactly how that was, and don't bullshit me that you don't."

I sigh and rest my forehead on his chin. "Yeah."

His lips kiss. "You think you need to be afraid of me, Annika?" His tone is tender. "Ever? In any way?"

I let out a breath. "No, Chance."

"You know—you *gotta* know that I'll take care of you. You don't have to be afraid."

I breathe a moment or two. "I'm not scared of it in the way you're thinking." I hunt for the words. "I know you'll be…gentle. I imagine it would…or will, I don't know—it'd be good. I have no doubt."

"*Good*?" He laughs the word. "When we kiss, is it just *good*? Or is it something a whole hell of a lot more than that?"

"It's something a whole hell of a lot more than that." I whisper it. "And that's exactly what I'm afraid of."

He buries his hands in my hair and begins massaging my scalp with powerful, gentle fingers. I let out a soft groan—the scalp massage is nearly orgasmic. He hums a laugh. "Like that, do you?"

I just moan again. "Yeah, you can go ahead and do this forever."

"What are you afraid of, Nik?"

"Nik," I whisper.

"Heard your mom call you that. Okay if I call you that?"

I hum an affirmative sound. "Yeah," I whisper. "I just…Mom, Erin, and Gram are the only ones who ever call me Nik or Nikki, and I…I like it. I thought I'd lost it when I lost them. So yeah, Chance. You can call me that."

"Right then," he says. "What *are you* afraid of, Nik?"

"Getting sucked in." I let out a breath, another moan as his massaging fingers move to my nape and the back of my neck, working out tension I didn't know I was carrying there. "Liking you too much. Wanting too much. *Being* too much."

"How is any of that bad, babe?"

"I lost myself, Chance. For a long time. I know you get that, how you lose who you are when you're a user."

"Sure as fuck do. But you ain't a user anymore, Nik. And neither am I."

"But I…I have major trust issues, Chance. I don't trust anyone. I don't even trust myself. My dad left us when we were little. I don't even really remember him. I was four, maybe, when he left. Erin wasn't even a year old yet, I think, so maybe more like three. He just…left. For another woman, probably. A younger one with no kids, I guess. I don't know. I've never really looked for him. Mom doesn't talk about him, none of us do. And I guess that just…it fucked with me on some kind of deep level, you know? Not having a dad, the fact that my dad abandoned us without ever really giving us a chance. Or whatever the case was. I don't feel like there's much excuse for leaving your whole family and never looking back. Like, how can you do that? How could any man have a wife and two little girls and just…leave? Not even a wife. He never married Mom. Just knocked her up twice and then vanished like a piece of shit."

"Nik, I get that, but—"

I shake my head. "You had both parents. And they were taken from you. They didn't abandon you willfully. Even your mom, not excusing her addiction, but we both know that's a disease, and some people are just never able to beat it. So you *don't* get it—you *can't*. Just like you've got shit I'll never get—like PTSD from combat." I sigh. "Chance, I just…I've had to be this person for so long. The athlete always striving for more, to be better. The perfectionist never content with where I'm at. Then it was taken away from me, everything I ever fucking wanted, everything I was, everything I had. Gone. Through no fault of my own, and I had to cope with that. I failed to cope with it. All that shit led me here, Chance…and it's turned me hard. Closed me down. Made me wary of men, of letting anyone close. Mainly because after I became an addict, no one wanted to *be* close to me. No one wanted me." I swallow hard. "No one wanted me. Except men who thought they could use me. So now I'm not that person. I'm not someone who can think about being *wanted*. Not anymore. Nor can I bear thinking about wanting anyone. It's all too much."

He allows silence to breathe between us, still gently but firmly massaging my scalp. Then, after a while, he stops. Withdraws his hands from my hair, rolls sideways so I land on the mattress and he's angled over me on an elbow. His long loose wild black hair drapes around my face and sticks to his beard. "Annika, honey. You're not answering the question. What...are you...*afraid* of?"

"Being abandoned again!" I shout. "Not being wanted. I'm afraid of wanting more than....more than anyone can give me. I'm afraid of..." I cover my face with my hands. "I've always felt like I take up too much space in this world, Chance. I don't know how to explain it. It's not just about being tall. It's just...*me*. My emotions are too much."

"Keep talking, mama. I hear you. I'm listening." His voice is tender and soft. Quiet and powerful and intimate.

His heat warms me. His weight, the little bit of it he's giving me, presses me into the bed. He tugs my hands down, and I have to look at him.

"I'm too much. Boyfriends, hookups, dates, one-night stands, whatever, I've always felt like I'm too much. Like I can't...I can't let on how much I'm feeling, how intense my emotions are. Sexually, I...I've never felt...matched. Like anyone could ever fill me up—I don't mean it *that* way, just...well, maybe I do. That's true, too. But I mean..." I shake my head. "I don't know the words, Chance. I've always felt like I'm too much and everyone I've ever been with just isn't enough. And how do you tell someone that?" I toy with his hair, pulling my fingers down through the inky black locks, searching his face, his eyes for what he's feeling. "I'm afraid of myself. And I'm afraid of everyone else. I'm especially afraid of you, because...because part of me wants *so fucking badly* to believe you could be the first man, the *only* man I've ever known who could...who could handle everything I am, physically, sexually, my ugly, filthy fucking past, emotionally. Everything. And I want that, Chance. I want you to be that *so* fucking bad it hurts. So bad it scares me absolutely senseless. Because what if you're not? What if..."

I trail off when his finger touches my lips. "Nikki baby." His voice is...tender and understanding. "I get that more than you could ever know. All of it."

"But Chance—" I start.

"Hush, babe—my turn." He holds my gaze, his unwavering, open, and deep. "Here's a few things I've learned in life. Okay? One, no man is an island—we need community, even just a few people who see you, know you, and accept you. Two, conversely, we absolutely *are* islands—no one can ever truly know the absolute entirety of another person. We have to continually choose to show other people who we are, what we want and allow them to see us. Three, you can't ever know for sure if you trust someone until you just take the leap and trust. And that's scary. This one, I've learned by watching Rev and Myka and then Kane and Anjalee. Rev...he's like me, in a lot of ways. Damaged, hardened, and just...not someone who's easy to know. Myka is the opposite. She's an open book. To meet her and spend one fuckin' hour with her is to basically know who she is.

She just lets it all hang out. It took a lot of courage for her to trust Rev with her heart, and even more courage for him to trust his with her. Because you can't know if a person is gonna accept you and stick by you and really fuckin' truly love you until you try. And I saw that end up being worth it for them. I know Rev was scared out of his fuckin' mind to let Myka in, to let her have the darkest parts of who he is. But he did it, and, Nik? Trusting Myka? That was an act of bravery for him. Because he's got some dark shit. Like me. Like you. So does Kane, and so does Anj. We all do. The only choice we got is to just *try*, babe."

"Just…jump? And hope?" I ask.

He nods. "Yeah, mama. Just jump and hope. You jump and you hope that I'll catch you. You jump, trusting that even if I don't, you're strong enough to survive that. Because I can tell you till I'm blue in the face that I've got you, that I won't let you down, that I can handle you, all of you, that I've got enough to give to fill you all the fuckin' way up, and that I'm man enough to accept all you've got to give. I can say that, but you won't really know it, you won't really truly be able to trust that it's true until you just…give me a shot."

"If I do, and you let me down, you discover you can't or don't want to…" I swallow, eyes burning again. "I don't think I'd survive that, Chance. I've been through too much. I don't know if I could—"

He silences me by kissing me. This kiss is unlike the others. This one is…slow. Deep. Exploratory. Giving. It's meant to prove something.

At first, I just accept it. I let him move his mouth on mine, let him taste my lips, trace my teeth and my tongue with his. But he's not content with that. He demands more…not from me, however. He demands I accept more from him. His mouth soars on mine, the kiss deepening. I can't help but respond, and my heart clamors and hammers in my chest, physically, and my heart swells and cracks within me, metaphorically.

This kiss *means* something. He's telling me something. Showing me.

It is in no way aggressive, nor is it sexual.

It's an emotional kiss. It's for the space where words fail, for the things language can't express.

My hands shake, and lift into his hair, dig into his scalp at the back of his head, cling tight. Pull him closer. Demand more.

My mouth opens and my tongue surges against his, responding to his demand—giving. Taking. His palm curls under my head, and then his whole arm snakes beneath me, curling, cradling me in a sheltering embrace, his mouth never leaving mine. His other hand cups my face, spanning from pinky near the base of my throat to thumb brushing over my eyebrow and temple.

His hand is rough, sandpaper and leather and stone against my softer skin, yet his touch is tender.

I have to break, to breathe—I pull my lips away and gasp into his mouth. "Chance," I breathe.

"You with me, mama?" he whispers. "You feel me?"

I don't know if he means the second question literally or metaphorically. Either way, the answer is the same. "Yes, Chance. I feel you."

He tugs me into the nook of his arm and shoulder. "Heavy talk for first thing in the mornin.'"

I laugh. "No kidding."

I realize I have no clue what time it is. I glance toward the window and see yellow sunshine—late morning.

"So." His hand roams from shoulder to hip and back, again and again. "What do you want to do, darlin'?"

"See Kelly." It's immediate.

"And then?"

I shrug. "I don't even know. I've been subsisting and dealing with Alvin for so long I don't even know…what to want. Where to go. Who I am. What's next in my life, Chance? I've never thought past the next day, because I…I was always too scared of what the next day might bring."

He lets out a long, slow breath. "I feel ya there, mama," he rumbles. "Because same." A moment or two of silence. "Maybe we just…take some time. Travel just for the sake of being anywhere, you know?"

I blink. Think. Breathe. "I…that sounds…" I swallow. "I don't have any money, Chance."

He glances down at me. "Funny—I know you inside and out, in some ways, but in others it's obvious we barely know each other. Like, where do you live? You have a car?"

I shake my head, roll a shoulder. "I…I live in my car." I swallow again. "I have a part-time job as a ticket taker at a theater in downtown Vegas—one of the few jobs I could do without experience and with my knee the way it is. But mostly, I was working for Alvin. He'd tell me, okay, you run this package to Barstow or Reno or LA, and he'd tell me the whole job is worth twelve hundred. He'd give me two hundred and tell me a grand would go to my debt."

"Was there any kind of real accounting involved?"

I laugh. "No. Just his word. I have a running tally in my car somewhere. I used to owe him thirty grand, but over the past few months I've done enough work for him I've knocked five grand off. But it was just…it felt impossible. Like I'd never catch up."

"Because he was just making shit up, honey. He didn't want you to pay off your debt, so he was fucking you over, making up numbers." He sighs. "So you're homeless?"

I nod. "Yeah. I've been trying to save for a place, but… every time I get a bit saved, something comes up. Usually my car takes a shit."

"What do you drive?" he asks.

I laugh. "My one halfway decent possession, and it's the only thing I ever managed to not fuck up, lose, sell, or trade for drugs. And that's only because it's been my home since I got kicked out by Mom." I nuzzle closer to him. "It's a twenty-fifteen 4Runner. I bought it used with endorsement money. Mom convinced me to buy used, nothing fancy, something I could buy outright, and something practical. I wanted to get, like, a Mercedes Benz or a Porsche or something—when I was a professional athlete and had endorsements and shit, I could've gotten one. Mom convinced me to stay within my cash means and buy something practical. Thank god she did. I parked in Alvin's driveway a lot of nights. Walmart parking lots, most other nights." I shrug. "I shower at rest stops, campgrounds, public parks. Anywhere I can scrub off, get my hair clean. If I'm truly desperate for a real shower in an actual house, yeah, guess who? Alvin again. I've been dependent on that man for so much." I swallow, nauseated at the memories. "He'd peek. I knew it, but I guess…it felt like letting him peek was worth being able to get clean and have time and space to actually get my hair done something like properly."

His eyes bore into me—I feel it. "That shit's over with, Nik."

"What shit?"

"All of it. Being homeless. Needing that fuckin' pissant *Alvin* for goddamned anything, ever fuckin' again." He sits up, taking me with him—I'm forced to sit on his lap, straddling him, facing him. "Listen to me, yeah?"

I meet his eyes; hyperaware of his size, his masculinity, his hardness. "I'm listening, Chance."

"Are you with me?"

I frown at him. "I'm right here."

"No. I mean, are you *with* me?"

I swallow, starting to understand his meaning. "Chance, I..." I close my eyes. "I will be beholden to no one, ever again. I have to make my own way."

"Bullshit. What you mean is you need to know you can stand on your own two feet. Right?"

"Yeah."

"Not what I asked. I asked are...you...*with me*?"

"As in, together?"

He nods. "As in together."

"We just met."

"And we've been through bloodshed, faced our addictions, you reunited with your family. We've bared our fuckin' *souls*, mama." He holds my face in both hands. "I don't need to have known you for months or years to know my soul is meant for yours, and yours with mine. I feel that shit. Scary as fuck, sure, but I'm gonna grab on tight and I ain't lettin' go, not for anything. There's nothin' you can do to get rid of me, to lose me, to scare me off. I've seen the worst this world has to offer, and in you, Annika, I see the best it has to offer."

I shake my head. "You're crazy. You can't see that. Not in me."

"Can too. Because I do."

"Fine, then, what do you see in me?" I ask, throat thick.

"I see a smart, strong woman with the soul of a warrior. I see a woman who's faced hell head-on and conquered it. You walked through fuckin' hell, honey. And here you are."

I nod, sniffing. "Here I am. Broken. No future. Homeless. No friends."

"You got friends, woman, shit. You got me. You got Rev. You got Kane. You got Myka and Anjalee. The other boys may take a bit longer to warm up to you, but they'll get there." He brushes my lips with his thumb—a gesture I feel in my soul every time he does it, for reasons I can't quite figure out. "You have a future now. And most of all, you have a home."

"I do?" I ask. "Where?"

He curls his arms around my shoulders and pulls me against his chest, my legs wrapped around his hips. "Here, mama."

"Dammit," I whisper, choking on emotion, which is lodging in my throat and trying to come out through my eyes. "I'm so *sick* of being so emotional. I *hate* crying. I don't cry."

"You're allowed to cry, though."

I shake my head. "Hate it. Won't do it."

"Gotta let it out, honey."

"No." I shake my head again.

He sighs, almost annoyed, but lovingly so, amusedly so. "You have a home, Annika. With me. My bed. My arms."

I shake my head. "That's nuts."

"Sure. Doesn't mean it ain't true."

"Love at first sight is bullshit," I whisper.

"Never said I fell in love with you at first sight." He lets that sink in a moment. "I said my soul recognized something in yours. Like a piece of a puzzle fitting into place. It's nuts. It's scary. And it's real."

I shake my head again. "I'm fucked up, Chance. You can't possibly want anything to do with me."

"I've lived in the basement of a nightclub because I was too scared to go outside. You think I'm not fucked up?"

"Chance…"

"All right. Fine." He sighs. "I'll bring you back to Vegas and drop you off at your car, if that's what you want. You can go. Do whatever you want. Say the word, you'll never see me again. Shit, I'll leave you here if you want. Drive back home to Sin on my own."

Panic sears through me like wildfire and I yank back, the tears I've been fighting springing out, trickling down. "No," I whisper, hands on his chest, lifting my gaze to his, finally. "No. Please. No."

He smiles. "Feels wrong, huh?"

I laugh and sob at the same time, thudding my forehead onto his chest. "Jerk."

"That visceral reaction to me leaving? What's that tell you?"

I grouse an aggravated sigh. "Shut up."

He tilts my face so I have to look at him. "I'll ask you again, honey. You with me?"

I have no choice but to answer him honestly: "I'm with you, Chance."

"Then you'll never need anything again. You got a home. You got family. Not just Gram and your mom and Erin, but all of us at Sin. We'll get you working. Something you like doing. You'll get paid to do it, and paid well. You'll have a home, a real home. A bed, and me in it every night, keeping you warm. Making sure you sleep like a goddamn baby."

"I do sleep better with you than I ever have in my life."

"'Cause you know you're safe. You know you *belong*, mama." He kisses me, a quick touch of lips. "Your soul knows. You just gotta let your mind and your body catch up."

Our eyes meet. I search my heart, and I realize he's right. "Okay, Chance."

He smiles. "Okay?"

I nod. "I'm with you."

"You're with me?" The smile on his face could light up the sun.

"I'm with you." I find myself smiling as well—helplessly, and brightly.

8

FRAGILE, HANDLE WITH CARE

Chance

WE SPENT THREE DAYS IN LA, WITH GRAM, and with Emily and Erin. Most of that time was spent at Gram's house, talking. There was a lot of Annika slowly giving her family the story of what she's been through, including the turmoil of her debt to Alvin. She learned more about Erin's fiancé, and their plans to get married next summer. Her mom talked about her plans for the future. There was a lot of reminiscing about old times, before the accident.

I listened, mostly. The women drew me into the conversation, and got me to talk about my parents, Mom's addiction, their death, my time on the streets with Rev, some lighter shit from my time in the Corps. I kept most of the stories away from the really gritty shit, but I think they understood well enough.

Now, after a pit stop at Target where Annika went on a brief shopping spree with my debit card—she got herself a new outfit of shorts, a tank top, flip-flops, and underwear, and got me a new pair of shorts and a tank top, just so we can go in somewhere together—we're heading south to San Diego.

I'm hyperaware that I'm technically driving a stolen car, so I make sure to keep my eye on the speedometer. I don't imagine Alvin is going to report it stolen, but I don't much like the idea of trying to explain how I came to be in possession of the car and why I don't have insurance or registration for it. I mean, it's in the glove box, but still.

It's an easy time, her and me. She holds my hand as I drive, our fingers tangled. Alvin had a cord plugged into the aux and the end fits Annika's phone, so she turns on music from her library—her choice surprises me: old-school punk, mostly. Dead Kennedys, Black Flag, Misfits, Ramones, Bad Brains. Suits me just fine, as my taste in music varies as widely as my taste in books.

The sun is shining, the ocean's on our right, windows down and the salt breeze on our lips. I feel free. And, looking at Annika as I drive, I can tell she's getting there too. One more hard conversation to have, and then we can work on us. I can work on thawing that icy wall she's got around her heart, keeping her body locked up tight. Keeping her libido imprisoned. She's a feisty one, I can tell. Deep down, in her thawed, freed, natural state, she'll be passionate. Wild. I just have to get her there.

That does mean working through my own shit regarding the topic of physical intimacy. Which I don't exactly relish the thought of, but if I can expect Annika to sort through her shit and give me herself and be vulnerable, I know I gotta do the same. If we can both get through all our respective baggage and find that physical connection, I have a feeling the result will be out of this fuckin' world. There's just a lot of shit standing in the way.

And I know I gotta be the one to lead the way. She's too scared, too traumatized. She's fragile, in a way, despite being one of the toughest people I've ever met. I have to handle her with extreme care.

I feel her looking at me. Cut my eyes to hers, lift an eyebrow. "What?"

She just shrugs, looks away. "Nothing. Just…"

I snort. "Don't 'nothing' me, Nik. Tell me what you were thinking."

A long sigh. "You don't miss a thing, do you?"

I grin. "Try not to."

A moment of silence as she considers what to say and whether to say it. "You promised me you wouldn't make the first move, sexually."

I nod. "Yeah."

"You seemed certain I'd end up wanting you."

"I am."

"Why? What makes you so sure?"

I look at her. "Not sure you're ready to hear the truth on that one, mama."

She frowns. "That sounds awful condescending, Chance."

"It's not, I swear. I'll tell you whatever you wanna hear, but don't say I didn't warn you if it's more than you can deal with." I slide my free hand out of hers, rest it on her thigh, the bare skin warm and smooth. "At first, I admit it was mostly just bravado and bluster. I'm crazy fuckin' attracted to you, physically, that ain't no secret. I was throwin' down a challenge. Tryin' to get you thinking with your body, not just your mind or your emotions."

"So you're admitting it was an attempt at manipulation."

"You wanna call it manipulation, I guess you could make a case for that, yeah. But it wasn't, like, nefarious."

"You said at first. Meaning it's different now?"

I nod. "Yeah, it is. Now I feel like I know you. We been through some heavy shit together. You're still locked up tight, darlin'. Closed up and shut down. Walls a mile high around that heart of yours, and I get the feeling that with you, if your heart ain't there, your body sure as shit won't be. But I know something." I wait before saying it.

She quirks an eyebrow at my pause. "And that would be what? Don't keep me hanging, here, Chance."

"You were made for me, mama. Your life. Your experiences. Your mind, your heart." I glance at her, meet her eyes. "Your body."

"Chance," she murmurs, her tone containing a hint of a scold, and more than a hint of skepticism.

"Don't tell me you ain't felt it, you ain't noticed it." I cup her thigh, squeeze, let my fingers dig into the warm flesh and dense muscle—a few inches above her knee, yet still short of the hem of her shorts, which are very short and very tight, molded to her thick, juicy ass and showing a hint of the lower edge of her ass cheeks. "You've never been satisfied, Annika. You've never met a man who can be what you need—who just *is* what you need."

Her cheeks turn pink. She looks away. "How do you know that?"

"Because it's true of me. Physically, no one's ever fit me. Matched me. Not the way you do."

"Chance," she whispers. "Stop."

I slide my hand higher. She clutches at my hand, but doesn't move it. "I know you want me, Nik. I can tell. You're ignoring it. Pushing it away. Pretending it's not there. But I can tell. I see you—I feel you responding to me. That's how I know you'll open up for me, eventually. And once you open up, you'll let me in, and when you let me in, you'll accept you want me. But I won't push it. I'll wait. I'll keep showing you that you can trust me, that you're safe with me, and that everything you need, everything you want, you can find...*in me*. And that's when you'll let yourself have what you want—me. Us. The physical connection to match our emotional one."

"I don't *want* to want you," she whispers.

"I know. And that's okay. I don't take it personally." I grin at her.

"It's not a joke, Chance. You scare me."

"Wanna elaborate on that?"

She shakes her head. "No, not really."

"Tough. Do it anyway." I squeeze her thigh. "Why do I scare you?"

She shakes her head. "I'm not sure I can."

"Try."

"I already have. We've been over this."

"Explain it again, but this time go deeper."

"I'm terrified of how much I want you," she says, not looking at me but out the window at nothing. "Physically, it just scares me. Because I've always felt like I'm too much, I told you this. I feel too much, want too much—*am* too much. And with you, I feel everything a million times more intensely, and I don't know why, I think it's just something about you, and that scares me shitless, because...because if I open all that up to you, give in to it and show it to you and let you have it, let you have *me*, you'll be getting a version of me no one's ever had, a wilder, more intense version. And the toned down, scaled back, dimmed version of me I've shown every other man I've ever been with was too much for them. What does that mean for the fullness of me, the real me you seem to bring out of me?"

"You're mincing words, Nik." I reach up and touch her jaw. "Give it to me raw. Unfiltered."

She just looks at me out of the corner of her eyes for a long, long time, then away again with a hard swallow, a shake of her head, and a huff. "Fine. Sex has never been fulfilling. The best it's ever been has only been good enough to make me feel like…like I'm only getting a taste of what it should be. What it could be. I exhaust men. I always want more. I want it harder. Slower. Longer. Deeper. I want to be fucked, and I want to be made love to. One, the other, and both at the same time. I want to be held and treated like something precious, and I want to be used and treated like a slut, fucked hard and rough." She's spewing her words at me, trying to shock me, shocking herself with the vitriolic truth. "Is that what you want to hear, Chance? That no man I've *ever* fucked has been good enough for me? No one's ever been man enough, big enough, strong enough, gentle enough, sweet enough. I want it all. I want a man who can be a macho jackass alpha who takes me how he wants me and doesn't ask first, doesn't ask permission and doesn't ask if I want it or like it, because he *knows* what I want and how I want it and he knows I'll like it, knows I can take what he's giving me. And I also want a man who can be sweet and kind and thoughtful and attentive, who takes care of me like I'm helpless and fragile. That man doesn't exist, Chance. You're not that man. No one can be all of that. But yet, that's what I want. And every man I've ever let even *close* to me has let me down because *he's… not…that.*"

"Keep talking," I murmur. "I hear you, Nikki."

She shakes her head. "What else is there to say, Chance? Only that deep down, I...I *want* you to be that guy. I do. But it's an impossible, unrealistic expectation, I realize that. I'm holding you and every other man up to what I know is an impossible standard and yet I'm still continually disappointed."

This an arena where words fail. So, I pull over onto the shoulder, surf churning out the window. Put on the flashers and shove the shifter into neutral and yank the e-brake.

"Chance, what are you—"

I cut her off with a kiss. For a moment, she's stiff and shocked, unresponsive. Mouth closed. Body tight. I'm patient. I trace her lips with my tongue and slide my hand along her jaw. Up to her nape. She's got her hair knotted at the back of her head in a wild spray of copper curls—I yank it free and slide the thick stretchy band around my wrist before shoving my hand into her hair. Grip, tighten, pull her closer. Demand her mouth to open with my tongue, even as my other hand cups her jaw and my thumb traces her cheekbone. A low whimper escapes her throat, and her lips part. Her body softens, just a hint. It's all the opening I need.

I pull her harder against my mouth with her hair, my grip tight enough to control, to remind her of my strength, but not enough to cause pain. My tongue pushes into her mouth, and with another low moan, she opens for me. I taste her. Scour her mouth with my tongue, and her mouth opens, and she instinctively deepens the kiss.

It's wicked and wild, then, and she's pushing back at me, her hands now yanking my hair from the loose topknot and delving her fingers through it. She leans into me, kissing me hungrily. When I respond with equal need, she growls, surges against me. The air in the vehicle is suddenly charged with erotic need, hers and mine, chaotic and demanding and crackling between us.

I reach over and pull her toward me. Without breaking the kiss, she slings her leg over the console between us and over me, sliding to straddle me in the driver's seat, both hands on my face, cupping my bearded jaw. Holding me in place and pressing me back into the seat as if to prevent me from escaping, from denying her the kiss. Her weight settles on my thighs, and I finally allow myself to explore her sweet, lush, curvy body. I run my palms up her thighs and around her to ass, which I cup, grip. She's mewling into the kiss, suddenly wild, desperate for me, as if our conversation and then my kiss and now my touch have unlocked something in her.

I'm hard, achingly erect. Her shorts are thin, stretchy athletic shorts, and I know she feels it at her core. I feel her, for fuck's sake. I feel her sex. The heat of it. The tight V against my cock, layers of material between us. Her breasts press against my chest. I tuck a hand under her shirt and roam the hot expanse of her back, over her bra strap, back down. Her hands dive into my hair, fist there, and she clutches at my face and pushes me deeper against the seat, the kiss gone supernova, wild and heated and almost angry. Desperate.

Our teeth knock, tongues war.

She grinds against me, core scraping against my cock, and I groan. I feel her need. She's soaked with desire. I can *smell* her need, and it's the most intoxicating thing I've ever smelled. She grinds again, angling for maximum contact, and she whimpers into my mouth. I span her hip with my hand, brushing my thumb over the front of her shorts. She tips her hips back, giving me access. Wanting me to touch her. I want to. I want to feel her warmth, want to watch her squirm, want to hear the gasps as she comes for me.

One touch is all it'd take, I think—she's fucking primed, ready to detonate.

But I made a promise, and so I hold back.

"Chance," she whispers.

"What?" I whisper back.

She moves her hips, pushing against my thumb where it rests about an inch above where she wants it. "I…"

I twist her hair in a knot in my fist, yank her back for another scorching kiss. Break it after a beat. "You what, Annika?"

Another pivot of her hips. A plea. I know what she's asking, silently. Any other circumstance, I'd give it to her without hesitation, without making her even say it. I'd give it to her before she even knew she wanted it.

Not now. Not her. She has to break through those barriers herself.

She whimpers. Rolls her hips, seeking relief. "I need…"

"Tell me, Nik. Tell me what you need." I touch my lips to hers, not a kiss, but a reminder, a tease of a kiss. "Tell me, and I'll give it to you."

She rolls her forehead onto mine, gasping. Whimpering. Hips grinding. The friction is delicious, and not enough, and too much. "Please." It's a hissed syllable, so quiet I barely hear it.

"Gotta say it, mama. Gotta hear the words. Gotta know what you mean, what you want. Just this once, you gotta gimme the words."

"Don't make me," she pleads. "You *know*."

"Yeah. But I made you a promise. What kinda man would I be if I broke that?"

She cups my face, arms resting on my shoulders, forehead to mine. Straddling me, knees into the seat, steering wheel at her back. Cars whoosh by occasionally. "Chance, dammit." Another grind of her hips, pushing her hot, covered sex against my cock. "Please."

"Say it, Nikki baby. Tell me what you need so I can give it to you."

"I want you."

"I'm right here."

"No." She shakes her head, a clumsy roll of forehead to forehead. "I *need* you. I need *you*."

I rub her thighs, then grasp her big, beautiful ass and lift her, settle her lower, help her grind against me, teasing what we could have. "I'm right here, mama."

"Fuck. Fuck." A breath, a soft exhale, then, angrily— "*Fuck*." She moves my hand, guiding it to her front. To her sex. "*Touch* me, goddammit. I want to come—I *need* to come. Make me come, Chance. Please, *fuck*, help me come."

I capture her mouth and kiss her with furious need, all hot mouths and wild tongues, depth and intensity unmatched, giving her the full force of my hunger for her. She groans into my mouth, lifting her hips, tilting them back to offer herself to me.

I slip my hands down into her shorts and find her wet sex slick with need, delving my middle finger into her. Softly, gently, slowly, I enter her with my finger, just one at first. She whines into my mouth, breaking the kiss. My index and pinky fingers press into her inner thighs on either side of her sex and she widens her thighs, lifting up on her knees and angling toward me to give me the optimal geometry. She's tight, wet, and hot around my middle finger.

Her head touches the ceiling of the car, her mouth against my ear. "Ohhh fuck, Chance. Yes, god yes."

She's a goddess gone wild, and I've barely touched her. She's everything. Pure honey, pure fire. The feel of her pussy around my finger is wondrous, slick and wet and hot and slippery and clenching around me. I press deep, draw out slowly, curling to drag my fingertip against her inner wall. I find it, that spot, instantly—I know I've found it because she surges against my touch and cries out, her already-clenching core spasming around me. I drive my finger back in, and press my thumb against her swollen clit. She cries out.

I shove my other hand under her shirt and yank down the cups of her bra, freeing her tits. I pinch her nipple and then cup the full, heavy weight of her breast, and she arches her spine, pushing into my hand.

"Fuck, fuck." She presses her lips to mine, but she's too fraught to kiss. "More."

I give her what she wants—an added finger, my ring finger with the middle, stretching her tightness. My fingers slide in and out, my thumb circling while I play with her breasts, one and then the other, squeezing, kneading, fondling, pinching, rolling.

As my fingers work her pussy, she rests her mouth on the top of my head, huffing. Her hips roll, gyrate, responding beautifully. Faster she drives, taking and taking. Guiding me to her perfect pace, slowing when she wants to back away from the edge, grinding faster when she needs it faster. Her hands clutch the back of my head, and her hot breaths come fast on my scalp as she gasps, groans, whimpers.

"Oh my fucking god, Chance. It feels…*so* good. So good. Don't stop."

"I won't stop till you've seen Jesus, baby." I drill my fingers in and out hard and fast, driving the heel of my palm against her clit. "Let me see you come, Nikki. Come for me, mama. Come for me."

I feel her fingers join mine, pressing against her clit and taking over, circling a fast light touch; I continue using my fingers to pleasure her while she gives herself the added touch she needs. I pinch and twist her nipples, tweaking harder and harder the closer she gets to her climax.

All at once, she throws her head back, spine arching, screaming, grinding her slick squelching pussy against my hand while her fingers fly over her clit. "Chance! Fuck, fuck, *fuck*, Chance ohmygod I'm coming, I'm coming, oh fuck I'm coming so hard!"

"Gimme your mouth, Nik," I command. "Kiss me while you come on my fingers."

She slams her mouth onto mine and shoves her tongue between my lips and then sucks my tongue into her mouth, and her hips drive and grind, fucking my fingers. Her pussy squeezes around my fingers and her breath comes in shrill pants.

Slowly, her climax subsides, leaving her quaking every so often with the harsh tremors of aftershock mini-orgasms.

"Holy fuck," she whispers, lips against my ear. "Holy fucking fuck."

"Got a bit of a potty mouth on you when you're turned on, mama," I murmur.

She shudders again, burying her face deeper into my neck. "Sorry."

"Better not apologize for that shit, baby, it's hot as fuck."

"It is?" She pulls back to look at me.

"To me, yeah." I restrain the need to adjust my raging hard-on—I don't want to draw attention to it, because this wasn't about me.

She blows out a breath. "Chance, I…" She shifts, and I pull my fingers out of her sweet wet sex and out of her shorts. Her eyes go to my fingers, glistening wet with her essence. "Oh god, gross. I wonder if there's a napkin in here." She moves to twist off me, reaching for the glove box.

I grab her wrist with my other hand, pull her back down to me. "Why's it gross, Annika?"

She wrinkles her nose at me. "My…my…*stuff* is all over your fingers. It's gross."

I hold her eyes as I put my two middle fingers into my mouth and slowly pull them out, licking them clean. "Mama, ain't a damn thing about you is gross to me. It's fuckin' delicious, is what it is. Tastes like fuckin' honey."

Her cheeks go pink, her lower lip clamped in her teeth. "Chance, Jesus." She's mortified. But also turned on.

I put my fingers to my nose and inhale. "Annika, you gotta understand me, baby girl. What I just gave you, that cute little orgasm you just had? Tip of the fuckin' iceberg. A cute little baby O, compared to what I'm gonna do to you the second I get you to a bed."

"Cute?" She grabs my hand and tries to pull it away from my face, using both hands, yanking. "Stop sniffing your fingers. And it wasn't cute *or* little. That was…" She shakes her head and keeps hold of my wrist with both hands as I press my palm to her cheek, and she nuzzles into my hand. "That was...I've never come like that in my life."

I grin at her, pleased with myself. "You ever been eaten out till you can't come anymore, Annika? Ever come so many times you gotta beg your man to stop?"

She shakes her head, adorably embarrassed, burying her face in my neck again, arms slinging around my shoulders, fingers in my hair. "No. Not even close. I've honestly always thought multiple orgasms were, like, a myth, or... or made up for movies or trashy romance novels."

I laugh. "You've never come more than once at a time?"

She shakes her head against my throat. "Nope."

"I can guarantee you they're very real, and I guarantee you, I'll show you exactly how real they are."

She rolls her hips, grinding on my still-hard but bent painfully sideways cock. "What about you?"

"Don't worry about me."

She pulls back. "But...It's your turn. I can feel you... you're hard as a rock. Don't you want to..." she trails off, shrugs uncomfortably.

"You're shy about this shit, aren't you?" I say.

She shrugs, nuzzling my throat, a sweet, adorable gesture that has my heart clenching in my chest, swelling. "I guess, a little?" She looks away. "I...I had a few boyfriends here and there in high school, and I'm obviously not a virgin or even close, but my focus was always volleyball. And then things sorta went...you know. South. Terribly, terribly south. So I guess what I'm saying is—"

"You're not very experienced."

"No." She shakes her head. I can feel her embarrassment, her blush. "Not very. At all."

"Wanna talk about it more?"

She shrugs. "And say what?"

"Talk about experiences. What you liked, what you didn't. How many, when, whatever. I'll tell you anything you wanna know."

She pulls back and holds my eyes. "You really don't want me to return the favor?"

I shake my head. "Nope, not right now."

"Why not?"

"Because this was about you. I ain't worried about me. I'll get mine." That's not entirely true. I have my own sexual hang-ups and I want to deal with them later on and elsewhere…not in a car on the side of the highway.

"But you're worried about me."

"Semantics, baby. Point is, this was about you. Making you feel good. Showing you that I can make you feel good. That it's gonna be good with me. I can take care of you." I cup her chin in my finger and thumb. "I *got* you, Annika. You're safe with me. I can handle you."

She spends a very long moment staring into my eyes, searching me. "I'm scared out of my fucking mind, Chance, but…I'm going to take a risk and trust you. I'm going to try to trust you. Just…" She squeezes her eyes shut, and tears leak out, one from each eye. "Don't let me down, please. *Please*. Don't fuck with me, Chance. I'm just starting to get my feet under me. I'm just starting to feel like…like I can have a real life again. So please, please, fuck, *please*, don't fuck me over. Okay?"

9

FORGIVING YOURSELF IS THE HARDEST PART

Annika

HIS EYES ARE THE SOFTEST, WARMEST BROWN I've ever seen. They sear me to the bone. Down to my soul. "I *got* you, mama." His voice is softer yet.

I shake my head, tears leaking down my cheeks. I hate crying. Hate the weakness, the burn in my eyes and the sting on my cheeks, I hate the snot and the puffy eyes. I hate the way it wells up inside me like vomit, surging up and out, decimating my control. Pushing past my grip on my emotions, turning me into a sobbing, hiccoughing mess.

He pulls me against his chest, tucking my head under his chin and he cradles my face in a huge strong hand. "Annika, you're okay. It's okay."

"It hasn't been okay for…a long time," I whisper. "A long fucking time."

"Nah, honey, I know that. What I meant was, it's okay to let it out." He tugs my hair away from my eyes and brushes a thumb over my cheek, through the tear tracks. "Cry about it all you want, Nik. It's all right."

"I h-h-hate crying."

"Who doesn't? But sometimes you gotta, and I'm telling you, you've got a safe place to let it out, honey. Right here." He squeezes me—it's a gentle thing, but he's so strong it's like being crushed in a vise.

It's an awkward, uncomfortable space, the steering wheel digging into my back, the console hard against my thigh, the door on the other thigh, and the ceiling brushing the top of my head. But I just can't bring myself to leave the shelter of his arms. I'm not sure what I'm crying about anymore, to be honest. I'm just…crying. For everything, I guess. For all the things I refused to cry about for years.

I don't even know how long it lasts, but it's long enough that when the tears finally stop, my legs are cramped and aching from being curled up underneath me. I lean back and rub my face. "Chance, I…"

"Nik, baby." He cuts over me. "Look at me and listen good, yeah?" I nod, let out a deep sigh, blinking hard, and he rubs a thumb over my lips, across my tear-stained cheek. "Thank you for giving me that. For trusting me with yourself like that."

"Are we talking about orgasms or me ugly crying?" I ask, meaning it as a joke to lighten the mood.

He doesn't seem to find it funny. "I look at both as precious fuckin' gifts, for one thing, and for another there ain't a single goddamn thing ugly about you lettin' yourself cry about all the brutal fuckin' shit you been through, mama. I know you were just joking, but it ain't funny to me."

I slide off of him, brushing the back of my wrists against my eyes, sniffling. "You can drive, now." I buckle up again.

He does the same, lifting his hips and plucking at the front of his shorts, blatantly adjusting the lay of his cock.

Which, my god. Even hidden behind underwear and the baggy shorts he's wearing, it's obvious he's as massively endowed as the rest of him is oversized. I mean, I felt it under me while I was straddling him. Thick, long, hard as a rock.

I look sideways at him as he settles again, putting the car into gear and angling back onto the road. "Chance, now that we've, um, opened the floodgates, so to speak, I really, really wouldn't mind returning the favor." I feel my cheeks heating, embarrassment and desire warring within me.

He grins at me, but it doesn't entirely match what I see in his eyes. "It ain't that I don't want you to. I do. A fuckin' lot. Trust me on that. I want you. I wanna kiss you and eat you out and watch your sweet little mouth take my cock, and I wanna fuck you and I wanna watch you ride my cock and I wanna make you come so hard you fuckin' pass out. I want all'a that, Annika. Want it, need it, and plan on making it all happen as soon as I can get you to a proper bed." He glances at me again, reaching over the space between us to caress my thigh from knee to shorts hem. "I'm not worried about getting the favor returned. I don't believe in keeping score, mama."

"Oh." I watch the seaside slide by out the window. "I...I've sort of been...shut down, I guess you could say. For a long time. Sexually, I mean. So, I...opening up and letting myself feel things, want things...it's not easy. And I admit I'm not sure where to start. What to do." I shake my head. "I'm not sure I even really know what I like or don't like. Other than maybe feeling like..." I shake my head again, hunting for the right words. "Like I'm wanted. Needed. Desired. Not just...there, not just an available fuck, you know?"

"Meaning, you been treated that way in the past."

I nod. "To varying degrees. I've just...I haven't always felt sexy, or desirable. Strong, powerful, yeah. Sexy? Not as much. A lot of men are just intimidated by me, by the fact that I'm six-three and a professional athlete, you know? I'm sure I've mentioned all this before."

He shrugs. "Sure, but it bears repeating in this particular context."

I snort and roll my eyes. "I guess I haven't always felt particularly...*feminine,* you know? Like I've said, I'm not a virgin. I've had sex. Good sex, too. Before the accident and the drugs, yeah, I had...not really boyfriends, I've never had what I'd call a serious long-term boyfriend. But there were guys I dated, slept with, all that. I know what I'm doing. I know I enjoy it. Or, I have in the past. But..." I let out a noise that's part sigh, part groan. "I'm not sure what I'm even trying to say."

"I ain't the jealous type, I can tell you that," Chance says. "Not in the sense that I'm gonna get all bent out of shape hearing about how things have been for you in the past. Ain't none of us lived in a vacuum. You had a life before me. You had desires, needs, all that. You had sex. Ain't somethin' to hide, and it ain't somethin' we oughta be shy about discussing. We gotta understand each other, Nik. And talking about shit is how we do that. So don't hold back. Not on my account." He watches the road, one hand on the wheel and the other draped on my thigh. "I get it, mama. I really do. Feelin' like something is missing but just not sure exactly what...shit, I've felt that way my whole life. Sexually, emotionally, relationally."

I watch him for a moment, and I see distance in his gaze, a kind of absence, like he's lost in thought and not entirely here in this moment with me. I give him another moment or two, then I rest my hand on his on my thigh. "Tell me what you're thinking about?"

He sighs. "Eh, I guess I was hoping to get into this shit later. But I suppose now's as good a time as any."

"Get into what?"

He shrugs. "You ain't the only one with issues about sex."

I hold my silence and wait for him to let it out his own way, in his own time.

"Growing up the way I did, being homeless and then in a gang, and then in the military, it kinda made it hard for me to have a ton of opportunities to connect with women. As I got into my teens, when most kids that age are flirting with girls and hooking up and learning how to take off a bra one-handed and whatever, Rev and I were just tryin' to survive. Find somewhere to sleep, find food, keep ahead of the cops. Once we connected with the gang, there was more opportunity, and we both started hooking up, mostly with chicks connected to the gang in one way or another. Ex-girlfriends, sisters, cousins, friends, shit like that. But it was few and far between for me. I wasn't confident, for one thing. I felt like I was a hundred feet tall, and I was gangly back then, all arms and legs and big ol' hands. Rev, now...I was jealous of him. He was—is—so damn good-looking he didn't need pickup lines, didn't need game. All he had to do was lift an eyebrow and wiggle a finger, and girls would just drop their panties for him. I had to work at it. I had to get game, you know? Talk smooth and be charming. But even then, I was just so much bigger than all them girls that I just...either it was me or it was her, or both, but it was just awkward, man. I was awkward. Sex was awkward. And that was before I bulked up."

I thread my fingers into his, my palm on the back of his hand. "I can relate."

"I know you can," he says. "But it only got harder once I joined the Marines and started eating regularly and lifting. I put on a good fifty pounds of muscle the first couple of years. So then I wasn't just six-foot-nine, I was six-nine and weighed close to three hundred pounds. I was fuckin' scary. I had short hair back then, and no beard. The long hair and the beard kinda soften me a little bit. Shaved? Women and children run screaming."

I laugh. "Oh, come on. Can't be that bad."

He snorts. Digs his phone out of his pocket and pulls up his photo library, trading glances from phone to road and back as he scrolls back to find a particular photo. After a minute of searching, he finds it and hands me the phone. It's a photo of a photo, meaning he snapped a picture of an actual physical printed photograph. It's him, Rev, and two other guys. They're all in desert camo fatigues, tan combat boots, tight T-shirts, and wraparound sunglasses. Rev looks pretty much the same as now. Chance, though...Jesus. He's quite a bit leaner in the photograph, still massive and muscular, but he's packing way less body fat. His head is shaved to skin, and he's a few days out from a shave, a dark stubble shadowing his jaw. His jawline is sharp, hard, and rugged, his eyes deep, dark, and wide. None of the men are smiling, all leaning on each other and scowling at the camera with ferocious intensity. He's right, I realize—he's downright frightening. The intense scowl doesn't help, I'm sure, but with his size, those muscles, those deep, dark eyes, and the shaved head and jaw...he's intimidating as hell.

I give him his phone back. "I mean, you are kinda

scary without the hair and beard. You're scary anyway, but yeah, I can see what you mean."

He laughs. "You're not supposed to agree."

I roll my eyes. "Well, I'm not gonna blow smoke up your ass. You do look way more intimidating. Not that you're not hot as hell, it's just in a slightly more 'holy shit he's gonna kill me' sort of way."

He snorts again. "Right. So what I'm saying is, I didn't have a lot of luck in the scoring chicks department. If I did, it was usually because Rev drew them in with that broody smolder thing he does. I got the friend who was a five and he got the ten."

I can't help a laugh. "I can't help but feel like you're sort of…objectifying, a little." I quirk an eyebrow at him. "I mean, scoring chicks? Really, right now?"

He rolls his eyes and shakes his head. "I'm making a joke out of it, Annika. The reality is, I had a hard time connecting with anyone, attracting anyone. And that was just the start of the issues."

I frown at him. "What else was there?"

He doesn't answer right away. "Hard to talk about."

I run my hand up his arm, over his shoulders. "Chance. Come on. I've given up all the deepest, darkest shit I have. I've dragged out all my skeletons. I've trusted you—I *do* trust you. Now it's your turn. You can trust me."

"It's not about trust. It's just…it's hard to talk about." He lets out a long breath. "Being a giant, basically…it can be hard. It's hard to find clothes. I don't fit in most vehicles. Like, right now, I'm fuckin' cramped." I look, and realize his knees are drawn up, nearly bumping the steering wheel, even though he's got the seat all the way back and tilted backward as well. "I worry about breaking chairs when I sit in them, because I have. I showed up late to a brief, this one time. Slipped in the back, trying to be quiet. Plopped into the chair, and it just gave out underneath me. So much for a quiet entrance, right? You know how fuckin' embarrassing that is?"

"God, Chance. That sucks. I'm sorry."

"I mean, it was funny as hell. But it was also totally mortifying." He shakes his head. "If I'm worried about breaking a chair, can you imagine how I feel trying to hook up with some cute little thing? It just…It doesn't work. I can't be on top, I'll fuckin' crush her like a grape. And… there is such a thing as being *too* well endowed. And I guess to most girls, that's me. They take one look at me with a hard-on, and they're like, 'no way, pal. *That* ain't fittin' in-side me.' And that's it. They're gone."

I stare at him in disbelief. "You've had girls just… walk out?"

He nods. "Yup."

"How could anyone be that bitchy? I mean, I get being a little worried, you know? You're a big guy, and I haven't seen it yet, but I've felt it, and yeah, I get the impression you're…um…a lot. But there's other things you can do. You know?"

He nods. "God, do I know. I'm an expert at those other things, Annika, mainly because things get started and I get worried about being…..rejected, I guess." He swallows hard, sighs, shakes his head. "Hard to feel sexy and confident when I've been literally told I'm too big to fuck. Too big in every way there is. Too tall. Too heavy. Too much cock. Too strong. Even when a girl's been will-ing to go through with it and fuck me, I gotta hold back, because I'm worried I'll accidentally hurt her. Because I can." He swallows again. "I have."

"You have, what? Accidentally hurt someone during sex?"

He nods. "I…was into it, you know? Feeling good. I'd made sure she got hers first, and she seemed into it. Making all the right sounds, not acting like…like I was doing anything wrong. I got a little too into it, I guess. When I was done, she left the bed and went into the bathroom and didn't come out. I heard her crying." He makes a low growling sound in the back of his throat, head shaking, eyes lost in the memory. "I bruised her. Fingerprints on her hips. Hurt her down there, you know? Like, I'd gone a little too hard, I guess. She never said anything, during. I swear she didn't. I dunno why. She got dressed and left, and I never saw her again."

"Damn, Chance." I look at him. "It kinda seems like it's on her, to a degree. Like, how are you supposed to know it's not feeling good if she doesn't tell you?"

He shrugs. "That was my thought. But…you can't imagine how I felt. Knowing I'd hurt her. Left marks on her. Made her cry. Jesus. Felt like trash, Annika."

I rub his shoulder. "Chance, I…I'm sorry."

He just wags his head yet again. "That was during my last leave before Rev and I got out. And to be totally honest, I…was never really the same. Any confidence in that area I may have had…gone. Toast. I've…at the club, there are girls. We lease them a room, give them a safe place to work, steady clientele with good money, and we only charge them a very nominal flat rate, and provide security. That's one of my primary roles at the club, is security for those girls. So, I've…I had a few moments with one of the girls. She's gone, now, got out of the sex work industry. But she and I had a little thing. Her name, her working name, at least, was Sindy. Like, S-I-N-D-Y. Obviously it was a made-up name. But she was…sweet, and very understanding. She really helped get me out of my head and regain some of that mojo. She's been gone for six months, though, and there's been no one else since her."

"Six months, huh?" I smile at him, but the smile quickly fades. "When I woke up in that crack house, and I realized what had happened, what I'd done…I…I swore two things to myself. One, I swore I'd get clean, and stay clean—I vowed I'd never use again and I'd clean up my life. The other thing I vowed to myself was that I wouldn't touch anyone. And I haven't."

"You swore off sex entirely?" he asks.

I nod. "I did. Seven months ago. So we're in the same boat." I glance at him. "Question for you."

He meets my eyes briefly. "Okay, shoot."

"When we met, you seemed pretty damn confident in your…abilities. Damn near cocky, like, absolutely certain I wouldn't be able to resist you. Were you faking that?"

He shakes his head, grinning at me. "Nope. Not faking that at all. The thing Sindy made me realize was that I've sort of overcompensated. I didn't trust women to let me actually sleep with them, so I got really good at what you might call foreplay. I know what I can do with my hands and mouth." He smirks at me. "I also happen to really, really get off on that shit, too. Big time."

I feel my cheeks heat. "Well, I can attest to the fact that you do indeed know what you're doing. I don't know if I've ever come that hard."

He brushes a thumb over my cheek. "Awww, you're blushing."

I bat at his hand. "Don't make fun of me."

"I'm not! It's cute."

I roll my eyes. "Cute. Great. I just *love* being called cute."

He grazes his thumb over my lips, gaze heated. "Just teasing, Nik. I need to pull over again and remind you how I feel about you?"

"Is that a threat or a promise?" I say, smirking back at him.

He drops his hand to my thigh, and slowly drifts it upward, higher and higher, until his fingers dimple the tender flesh of my inner, upper thigh. "What do you want it to be?"

I trail my fingers down his arm and then to his knee, mimicking the journey of his fingers on my leg. Up, up. My heart pounds. I haven't touched a man in so, so long. I haven't been touched in so long.

"The last time I remember being with a man, in a conscious, voluntary sort of way..." I say, dragging my fingers down his thigh again, to the hem of his shorts and under, fingertips ghosting over the hard muscle, up, up, until I feel his manhood bulging behind his underwear, "...was actually a few months before that business with Alvin and his buddies. I was in a shelter, and there was a volunteer. It was...not great. I was jonesing pretty hard, he lasted about a minute, and we were in a supply closet. So it's actually been almost a year since I've been with anyone in a way that actually counts."

Chance huffs, glances at me. "What are you playing at, Nik?"

I run my fingers over his bulge, and at my touch, it twitches, hardens. Strains. "I'm not playing at anything."

"Don't start nothin' you don't plan on finishing, mama," he growls.

"What if I do plan on finishing what I start?" I ask, feeling bold. "You opened the floodgates, Chance. I've turned off my sexuality. I've been focused on staying clean and trying to get out from underneath my debt to Alvin. But now…now you made me feel things. Emotions I've been ignoring. Desires and needs I've been suppressing." I trace his length…it's curled, furled inside his underwear, unable to straighten. "You touched me. You made me feel good. You reminded me that I'm…that I'm a woman, that I once liked and wanted and needed sex. That I still do. You make me feel beautiful again, Chance."

"I'm just pointing out the truth, Annika. You *are* beautiful. Fuckin' breathtaking, is what you are." He lifts his hips, gripping the wheel with both hands now. His jaw tightens. He growls. "Fuck, Annika. Killin' me, teasing me like this."

"Who's teasing?" I say. "I'm just….exploring."

God, he's huge. I can't even begin to fathom the size of the organ my fingers are discovering. The length of it, the girth. I cup the bulge, and then run my palm over it. It hardens further, but it's trapped inside his underwear.

"Pull over," I murmur.

He does, sliding onto the shoulder and shoving the shifter into neutral, then yanks the parking brake. "Annika, babe, I told you. There ain't no 'returning the favor' going on, okay? We can wait. Get to San Diego, get a hotel."

My heart is hammering, but desire pounds inside me even harder. Driving me to touch him. It's an urge, a need. I feel like I've woken up for the first time in years. His touch did something to me, ignited the pilot light of my libido.

"I'm not returning the favor," I say.

I slide my hand out from the leg of his shorts and hook my fingers into the waistband, pull it away from his body.

He angles his hips again, and his cock straightens, slapping upright against his belly. I pull at his shorts, and he lifts up. I tug them down, and he's bared for me. "No? Then what are you doing, honey?"

"This is for me." I meet his eyes, reaching for him. "Because I want to touch you. I *want* to, Chance."

Good fucking god. He's absolutely massive. So long, so thick. Veiny, with rippling brown flesh. Hard as steel, yet as I touch my fingertips to him, his skin is soft and warm. He closes his eyes, tight, jaw clenching. And then, as I curl my fingers around him, he inhales on a hiss. My fingers don't meet as I grip him. God, he's going to stretch me so tight, when I finally get him inside me.

"Fucking fuck, Annika," he growls, as he unbuckles his seat belt and lets it retract. "Your touch. God, your hand."

I give his length a slow, gentle caress tip to root. "You like that?"

He smacks his head backward against the headrest. "Do I like it? Feels like heaven, Annika."

I twist in the seat to face him, wrapping my other hand around him now, too. I twist my upper hand around the fat plump head of his cock, and the other I slide down, down, down the many, many inches of him.

He groans, a long, ragged sound from deep in his chest. "Jesus, Annika."

Both hands, then, gliding up together, and down

again. My core tightens, heats, drips. God, he's beautiful. I want him inside me. I want to watch him come. I want him above me. I want to ride him. I want his mouth on me. I want to get naked with him and come together until we're both too exhausted to move.

I want him to come.

Right now.

The need for him is sudden. Immediate. Intense. It's hitting me out of nowhere, a raging inferno of need for Chance. For his body. His touch. His pleasure. I caress his length with both hands, twisting occasionally, marveling at the sheer size of his cock. I couldn't even guess at how many inches it is, and nor do I care. All I know, all I care about is that I get to touch it.

He groans again, and his hips lift, pushing him into my touch. "Fuck, Annika. Fuck. Been a long time. Can't hold back much longer."

"Don't hold back, Chance." I pump at his base, using my other hand to twist around the head again, twisting and plunging, twisting and plunging.

"Gonna make a mess in about thirty seconds," he warns.

I keep my touch slow, gentle. Unhurried. Just enjoying the sight of him, the feel of him. "You're beautiful," I say. I squeeze oh-so-lightly around the head in gesture. "*This* is beautiful, Chance."

His eyes open, find mine. "Annika. Fuck. Jesus, fuck."

He's beginning to thrust, to buck. Jaw clenched tight, he knots his hands into fists behind his head. Gasping, growling, groaning.

"Fuck. I'm—I'm gonna come, Nik."

"Lean the seat all the way back and pull up your shirt," I tell him.

He levers the seat to not quite horizontal and tugs his shirt up around his chest. Hands behind his head, eyes locked on me, on my hands as I caress his thick, hard length. One hand around his balls, cupping and massaging, I keep my strokes slow, tip to root, squeezing at the tip and twisting at the root. As he nears the edge, he thrusts into my hand, wanting it faster, needing it harder. Instead, I go even slower.

I want to taste him. But...perversely, I make myself wait. For now, just this.

"Annika..." he rasps, his voice ragged and raw with tensed energy. "Fuck, the way you touch me. Never felt anything so amazing as your hands on my cock, Annika."

"You gonna come for me, Chance?" I murmur, plunging short, shallow strokes around the tip of his cock.

"Right now, oh fuck, oh fuck, Nik...fuck, I'm coming." He arches, and then his ass lifts up off the seat, and now I give it to him hard and fast, my fist a blur around his cock.

He comes in a jet stream, laying a thick white stripe up his brown belly and onto his diaphragm. As he comes, I slow my touch again, squeezing his balls and giving him slow twisting strokes at his base. He spurts again, and his breathing is ragged, panting gasps cut through with snarling groans of blissed-out release.

"Oh my god, Annika, baby girl." He opens his eyes and looks at me. "Jesus. You ruined me."

I grin my pleasure at him. "That was fucking hot, Chance." I can't help it—I lean over him and fit the tip his cock into my mouth, running my tongue over the slit of his opening, tasting the tang of his leaking droplets of cum. "Next time, all mouth," I promise him.

"Next time, I'm gonna fuck you into next week," he shoots back.

"I love it when you threaten me with a good time," I say, smirking. "Hold still. Let me see if there are napkins or something in this car."

I open the console between our seats and find a stack of brown paper napkins from a fast food drive-through, and I use them to clean him up. When he's clean, he tugs his shorts back up, drops his shirt, and levers the seat upright. Letting out a gusting sigh, he reaches over, cups my jaw, and pulls me to him, claiming my mouth in a harsh, rough, demanding kiss.

I think he meant it to be hard and quick, just a brief kiss before he gets us back on the road. I have other ideas. I clutch his neck and lean into him, give him my tongue, feel him suck it into his mouth, tangling his against mine. Ignition, then. All tongues and teeth and lips, battling and clashing. He pulls me closer yet, so I'm lying halfway across the console at an awkward, uncomfortable angle.

"I can't get enough of your fuckin' mouth," he growls, breaking the kiss. "Can't enough of *you*."

"Same," I whisper. I yank away from him and plop back into my seat. "Drive. Before we get carried away again. Just…drive."

He shoves the shifter into gear and nails the accelerator a little too hard—we fishtail and the tires spit gravel and then squeal and smoke as we transition from shoulder to pavement, rocketing forward as the tires catch and the powerful engine roars, propelling us down the road.

Once we reach highway speed, he lets off, raking his hand through his hair and then down through his beard.

"You know," he says, glancing at me. "That's the first time I've ever messed around in a car."

"Been a long-ass time since I have," I tell him.

"It was fuckin' hot as hell, but I think overall I prefer a bed." He grins at me.

"Me too. Car sex is always a lot more awkward and uncomfortable than you'd think, in my limited experience with it."

There's quiet between us for a while, companionable and easy.

"You, um…" he starts, trails off, starts again. "You said I was…beautiful."

"Yes, I did." I meet his eyes. "I meant it."

He furrows his brow. Puzzled, perhaps. I'm not sure what he's feeling, so I wait for him to speak. "Never been accused of that, before."

"Chance…"

"Big, yeah. Obviously. Scary. Intimidating. But… beautiful? Never."

"Well, you are." I take his hand, thread our fingers together, palm to palm. "All of you is beautiful, Chance. For real. I mean it. But, just to be clear, what I said was, your cock is beautiful." I grin at him. "But the rest of you is beautiful, too."

He snorts. "Never heard a woman describe a dick as beautiful, before. That's a new one."

"Well, yours is. It's absolutely perfect. To me, at least."

He eyes me. "Tryin' to decide if you're blowing sunshine up my ass or not."

"I wouldn't do that."

He nods. "I guess I know you wouldn't, at that." He shrugs. "And I'm glad you think so."

"I'm not like the other women you've been with, Chance. I'm not gonna get scared off." I squeeze his hand.

"I'm starting to understand that."

More silence.

A thought bubbles up, a question that's been percolating in the back of my mind for a while now. "Chance?"

"Hmmm?"

I hesitate to put it out there. I'm scared of the answer. "We get to San Diego, I make amends as best I can with Kelly…then what? Not just for me, but…us. I…what is this, with you and me?"

"We go back to Vegas and…figure things out, I guess. We find you a job at the club—I'm not sure what, but we'll find something." He shrugs, looks at me. "As for you and me, and what this is? I don't know, Annika. I've never…I've never been in a relationship, not a real one, not something I thought would last. But…you're different. It's different with you. I told you when we first met, I feel a connection with you. An emotional one, a mental one…and obviously we have a physical connection."

"Chance, I…I don't know how to…be in a relationship. I've never been in one either."

"Then I guess we just take it one step at a time and figure it out together."

My throat is tight. "You…but you want that. With me."

"Fuck yeah, I do, mama. You think I'd be doing any of this shit for just anyone? Hell no. You got me out of the club for the first time in over two years, and I honestly wasn't sure I'd ever leave. So fuck yeah, Nik—I want a re-lationship with you."

Now that I've opened the box on my emotions, they're spiraling, boiling. Questions, doubts, fears, needs—where before I was numb and shut down, feeling only the drive to survive and stay away from Alvin as much as I can, now I'm just awash with a maelstrom of feelings. And I don't know what to do with them all.

He seems to sense it, looking at me, taking his hand from mine and squeezing my thigh. "Talk to me, mama."

"I just…it's a lot."

"This whole thing? Or what you're feeling right now?"

"Both."

"So tell me what you're feeling."

I look out the window and try to find the words. "I wasn't sure I'd ever be able to have this. I wasn't sure I wanted it. I wasn't sure I *deserved*…to be happy, to feel hope again. To feel…wanted, I guess. The accident changed everything, and for a long time, there was no room in my life for…feelings."

"For love, you mean." His eyes meet mine. Deep, dark, soft, inviting me to fall into him and never surface again.

"Yeah," I breathe. "Do I even believe in love? I don't know. How could I ever love you when I don't even like myself?"

"What's not to like?" he asks. "You're strong, you're smart, you're beautiful. You're a survivor. You're funny. You're brave. You've been through hell, you never gave up, and you're still here." His eyes cut to mine, serious and in-tense. "We're more than our mistakes, Annika."

"No, of course not." I shake my head. "You're an amaz-ing man, Chance."

"So, if you can see me as amazing, even though I've done some seriously fucked-up things—if I can be forgiven and deserve to be seen as more than just the worst shit I've done…then you can damn well give yourself that same grace."

"It's not that easy."

"No? Why not?"

I shake my head again. "I'm not…I'm not *good*."

"Who *is* good? Fuckin' nobody, mama. Ain't one single goddamn person who's ever lived been *good*, unless you believe in Jesus. The rest of us are just different shades of fucked up. You gotta forgive yourself, Nik. You can make amends all you want, with your mom, your sister, Kelly, anyone and everyone. That'll make some space in your soul. But if you wanna get free of all the bullshit keeping you chained to feeling like a piece of shit, you gotta forgive yourself."

My lip quivers, my eyes burn. "Have you? Forgiven yourself?"

He rolls a huge, heavy shoulder. "I'm workin' on it, mama. It ain't easy. I don't think it's a one-time thing. I think it's a process."

"Where do you even start?" My voice is low, cracking, breaking, hoarse. "Where did you start?"

He doesn't answer for a long time. "I did some online therapy, actually. Legit, no one knows, not even Rev. But I did. It was just a couple sessions. I was having trouble sleeping, you know? Like, I'd lay there awake at night, wrestling with this shit. Hating myself. Going over all the awful shit I've done, replaying it and just…hating myself. I never let on to anyone that I was feeling any of that shit. I'm a master at acting like I'm fine, like nothing fazes me.

But secretly, alone at night, man…I was fucked up. So I talked to this therapist via Zoom, right? He was a former soldier, too, so I know he got that part of it. And he had me write it down. Like, in so many words—'I forgive myself.' You gotta say it, mama. That's what he taught me. You gotta make it real. When you make amends, you gotta say the words, yeah? Ask for forgiveness, so you can make amends and move on to the next step. Well, it's the same for forgiving yourself. And no, it doesn't magically fix anything. But it's a start. And honestly, I think forgiving yourself is the hardest part."

I mull that over, watching the scenery slip past the window. Chance gives me the time and space to sort through what he's told me and how I feel about it—he just drives, radio off, silence simmering between us, his big gentle hand possessively and affectionately resting on my bare thigh, his fingers occasionally dimpling into the flesh and muscle, thumb rubbing in circles, back and forth.

I forgive myself. It's nearly impossible to even think the words in the confines of my own mind.

I made mistakes. A lot of them. But…I was hurting. I was lost. I'm not making excuses, I just…yeah. Around and around I go, trying to justify and excuse the shit I did, and then getting angry at myself for doing it.

Eventually, I come to some conclusions.

I was in pain. I was angry. Confused. Lost.

That doesn't excuse or justify what I did—nothing can and I'm not trying to. I did have reasons, right or wrong. But it's done—I did what I did, and here I am, for better or worse. I survived. I'm clean.

I'll never, ever go back to drugs.

I want to have a life—a semblance of normalcy. I want to have friends. A job.

I want…I want to be loved, and I want someone to let me love him.

I want that. Fuck, do I want it. To love, and to be loved.

I want….*life*. Not just existence, or subsistence, or basic survival. But a real, full life.

And the first step on the path to any of that?

I forgive myself.

I don't need to write it down. I don't need to say it out loud. It's enough to know it, to speak to my own soul.

I forgive myself.

Tears leak down my cheeks, and I let them. Chance notices, and as if he can read my mind or see what I'm feeling, he knows there's nothing he can or needs to say. His presence is enough. He caresses my thigh and he drives, and lets the silence breathe.

For the first time since that car smashed my knee into dust, I feel like maybe, just maybe…

I'll be okay.

10

Chance

W E'RE IN SAN DIEGO, PARKED NEAR A BEACH not far from downtown. Annika is staring at her phone, her thumb hovering over the green call button, Kelly's phone number displayed across the screen.

"You can do it," I tell her. "It's okay. Just…go into it knowing the worst thing that'll happen is she might say she doesn't want to see you. She may not be able to get over it. That's a possibility. Once you accept the worst possibility…" I shrug. "You're more than halfway there."

She wipes her face with one hand. "I'm scared. In some ways, her forgiveness means more to me than Mom's, or Erin or Gram." A shake of her head. "She wasn't family, she was…my best friend. More than a best friend, more than a sister. I was closer to her than anyone else on the planet. And when she cut me out? I honestly contemplated suicide, after she told me not to call her again—losing her was that painful."

"All you can do is try."

She nods. "Actually…" She frowns at the phone. "Can I call her from your phone? This is the same number I've had for years, so there's a good possibility she won't answer if she knows it's me."

I unlock my phone and hand it to her. She dials the number, hesitates, and then she stabs the call button with her thumb, as if to do so before she can chicken out. She holds the phone to her ear, letting out a long, slow, nervous breath.

I hear it click, and faint voice say, "Hello?"

"Kelly?" Her voice shakes, threatening to break. "It's me. It's Annika." She puts it on speaker, presses the top edge of the phone against her forehead, eyes shut, leaking tears.

Kelly's voice is hard and cold as ice. "Annika, I told you—"

"Please, Kelly, just…listen. For two minutes, please."

A sigh. "Fine. What, Annika? You gotta know I'm not giving you money."

"No, I…no. Kelly, I'm clean. I've been clean for almost eight months."

"Congratulations." Pause. "Is that it?"

"No—Kelly, I…I don't want anything from you. Not…not like that. I just…I need to see you. Please? I want to talk to you in person. I'm in San Diego. I drove here to see you, because the things I need to say you to I need to say face to face."

A longer pause, a shaky breath. "Goddammit, Annie. I promised myself I was done. With you. I can't…I can't go through that again, what you put me through."

"I understand, Kel. I swear I get it. And if you still don't want to be in my life after we talk, I'll understand that. But part of my…part of the process of moving on from all that shit is making amends. Asking for forgiveness from all the people I fucked over. So I can let it all go and put it behind me. Please. Just…give me fifteen minutes, face to face. Please. If that's all you can give me, then I swear I'll leave and you'll never hear from me again, I just—"

"Fine," she snaps over me. "God, *fine*. But if this is all some scam, Annie, I swear to fucking god…"

"It's not. I promise."

"Double pinky swear, cross your heart?" There's a teasing, hopeful note in Kelly's voice, which even I can pick up on, and I don't even know the woman.

Annika laughs, a soft sniffling, tearful laugh. "Yeah, Kel. Double pinky swear, cross my heart, no take backs."

Kelly laughs, and then says, "I'll send you a pin. Is this a new number, or is this someone else's phone?"

"Someone else's. My number is the same."

"You figured I wouldn't answer if your name came up on the screen."

"Yeah, pretty much."

"That's fair. I wouldn't have." Kelly hesitates. "Who is he?"

"You're on speaker," Annika says. "His name is Chance. And he…it's…"

"Ah," Kelly says, understanding her voice. "Is he good for you?"

"We're still figuring things out," Annika answers, her eyes on mine, "but yeah. He's good for me. Really, really good."

"Don't make me regret giving you this opportunity, Ann. Please. I'm begging you. If you're lying to me, just… don't show up." Her voice drops, trembling. "Don't make me regret this."

"God, Kel. You won't regret it."

"Sending you a pin. I'll see you in a few minutes." She clicks off, then.

Annika hands me the phone back. She sniffles, rubbing her face with both hands. "God, that was hard. But good. She didn't say no."

"She calls you Annie?"

A nod. "Yeah. Everyone else calls me Nik or Nikki. But Kelly likes to be different, so she always called me Ann or Annie." She gives me a droll side-eye. "Kelly's the only one who gets to call me that, so don't get any ideas."

"Noted."

Her phone pings with an incoming message—a pin to Kelly's house. "She's thirteen minutes from here."

"You want to go alone?" I ask.

She shakes her head. "God, no. I don't know if I could do it alone, if I could face her on my own."

"You can, though."

"I don't want to."

I brush my thumb across her cheek. "All right, then, mama. I got you." I hand her the aux cord. "Plug that shit in and let's go see your girl."

The head unit is a brand new aftermarket touch screen with all the newest CarPlay software, and when she plugs her phone in, the directions from her nav app pop up on-screen. I follow them across town to a cute, tidy little sub-division not far from Camp Pendleton. The houses are modest, one-story ranches and the occasional two-story Colonial or Craftsman. The pinned location is a nice little ranch with pale yellow siding, white shutters, a big picture window in front beside a lavender-painted front door. Neat flowerbeds on either side of the walk and front porch are filled with daisies and hydrangeas in front of small, square-trimmed box shrubs. The lawn is freshly mowed, and a newer, silver, four-door Audi sedan sits in the driveway outside the detached garage.

We park on the curb, and Annika waits a moment, eying the house. "She's doing well for herself, it looks like."

"Yup."

She looks at me, gnawing on her lower lip. "I'm scared."

"You already did the hard part. Breaking the silence and reaching out first—that's the hard part." I squeeze her knee. "It's gonna be okay, mama."

She nods. Lets out a breath. "Promise?"

I shrug. "I mean, she agreed to see you. If she wasn't ready to forgive you, I don't think she'd let you come to her house."

"True."

While we're talking, the front door opens, and a woman steps out to stand on the front porch. She's as tall as Annika, or very nearly—over six feet. She's blond, her hair cut straight at her chin in a sharp bob. She's beautiful, with clear blue eyes and fine features. She's more svelte than Annika, dressed in skin-tight athletic leggings and a sleeveless tunic coming down to mid-thigh, belted at her waist, barefoot.

Annika lets out another breath. "I can do this. I did the hard part." This is to herself, not to me.

She reaches into the back seat and grabs her cane, shoves open the door, plants her good foot on the ground and then her cane, and forces herself to her feet. We've been in the car for a long time, so I imagine she's got to be stiff—she bends and extends her bad knee a few times, then shakes it out.

A fraught, awkward moment, then—Annika is frozen in place, leaning on her cane; I can see her free hand trembling, and her chest is rising and falling swiftly as she fights an onslaught of powerful emotions.

Kelly is frozen as well, hands over her mouth, eyes wide and tearful. Kelly is the first to move, trotting down the two steps to the walkway and then jogging across the small lawn, slamming into Annika so hard Annika stumbles back a step, catching herself with her cane. I can hear them both talking over each other, both crying and laughing at once.

Kelly pulls back first, grabs Annika's wrists and examines her forearms, then touches her face, like her mom did. "You look good, Ann," Kelly says. "You look healthy. You're really, actually clean."

"I am. Eight months, or close to it. Seven months, two weeks, and a couple days." Annika brushes her fingers along the straight line of Kelly's bob cut, along her jaw. "I like the short hair. It looks good on you."

"Thanks." Kelly tucks her hair behind her ears. "It's new. I'm not used to it quite yet."

Another hug. It's obvious Annika doesn't even need to say the words—all is forgiven. But I know she needs to say it, for herself, and needs to hear it.

Kelly ducks to glance into the car at me. "Well, come on in. Luis is at work."

Annika blinks at Kelly. "Luis?"

Kelly holds up her left hand, wiggling her fingers. "I'm married. Luis is my husband."

Annika swallows hard. "You…you got married?"

Kelly ducks her head, nods. "Yeah. I…I thought about inviting you, but…I just couldn't. I'm sorry."

"When was it?" Her voice is subdued, carefully shielding the hurt.

"A year ago next month." Kelly rolls her shoulder. "It was my family, his family, and that's about it. It was in his parents' backyard. Super small."

"I wasn't clean a year ago next month." Annika nods, squares her shoulders, making a monumental effort to put the hurt away. "Congratulations. You'll have to tell me about him." She looks at me, then at Kelly. "He's good for you, though?"

Kelly lights up, nodding eagerly. "Yes, god yes. So good. He makes me a better person in every way. When you called and texted a few months ago, he wanted me to answer. He told me I had to forgive you, even if I never saw you again. I was too…upset still, I guess, so I didn't. But I should have. It's bothered me ever since." She ducks again to look at me, gesturing to me. "Come inside, you guys."

I shut off the engine and exit the car—as I rise to my full height, Kelly's eyes widen.

"Holy fucking shit, you're *huge*." She looks to Annika again. "I thought *my* man was tall, but god*damn*. What are you, seven feet?"

"Not quite. Six-nine."

"Jeez." She pulls a face. "Sorry, I'm sure you get sick of that kinda thing, huh?"

I laugh. "Nah, it's fine, I'm used to it." I extend my hand to her. "Chance Kapule."

She takes it, and I'm careful to grip very gently as I shake her hand. "Kelly Conrad." She heads for the house. "Well, come on. No sense standing around outside."

The interior of her house is as neat, attractive, and tidy as the exterior—open concept, white walls, dark wood flooring, dove gray living room set with colorful toss pillows and throw blankets, slate kitchen appliances, white marble countertops streaked through with gold veins. There are clusters of framed photos on the mantle over the fireplace and on couch-side tables, of Kelly with longer hair next to a tall, built Hispanic man sporting a high and tight hair cut; most of the photos are a variation of the same. In several of the photos, her husband, Luis, is wearing Marine Corps uniforms—Service Charlies or Bravos, or PTUs; in one of the photos, I can make out the single gold bar of an O-1, a Second Lieutenant.

Annika stands beside me, both of us examining the photos together. "Your husband is in the Corps, huh?" I say. "O-1?"

Kelly beams with pride. "He just got his silver bar a few weeks ago, actually. He's O-2, now."

"Nice," I say. "Congrats to him. O-2 is a hell of an accomplishment. I was E-6, Force Recon."

Annika glances at me, the question in her eyes. "E-6? O-2?"

"E-6 is Staff Sergeant," I explain. "Quite a few ranks below your girl's husband. O-1 is Second Lieutenant, O-2 is First Lieutenant."

"Force Recon? Impressive. Luis is JAG." Kelly gestures at a Keurig on the counter, glancing at me. "Coffee, Sergeant Kapule?"

I wave at her. "Just call me Chance, please. And yeah, I'll never turn down coffee. Thanks."

She gestures at the four-place round table in the nook off the kitchen. "Have a seat. Coffee, Annie?"

Annika nods and takes a seat, as do I. "Sure, please."

A few minutes later, we all have mugs of coffee, Kelly sitting across from me, next to Annika.

A moment or two of silence. And then Annika clears her throat, sips coffee, turns her attention to her friend and former partner. "Kel, I...god, where do I even start?" She blinks hard, looks away from Kelly, into her coffee. "I'm sorry. That doesn't even come close to..." She shakes her head, trailing off. Starts again. "I...took money from you and used it for drugs. I stole cash out of your purse. I almost stole your car, but I talked myself out of that one. I lied to you about being clean so many times. I know I don't deserve your forgiveness, but I hope to god you can find it in your heart to give it to me. You were like a sister to me, and I fucking...I betrayed you time and again. I love you, Kelly. And I'm sorry for all the awful shit I did and said to you."

Kelly doesn't answer for a long time, tears streaming freely down her face. She grasps Annika's hands in hers and squeezes. "I forgive you, Ann. I wasn't sure I ever could—I was so angry at you for so long. They say those you love the most have the capacity to hurt you the most, right? And you...I would have died for you, Annie. You...you saved my life, Annika—don't think I don't know that, don't think I've forgotten. You've never said a word about it. Even when you were using, you never tried to play that card. But...when I realized you were lying to me, that you were using...I watched you take the cash out of my purse. I didn't stop you. I should have, maybe. I don't know. I just...I felt so betrayed. I thought you'd tell *me* the truth, out of anyone. If you'd told me you were an addict and you needed help, I'd have moved heaven and earth for you." Kelly halts, shuddering. Starts again. "But I know better. My mom was addicted to Oxy. And I watched her. I saw what happened. She couldn't help herself, and she refused to ask for help. I tried. Dad tried. Gram and Papa tried. Aunt Marnie tried. Mom wouldn't accept the help. Just kept spiraling. So, I knew if you didn't ask for help, there was nothing I could do. And honestly, it was hard, watching you, having watched my mom damn near kill herself."

"Your mom got sober, though, eventually, right?" Annika asks. "I remember you saying she'd been through rehab."

"She went through a methadone clinic. The treatment was...rough. But she got off the Oxy, at least." Kelly lets out a ragged sigh. "Of course, she's an alcoholic, now, so I still don't see her."

"Jesus, Kel." Annika leans into Kelly, rests her head against Kelly's.

"Some people just...seem to need to be addicted to something. At least with the drinking, she can hold down a job and is something approaching functional. When she was hooked on Oxy, she was...fuck, she was a disaster."

Annika blows out a breath. "I get that. It was pills that got me into trouble, actually. It hurt so bad, and it never stopped hurting. The pills were the only relief I ever got, but I very quickly realized I was taking more than I should. I knew I was addicted, like, immediately. So I tried to quit." A shake of her head. "Quitting the pills was pure hell. My knee killed me, literally every moment of every day, so bad I couldn't sleep. So I started drinking. And then one day, at a party, it hurt so bad I couldn't see straight and I was going crazy. And the guy I was with offered me a pipe, and he told me it would make the pain go away." A bitter, harsh, angry laugh. "It did. I felt *amazing*. For the first time since the accident, I didn't just not have pain, I felt *good*. That

was short-lived. It was worse than the pills. The *need*…
fuck, you can't imagine. It's…it's kinda like being on fire,
and the only way to *not* be on fire is to get a hit."

I nod. "That's a good way of putting it, actually," I
chime in. "It's a hell of a lot like being on fire, just on the
inside. And the outside. Your brain, your skin, your fucking *organs*…every last particle of your being just…*needs*
that hit. It's all-consuming."

Kelly's gaze is sharp as it cuts to me. "You too?"

I look at Annika as I answer Kelly. "Me too. It's part
of what connected Nik and me."

Kelly looks from Annika to me and back, wiping beneath her eyes with her middle fingers. "And now you're
keeping each other accountable?"

I shake my head. "Nah. Nothing like that. If she don't
wanna be clean, ain't a damn thing I could do. Same for
me. She's clean because she don't wanna fuckin' die. I'm
clean for the same reason. We just get each other, because
nobody can ever understand an addict like another addict."

Kelly nods. "So, what's next in your life, Annie?"

Annika shrugs. "Still working on that." She looks at
me. "Honestly, I don't know. Chance…he set me free in
a very real way, and I'm still processing how that feels."

Kelly tilts her head to the side. "Set you free in what
way?"

Annika is obviously reticent to discuss it. "Um. I owed
a lot of money to a very bad dude. Chance…convinced
him to, um, relinquish his claim, you might say."

Kelly arches an eyebrow. "Do I want to know what
that means?"

I roll my shoulders, curl my hands into fists. "Look
at me. I have a way of making people see things my way."

"The shotgun in his mouth certainly seemed to help convince him," Annika adds.

Kelly's eyes widen. "Oh. Um. I see."

"He's alive," I reassure her. "He ain't gonna enjoy being' alive for a good long while, but that's his problem. He was a filthy piece of useless shit. He got way less than he deserves. Nikki just wanted to be free of him."

"I don't claim to know much about this, but I feel like people like him don't give up all that easily," Kelly says.

I shake my head. "Not usually. I think in this case I was...very convincing."

Kelly nods. "I think I'm better off not knowing the details."

Annika snorts. "I think you are too, Kels."

Silence, then.

"You're married to a hot guy, you've got a nice house, a nice car..." Annika bumps Kelly with her shoulder. "What else have you been up to?"

Kelly smiles. "I'm a research assistant for a high-profile lawyer in the area, a friend of Luis's. Mostly, I get to work from home, which I like. I go into the office a couple times a week to report in with my progress on whatever I'm working on. I make my own hours, and it's always interesting."

"You always were good at internet stalking," Annika says, laughing. "Remember when you were dating that guy and you didn't think he was being honest about stuff, so you hunted him down online and discovered he was lying about literally everything?"

Kelly nods, snorting a laugh. "Yeah, well, now I get paid to do basically that. God, that guy was such a *liar*. He pretended he was a cadet in the police academy when he was a convicted felon, he pretended he was the heir to all this money when he didn't have two pennies to rub to-gether, and oh, by the way, he was one hundred percent gay and pretending to be straight. I still can't figure out why he'd lie about his sexual orientation...*he* tried to pick *me* up. If he was gay, fine, whatever, don't lead me on."

"Some people are just pathological liars," I say.

Kelly nods. "I don't get it. Just be real, right?"

"I never got it either," I say. "I get lying about shit you're embarrassed of or to protect a secret or some shit. But just lying about random nonsense that don't fuckin' matter. Makes no sense to me."

Kelly looks at Annika, then. "It's really, really good to see you, Ann." She swallows hard. "It's especially good to see you looking like yourself again. Last time I saw you, you were..." She shook her head. "I wasn't sure how you were still alive. You looked half dead, strung out...god, Ann, it cut me to the fucking bone seeing you like that. I looked up to you, you know that? You were...you were a freaking goddess, to me. The shit you could do on the court? God, Annie. No one—but *no one*—could kill like you."

Annika laughs bitterly. "Yeah, well, that's long gone." She lifts her cane and twirls it. "This is me, now."

Kelly sighs sadly. "That's not *you*, Ann. That's *part* of you, but it's not *you*. You pushed me out of the way and saved my life, you took the hit instead of me. And in the process, your whole life got fucked up."

Annika frowns. "Don't you *dare* try and tell me you feel any kind of guilt about that, Kel."

"How can I not? I didn't cause it, I know that, but you were permanently handicapped saving my life." Kelly plants her face in her hands, shaking her head, bobbed hair shaking. "I can't help but feel…I don't know, Ann, not guilty per se, just…shitty."

Annika grabs Kelly's hands in a death grip and pulls them away from her face, clutching and shaking, her voice quavering with raw intensity. "I'd do it again, Kel. In a fucking heartbeat. You absolutely cannot feel bad about it. It was my choice, my action. And honestly, it wasn't even a choice. I just…it just happened. But even knowing what I know now, what I've been through, what I've done…to save your life?" She chokes, weeping, shaking her head. "I'd do it again." A bitter, cynical laugh. "The only thing I'd do differently is say no to that fucking meth pipe."

Kelly reverses their grip, holding Annika's hands and kissing her knuckles. "I just feel like after the accident, I should have been there for you."

Annika shakes her head, bumping her forehead against Kelly's. "Stop, Kels. Just stop. You're not responsible for my fucked-up choices. Don't try to take any of this on." She pauses, then continues in a much quieter voice. "For what it's worth, you were right to cut me out. I don't harbor any anger or resentment, at all. I harbor guilt, if anything. I would have kept using you, and that's the fact. You did the right thing, you did what you had to do for you. Just so that's clear."

Kelly nods, sniffling. "I know. I'd been down that road with Mom. So I know it was the only thing I could do. It just…that doesn't make it any easier. I loved you—I *love* you. I never stopped. I just had to put it aside." She inhales slowly, lets it out. "I don't think I ever gave up hope that *this*—" she shakes Annika's hands, still imprisoned in hers, "would happen. I always hoped, down deep inside. I was just…scared it wouldn't."

Annika fights back another sob. "I was so scared you'd—you wouldn't..." She shakes her head, letting out a soft, shuddery breath. "I was so scared I'd come here and you'd reject me again. I know, I know—it was self-protection, it was what you had to do, but that's still what it felt like, even though I did know and do know that's not what it was. Emotions aren't always logical."

"Well...here we are, now." Kelly pulls Annika into a hug. "It's behind us, now."

There's coffee and conversation, then. I mostly sit and sip and listen, and let Annika and Kelly catch up. Kelly is funny, in a dry, sarcastic kind of way. She and Annika quickly fall into a routine, making each other laugh and trying to outdo each other, make the other person laugh even harder, until they're both breathless and wiping tears of hilarity from their eyes. It's amazing to see the way Annika lights up around her friend, how at ease she is in her own skin with her.

Before we know it, it's dark outside and hours have passed, and the side door off the kitchen opens, Kelly's husband Luis enters. He's tall—six-four, maybe—and very fit, with hard, intelligent dark eyes. He's in dress blues, carrying a leather briefcase, a cell phone pinched between shoulder and ear as he enters. He marks our presence, but beelines for Kelly, setting his briefcase on the floor and snagging his cell with one hand, cupping his wife behind the neck as he bends to kiss her.

He straightens after kissing her, hand resting on her shoulder as he focuses on the person on the line. He speaks in rapid Spanish, listens, answers again, and then ends the call. He tosses the phone onto the table, his attention turning to Annika. His guarded expression says he knows exactly who she is.

"Baby," Kelly says, reading her husband's hesitance, "it's all good. Promise."

Luis's focus is laser-like, scanning Annika, scrutinizing. "She's clean?" It's addressed to Kelly, even as he continues to eye Annika.

"Yes, my love. She wouldn't be in our home if she wasn't." Kelly moves in front of him, touches his face. "It's all good. I promise you. We've made up. She apologized and I've forgiven her."

Luis's scrutiny is now on his wife; apparently what he sees on her face appeases his protectiveness, because he nods, kisses her again, and then moves toward me. "Luis Alvarez."

I rise to my feet and we shake hands. "Chance Kapule."

His eyes cut to my left bicep and my USMC globe, anchor, and eagle tattoo. "You're in the Corps?"

"Yes, sir," I say. "Force Recon, honorably discharged."

He eyes me. "You must have just barely made the height and weight cutoff."

"I joined at seventeen. I wasn't done growing, apparently, and I weighed about a hundred pounds less back then."

He nods. "Force Recon, huh? Saw combat?"

"I did two tours in Iraq as an infantry grunt before we made the Recons. Saw more than plenty combat with the Recons, as well."

"Three tours in Afghanistan." He taps his left thigh. "IED shrapnel nearly severed my leg. Ended up switching tracks—out of the infantry and into JAG."

"Oorah."

"Oorah," Luis returns. He kisses his wife again, then heads out of the kitchen. "Gonna change. You guys are welcome to stay—we have a guest room."

Annika looks to Kelly. "Are you sure? I don't wanna impose or...press my luck, I guess."

Kelly waves her hand to dismiss Annika's question. "Annie, come on. Of course you're staying. You're family."

Annika blinks hard. "Just like that?"

"You never stopped being family, Annie. Never. I had to put up boundaries to protect myself, but I never stopped loving you. I just couldn't have you in my life because it wasn't healthy for me. Now that you're back to being yourself, there's nothing I wouldn't do for you."

Annika presses the heels of her palms into her eyes. "God, I'm so sick of crying."

"You're letting things out that you kept bottled up for years," Kelly says. "You just have to let yourself process all this shit. It was gonna come out one way or another, at some point."

Annika nods, breathing slow, deep breaths. "I know. I just...I've cried more in the last week than the rest of my life combined. It's getting old."

Luis returns to the kitchen, then, wearing gray shorts cut off from sweatpants with a USMC T-shirt—a gnarly scar is visible on his left thigh. He reaches into the fridge and pulls out a bottle of beer, then hesitates, glancing at Annika. "Wait, shit. I can have something else."

Annika laughs. "I appreciate the consideration, Luis, but alcohol was never an issue for me. I can't touch anything stronger than aspirin, and obviously meth, but I'm fine to have a few drinks, and you certainly can."

He continues to hesitate. "You're sure?"

Annika nods. "I'm sure. Alcohol has never triggered cravings for me. I promise." She smiles at him. "But, I don't want to make you uncomfortable. If it would make you feel better for me to not drink, I'm fine with that. This is your home. I've just made amends with Kelly. I'm not going to risk that over a beer."

He nods, and then pulls out four bottles of a locally-brewed IPA, pops the tops, and hands them out. What follows is a meandering conversation. Kelly and Annika continue their attempt to make each laugh so hard they pee, and Luis and I swap war stories. Annika is true to her word, accepting a second beer but refusing a third, switching to a can of LaCroix. I'm nursing my drinks, which is overly cautious of me since I could drink a case of beer on my own and stay on my feet, but it's a delicate situation and I don't want to cause any issues, so it seems wisest to play it safe.

Eventually, Luis glances at the clock on the microwave. "I gotta get some sleep, I have a hearing at oh-eight-hundred." He looks at Annika. "It's really good to see you clean and healthy, Annika. I can't tell you how many nights my wife has spent awake, worrying about you, wishing she could help you and knowing she can't."

"Luis," Kelly snaps. "Don't. We're past that."

Annika makes a face that's not quite a smile, more of an expression of understanding. "It's okay, Kelly. He's allowed his feelings."

Luis nods. "Appreciated, Annika." He kisses Kelly as he leaves his chair. "Love you, babe. Have fun with Annika." He nods at me. "Chance. Good to meet you, brother."

"You too, Luis."

The conversation winds down, then, and Kelly starts

yawning. "I get up with Luis at the buttcrack of dawn, so I'm going to bed too."

Later, I'm settling into the guest bed, and Annika is braiding her hair, sitting on the edge of the bed, gaze vacant, lost in thought. She's in a T-shirt and underwear, fingers moving swiftly. Her posture is tense, her shoulders hunched.

I twist on the bed, swing my legs to either side of her hips and begin massaging her shoulders, digging my thumbs into the knots of muscle. "Jeez, mama. You got some crazy fuckin' knots goin' on here."

She snaps a hair tie into place at the tip of her braid, and then slumps, moaning. "God, that feels good." She lets out a sigh. "I guess I was more stressed about talking to Kelly than I even realized."

"She didn't make you work for it at all," I say. "It's obvious she loves you."

"I was so scared she wouldn't, Chance."

"But she did. You can breathe, baby."

I start in on the back of her neck, and she drops her head, letting it hang as I work my thumbs into the muscle. "Thank you," she murmurs, after a while.

"For what?"

She pulls away, pivoting to face me, nudging me to lie down. When I do, she curls up against me, resting her head on my chest. "Everything…just everything. What you did with Alvin. Driving me all the way here. Being here with me and supporting me through all of this."

"Anything you need, mama. Anything."

She sighs. "I don't know where I'd be without you." She barks a bitter laugh. "Well actually, yes, I do. Alvin would have—"

I cut in. "But he won't. He's out of your life. I *got* you, Annika. No one is ever gonna hurt you again, I swear on my fuckin' life." I turn my face to her, kiss her cheekbone, her temple. "You're in a new chapter. Good shit is coming for you. You got your family back, you got Kelly back. You don't owe anybody anything. You're safe. You can dream again."

She shakes her head against my chest. "I don't know what to dream *of*, Chance. What do I want for my life?"

"I don't know. I can't tell you that. Only you can decide that."

"That's just it, Chance. I don't know."

"You don't have to know. Not right now. You can take time to figure it out."

"What if you get sick of me?"

I laugh. "We've spent every moment of every day together since we met at the club, and I feel like I'm just starting to get to know you."

She sighs. "I've been weighed down for so long, this feeling of freedom is…it's almost disorienting. Like being unexpectedly weightless."

"I know what you mean, sorta. When Rev and I got out of the Marines, we were so used to having our life ordered down to the minute that we didn't know what to do with ourselves as civilians. It took time to come to grips with that." I tip my head to the side. "Not the same, I know. But similar."

She breathes out slowly. "I'm glad I met you, Chance Kapule."

"I'm glad too." I cup her hip.

"I want you," she breathes. "But I'm not sure—"

"Not here," I murmur back, feeling sleep stealing up

through me and over me. "Not here, not now. I want you too, but that ain't goin' anywhere, mama. Tonight, we just hold each other."

She nuzzles closer to me, throwing a soft, heavy thigh over mine, her hand on my belly, her breath slowing.

When I'm sure she's asleep, I let myself drift off, too.

11

Annika

L UIS IS GONE BY THE TIME I WAKE UP AND DRESS. Chance is already out of bed, sitting shirtless and barefoot on the front porch steps sipping coffee and browsing on his phone. There's more coffee in the pot, so I hunt down a mug and pour myself some, and then join him on the porch.

"Your girl is out for a run," Chance informs me.

"I miss running."

Chance barks a laugh. "Not me. I fuckin' *hated* PT. Running sucks. I'll pull iron all day long, but fuck me if I'll ever run another goddamn mile. I can't tell you how many fuckin' miles I've run, marched, and rucked."

"What do you mean by rucked?"

"Running is running, obviously. Marching is in formation, in cadence. Rucking is like hiking, but carrying fifty-some pounds of gear in a backpack, or a rucksack—therefore, rucking."

"That doesn't sound fun," I say.

He bobs his head to the side. "Eh. I bitch about it, but you really get close to the guys in your squad on long rucks. When you share misery, it forges a bond."

"Is combat the same way?"

He doesn't answer immediately. "That's a little different." He sighs. "There's no way to explain that bond. I'm not tryin' to avoid answering. There's just really no fuckin' way to explain it to someone who hasn't lived it."

"I can sort of understand, in a very minor way. The Olympics tryouts and qualification rounds…you're in very close proximity to the same people day in and day out. It's why Kelly and I are so close. We lived together, trained together, partied together."

At that moment, Kelly jogs up, dressed in very tight, very short workout shorts and a sports bra, earbuds in, checking her smart watch as she puffs to a stop. "Five miles in thirty-five minutes. Not too shabby," she says, dragging her wrist across her forehead.

"Nice," I tell her, extending my fist for a fist-bump. "You've gotten faster."

Kelly nods, tapping her watch to stop the run and kill the music, then stretching out on the lawn. "Most mornings, Luis and I run together. He has court this morning, though."

"He can run with that leg injury?" I ask.

Kelly nods, bending over her right leg, stretching her hamstring. "It took a lot of rehab and PT before he could jog again, but yeah. He's not as fast as he used to be, but he puts in a few miles almost every day."

I can't help a bitter huff. "I can still barely walk, and that's with a limp and a cane."

Kelly finishes with her hamstrings and moves to sitting, grasping her toes and slowly extending forward. "Ann, yours is a totally different injury. Your entire knee was basically dissolved. You're lucky you didn't lose the leg from the knee down. Walking at all after what happened is a miracle."

"Yeah, I know. It's just hard. In my soul, I'm still an athlete. My body just can't do what I want it to."

Kelly grimaces at me. "I'm sorry, babe."

"At some point, I think you oughta see another physical therapist," Chance tells me. "Get an assessment. See if you could rehab it any further, you know? Get more mobility. And if not, at least you know, you know?"

I frown at him. "With what health insurance and what money?"

He frowns back. "We know people, mama. We can get you in to see the best physical therapist in Vegas, I fuckin' guarantee. And you ain't gonna worry about the cost. We'll take care of it."

Kelly eyes Chance questioningly. "We?"

"Where I work. We're a close-knit group, mostly combat veterans with issues that make it hard for us to stay gainfully employed at a normal business." He glances at me, likely considering how much to tell her. "It's a nightclub. We work security. It's good work, good pay, and the owner provides living quarters for us all together, underneath the club. It's a good gig for fucked-up dudes like me, for whom normal socialization ain't really an option."

Kelly looks at Chance thoughtfully. "You seem well adjusted enough to me."

Chance laughs. "Trust me, I ain't."

"So, should I worry about Annie, with you?"

I answer for him. "No, Kel. You don't need to worry. Chance is...he's good. I'm good." She smiles at me. "We're good. Promise, babe."

Kelly looks between Chance and me. "I don't mean to question you, I just...my girl's been through enough. I don't want to see her go from trouble to trouble, you know?"

Chance nods, unfazed. "I getcha, Kelly. And I appreciate you lookin' out for Nikki. All I can do is promise you that while I may have my issues, I wouldn't ever do anything to hurt Nik. Not anything, not ever." He looks at me. "I care about her, a fuckin' lot. Ain't known her for a long time, but...I guess my heart don't seem to know that. My heart seems to feel like I've known her my whole life. I'll take care of her. You got my word of honor on that."

My heart squeezes, clenches, flip-flops. Words bubble up and stick in my throat. "Chance..."

He rests his mug on his knee and slings an arm around me. "I told you, mama. I fuckin' *got* you."

I sniffle, turn my face into his arm. "Dammit. *Again.*"

Chance just laughs softly, kissing the top of my head. "It's all good. You lived under a heavy-ass cloud for a long damn time. Like your girl said last night, it's gonna take time to process all the shit you got pent up in there."

I just shake my head against his arm. "Don't want to. It's too much."

Kelly moves to sit beside me. "If you can come here and reconcile with me, then you can do anything." She leans against me. "You talk to your mom, or anyone else?"

I nod. "Mom, Gram, and Erin." I sniff a laugh. "I saved the hardest for last."

Kelly laughs with me. "You always did like leaving the hard stuff for last."

"Once the easy stuff is out of the way, I can put all my

focus onto the hard thing." I laugh. "In this case, though, I just had to work up the courage."

"I love you, Ann." Kelly kisses my cheek. "Unfortunately, I have some research to do that I can't do from home."

I sit up and wipe my face with both hands. "I love you, too."

"Luis and I can come visit you, maybe? Where are you living, now?"

Chance answers for me. "She's living with me in Vegas."

I eye him. "You're sure about that?"

He just nods. "Yup. Now that I've got you, I'm not letting you go. You're stuck with me, mama."

Kelly laughs. "Send me an address, and I'll talk to Luis. We'll find some time to come out and see you. We'll send the boys to go be macho Marines together, and you and I can go tear up Vegas together."

I nod, yet again feeling emotional, this time at having to leave. "You got it. It'll be fun." I work to my feet, and Kelly and I hug for a long, long time. Eventually, I pull away. "Thank you, Kel. After how I treated you, I don't deserve your forgiveness, and I'll be eternally grateful that you gave it."

"That's the thing about forgiveness, honey—we never deserve it. We don't forgive for the other person, we forgive for ourselves. And in your case, I love you." She cups my face. "Down to my bones, bitch. No take backs. So, yeah."

"Down to my bones, bitch," I echo—how we used to say we loved each other, back in the day.

She pulls back, blinking hard. "Okay. Go. I gotta shower and hit the library." She hugs me again, takes my mug from me, and then gently pushes me backward. I turn away and she smacks my ass, hard, the way she used to.

I laugh, giving her the finger. "I did *not* miss that. Your ass-slaps still sting like a motherfucker." I look at Chance. "Your shirt and shoes still in the house?"

He shakes his head. "Nah. In the car. I figured we'd say our goodbyes after she got back from her run."

Kelly pulls a face. "I don't mean to send you packing, it's just I'll be working till late, and then we have plans for tomorrow we can't cancel."

I shake my head. "It was a surprise visit. I'm just so glad I got to see you at all." I pull my phone from my back pocket. "Text me, yeah?"

Kelly takes Chance's mug as well, looping them over her index finger. "Will do. Love you, babe."

I don't look back, just wave without looking. "If I say anything else, I'll start bawling again, so I'm gonna let you have the last word."

Kelly just laughs, and I climb into the passenger seat. Chance slings in beside me a moment later, starting the engine.

"You ready?" he asks.

My eyes burn. "Nope. Let's go."

He says nothing, just drives away.

◆

We end up getting breakfast at a little cafe in Old Town. We don't talk much—it becomes apparent Chance has something gnawing at him. I decide to let him bring it to me when he's ready. After breakfast, we walk around Old Town for a bit, and eventually end up at the end of a pier. Chance plops down to his butt, and holds a hand up to me—I hesitate, but then figure fuck it, and grip his hand and let him help me, let him support my weight as I shove my bad leg out and lower myself to my butt beside him. Silence curls around us, settles between us. Behind, cars rush, people chatter, skateboards growl across the sidewalk, seagulls caw, waves crash. It's not awkward, it's just…silence.

After almost five minutes of Chance staring out at the ocean, one foot idly kicking over the edge of the pier, he looks at me. "Not many people could sit in silence for that long."

I shrug. "Feels like you needed it. You've given me so much already, Chance. I can give you some quiet to think."

"You gonna ask?"

I shake my head. "You'll tell me when you're ready, or not. I'm not gonna push."

He snorts. "Well that's fuckin' dumb."

I twist away, startled by his unexpected response. "What the hell does that mean?"

"It means, I appreciate you givin' me space and time to think about the shit in my stupid fuckin' head. But, at this point between us, I kinda expect you to push me a little. I'm used to keepin' shit to myself. I'm closer to Rev than I can even put into words, but our relationship ain't like that. We're dudes, for one thing, and dudes don't tend to share this kinda shit very easily. Honest truth is, Annika, you're gonna have to pull things out of me. It's hard for me to open up. I can get you to open up and trust me and all that, but hypocritically enough, I ain't so good at doing the same in return."

"So you're saying you want me to…I dunno…force you to open up to me?"

He nods. "More or less."

I take his hand in mine, palm to palm, and tangle our fingers together. "All right then. Out with it, buster. What's eating you?"

"Forgiveness."

When he doesn't immediately elaborate, I roll my free hand in a circle. "What about forgiveness?"

He sighs, a long, bitter, resigned sound. "My cousins, and my uncle. I'm *so* fuckin' angry at them, Nik. It burns inside me like acid. It's like that sour stomach the day after you've had way too much to drink, but worse. It's eating away me from the inside and I don't know what to fuckin' do about it." He shakes his head. "Your girl, Kelly—earlier, before we left, she said somethin' that's stuck in my craw. She said that we don't forgive people so *they'll* feel better, we forgive people so *we* will."

"And you're thinking, if you can figure out how to forgive the people who got you hooked on meth and fucked up your life, maybe you'll finally feel…" I trail off, unsure how he'd feel.

"Free," he fills in. "I'd finally feel truly free. Being angry at them, blaming them…it's weighing me down. It's got me trapped in this fuckin' cycle of bitterness and resentment and guilt. Like, I made that choice. I did that. No one else but me. So it's not their fault, it's mine. But then a little voice starts whispering that I was fuckin' wasted, I could barely stay on my feet—and mama, you got no clue how much booze it takes to put me in that state. Bottles of whiskey, I'm talking—bottle-z, plural." He shakes his head. "I was so far gone I think I'd have done anything I was told. I think I thought it was pot. I don't even remember smoking it, to be honest. It's just this hazy, vague memory of the whole world spinning and my cousin Eddie handing me a pipe and telling me to try it. After that? Nothing. And that little voice is like, it's Eddie's fault, not mine. I wouldn't have hit that pipe if I'd known what it was. But I didn't ask. And I was the one to get myself so shit-faced I was incapable of even asking. So I just…I go in circles, and I get angry at them and at myself…" he trails off, shrugging.

"Do you think you have PTSD?"

He frowns, paws a hand through his loose, wild, tangled, wind-blown black hair. "I mean, yeah. You don't do the shit I've done, see the shit I seen, and not have some kind of trauma from it. I have nightmares. Not all the time, but I have 'em. I get flashbacks. But…" He shrugs, groaning a sigh. "I just think of my buddy Jameson. He tried out for Recons with Rev and me and a few others. Good dude. Solid. Dependable. Funny. Then one day he just…couldn't handle it anymore. We got back from an op and…he never came back from the shower. I went to check on him, and he was just standing there, staring at nothing, shaking all over. The water was ice cold, but he didn't notice. He pulled it together, to a degree. Rotated out, went home. His family has a ranch in Oklahoma and I guess he was okay for a while. And then he snapped. Thought he was downrange, in combat. Totally lost in his head, in the past, I dunno. I guess eventually through a lot of therapy and getting a support dog, he's able to function again, but…he ain't the same." He shrugs, flipping a palm to the sky. "I'm not there, and so I guess I figure I'm fine. Like I said, I have my moments, but for the most part, I'm okay. I think in part, because Rev and I came from such a fucked-up life already, combat wasn't so much of a shock to either of us. I dunno, though, I'm just guessing."

"I guess I just wonder if maybe it's a spectrum, right? And it manifests in different ways and maybe for you it's not overt, not like your friend Jameson, but it's still there, and the drinking and getting hooked on tweak…maybe that was part of the way you were trying to cope with it. I'm obviously not any kind of an expert, but…"

He nods. "I think you're right. I just…I can't use it as an excuse."

"No, I'm not saying it's an excuse. You and I, maybe more than anyone, understand the necessity of taking responsibility for our choices and not trying to excuse or justify them. But I think we can allow for mitigating circumstances. Not excusing, just…explaining, maybe. Or…understanding, for ourselves, how we got to where we were. Because before you can forgive your cousins, I think you gotta forgive yourself." I grin at him. "Weren't you the one telling me about Rev learning to forgive himself?"

He groans a laugh. "Like I told you, I'm good at knowing the right thing to say and being there for other people. I ain't so good at taking my own advice."

I curl my arm around his and rest my head on his shoulder—I feel self-conscious doing it. Silly. Girly. I've never been that girl—never had a boyfriend of the cuddling and PDA variety. I've never been…good at overt displays of affection, receiving or giving. My mom and Erin aren't that type, either. In fact, the only regular hugs I ever got were from Gram.

But with Chance, I feel an opportunity to be someone new. To be different. And I remember a conversation we had back when we first met—not that long ago chronologically, but emotionally, it feels like ages ago—about how Myka gave Rev a kind of sweetness that cured the darkness in him. Or, at least, helped him emerge from the darkness and find a new version of himself. Or something like that.

I told Chance he'd never get that from me. Because I've never gotten it from anyone. Mom loves me, Erin loves me, Gram loves me, but it's not that kind of love. And I thought, then, when I had that conversation with Chance, that I'd lost forever whatever love I may have had from them.

But now…

Things feel different.

For me.

For him.

For *us*, because somehow, I feel like an *us* may actually be possible.

And I don't think he'd ever come out and say it in so many words, but he wants, maybe even *craves*, that tenderness he's seen Rev and Kane both receive. He saw what it's done for them, and he wants that for himself.

God knows he's earned it, from me. Why he wants it with me, what he saw in me, I'm not sure. But I'm not going to argue anymore. I can't. Because I want what he's offering.

Fuck, I *need* it.

I need to feel loved. Not just by my mom or Erin or Gram or Kelly…

I want and need what Chance is offering me. The word "love" hasn't been floated. That'd be nuts—we just met. But it's there, in the ether between us.

That's what this could be.

And so, I suppose for me, the next step is to try on for size the act of showing sweetness to him.

When I lean into him and rest my cheek on his huge, hard, solid bicep, he twists and kisses the crown of my head.

And it's a kiss I feel down to my bones. It makes me shudder all over, because it seems to melt something inside me. Rattles the walls around my heart.

"I need to go to Hawaii," Chance murmurs.

"Well, I've got nowhere to be, and I've always wanted to go to Hawaii." I feel shaky and nervous, as I try out another attempt at showing him sweetness—I palm his cheek, turn his face down to mine, lift up, kiss him.

Not hungrily, not hot and wild. Soft. Tender. Slow. Just lips damp and warm on his, my fingers drifting around to the back of his neck, into his hair, curling over the shell of his ear, tracing the line of his jaw and the soft scratchiness of his beard.

When the kiss breaks, our foreheads meet, rolling together. "Wow," he murmurs. "That was…a hell of a kiss, mama."

"Yeah?" I whisper, blushing so hard my cheeks burn.

His thumb brushes over my lips, eyes searching mine. "Yeah."

I feel vindicated, seeing the emotion in his eyes and on his face, the emotions I don't think he knows to express—emotions catalyzed by my sweet little kiss.

He sees what I'm doing. Why I kissed him like that. And it makes him feel so much, so many things, he doesn't know how to put it into words.

I don't mind. I don't need words. I just need…god, honestly? Him. I just need him.

———— ✦ ————

We're seated in the boarding area outside our gate at San Diego International Airport, waiting for our flight to board—we got lucky and snagged the last two seats on a flight bound for Honolulu in a couple hours. Chance paid for the tickets and wouldn't hear a word of argument from me. Not like I could afford my own ticket anyway.

"I gotta call Inez," Chance says, bringing his phone to his ear. "Hey, Inez, it's me. How are things at the club? Ya'll gettin' along okay without me?…Yeah, things with Annika are pretty much settled, but I…um, shit, this is hard." He barks a laugh. "God, Inez, I swear to fuck you're psychic or something. Yes, I need to go to Hawaii. I've got some shit I need to settle. No, no worries about that. I just…I gotta see them. I gotta…forgive them, and myself. I'll never be able to really move on if I don't…yeah, just a day or two… well, if you're sure, yeah, that'd be great, honestly. All right, cool, we'll make it three days. Nah, I'm good. You make sure you call me if anything comes up. And tell the boys they can call me if they need me. Thanks, Inez. Yeah, bye."

He hangs up and grins at me. "How's three days on the beach sound to you?"

"Sounds like I'll need a bathing suit," I answer, feeling almost embarrassingly giddy at the prospect.

His grin is wicked. "Not where we're going, you don't."

I arch an eyebrow at him. "Um, what?"

"It's not just my uncle and his deadbeat kids who live in Hawaii. My grandma, my great-aunt, and some other cousins all do, or did. There's a little plot of land that's been passed on through the family. It went to my dad, and when he passed, it went to me. It ain't much, but I've been paying for a local friend of the family to keep it up for me. Uncle Joseph, Eddie, and Rico never knew I owned it. I think they just assumed it went to another cousin, of which I've got an actual shit-ton. And back when I was in Hawaii last time, I was…" He frowns, sighs. "I was honestly too chicken shit to go. My dad brought my mom there for their honeymoon. The only vacation they ever took. She was sober, then. My grandma passed away there—peacefully, in her sleep, so there's nothin' creepy, it was just where she wanted to be when she passed on. I guess it just seemed like there would be too much there, and I was…I was scared to feel it all. Joey, Eddie, and Rico, they seemed safer. They knew my dad, and I thought I could connect with him. Only, what I discovered was the reason he left in the first place. Those assholes are toxic as hell, and always have been. But now…I think I'm ready to not only face them and show them I'm not that fucked-up bastard I was, but also to visit the family property."

"What does that have to do with not needing a bathing suit?" I ask. "I mean, I'm all about you doing what you need to do, and I'll be there to support you every step of the way, but…if we're going to the beach, I need a bathing suit."

He just grins again. "The property is a tiny little place on the beach. You gotta fly into the big island and then take a puddle jumper to Kaua'i and then you need a four-by-four to get to the property itself. It's remote, isolated, and very, very private. So, what I mean is, you won't need a bathing suit, because we won't be wearing a stitch of clothing for the next three days."

"Oh," I whisper, blushing again. "I see. Sounds…fun?"

He laughs. "Mama, you don't even know."

"You've got plans, I take it?" I meet his eyes, see the twinkle in his, mischief and arousal.

He brushes his lips against mine. "Nikki-baby, you got no fuckin' clue."

"I think I may have a few ideas of my own," I murmur.

"Been dreaming of getting you alone since the day we met," he whispers. "And baby girl, the things I want to do to you…"

I tug my fingers through his beard, and then use his beard to pull him closer, so my whisper is almost inaudible, felt more than heard. "I…can't…*wait*."

12

LAST OF THE DEMONS

Chance

OUR RENTED WRANGLER BOUNCES AND JOUNCES along the rutted, muddy two-track. Mud splatters, and the suspension works overtime to absorb the deep pits and divots and ruts in the path. It's barely a path, honestly. The only way you'd even know the two-track path is even there is if you know it's there to begin with. Otherwise, it's just a narrow gap in the dense tangled tropical forest way out in the middle of nowhere on the northern edge of the big island. There's an old, faded white sign nailed to the tree near the opening, which at one time said "Kapule" on it, but at this point it's just black paint faded into illegibility.

Annika clutches the oh-shit bar with both hands, sometimes grabbing her chest with one hand to hold her tits down when we go over a particularly nasty series of bumps and ruts.

"Jesus shits, Chance, where the fuck are we going?" She glances at me, annoyance rife on her face. "We left the main road almost half an hour ago."

I laugh. "Almost there, mama. Uncle Joey and the boys live on the old family homestead. It's about twenty acres in the middle of nowhere. They only got indoor plumbing and electricity a few years before I was born, and I think they got satellite internet only like five or ten years ago. It's…rustic, let's say."

She eyes me, and then spies another series of ruts ahead, and braces, one hand on the oh-shit bar, the other clamped over her chest. "When I think of Hawaii, I think of beaches and surfers and Magnum PI. This…" she nods at the road with her head, "makes me think, paddle faster, I hear banjos."

I cackle. "Understandable misapprehension for folks who've never been to Hawaii, or who never leave the touristy areas. That's why they live way out here—no visitors. No tourists. And honestly, no authorities, for the most part. They get left alone, mainly because it just ain't worth the trip all the fuckin' way out here, even for cops. I mean, it's a locally open secret Joey and boys are…not the best sorts. I think they cook meth, probably grow pot, too. But they keep to themselves, so they get left alone."

She frowns hard at me. "Neither of us need to be anywhere fucking close to these assholes, if they're cooking."

I nod. "We're gonna be here just long enough for me to say what I gotta say to Joey and the boys, and then we're outta here. I don't know that they cook for sure. If they do, it ain't gonna be near the main house. They know better than that—that shit is volatile."

She doesn't look appeased. "I don't think I'm gonna feel tempted. I just…I want that shit out of my life, Chance. For good. Completely."

"Me too, mama. But I gotta do this. If you get bad vibes or anything, you just park your fine ass in the Jeep and let me do my thing. I promise I'll be quick, and we can get to the good stuff."

She nods, letting out a breath. "That would be good. I need the good stuff, Chance."

I point ahead, where the path bends sharply to the right, passing between a towering pair of Banyan trees, to which are nailed matching "Private Property KEEP OUT" signs. "We're here."

We bounce between the trees, around another sharp bend and down a steep hill, and then the path opens into a wide circular clearing. At the far end of the clearing is the sprawling, ramshackle structure of the main house—decades of additions by subsequent generations, all hand-built, nothing to code, made from cast-off and repurposed materials, much of it recovered via trawling dumpsters and neighborhood trash days. There's no cohesion to the structure, no pattern, just various rooms and expansions and additions tacked on willy-nilly, made from plywood boards, sheets of corrugated iron, sections of sheetrock and bare two-by-fours and exposed, un-mudded, mold-dotted drywall, which is obviously not meant as an exterior product. The roof is much the same. Most rooms leak in the corners during heavy rains, which is just about every day. There's more than one hazardous, not-to-code fireplace.

Next to the main house is a hand-built carport, just four heavy-duty posts concreted into the dirt and a make-shift roof, sloping down to a partial back wall, with open sides. Behind and off to the side, in the woods aways, is a barn, the oldest structure on the property, dating back to the eighteen hundreds, or so goes the family lore. It's leaning atrociously, and daylight shows through gaps in the walls. Inside is a jumble of shit—old bikes, rusting hulks of cars, massive piles of building material in case the house needs patching, which is all the time, old TVs, fridges, couches…you name it, you can find it in the barn.

Parked in the carport is Joey's ancient deathtrap, a 1986 GMC Jimmy, more rust than metal, with a suspension kit and off-road tires worth more by triple than the vehicle itself. Eddie's Bronco is next to that, and Rico's El Camino.

"The gang's all here," I remark, pointing at the lineup of rusting, lifted, battered old vehicles, which are kept running through stubbornness and what Uncle Joey calls "redneck ingenuity."

"Great," Annika mutters. "I'm so excited." She watches me as I park in the middle of the clearing. "You okay?"

I blow out a breath as the door of the house creaks open and Joey appears, tall and gaunt, long black hair streaked with silver and tangled and matted and greasy, wearing cut-off jean shorts and a dirty white tank top, a cigarette smoldering in the corner of his lips and a sawed-off shotgun in his hands. He's lost a lot of weight since I last saw him—too much.

"Nope," I admit. "Now that I'm here, this is starting to feel like a bad fuckin' idea."

"We can go." She grabs my hand, squeezes. "Just turn around and go."

I shake my head. "Nope. No can do. Gotta face the demons, mama." I jerk my head at Uncle Joey, who's glaring death at me. "And there's one of 'em." I open the door, glance at Annika. "Just stay in the car, I think. Now that I'm here, I don't think I'm gonna go in."

She just nods, reaches out and rubs my arm.

I heave myself out of the car, leaving the engine

running, and tug my hair away from my face. The air is still, hot, and humid. Joey says nothing. Eddie pushes into the doorframe, and Rico appears behind him.

"Figured you was dead," Uncle Joey says, after a moment. His voice is ragged, hoarse.

"Nope. And not for lack of tryin'," I say. "Joey, Eddie, Rico." That's about all the greeting I can muster.

"Whaddya want, boy?" Joey grumbles. "Ain't nothin' for you here."

"No shit," I say. I lean back against the grill of the Jeep, heat blowing out against my backside. "Just here to say a few things to you three."

The trio spills out almost as one unit, Joey hooking the butt of the shotgun under his armpit, grabbing his cigarette and tapping ash off. Eddie looks like hell— he's almost as tall as me, and back in the day he was quite a figure, heavy, rough, and muscled; he's wasted away in the intervening years, scabbed and dotted with sores, unwashed, visibly jittery, skin sallow and sagging and prematurely aged. Rico looks much the same, still with the family height, but lean and fairly healthy looking, bulging beer belly notwithstanding.

Eddie is still on tweak. Rico, probably not. Joey, maybe, more likely, lots of booze and pot.

"Well?" Joey demands. "You came all the way the fuck out here to say somethin', fuckin' say it. Ain't got all day."

I shake my head. "Don't know where to start, now that I'm here." I swallow hard. "You three took me in after I got out of the Marines. I was a mess. You gave me somewhere to be, and…" I shake my head again. "Eddie, you got me hooked on meth."

Eddie's eyes narrow. "Looks like you got off it."

"Yeah, I did, and it nearly fuckin' killed me. I harbored a lot of anger at you for a long time."

He spits into the dirt. "All I did was offer it to you. You the one who smoked it."

"I know." I nod, drag my hair back again. "I fuckin' know. But you still put it in front of me, knowing I was fucked up. Knowing you were hooked on it yourself. You still gave it to me. But yeah, Eddie, it was my choice, too." I swallow. "I want you to know I forgive you. That shit damn near ruined my life, as if it wasn't fucked up enough to begin with. You're to blame for that as much as I am. But I need you to know I forgive you, and I hope you find your way. Life is better without it, man. Trust me. Once you're off of it, life is better. But I can't make you and I sure as fuck ain't gonna try. I just can't hold on to the anger at you any longer."

Eddie spits again. "What the fuck ever. Fuck you." He goes back inside, the screen door slamming noisily. I hear a bottle smash, and then another door slam.

Joey lifts his chin in my direction. "Who's she?"

"No one you'll ever know," I growl. "She's freedom and salvation. She's a new kind of future."

"Come to rub it in my face?" he sneers. "That you're so much better off without us? Clean, fat as fuck, with a pretty girl?"

I shake my head. "No. I just had to come back here and…" I shrug. "Stay what I gotta say. Look the past in the eye and know that I've beaten it."

"Always did think you were better than us," Rico grumbles. "Never said it, but I felt it."

"I'm not. I don't think that." I frown, shrug. "Well, maybe I do, and maybe I am, in a way. I got clean. I have a job. I have a place to live. I have friends—brothers. People who care about me and won't let me do shit that'll fuck me up. You're family. You guys oughta have been that for me. But you weren't. You pulled me down into your shit, in this...darkness." I gesture at the house. "Sell the land. Get real jobs. Get off the sauce and off all the other shit. Start over. Do better—*be* better."

"I ain't sellin' shit," Joey snaps. "Family been born here, lived here, and died here for four generations. Ain't much but it's my home." He spits into the dirt, like Eddie did. "And besides, this land ain't worth shit to anyone else."

"I'm just sayin'. You can do more than whatever it is you do here."

Joey drops his cigarette butt to the dirt, grinds it out with his bare heel, plucks a soft pack from his shorts pocket and lights another, swaggering a few steps closer to me; I can smell the booze on him from ten feet away. "Listen, boy. You found Jesus or some shit, good for you. You got clean. You're healthy, you got a girl. Good for you. Happy for you. But fuck off with your opinions on my life." He glances over his shoulder at the house, then back at me. "Yeah, Eddie's got a problem. But that's his problem and *my* problem, not yours. I wanna drink and smoke myself to death, what's it to you? You're about to drive off and never come back, now that you said your piece." He pulls from the cigarette, blows it out of his nostrils, speaking as he does so. "You needed to come here and prove to yourself that you...what? That you won? Well, boy, you won. Good for you. This is our life, and you ain't gotta like it."

"I ain't judgin' you—" I start.

"I don't much give a fuck if you are or not." He taps ash off. "Look. You need forgiveness? Be forgiven. You need to give forgiveness, well, you done gave it. For me, for Eddie, for Rico. Great. Thanks. But don't sit there and preach at me, all right? You go live your life, and feel good about yourself knowing you made more of yourself than us."

I sigh. "Uncle Joey…"

He turns away. "Wait a second. Got somethin' for you." He vanishes into the house with a creak of springs and a slam, appearing a minute or so later with a file box, a thick cardboard box used to store papers. "Your aunt Lu passed a few months ago. Cancer. Your dad was close to her, exchanged letters with her up till he got himself killed. When she passed, your cousin Angie brought this by, fig-urin' I may know how to get it to you. It's some letters and photographs and shit. Personal shit from your dad and ma."

I take it from him, finding it heavier than expected. My heart pounds as I prop it on my hip and tug the lid off—within are piles of envelopes, a few dozen of them, along with a haphazard pile of photographs…I see Mom, Dad, myself as a little kid. There's an old Zippo lighter, a tarnished gold ring on a thin, cheap silver chain. A framed photograph of Mom, Dad, and me, from a Walmart photo booth or something like that.

My eyes burn. "I…thanks, Uncle Joey. When they were killed, their shit was sold or impounded or lost in the shuffle when the apartment was repossessed. I never was able to get anything of theirs. Not one damn thing."

He nods. "Well, there ya go. Whole box of shit." He taps ash, sucks smoke, exhales, spits. "Your dad was the best of us. Shoulda been somethin'. That no-good drug-ad-dled bitch drug him down, got him killed. He loved her, even though he knew it was some toxic-ass shit she was mixing him up in. You deserved better."

Coming from Uncle Joey…that's some harsh criticism.

"She loved him, and me."

He nods. "I know it. But I figure after what you been through, you know that sometimes, that ain't enough. Wasn't enough for her. You're stronger. You got away." He slugs my shoulder. "Get outta here, Chance. Leave us in the rear view. Be what your dad never got to be. I know you mean well. But…" He shakes his head, glances at Rico, who's been by the front door this whole time, silently watching and listening. "You got your path, we got ours."

"Eddie's gonna die, Joey," I say. "You gotta know that."

He nods. "I do. We don't cook no more." Ash, inhale, exhale. "I done tried it all. Kicked him out a bunch of times, after you vanished. He's been arrested, even tried rehab once, which damn near bankrupted me." A shake of his head. "He won't never kick it. So, all's I can do is…be there. He chose his path. I can't change that. Rico can't. You sure as fuck can't. Don't like it, but it's better he's here with family who gives a shit about him. I can try to keep him alive as long as possible. But I know, sooner or later, I'm gonna find him done gone and croaked. Breaks my damn heart, boy. Breaks my damn heart."

I shake my head. "That shit is pure evil, Joey."

"I know it. God almighty, do I know it." Joey flicks the butt to the dirt and grinds it out, pulls another and puts it to his lips, but doesn't light it. "Now go on. Git. Take that pretty girl you got there and go love on her. Thomas has been keepin' up the place on Kaua'i for you, yeah?"

I nod—I guess he does know I own it. Which doesn't

surprise me all that much, really. "Yeah. That's where we're going next."

He nods. "Good. Glad it's being taken care of." He eyes me. "When he's gone…I'd like to put him to rest out there. Next to my ma, and my Connie, God rest her."

Connie—my aunt, his wife, who was killed in a car accident when the boys were little.

I nod. "Sure. Course. He should rest with family."

"God willin', it'll be a while, yet."

I palm the back of my neck. "I'm not sure what I was expecting from you, Uncle Joey, but I gotta say you've kinda surprised me."

He rasps a hoarse chuckle. "I'm not all bad." His eyes go haunted. "And…watchin' Eddie has…" He shakes his head, pulls the unlit cigarette from his mouth and toys with it, staring at it rather than meeting my eyes. "And knowing that he got you on that poison?" Another shake of his head. "Coulda killed him, and I did whup him, after you disappeared. Thought for sure you was dead."

"To be honest, I should be. Just about was. I was… saved."

"Well, I'm glad you were." Somethin' good's gotta come outta this place."

"Uncle Joey…"

He lights the cigarette, sucks smoke, coughs on the exhale in a way that makes me wonder if Eddie's not the only one with one foot in the grave. "Get on outta here, Chance. Take that girl and git. You said your piece. I said mine. Nothing else for it."

I nod, heft the box. "Thanks for this."

"Hope it brings you some kinda peace about your old man. He really was the best of us." He heads for the house.

"Goodbye, Chance. Have yourself a good life." The screen door slams after him.

Rico hesitates. "Dad is…"

I nod. "I know. I heard it."

"Won't be no funeral. So…don't come."

"You think Eddie'll…" I trail off.

Rico nods. "Yup. He barely gets outta bed most days. Won't be long."

"What are you gonna do, after?"

He shrugs. "Hell if I know." He glances at the screen door. "Probably sell this place. Won't tell Dad, but…I couldn't stay here on my own."

"I wouldn't either."

He holds the door open, glances at me. "Good to see you healthy, Chance." That's all the goodbye I'll get from Rico—he was always shy on words.

I head back to the Jeep. Set the box on the rear floor well, get behind the wheel. Make the turnaround, head away. Annika watches me for a long time without speaking.

I reach out and take her hand. "It was good, mama. I'm good."

She keeps watching me. "You sure? That sounded intense."

"It was. Eddie is not well, and neither is Uncle Joey. Eddie…that's a lost cause. He's…he's gone. Way down the hole and doesn't plan to come out of it. I think Uncle Joey is sort of seeing mortality himself and he's sorta…" I lift a hand. "Thinking on things. Rico…he's always been a bit…aloof, I guess. Not sure where he's at. But I'm glad I came. I can see that Eddie never really…" I shake my head, sighing. "I don't know. I guess what Joey said is the best way to put it—he chose his path."

She nods. "Yeah, that's the way of it sometimes. I don't want to use the phrase 'lost cause' but…"

"If it were to ever apply, it applies to Eddie." I scrub my face. "And I think me getting addicted was…collateral damage."

"What's in the box?" she asks.

I sigh. "Uh, so I guess Dad was pretty close to my aunt Lucy, who we all call Aunt Lu. I guess he exchanged letters with her for years, sent her photos of us. When Aunt Lu passed, her daughter, my cousin, brought the box to Uncle Joey, I guess figuring if I was gonna maybe see him."

"So how many aunts and uncles and cousins do you have?"

I laugh. "A fuck-ton. There were six in my dad's family. Uncle Joey's the only one left. Aunt Lu…she was complicated. When I came here, after I left the Corps, I tried to connect with her, but…" I sigh, frowning. "I guess I reminded her of my dad and it was hard for her, and she didn't really want to…I dunno. She couldn't deal with that, so our connection sort of fizzled. Or at least, that's all I can really come up with. She just didn't want to see me, which I admit both hurt and pissed me off. All the others have passed—two before I was born, one when I was kid, another a few years ago, then Aunt Lu just a few years ago." I sigh. "And Joey ain't long for this world either, I don't think. Rico hinted at the fact that he's sick, and I could tell, too. He's lost a lot of weight, he's been a chain-smoker for as along as I've been alive, and he's got a nasty cough." I shrug, shake my head, glance in the rearview as the two huge banyan trees recede from view. "This is goodbye for good to this place, to this part of my life."

She touches my arm briefly, a brush of her fingers

before grabbing the oh-shit bar and her chest once more. "How do you feel about that?"

I twist the wheel in my fists. "Mixed. I mean, when I lived here, I was...even before I got hooked on tweak, things were not great. Bleak. I was depressed. I was struggling with becoming a civilian. Nightmares. Seeing threats around every corner." I laugh. "PTSD, I guess, now that I think about it."

"Chance..." her voice is soft, sad, compassionate.

"Ain't gonna lie, mama, it was rough." I clear my throat. "That place back there? It's a fuckin' hovel. Leaks. Dark. Bugs, rodents, no A/C. Stank to high heaven, because it's fuckin' filthy, as you can probably imagine, since we both know addicts ain't exactly clean freaks." I shake my head. "I was drinking all the time, smoking pot...doing shady shit with Eddie and Rico. There were always fights. Eddie and Rico would get wasted and pick fights with me, or with Joey and I'd have to step in. There wasn't enough food, because what money there was went to booze, smokes, and drugs." I grip the wheel until it creaks and my knuckles hurt. "I...after I got hooked, it was easy for Eddie to manipulate me into doing shit I wouldn't normally do. Knock over liquor stores, put the hurt on someone who owed Eddie money." I shake my head. "Fuckin' shameful, the shit I did. No excuse. I just did it because if I did, Eddie would give me a hit. He used me, strung me along, kept me strung out and made sure he was the only place I could get my fix. He used me. But it was still me who did that shit."

She rests her hand on my thigh, knowing there's nothing for her to say; it's all been said. I just need to get this out.

"But, as awful as it was, they took me in. I had nowhere

to go. I'd never had to fend for myself, in the sense of living independently. I was homeless, then I was in the gang, and then I was in the Marines. The gang had a few different places where we could crash, and Rev and I just bounced around. We never had a home, per se, like our own place, but we always had somewhere with a roof and a bed, or, at least, blankets on the floor. I got out of the Corps and I had no fuckin' clue where to go, what to do. Rev and I had a disagreement about that, and we went our separate ways for awhile. Thank fuck we did, because it means Rev never saw me as an addict." I shake my head and shrug again. "They took me in. But there was a cost to it, I guess. So like I said, mixed. I am glad I came, though."

She relaxes a bit as we go through a less bumpy stretch. "You feel any kind of closure?"

I nod. "Yeah. I do, actually. Seeing Eddie, telling him I forgive him, seeing Uncle Joey and…I dunno. I guess I feel so grateful I got out, I survived, got clean, and got a new lease on life, at the risk of sounding cliché. They're stuck in place, stuck in time. I wish I could help them, but I know I can't."

Annika gives me sharp, piercing look. "More to the point, do you forgive yourself?"

I nod, then bob my head to the side. "Yeah. Well… working on it. I think forgiving Eddie is a big step in the right direction. I feel lighter. I was harboring a lot of anger and resentment and blame for him, and now I just feel… sad, I guess. He's sick. It's a disease, addiction is. And it's just clear he's dying from that disease, and seeing him like he was just now…yeah. I'm not angry at him anymore. I'm just sad for him, and for Joey. There's hope for Rico, maybe. I dunno."

"I'm sorry you went through that, Chance."

I glance at her, and she smiles at me, softly, sweetly. "Led me to you, so…"

Her brow furrows. "So…? What?"

"I'm just glad we met. I feel like…when I'm around you, I guess I feel like…" I swallow hard, pull hard to get the words past my teeth. "Like I can be my best self. That there's possibilities. Not just…alive. Not just one day to the next, working, hanging out with the guys, wash-rinse-repeat." It's so hard to put this into words. It's vulnerability, which is scarier to me than combat or anything else; I've relied on no one but me my whole life. "You make me…" I trail off, shake my head as if to clear it, "you make me want *life*, Nik."

"But you seem to be saying that having met me almost…" she laughs, a dry, sarcastic bark. "It almost sounds like you're saying it's worth it. Having met me."

"Would that be so crazy?" I ask, looking at her. "You and me, this thing with us…it's barely begun. But…if it could be what I see Rev and Myka have, what Kane and Anj have…then yes, Annika. It would be worth it. And I'm willing to work for that, to build us up to that."

She shakes her head. "You're crazy, Chance."

"Why?"

She swallows hard, blinks harder, turns her face away, covering her mouth with her palm, other arm curled across her torso protectively, shelling herself. "What if I don't feel the same way?"

"Hey, you're allowed to feel however you feel." I reach out and grab her thigh. "If you don't want this with me, that's okay. I'll be okay. I'd be sad. It'd…that would fuckin' suck balls, not gonna lie. But I'd let you go if that's what you need. I'd help you get set up somewhere. San Diego, or LA, or whatever you need. And I'd wish you well and tell you I hope your life turns out fuckin' magical, mama."

She looks at me, eyes hazy with unshed tears. "No, no. No. I'm not…that's not what I mean." She turns away again, dashing at her eyes with the back of her wrist. "I'm *so* sick of crying, goddammit," she mutters. With a shake of her head and a gruff clearing of her throat, she tries again, stronger. "I just…I don't know if anything is worth what I went through. The accident, addiction, Alvin. It was pure hell. And…" she trails off, looks at me, starts again. "You mean a lot to me. I like being with you. I want more of what we have. The idea of saying I want a relationship with you scares the absolute hell out of me, Chance. I don't know how to be a…god, girlfriend sounds so trite and childish. How to be a lover? How to love someone? Is that what this is, what we're looking at, here? I don't know how to love someone. I'm not sure I even love myself. Shit, I don't know if I *like* myself."

"Can I say I love you, or that I'm in love with you, right here, right now?" I shrug, shake my head. "No, that'd be premature. But can I see it going there with you? Absolutely. And very quickly. And I want that. More than I've ever wanted anything in my life, I want to be with you. I like being around you. I already said it—you make me feel…just better, about myself, and about life. And I like that. A whole fuckin' lot."

"I feel the same way," she whispers. "I just don't know if I'm at a place yet where I can feel like *anything* is worth what I went through. That's not anything against you, Chance. You're…you're the best thing that's ever happened to me."

I grin at her. "Hey, mama. I didn't say it *was* worth it. I said it *could be*." I jostle her leg. "I wouldn't wish what I went through on my worst enemy. And I sure as fuck wouldn't repeat it. I just mean I'm more thankful than I can say that I met you."

She smiles at me—it's wobbly, a little shaky. "I can agree to that."

I slap the steering wheel. "So. The hard shit is all done. You've reconciled with all the people you love, Alvin's out of the picture—and I can protect you if he decides to try something—and I've faced the last of my shit. Now, we have some fun."

Annika laughs, resting her head against the headrest. "Fun. When was the last time I had *fun*?" She smiles at me. "I'm ready for fun and relaxation."

"Me too, mama. Me too."

13

JUST TRUST ME, MAMA

Annika

SALT SPRAY WETS MY FACE AS THE PROW OF THE rented powerboat smacks into the white-capped waves and then lifted, pointing skyward, only to smack back down again. Above, the sky is mostly clear blue with a few high puffs of gray-white clouds scattered here and there; the sun shines bright and hot, and here on the open ocean there was long stiff wind blowing. My hair is bound back in a thick braid, which whipped crazily. Behind me, we have a single duffel bag containing—despite Chance's sexually charged teasing—a new bikini for me and a pair of board shorts for him, and a couple more changes of clothing for both of us, along with some toiletries and a few odds and ends. A large white Yeti cooler contains a variety of groceries—a carton of eggs, a bag of ground coffee, shredded cheese, deli meat, bread, some green and red peppers, a package of chicken breast, a bag of rice, a head of broccoli…enough food for three days. There's also a couple of red containers of gasoline for the boat, and few other items—a cast iron skillet, a spatula, matches, a lantern, and some other stuff I wasn't sure of.

Chance paid for it all. When I questioned the amount

of money he was spending, he admitted he had spent very little of his military salary, and was paid exorbitantly—his word, not mine—for his work at the club.

"I'm flush, mama," he'd said. "No worries."

I didn't like it. Part of me worried he was keeping a tally in his head, and someday, it'd come up. He'd hold it against me. Expect it from me.

He'd smelled that from a mile away. Looked at me, eyebrow raised. "I hope you don't think I'm keeping track. I ain't Alvin, baby. I'm taking care of you. It's just money, and I don't got any reason to spend it. Till now, it's just been sitting in my account collecting dust."

I'd snorted. "Earning interest, you mean."

"Whatever. Point is, I ain't worried about it, and I don't want you holdin' on to any kind of worry.

I'd rolled my eyes. "Whatever."

He'd cupped my jaw. "Mama." It was a scold.

I'd breathed a sigh of annoyance and resignation. "Fine, yes. That's exactly what I was thinking. What are you, psychic?"

He'd shaken his head. Brushed his thumb over my lips. "No, I can just see it on your face. See you gettin' all twisted up inside."

"It's conditioned into me by now, Chance," I'd whispered.

"I know," he'd murmured. "Fight it. It ain't your reality no more. I got you. Okay? Try to trust that."

"I'll try."

Now, we're following the coastline toward his beach property. We'd left the marina at Hanalei behind a while ago, and I'm not sure how long it would take to get there. I don't really care, to be honest—I'm enjoying the ride. The island on our right was lush, dense, and mountainous, almost eye-wateringly verdant and beautiful. I've never been anywhere so beautiful. Behind me, Chance has long-since shed his shirt, kicked his flip-flops off, and taken his hair out of its ponytail, letting the wind whip it behind him in a long black streamer.

I sit twisted on the seat, so I can watch the coastline unfold ahead of us and also soak in all that was Chance.

I've been blocking myself from really opening up to how I feel about him, I'm realizing. How deeply I'm starting to feel about him.

How attracted to him I am.

He's got one hand on the tiller of the outboard motor, the other slung forward along the side of the boat. His brown skin glistens, moistened by the spray, mountains of muscle bulging and rippling, black-and-white tattoos seeming almost alive. His beard is thick, recently trimmed and brushed. His eyes are deep and dark, constantly moving, scanning, assessing. He seems…at peace, in a way that's new even since I met him. As if some of the shadows swirling behind his eyes have fled, dissipated.

He's handsome.

Rough, rugged. Immensely powerful. Hewn from granite, the steel of him forged in the fires of life…yet despite all that, he's gentle. There's a sweetness to him. A tenderness belied by the colossal enormity of his physical presence.

I feel safe with him. And I can't even put into words how long it's been since I've felt safe. But I don't just feel safe—I feel taken care of. I…*belong*.

Something is unlocking inside my soul, as I sit in this

boat and let my mind wander and my heart finally escape the suffocating prison I've had it locked away in for so long.

I could be happy. With him.

Shit. Shit, shit, shit—I *am* happy with him. I don't have it all figured out. I don't know what I want to do with my life, but…with Chance supporting me, I can figure that out. I can learn to dream again. I can't be an athlete anymore, but I can find something else to fulfill me.

Maybe it'll just be…life. Being with Chance.

I feel a glimmer of what that might be like. Scraps and shreds of a vision: the train of white dress, a black tux…a hospital room, a tiny little head with damp dark hair…a home, a future…*life*.

Someday.

For now, I just want to learn how to be with him. How to trust him with all that's me. How to give him myself, my heart. My body.

I'm eager to explore our relationship. Not just the emotional outlines of it, but the physical depth of it. What it's like to have a sexual relationship with someone I care about. I've never been with a man in that sense. It's scary, but exhilarating.

He catches my eye, and I realize I've been staring at him. "Thinkin' deep thoughts over there," he calls; the motor and the crash of the waves against the hull and the wind is loud, making normal conversation pointless.

I nod. Smile. "Thinking about you," I call back. "Life." I hesitate. "Us."

He opens his mouth to answer, but his eyes flick over my shoulder, fix on something, and he points. "There it is."

I twist the other way and follow his gesture. The mountains descend dramatically in a V, with lush, dense jungle filling the space between them, the peaks curling around the coastline in either direction, leaving a wedge of lowlands extending toward the ocean. There's a short but deep stretch of white sand beach, jungle trees swaying in the wind at the edge of the beach, casting shadows on the sand. As we approach, I can see, tucked into the trees, a small hut, built up off the ground on stilts. The roof is thatched, and the walls seem like they can be rolled up down somehow—I'm not sure, it's still too far to see clearly. Against one side of the hut, there's a wooden rack with surfboards and standup paddleboards tipped up on end; the boards are colorful, beautiful. A few minutes later, we're scudding up toward the beach—Chance tips the motor up out of the water, and we coast up onto the sand with a noisy scraping sound. Chance hops lithely out of the boat and into the water, grabs the prow of the boat with both hands and pulls powerfully backward, dragging it up further onto the beach as if it weighs no more than a bag of laundry. There's a long, wrist-thick rope tied to a tree, the bitter end coiled just out of reach of the high tide line, and Chance uses it to tie the boat off.

He stands ankle-deep in water, hands propped on his hips, taking in the scene. "God, but it's good to be here."

I don't have words for how peaceful it is. The only sound is the susurrus of the surf, a gull keening in the distance as it tilts on a wingtip just above the water, and the wind playing in the trees. I've never been anywhere this remote. I don't think there's anyone for miles in any direction.

I sit on the edge of the boat and twist, slip down into the wet sand, the water curling around my bare feet. I move up to Chance's side, and somehow I end up leaning into him, his arm low around my hip, fingers toying at the hem of my shorts, teasing the bare skin.

"Thank you for bringing me here," I murmur.

He huffs a laugh. "Been here thirty seconds, mama. Don't thank me yet."

I inhale until my lungs won't hold anymore air, and then let it out slowly. "It's *so* peaceful."

He nods. "My favorite place on earth, right here. I came here with my *tūtū* and Aunt Lu a few times."

"What happened with your aunt Lu?"

He shrugs. "I dunno, exactly. We spent some time together when I first came to Hawaii, but she just sort of... pulled away from me. She didn't really believe in doctors or hospitals or any of that, and I think she was sick a long time before she passed. Maybe she was just..." He shrugs, waves a hand. "I dunno. Doesn't matter. She left me the deed to this place in her will—it actually originally went to my dad, but he died, so it went to me, or...I don't know. Back to her and then me? I don't know. I just know I got the notice that she passed, and I had to mail out some paperwork to take ownership of this place. But I never thought I'd be here again." He looks at me. "For a while, I wondered if I'd ever leave that club. You got me out of there, Nik."

"Because my pathetic ass needed saving," I quip, laughing.

He doesn't seem to find it as funny, dark eyes peering down at me, glinting with intensity. "We saved each other, mama. You saved me every bit as much as I did you."

I wrap my arm around his waist, rest my chin on his chest, and enjoy the feeling of being the small one. "Okay, Chance. You're right." I scratch my fingernails up and down his back lightly a few times. "Show me around."

He tips my chin up and kisses me softly, quickly, and then gently pats my ass. "Good plan. Come on. You grab the duffel, I got the rest."

I grab my cane and the duffel bag, and then watch, amazed, as he heaves the huge, heavy white Yeti onto one shoulder, dips at the knees, and somehow manages to scoop up the rest of the bags of supplies with his other hand. He strides easily toward the hut, as if entirely unencumbered, while I hobble far less gracefully after him.

And that's when I make the vow to myself that if it's possible to rehab my knee into increased mobility, I'm damn well going to, as soon as possible. I'm fucking done limping around and feeling sorry for myself.

This feels like another shift within me, leaving behind some old, sad, broken part of myself, like choosing the bright new future of what could be rather than clinging to the darkness and futility of what was.

There's a few steps up into the hut, which he takes in two strides, and then sets the load of goods down. The walls are made of overlapping slats backed by screen netting, which can be rolled up and tied into place, or let down and tied down, with thick, heavy duty exterior storm shutters which can be latched in case of bad weather. Currently, the walls are open to let in the light and the breeze. It's significantly cooler inside, with a breeze coming in off the water. There's only one room—it contains a king-size mattress on a raised platform in the center of the space, freshly made with white linen sheets and a pale green handmade quilt. In the back right corner, there's a small metal sink with a well-pump handle, surrounded by a short L-shaped span of countertop, cabinets built in underneath. There's a two-burner propane stove, on which sits an old-school camping-style coffee percolator and a kettle. From the raf-ters overhead hang a few old, battered, but well-loved pots and pans. There's also a very small fridge in the kitchen-ette area, and a leaf-bladed fan with a lightbulb over the bed, which I assume must run on some kind of generator.

He gestures. "Here we are. Rustic, at best. But it's peaceful, and quiet. No cell signal, no TV, no past or fu-ture. Just you and me, here and now."

"Um, yes, but…is there a bathroom?"

He laughs, moves toward the back of the hut, point-ing. "Outhouse." He grins. "It ain't an all-inclusive five-star resort, I know."

I shake my head, smiling. "It's perfect. Outhouses don't bother me too much, as long as nothing climbs up and bites me in the ass."

He laughs. "Nah. Like I said, we got a guy who lives here on the island. There's a little track you can use to get here. Thomas comes every couple weeks to check on things, make sure the generator is fueled up and working, make sure the outhouse is nice and tidy. I emailed him to make sure he checked up on it for us." He points to the wall where the kitchenette is—such as it is. "There's an outdoor shower, too. Once I fire up the generator, we've got a little hot water tank that mixes with the well. You gotta keep it short, but you can get a good five minutes of hot water out of it."

"Wow, that's fancy," I say. "This place is amazing, Chance."

He nods, proud. "Been in my family for a long, long time. Everybody who's owned it has done something to improve it, but being that we're way out here, there's lim-itations. Won't ever be electricity or plumbing or internet."

He shrugs. "I guess you could maybe get one of those new portable satellite things for internet if you really wanted, but I guess I like it this way. Makes it a real getaway from life, you know? I don't wanna know nothin' about nothin' but sittin' my ass on the beach, surfing, sleeping…" he gives me a broad, suggestive wink, "gettin' it on with my lady."

"It's perfect." Ridiculously, childishly, embarrassingly, I feel myself blushing at his last statement.

He touches my cheek with his thumb. "Ah, god, you're blushing?" His grin is hot, teasing. "I dunno how, but you manage to be cute and fuckin' sexy as hell at the same time."

I frown up at him. "Cute?"

His big, hard, rough, strong hands frame my face, thumbs brushing over my lips in that gesture of his, which always makes my heart flip and my chest ache. "Yeah. Cute. Adorable. So fuckin' unbearably goddamn cute it makes it hard to breathe." My pulse hammers as his hands slide down to cup my neck, thumbs now ghosting over my throat in an exquisitely gentle touch. "And then at the same time, you're so fuckin' sexy, so hot, I don't know what to do with myself around you. Never in my life have I known a woman like you, Annika Scott. You turn me on in a way there ain't a chance in hell of ever turnin' me off."

"Chance…" I breathe.

"I fuckin' need you more than I need my next breath."

Now that we're here, alone, with no possibility of interruptions, the prospect of being laid totally bare for him, of being held, touched, fucked…loved…it's overwhelming. I can't breathe. I'm frozen in place even as my cheeks flame and my core goes molten. My pulse pounds so hard and so loud in my ears it's all I can hear. My hands shake. I can't look away from his fiery, fierce, unrelenting gaze.

He steps into me. Cups the back of my neck and tips my face up to his—and kisses the ever-loving hell out of me. He has a variety of kisses—quick, long, soft, hard, deep, questing, scorching, and any combination of them all. This one is…everything. It steals my breath and gives it back at the same time, sends heat swirling through me, lips to belly to sex. It makes my hands tremble and my pulse flutter.

I feel his hands moving—tugging the hair tie free and tossing it blindly in the direction of the bed, then feathering through my curls to loosen the braid until my hair is loose and probably wildly voluminous. Then, those hands curl up into my hair against the scalp, fingertips massaging, then raking through the locks. He breaks the kiss for a moment, eyes piercing mine, assessing me for demurral. All I am capable of is looking back at him, totally overwhelmed. I feel too much. I need too much. It's an overload of emotion and need, a manic flux of erotic lightning in my blood and muscles helixed around a soul bond, a heart-match, a sense of unity with the man towering over me, making me feel safe, looking at me with such need that it makes my knees turn to jelly.

I swallow hard, blink, squeeze my eyes shut. "Sorry, I…I'm just…I want you, but I'm—"

He shakes his head, touching my lips with a forefinger. "Hush." He nips my lower lip. "I got you. You don't gotta do a damn thing but stand there and let me worship you, Nik."

"Worship…" I whisper. "I…I want that."

"Then all you gotta do is let me give it to you."

He nuzzles his forehead against mine, and then his lips descend to the side of my neck. Tongue dips against skin, tasting. My breath stutters in my throat. Fingers find skin between shorts and sleeveless cotton button down, tease, trace. Another kiss, to the divot at the base of my throat. I tip my head back, offering, begging. He kisses up my throat and back down, and his fingers work the buttons of my shirt, nimble and sure. The blouse drapes open, and his palms skate over my shoulders to brush it off, and it flutters to the floor.

A seagull caws, out on the water, and is answered by another. The wind moves and twists and flurries, warm, carrying a hint of salt.

His lips move to my chest, touching a freckle here, a freckle there in delicate little kisses. His palms scrape over the skin at my sides, my belly, around to my back. Teasing down my spine. Molding over my shoulders. Skipping the bra strap, down to the edge of my shorts. Around again to my belly, palm flat, fingers trailing. Kisses sloping down one breast to the cup edge, then over to the other breast. One finger drags a hot line over my shoulder, nudging the strap off. Then the other side, and my breasts descend under their own weight without the support. Chance kisses that tender no-man's-land that's not quite chest, not quite shoulder, just beside my underarm and just above my breast. Apparently, that's an erogenous zone, because my pulse quickens until my breath catches in my throat, and my hands reach out to balance myself against him.

He rumbles in his chest, a smile curving his lips against my flesh—and he kisses there again, now with his tongue flickering wetly, teasing, hot. Then, the other side, mirroring. My lungs are stuck, mouth hanging open. And then, without warning, he flicks open my bra. It slides off, drooping between us, catching where my hips press against his. My bare breasts brush his chest, sensitive, hardened nipples against his smooth hard muscle. He leans back a couple inches, letting the bra hit the floor, his gaze hungrily soaking up the vision of me, topless for him.

"Fuck, you're incredible." He gives me no chance to respond, palms rubbing up my belly to catch my breasts.

He lifts them, hefting their weight, thumbs rolling over my nipples, dragging a gasp from me—lightning sizzles in my veins at his touch. And then his mouth is there, right where I didn't know I needed it, suckling around a nipple while his huge gentle hand kneads the other. He kneels in front of me, mouth moving to my other breast, nipping and licking and sucking my nipples until I throw my head back and moan, gasping. He unbuttons my khaki shorts, tugs down the zipper. Yanks the shorts off to pool around my ankles. I grasp his shoulders for balance—he pauses to gaze up at me between my breasts.

"Chance," I murmur, licking my dry lips. "Please." I have no idea what I'm asking for; I can only hope he knows what I need, because I don't.

He does.

Fingers curl in the elastic of my underwear, pulling them down, rolling them over my hips and ass; they catch where my thighs rub together, and then they're down with my shorts. I kick the puddled bundle of clothing aside, and I'm naked for Chance.

He sits on his knees and leans back, hands resting on his knees, and just looks at me. "Holy fucking hell, Annika." His voice is thick, brows furrowed. He shakes his head, as if overcome with awe. "You're fucking *perfect*."

"I'm not." I hold myself steady on his shoulders. "I'm really not."

"You are to me." He shuffles closer, and my breasts

hang in front of his face. He nuzzles them, and then kisses them—not to arouse, but to lavish affection. "Perfect."

He moves his mouth lower, down my centerline to my belly button, kissing, kissing, hunching lower until his mouth ghosts over the seam of my sex. Then, his tongue flits out against my clitoris, sending a wrenching jolt of electric heat through me—his lips seize my sex, suctioning around my clit, tongue circling mercilessly. I cry out, fingernails digging into his shoulders.

"Perfect." It's a grumbled whisper.

His hands skate up the outside of my legs to my hips, clutching there, and then he gently but firmly pivots me in place so I'm facing away from him. I can't imagine what he's going to do next; he presses a kiss to my lower back, his hands framing my buttocks. Again, my breath catches as he slides his lips over the swell of one cheek, kissing, kissing, kissing. The other side, then.

"Perfect." Another rumbled whisper.

He twists me in place again to face him once more, and then surges to his feet, scoops me up in his arms and takes one long step, one knee in the bed as he bends to lay me down. His mouth claims mine, eyes blazing. "You—are—*perfect.*"

My eyes burn, vision blurring. "Goddammit, Chance," I breathe.

No quarter, no mercy. He cups my breasts, squeezing them together inward and kisses each nipple slowly and with his tongue moving in deft thrilling wet circles, then releases them to bounce away to either side, kissing down my torso to my sex. No buildup, just his mouth devouring my pussy. A finger slides over my seam, through the lips, and delves into me. I gasp, spine arching as I'm filled by his finger and licked by his tongue. I cry out, heels scrabbling at the quilt. He drives an arm under me, one hand lifting me by the ass, pressing me against his hungry mouth.

Right to the edge then, hovering at the cusp of ecstasy, lights flashing behind my eyes, my belly clenching, sex pulsing and weeping, spine bowed upward, heels digging into the mattress—my knee protests the use of it but I barely feel it.

And then his finger is gone and his tongue is lazily swiping up my nether lips, a tease of a lick, barely flicking against my clit—again—and again—and again, each touch of his tongue to my sensitive, throbbing center a tease, a taunt.

"God, Chance, *please!*" I whimper.

"Please what, baby girl?" His words are a murmur against my flesh.

"Stop teasing me," I breathe.

He laughs, a hot huff of breath on skin. "Just trust me, mama."

And then his tongue dives in against my clit, pressing, circling, flicking, thrashing side to side. His rough-yet-soft beard scrapes my inner thighs and the lips of my sex, his nose nudges me, his breath washes over me—a kaleidoscope of sensation. When I'm spiraling up to the edge, he suctions his lips around the bud of nerves and slowly softly delicately…makes out, I think is the only accurate term…with my clitoris. And while he's doing this, he slips a finger into me, gentle and cautious, in and curling, withdraw, in and curling, withdraw…and then he adds a second finger. His mouth moves unhurriedly on my center, suctioning and kissing and tonguing while his fingers drive in and out of me, his fingertips scraping that magical hidden place inside me.

I'm flung helter-skelter to the edge, hips bucking, breasts bouncing. "Fuck, fuck, fuck!" I cry. "Chance, yes, please, yes, please fuck, god, please yes!"

He pulls away entirely. "Not quite yet, mama. You're not ready yet."

My thrashing subsides and I do an ab curl to glare down my body at him. "I'm gonna kill you if you don't let me come, you sadistic bastard."

He just laughs. "You'll thank me when I'm done, I promise."

He skims his mouth up my belly and cups each of my breasts in a hand, laving his tongue over one nipple and then the other, alternately pinching and licking and sucking on them until the sensation is nearly enough to make the orgasm he's building inside me start rising again.

As it is, it leaves me gasping, clutching at his head.

But it's not what I need.

As if he knows I'm about to have a tantrum on him, he wedges his massive shoulders between my thighs once more, pulling my ass to the back edge of the mattress and hanging my knees over his shoulders. My ass is suspended in the air, only my torso on the bed, the rest of my lower half entirely at his mercy. He kneels in front of me, brings his mouth to my sex.

A lick.

A kiss.

A breath of hot air, a finger delving into me and withdrawing again entirely.

Tease, tease, tease.

A series of slow licks with a flattened tongue, and then

a few quick light circles, and then his finger plunging into me.

The orgasm is a pent-up wildfire, now. I feel it pounding behind my belly, swirling behind my eyelids. Pulsing against my lower back. Throbbing in my sex. Tingling in my tight breasts.

When it comes, it's going to rip me apart.

He is purely patient, masterfully tactical. Each moment, each touch drives me higher, closer, deeper. Builds the orgasm to frenetic desperation. Even when I'm not at the edge, I'm gasping, wild, hips bucking and thrashing. The edge is always there, now, and with each switch of tactics he brings me closer and backs me away, up to the cusp of climax and away, again and again.

Time dissolves.

I become aware of a sound—a keening, a low weeping whimper. Me. It's a pleading sound. Helpless, unconsciously emitted.

"Please, please, please," I beg. "I need to come, I need it, I need it." I hear my words, uttered in a ragged, hoarse whisper. "Chance...*please*."

"Now?" he murmurs. "You think you're ready?"

"I'll die if I don't get to come," I gasp. "I'll fucking *die*."

"Wouldn't want that." He surges up over me, pulls me fully up on to the bed, and then cups a powerful hand under my neck, lifts my head to savage a wild, starving kiss to my mouth.

His fingers drive into me, two of them hooking deep while his palm drives against my clit.

I detonate.

I scream, a full-voiced throat-shredding cry, my entire body bucking up off the bed. Lights and heat flash behind my eyes, and my pussy clenches around his thrusting fingers. His palm rubs against my clit as his fingers drive into me, and he swallows my scream. Moves down to my breasts, using his free hand to bring a breast to his mouth, sucking hard, pinching the bud with his teeth until I gasp at the sharp nip of pain that only makes the pleasure explode all the more potently. The other breast, the same treatment.

To use the word "orgasm" for what I'm experiencing is to dull the razor sharpness of it, is to dim the brilliance of it, is to domesticate the wildness and mute the roar.

I'm torn apart, shredded, dissolved.

I heave, my hips thrash.

He descends my body once more and as I'm rippling through the peak of the orgasm, he seizes my clit in his mouth sucks it though his teeth, and then thrashes his tongue over me, side to side, violently.

The universe itself coruscates inside me.

I come all over his mouth, and keep coming.

He gives me his fingers again, and now something snaps inside me. Breaks.

Helpless to stop it, I feel something gush out of me, wetness spurting in short, hard spasms.

I curl in on myself, unable to tolerate any more. I'm gasping like I've sprinted a hundred-yard dash in record time. Every muscle is clenching and releasing, my eyes squeezed tight, hips helplessly thrusting.

Chance hauls me into his arms and rolls to his back, bringing me on top of him. His giant arms shelter me. My hips fit against his, between his raised thighs, feet planted with knees bent. I'm partly on my side, aftershocks make me twitch spastically.

He holds me. Smoothes his fingers through my curls.

After a moment or two, I gather enough wherewithal to straighten, lying on my belly on him, leaning on my forearms on his chest. I feel his arousal pressing huge and thick against my thigh and sex and belly. Straining. Begging.

Tear tracks stain my cheeks I know, which are likely flushed pink. "Chance," I whisper, swallowing hard, shaking my head. "Good lord."

He grins, cocky, pleased and proud. "*That*...is an orgasm."

"That was so much more than an orgasm I don't think they have a word for it." I shimmy higher, breasts smashed between our bodies, my arms looping under his neck and head. "That was the single most incredible thing I've ever felt." I blush so hard my cheeks hurt. "I think I squirted." I mutter that last part against his neck, my forehead pressing into his jaw.

His hands roam my shoulders, back, hips, and ass in a soothing circuit of sliding palms. "Love watching you come, Nik. Most beautiful thing I've ever fuckin' seen." He shakes his head, turns his face to kiss my temple. "*You're* the most beautiful thing I've ever seen, and never more so than when you're coming."

Need pounds through me—for *him*. To join with him. To feel him inside me. To be connected to him, surrounded and filled by him. To give myself utterly to him. I need it more than I need to breathe.

I lean on my forearms again, bracing them on his chest. Hold his eyes, unblinking, as I slide my thighs, one and then the other, to the outside of his. He straightens his legs out onto the bed, allowing me to straddle him.

"Mama, all I care about is you. Making you feel good." His eyes are...not haunted, but...

Scared.

He's scared.

He'll make me come again and again, until I'm nothing but a puddle of jelly. But taking the step to make love to me, despite his promises and teasing? He's scared. He'll never say so. But he is. I can see it. He wants me. He needs me.

God, it's crazy, but I think he loves me.

I think he's underselling how often he's been rejected at this point simply for being too...much. Too giant, in every way.

I'm not scared.

I am thrilled.

Excited.

Ready.

14

A PRICELESS GIFT

Chance

MY HEART IS HAMMERING A CRAZY TATTOO IN my chest, my pulse so loud in my ears I can barely hear the surf outside. Her weight is negligible, straddling me, but it anchors me down, grounds me. Terrifies me. Her thighs are soft against mine. Her sex is a damp warmth against my painfully hard cock. Her breasts drape like hot silk against my chest.

I can't manage a full breath, can't quite swallow. Certainly, I have no fucking words.

I want her.

Want—what a pathetic scrap of nothing against the wild, crazed, nearly narcotic desperation I feel to have Annika wrapped around me, to take me inside her, to make love to her. I fucking need that.

But I can't do it.

I can't ask.

I can't move.

I've never told anyone, not even Rev, how many times I've had a girl try to take me and not be able to, or worse yet, not even try. The pity in their goddamned eyes…it makes me feel about two inches tall. Being a giant ain't all it's cracked up to be.

It hurt, every time a girl took one look at the size of me and my erection and noped the fuck out on me. Hurt, and hurt, and hurt—rejection for something I can't control. Even if they wanted to, but couldn't, it still hurt. But better that than me hurting them.

And that's an even deeper layer of fear—that I'll hurt Annika.

My hands tremble, and I clench them into fists, and then try to act casual and possessive and affectionate as I fill my hands with the beautiful generous curve of her ass.

I see a world of emotion in her eyes as she straddles me, her hands on my chest above my pecs. I can't enumerate the things I see in her eyes. Erotic promise, need, affection, awe, understanding...

That other word I can't bring myself to even think.

For all my physical strength and toughness, for all my mental resilience, I'm just not strong enough for this moment.

"Chance, honey." Her voice is soft but charged. "I need you, baby."

Honey.

Baby.

My throat burns, my eyes ache with holding back the haze. She's saying it, and she's meaning it. Saying those things to me with such delicate sweetness that whatever breath I had in my lungs evaporates.

Rev is the only human being who's ever shown me loyalty and love, but it's the masculine kind, the brotherhood of blood and trauma. Rough and ready, solid and unspoken. I'd put my very soul in his hands and not spend a moment worrying.

But it's not the same.

Not this delicate, feminine tenderness.

Hearing those words from Annika, and seeing clear as day in her eyes that she means them...

I almost can't hold it back.

"Nik, I..." I shake my head, words drying up in the heat of my fear.

She sees. She knows.

"Trust me?" It's a breathed pair of syllables, but they contain the universe.

I frame her beautiful face with my hands, and I can't hide that they're trembling. "Nik." I swallow. Her name is all I can manage, in a husky, guttural rasp.

Her smile is the sweetest thing I've ever seen. "Just trust me, baby." My words, back at me.

She slides one arm under my neck and touches her forehead to mine, eye to eye, breath to breath. Tilts her hips away from my body and reaches her other hand between us. Slides her touch around my shaft, forefinger and thumb pointed toward my root. Her touch is achingly soft, gliding down and sliding up, caressing my length. Again, and again, until I'm gasping.

"Fuck, Nikki." I close my eyes. "Your touch—so fuckin' beautiful. So perfect."

"Look at me, Chance," she whispers, but there's a harsh command in the words. "*Look* at me."

I open my eyes and meet hers. She lifts up more, angling her ass to the ceiling. Tilting her sex. She moves slowly. Never looks away from me, not for a second, not even blinking.

"Nik, baby…" My voice is rough, an unsteady rumble. I run my hands up her spine, then frame her waist.

My panic shows in the movement of my hands, the way they shake and the way they skate over her body, shoulders to spine to hips, again and again. Not daring to stop her, not daring to hope.

"I got you," she breathes—my words, again.

A kiss. Lips wet on mine, tongue soaring into my mouth, hot and wild and drowning.

As we kiss, she tilts my cock and brings the tip to her seam, nudging it there against her lips. I gasp out of the kiss. "Nik, are you sure you're—"

She silences me with her mouth on mine, and then bumps her forehead against mine. "Trust me. I've *got* you."

She flutters her hips in tiny little circles, rolling my tip against her sex, teasing, driving me inward in increments, like a taunting microdose of sex.

I grasp her ass in clutching fingers, my grip hard, bruising. She doesn't complain, doesn't seem to notice.

She's focusing entirely on me, on us, on what she's doing. The fluttering ceases. She buries her face in the side of my throat, both arms slung around my neck. With a low moan, she takes a little more of me. An inch. Maybe two at most. Pauses, breathing slowly, deeply.

Pulling her face away, she finds my gaze and holds it. "So good," she murmurs. "You feel *so* good."

Before I can say anything in return, she claims my mouth in a soft, sweet, slow kiss. And when she draws my tongue into her mouth and tangles hers against mine, she flutters her hips again in a slow roll—sinking down around me, taking more of me, inch by stretching inch.

"Oh god," she groans, breaking the kiss and slamming

her forehead against my breastbone. "Oh god…oh my fucking god, *Chance*." Her teeth nip at my skin and she groans again, pausing to let herself get used to me. "I've never felt anything like this. Anyone like you."

"Tell me you're okay," I growl.

A laugh. "Okay?" Another laugh. "*Okay?*" She clasps the back of my head and pulls my head up against hers, forehead to forehead. Groans long and low and feral as she slides her sex down my shaft, all the way, bottoming out to bump against my root. "So much more than just okay, Chance."

I'm trembling all over—she's taken all of me. "Annika." I swallow hard, fingers digging brutally into her ass. "You feel… There are no words. No words, mama. No words for how fucking amazing you feel."

She grabs my face in both hands and kisses me again, using the kiss and her grip on my jaw and cheeks and the kiss itself to brace against me as she slides herself up my length, drawing her slick hot wet sex up my aching, straining, throbbing cock. She's slick around me, drenched, clamping hard around me, pulling upward until only the head of me is left inside her.

"We're not using a condom," I say.

"Are you clean?" She whispers the question, and I feel her smile against my cheek, because she knows the answer.

"Yes. Hasn't been anyone in…a long damn time. And we get twice yearly checkups by a doctor who comes to the club—includes testing. I'm clean, I promise I am."

She feathers a few slow, shallow strokes with just the tip of me inside her. "I am too. After that incident…I got tested and there's been no one since. And I'm on birth control—the shot." She kisses my cheek, my closed eyelid, beside my nose, then finally my lip. "I don't ever want anything between us. Only you, only me." She slides down my shaft, just a little. "Touch me, Chance," she whimpers. "Touch me. Take me."

I shake my head. "I'll hurt you."

She shakes her head back at me. "You won't." She braces her palms against my chest and sits upright, taking me back down deep inside her tightness. "Watch," she commands. "Watch me."

She hangs her head, long wild red curls a thick curtain around her face—she's watching where we join, her sex and mine. Lifts up. All the way, slowly, inch by inch, drawing me out of her until I ache to have her wet pussy clenching around me again, needing it, desperate for it. And then she sinks down again, sliding me home.

Home.

Fuck, fuck.

She's home.

I swallow around a knot in my throat, watching my cock disappear inside her pussy. "Fuck, Annika. Jesus, Jesus." I groan, unable to hold myself back from pushing my hips against hers as she takes me to the hilt.

"*Yes*," she hisses, when I thrust against her. "Yes, Chance." She pries my hands off her hips, guides them up to her breasts. "Let go. Touch me. Take me."

I cup the silky weight of her tits in my palms, brush my thumbs over her nipples, and she jerks, groans, and grinds in circles on me.

"Yes," she moans. "I love your hands. I love the way you touch me."

She lifts, spine arching, head thrown back, belly and breasts pushing forward as she draws me out of her. At the apex, when I'm about to slip free, she rolls her hips in a wide circle, taking my cock with her—I have to thrust. I need her. I need her tightness back.

"Annika, fuck—fuck, you're perfect."

"Touch my clit."

I obey immediately, press a thumb to her clit, and she cries out at the first touch. Sinks down—and it's not a slow, gentle movement. It's rough, and fast. The slick squelch of her sex around mine is loud and wet and erotic.

"Jesus, Annika. Never...never felt this. Never knew it could be like this."

"Me...me either." Her eyes fly open and pierce me. "More, Chance. Harder. Take me. Fuck me."

She shows me the way, as if knowing I'm not there yet, that I don't trust it. That I don't trust I won't hurt her.

She leans forward onto her palms and pushes backward, sliding me deep. Draws forward. Pushes down. She goes slowly at first. Each time I bury into her, she groans, hoarse, breathless. I reach between us and press my middle finger to her clit, following her movements, circling the sensitive nub of flesh. I feel her respond, watch her rise to it—she speeds her movements, pushing down onto me and sliding forward faster and faster. Fucking herself on me. Fucking me.

Taking me.

All of me.

Faster and faster.

"Please, Chance. I need you." She whimpers as my cock slides home, and she pauses there, drives down harder, grinding against me, rolling her hips—taking more and more until I'm so deep inside her beauty it aches, hurts so good. "Please, Chance."

"Ahhh fuck, Nik," I groan, abandoning her clit to grasp her hips in my hands. "Heaven—you're heaven."

"Then *show* me." Her voice is ragged. "I need you."

"You have me."

"I need more of you."

"You have all of me."

She drags her palm down my cheek, rubbing her thumb over my lip in an echo of the gesture I always use on her; green eyes spark fire. "I want you to *fuck* me, Chance," she says, enunciating each word clearly. "I want you to make love to me. I want you to fucking *take* me. Because *I can take it*. I want that more than I've ever wanted anything in my whole life. Make me yours, Chance." She cradles my head in her arms, my face alongside hers, and begins moving on me again, sinking deep. "Because baby… you—are—*mine*." The last word is cried out, shrill, as our hips knock together.

That snaps something inside me. Breaks me. Shatters the last of my walls, dissolving my fear in the flashflood of…

Love.

God, it's love. She loves me. I love her. Fuck, it's real. It's true.

The knowledge explodes inside me, cracking my heart open in my chest and setting my blood on fire.

I grab her hair in my fist and bring her mouth to mine, and I kiss her, savagely, brutally, beautifully. She moans into the kiss, softening above me, mouth fusing with mine. My other hand grips her hip, squeezes an ass cheek, and pushes her down onto me, harder, deeper. She whimpers, my cock sliding so deep there's nowhere further for me to drive.

My balls ache with the need to release, but I hold it back with iron control. Not yet. Not even close.

I let go of her hair and seize her other hip. One arm along my chest with her palm on my cheek, her other slung around my neck with her hand tangled in my hair, she breaks the kiss but breathes against my mouth, lips and teeth mated. I haul her up, groaning as I lose her heat around me, lose her tightness like a vise on my cock.

"Please please pleasepleaseplease…" she chants—and I slam her down and thrust up into her. "Yes *fuck*, fuck, *god*, Chance, *YES!*" The last word is screamed.

"Annika—" I snarl. "Tell me if—"

"Shut *up*," she snaps. "You're perfect. You're everything I've ever fantasized about."

I slam my back head back into the pillows and then crane my neck so I can watch us, watch her spine moving in sinuous, serpentine ripples, watching her thick beautiful round ass rise and tilt upward as she moves up me and I haul her higher, and watching as her ass lowers and spreads apart to sink down around me, her sweet pussy taking me, swallowing around my cock, stretching and sliding.

"Oh fuck, Chance, *fuck*," she groans, and I love how dirty her mouth is when she's lost in our perfection. "So good. There's never been anything this good."

"Nothing," I agree on a gasp. "Nothing, not ever."

Faster, then. Harder.

I settle into the realization that not only can she take all of me, she can't get enough. She needs more. She's taking all that I am and demanding more of me.

She angles a hand between our bodies and finds her clit, letting me set the pace, now, and touching herself in quick rough circles, her knuckles moving against my belly just above where we're joined. She starts whimpering, sliding down to meet me faster and harder, and her head thunks down to rest on my chest and her breasts drag against my muscles and she moves and moves and moves, thrusts, fucks, groaning, whimpering.

I drive up to meet her, bracing my hands on her hips where they bend around to her thighs, pushing her down onto me as I thrust up into her. I feel it rising in me, now, and I can't stop it.

I don't try.

She comes apart first, voice cracking into a shrieking cry—I feel her pussy spasm around me, the impossible happening as she tightens harder around me. "Oh *fuck*, Chance, oh my fucking god, Chance—Chance—Chance…" she chants my name again and again as she loses control and goes wild, arms clinging to my neck and fucking me as hard and fast as her body will allow, her ass slapping against my hips with each repetition of my name, taking me and taking me as she comes all around me.

Just past the peak of her climax, she twists, trying to roll us. She has zero chance of actually forcing the leverage, but I allow it, rolling on top of her. I brace my weight with my hands on the mattress, but she has other plans.

Her thighs clamp around my waist, heels digging into my ass, and she clings to me, pulling me down. Her teeth sink into my shoulder as she comes yet still, and I can't help but move, driving into her.

"Come for me, Chance," she breathes into my ear. "Come for me. Let go for me, please—*please*, Chance. Please let go. Give me all of you. I want it all, every last bit of you."

I bury my face in her throat and give her what she's begging for.

I can't not.

I've never had this. Never been given such a priceless, precious gift as she's giving me in this moment—herself. Us. Abandon. Total vulnerability. Complete union with another soul.

I lose myself in her, then. I don't think about bracing my weight, or holding back the force of my thrusts. I just trust her. Give her all that I am.

Time ceases to have meaning. It could be thirty seconds, or an hour. I don't know. I just know it's the single most monumental moment of my existence.

"Annika…" I breathe, my voice nothing but a whisper on the wind. "Nik, I'm…"

Her thighs squeeze around me until it hurts, and her hands cradle my head to her breasts as I hunch to withdraw and arch to drive in, and her voice rides the breeze and weaves in with the surf— "Yes, Chance, yes. Come for me, my beautiful man. I want it. I want it."

I have absolutely no control, I'm decimated, reduced to cinders and rubble of the man I was. "Nik, oh god, *Annika.*"

I shatter with a snarling roar that's more animal than human. Everything I am explodes out of me and into her, into the lush, strong, incredible woman beneath me. I pour myself into her, strokes shuddering, all of me trembling, even my breath is shaky.

When I can't support my own weight anymore, I flop to the side and roll to my back, taking her back on top— I'm still buried inside her to the root. She sinks lower, driving her ass down my body, dragging her palms over my chest, lips stuttering over my skin. She takes me until I feel my balls press against her sex, my cock throbbing as her tight wetness grips me, clenches me.

There she stays, lips on my sternum, hands outstretched to rest on my chest. She wiggles her ass, as if in an attempt to get me deeper.

"Jesus, Annika." It's gasped, panted.

A soft kiss to my upper abdominal muscles. "I don't have words, Chance." Another kiss. "Well, that's not true. I can think of a few."

I tangle my fingers in her hair. "Such as?"

"Glorious. Life-changing. Perfect. Incredible."

I feel my cum leaking out of her around me, dripping. "Funny. That's exactly how I'd describe you."

I pull her up, but she shakes her head, dotting kisses all over my chest and stomach, keeping me inside her even as I soften. "Not yet."

She rests her cheek on my sternum, her hands rubbing soothing patterns on my chest and shoulders. Finally, she rotates her head to rest on her chin, smiling sweetly up at me. "You were right."

I almost can't handle the glutting overload of sensation and emotion—overcome, overwhelmed, shattered, destroyed and put back together, on fire yet liquid. "About what, mama?" I ask on a hoarse, harsh rasping murmur.

She touches her lips to my skin again, keeping her eyes on mine the whole time, and then rests her chin on me again. "You're worth it all. Everything I've been through that led me to this moment with you. It's all worth it to be here with you, like this, right now."

I squeeze my eyes shut, unable to stop the salt haze from leaking out. "Fuck, Nikki. Fuck. Jesus." I cover my face with my hand, embarrassment mixing with the intensity of my emotions and reacting together, heating my face and my tears until they burn like acid in my eyes and on my cheeks; my chest aches with unspent breath.

She lengthens on me, thudding her forehead on my chest with a long rough groan as I slide out of her. "Chance. Chance, baby." She crawls up my body and slides to my side, onto her back, pulls me over and onto her, pressing my face into her breasts and cradling me there, wrapping her arms as far around my shoulders as they'll go. "It's okay, it's okay. Feel it, Chance. Let me have this, too."

"So…so fucking—embarrassing," I grit out through clenched teeth. "I don't know why I'm fucking—" I'm so embarrassed I can't say the word.

"Yes, you do. Tell me why you're crying." She trails her fingers through my hair. Seems not to mind the fact that I'm wetting her chest.

"Because I'm a big fuckin' baby."

She laughs. "Nah, that's not it." She cups my jaw and tilts my face up to hers, but I resist. "Let me see you, Chance. Show me your eyes, baby."

I shake my head, everything burning, and rest my forehead on hers. "Can't. Too—too hard. Too embarrassed."

"No, no, no," she says, her voice a soft coo, like a mourning dove. Musical, gentle. "No embarrassment, honey. It's beautiful."

"That I'm blubbering?"

"That you're trusting me with this part of you." She cups my cheek. Brushes her thumb under my eye.

"Ruining…the—fuck." I clear my throat. "Feel like I'm ruining the moment, what we just had."

"You're not, I promise you're not. You're making it even more beautiful."

I shake my head. "How? God, you're crazy."

"I'll tell you, but it's gotta be an exchange."

"Exchange for what?"

"Well, one, you look at me. Two, you tell me what you're feeling." She shimmies down, so she's lower than me, and looks up into my eyes through her thick eyelashes. Her smile is exquisitely tender, achingly accepting. "There you are. Hi."

I choke, laughing and half sobbing. "Where did you come from? God."

She blinks in confusion. "What? What do you mean?"

"This…you. The sweetness." I swallow hard, breathe out a slow shudder. "Like…the others."

Her green eyes dance. "*You* did this. *You* made me safe. You've given me space to…" A shake of her head as she hunts for the right words. "To become this version of me. You made it possible. By…just being you. Everything that's happened. Everything you've done for me."

"What did I do? Kicked Alvin's ass. He's fuckin' lint out of my belly button, Nik. He's nothing." I shake my head. "What did I do to deserve you?"

"You brought me out of my shell," she whispers. "You showed me that it was okay to live again. *How* to live again. You gave me safety to be myself again. I don't really recognize this me, but honestly? I freaking *love* her. And you made it possible. So I'll do anything and everything I can to show you how much I appreciate it—how much I appreciate *you*."

I cover my eyes again, with both hands this time. "I'm feeling *so fuckin' much*, mama. Like all this shit that I've

been ignoring and pushing down my whole life is just…
boiling up. More than that. It's…you. It's us." I breathe out
again, slow, through pursed lips. "Being with you. Making
love with you—god, I never thought I'd call it that…I
never fucking *dreamed* it could be like that. That I could
ever just…*let go* and just be…me. For the first time in my
entire goddamn life, you've made me feel…accepted. Not
too much, too big, too…everything. You took all of me,
and you…" I trail off.

She lies diagonally across me, breasts squashed on my
ribs, pillowing her chin on her stacked hands, gazing at me
with fierce yet soft eyes like summer grass in the noonday
sun. "You make me feel fulfilled. Sated. More than that.
Good god, Chance, I can't explain it, how you made me
feel just now." A soft sigh. "You make me feel beautiful and
sexy and feminine and…*safe.*"

I shake my head. "I've never felt this way. Didn't know
it was possible." I look down at her, rubbing at my eyes. "I
didn't…I honestly thought I'd never find someone who
could…I dunno how to put it."

"Bluntly, that's how. Just tell me the truth."

"I never thought I could have sex like that. Fully into
it. Letting go. Not thinking. Not holding back, not worried about anything. I've always, always been so, so careful.
Always had to hold back, be gentle, be cautious."

She just smiles at me. "We fit each other. Matched
perfectly. I thought it was rom-com bullshit, but…I really
feel like we were made for each other."

I wrap my arms around her and crush her in a bear
hug until she laughs with a fake groan, and I release her,
but just enough to hold her as close as two people can be,
wrapped up, tangled together.

We drift together, then. Breathe, float, relax.

The wind sighs.

The surf crashes.

Gulls cry to each other.

I feel undone, but in the most amazing way. Like I was taken apart and reassembled, only to discover that I was never put together correctly in the first place. *Now* I'm correct. *This* is how I'm supposed to be.

It's beautiful.

15

LOVE LIKE STARS

Annika

WE DOZE TOGETHER. I SLEEP IN HIS ARMS through the afternoon, more sated and content than I've ever been in my life.

When I wake, it's evening, the sun an inch or two above the horizon, a huge red-orange coin, brilliant and bright. I can see the beach from my sheltered nook in Chance's arms, a deep crescent of white leading to gleaming, rippling, endless azure being slowly stained red by the sunset. A few gulls play above the waves, winging and wheeling and dipping and swooping, their calls sounding like laughter.

I feel Chance's mammoth chest lift as he sucks in a huge breath, and then we sink together as he lets it out.

I look up, and see he's awake as well. I trace the beard along the angle of his jaw. "Hi, you."

His smile is pure warmth. "Hey there, mama. Have a good nap?"

A stretch ripples through me, causing me to stiffen and spasm, straightening and then bending backward against him, a deep, almost orgasmic groan escaping me.

"God, yes. Best nap ever." I curl a thick strand of inky black hair around my finger. "You?"

He arches up off the bed in a stretching yawn of his own. "Fuck, I don't know if I've ever napped that hard."

I laugh. "Good." I wrinkle my nose. "I, um, need to hit that outdoor shower, though. I'm…um, crusty."

He grins. "I've got a better idea."

He rolls me onto him, belly to belly, chest to chest, and then sits up, twists, and stands. His hands cup my ass and hold me in place, and my thighs clamp around his waist. "Hold on, mama."

I cling to his neck and laugh as he strides out of the hut, down the steps, and toward the surf. "Chance, wait, I'm not—"

He ignores me and stomps right into the ocean up to his hips, and then twists and falls backward. I have plenty of time to suck in a deep breath and close my eyes before we hit the water. His arms are powerful bands around me, and as we go under, he kicks powerfully, swimming us toward deeper water, still on his back. He surfaces, planting his feet and standing up. The water is around his chest, and I'm still wrapped around him.

I laugh, holding to his neck one-handed and wiping at my face and scraping my hair away from my eyes. "It's so warm!"

"Middle of the summer, baby. Like bathwater this time of year."

His hair is sticking to his face, so I brush it aside, away from his face. "I was expecting it to be a lot colder. Not sure why. I swam in SoCal all the time and it wasn't *that* much cooler than this."

He releases me and I find my feet, grinning at him as

I duck under and swim away from him, angling for the sea floor and then kicking off with my good leg. Surfacing, I wipe my face and then scrub my skin, especially where I'm a little crusty from earlier. Not that I mind—far, far from it. In fact, I can't wait to have him inside me again. To feel him let go, to fill me with his cum.

I feel like he ignited something inside me. If my libido was dormant before, meeting him woke it up. Kissing him and getting back in touch with my own body lit the match. And now, having known the glory of being intimate with Chance? That once-dormant libido is fully awake, a ravenous monster that can't be sated.

It's almost a gnawing hunger in me—a sensation that feels a lot like a craving for meth. Except…the fix I need won't leave me sick and dying. The fix I need will make me more alive. More myself. More of everything good in this world.

My cheeks heat, my lungs expand in my chest, my heart—the metaphorical one—swelling and filling every nook and cranny in my soul, because my heart is full of him.

I look at him. He's a few feet away, in the act of surfacing after ducking under as I just did. His gargantuan shoulders and chest stream rivulets of water, the heavy muscles shifting and rippling as he runs his hands up his face and backward over his scalp, elbows flaring as he draws his hair backward. His thick beard streams water down his chest. His eyes catch mine, flaring with a wealth of emotion as our gazes lock.

"You're so fucking beautiful, Annika," he says. "You take my breath away."

Instead of answering, I kick off and swim to him, my

naked body slicing through the water. I reach him, and he catches me, gathers me close, as if he can sense the hunger rising in me. Our wet, naked bodies collide, and our mouths fuse in a wild, greedy kiss. My legs wrap around his waist and I cling to the cliff-face of his shoulders, feeling his hands slide up my thighs to my ass. He walks toward the beach with me, striding through the waves, kissing me.

I can't wait. I need him.

The water surges through us and around us as he walks us to the shore, and I reach between us. Find him ready for me. God, he's so fucking big. I'd be lying if I said I wasn't a little apprehensive, earlier, when I was preparing to take him inside me. But I should have known better. Everything else about us just *works*. This, too, seems to just work. To fit, perfectly, as if we are cut from the same cloth, created to match.

I grip the thick column of his erection and stroke him a few times, but I need him inside me. I don't want foreplay, I just want him. I lift, fit him to my opening. Bury my face in the side of his neck and let a cry loose from my lips as I clutch his neck and slowly sink around him, impaling myself on him.

His knees buckle mid-step. "Fuck, Annika...fuck, you're so tight." He catches his step as we reach the shore, or nearly. Halts, the water scudding up around his calves and receding. "God, Nikki. The way you feel..."

I just moan as he fills me. More, and more. Deeper, and deeper, until the aching burn of my pussy being stretched around the unbelievable girth of his cock, the length of him filling me until I think I can't take any more of him. But, I can. His big strong hands cup my ass—he pulls me apart, and I sink lower, more of the magnificent, massive perfection of his cock driving into me. I can't help but scream in pure ecstasy, and then it's too much and I sink my teeth into the thick cord of muscle at the base of his neck where it meets his shoulder, biting through my scream until he growls in protest.

And then I'm so incredibly full of him that I can't summon a breath, can't move, can't do anything but tremble around him as my pussy stretches to accommodate him. The burn is so beautiful, the ache so deep, so dizzying that I groan low in my throat, almost a feral growl, until my lungs are empty and I have to suck in a lungful of oxygen.

"Chance," I groan, rolling my hips, "I need you."

He slides an arm under my knee, and then the other, so my knees are hooked over the crooks of his elbows, supporting my weight easily. I feel so small with him, the way he carries me and handles me like I weigh nothing. He lifts me, drawing himself out of me with aching slowness. My arms lock around his neck, and I can't help but seize his mouth, demand his tongue. In this position, I can do nothing but surrender control to him, and I do so…willingly, gladly, eagerly.

He's so effortlessly supporting my weight that I feel safe to hook one arm around his neck and slide a hand down to my pussy. I find my clit with my fingers, and with one touch, I'm flying. He lifts me until there's only the plump head of his cock left inside me, and then he holds me in place a moment or two before gradually allowing gravity to drag me downward. He's so thick and my pussy is so tightly stretched around him that I feel my lips stutter around the veins of him. I whimper as he sinks into me to the hilt, bottoming out inside me. I swipe fingertips around my clit, feeling lightning gather in my core, building behind my sex, throbbing in my clit, aching my belly, rising up into my chest and tingling in my bloodstream, turning my veins effervescent. Stars dance behind my shut eyes, and now he pulls me up his body once more, so slowly, so gradually.

My fingers move faster, circling my swollen, sensitive clit with increasing speed, until the circles start to ellipse into side-to-side motions, and my hips try to rock, to gyrate, but I can't move, can only strain toward him, silently begging him to give me what I want, what I need.

"Chance, please," I whisper, my voice barely audible over the surf. "Harder, please."

His growl is one of disbelief. "Fuck, Annika. How are you real?" He releases his grip on me so I fall onto him, ripping a scream of delight from me and a grunt from him. "So fucking sexy."

"I need you, Chance. I need more of you. I can't get enough of you." I nibble his earlobe, a huff escaping as the first sizzling bolt of ecstasy lances through me, the precursor of my orgasm. "You know I can take it now, baby."

"Come first." He lifts me. Lowers me. Again. Again. Almost a rhythm, now. But nowhere near what I so desperately need—to feel him fucking me, to feel his huge cock plunging into me, taking me, claiming me, using me for his pleasure. "When you come, I'll give you what you need, mama."

I nuzzle against his throat, gasping, helplessly trying to thrust into my fingers as beauty swirls through me. "What if I can't come until you fuck me?"

He laughs. "You're about to come right now—I can feel it. I can feel this tight wet pussy squeezing me." He adjusts his grip, his hands digging into my ass, spreading me open for him, lowering me until I'm right where he wants me. "Give it to me, Nik. Let me feel you come on my cock."

I shake my head, groaning—I'm so close, but I can't find the edge. "I can't, Chance. I promise. I'm trying. I need you. Fuck, I need you." I slow my touch, overstimulated, momentarily bringing my fingers away from my clit entirely, sliding them downward until my middle and ring fingers are split around his cock, feeling it gliding between them as he dips at the knees and drives his hips to fuck into me—I whimper at the wonder of him filling me. "Please, Chance. God, please."

He nudges my chin with his nose, groaning, and then claims my mouth with his in a short but fiery kiss. "You can, baby. I need to feel you come."

"I will," I breathe. "I swear I will. But I need you."

He thrusts into me, finally giving me a steady rhythm. "This?" He grunts. "This what you need, mama?"

Our foreheads touch, and I nod against him. "Yeah, honey. That's what I need. More of that." I touch my clit again, and feel the edge there, just out of reach but drawing closer. "Fuck me, Chance, please. That's what I need."

He widens his stance, feet splashing in the surf as it licks around his legs, rising to his knees as it crashes in and receding to his ankles as it pulls away. I quicken my touch, and now I feel myself responding—wetness surges through me as I topple toward the edge, and the slow, steady sliding thrusts of his cock grow smooth and slick with the added lubrication.

"Fuck, you're so wet, Annika. So wet for me." He lowers me an inch or two, and drives into me, once, hard—a scream of bliss rockets out of me when he does it. "Ahhh god, baby, you like that?"

I nod, whimpering, so close to coming I can't find words. Or at least, not coherent sentences. "Please, please, please," I beg, ready to plead with him now; if only he'd fuck me how I need it, I could come, and I need this orgasm more than I need my next breath, more than I need anything. In this moment, reaching my climax is all that matters, and only he can give it to me. "Please, baby—fuck me. Please fuck me."

He groans at my words, at my pleading. Another hard thrust. "Like that?"

I nod, a sloppy roll of my head. "Yeah, yeah, like that. Again, baby. Again." I bite his lower lip. "You like it when I beg? Hmm? You want me to beg?"

He drives into me—twice. Hard. "Yeah, Nikki. Makes me feel like a god when you beg me to fuck you."

"You are," I gasp, nearly undone when he delivers another series of slow hard thrusts. "You are a god, to me. You want that? Then that's what I'll do—I'll beg, honey." I press my lips to his ear and whisper my pleas in a hot breath. "Please, Chance. I can't come until you fuck me like only you can. No one else on this earth can give me what you do. I'm begging you, honey. *Begging*—please, please fuck me. Fuck me hard and don't stop."

He growls—and obeys. His arms clamp around me, clutch me against him, position me where he needs me. Knees bent, he angles me away, buries his face between my breasts…

He fucks me.

Hard.

Fast.

Unrelenting.

It's exactly what I need.

I let myself scream until my voice gives out as a climax without parallel smashes through me. Lights shatter behind my eyes and heat billows through me. I feel my sex clenching around him spastically, squeezing like a vise, soaked and drenched and slick—I'm still so stretched around his cock that my sex is a ring of flesh. If he were even a tiny bit larger, I couldn't handle him, but since there is a god, she made him just big enough to be perfectly too big for me. I scream and scream, and when I can't manage another scream, I gasp until my lungs are full and then I can only moan long and low, the sound broken as he drills into me, again and again, tireless, his rhythm perfect.

Then something new and unexpected happens.

Another climax starts to build inside me. He hasn't come yet, and I'm about to fly apart a second time. "Oh god, Chance, Chance, I'm gonna come again."

He staggers forward a few steps and then drops to his knees, sitting on his heels. "Wait for me, mama…I'm almost there. Wait for me—come with me."

It builds fast, and I almost lose control over it, almost go flying into ecstasy again without him, but I hold it back. He releases my legs and grips my ass again, my heels hooking around his back as I sit on his thighs. He continues thrusting into me, then, beginning slowly and picking up speed. I don't need to touch myself anymore—I can't. If I do, I'll come.

"I can't wait any longer, honey," I whisper. "I can't hold it back anymore."

He growls, throws his head back. Snags a fistful of my dripping wet hair and roughly pulls my mouth to his, slashing a hot kiss so forcefully that I lose my breath. "Wait for me, goddammit," he snarls. "Don't come until I do."

I dig my fingernails into the rock-hard muscle of his shoulders and cry out, shaking my head, my whole body trembling as I fight back the onslaught of orgasm, leaning away to give him a better angle for his pounding thrusts. "I can't, I can't, oh god, Chance, please, I can't—I have to come. Oh god, I can't—I can't…"

I shudder, and despite all my efforts, I feel the orgasm tear open inside me, releasing a torrent of endorphins and ecstasy and wonder and dizzying splendor, all of it at once, too much at once. A ragged sob rips out of me. "I'm sorry, I'm sorry, I couldn't stop it, fuck, fuck, Chance, come with me come with me come with me—" I don't even know what I'm saying anymore, I'm lost to the mind-bending bliss of the climax.

I feel him find the edge, then. I feel it in the way his cock throbs thicker inside me, in the way he slams into me and his rhythm falters. I feel it in the way his fingers claw into my ass cheeks, digging in so hard I know I'll have bruises later—marks I'll cherish, knowing how I got them. And then he drops his head and I force my eyes open and find his gaze, and he holds my eyes and he fucks into me, deeper than ever, pulling my ass apart so he can get deeper and deeper.

"Annika," he breathes, the softest, highest, quietest sound I've ever heard him make, so awestruck it makes my eyes sting with tears. "My love."

He comes.

I'm still twisting and soaring on the heights of my orgasm, and when I feel him unleash inside me, I soar higher yet, sobbing and laughing and moaning all at once, and I feel him pour into me in wave after wave, and I come around him, on him, with him. There is only us, this moment, a connection between us drilling into our souls, merging us into something more than merely one flesh. He holds me down onto his thighs and drives into me without pulling out, only fucking deeper and deeper.

I hold on to his face and ride his wild bucking thrusts, half kissing him, moaning, sobbing, laughing from the sheer, unadulterated joyful wonder of it all.

After an eternity of breaking apart together, he falls forward, taking the fall on his forearm and rolling to his back. I'm cradled in his arms, then, his cock buried home, still hard inside me. I cup his jaw and shake all over and kiss his face everywhere—eyes, lips, nose, chin, forehead, temples, jawline, cheekbones, only ending with a searing kiss to his mouth after I've touched my lips to every part of his beautiful, rugged, handsome face.

We pull apart and his hand passes over my face, brushing my hair aside, thumb ghosting over my eyebrows, across my temple. "I love you, Annika." His voice is husky, rumbling.

I laugh and sob at once again, and fall helplessly into kissing his mouth until I can't breathe and have to pull away. "I love you too, Chance." It comes out a whisper, so I repeat it louder. "I love you."

"Never said those words to anyone before." He clears his throat. "Never thought I would."

"Me either," I answer.

He caresses my face with both hands, brushing my wet hair back, tracing my features. "I still can't believe you're real. That this is real." He shakes his head. "That I could feel this way."

I duck my head as a fresh wave of tears overcomes me. "Stop making me cry, dammit."

He laughs gently. "Yeah? Now whose turn is it?" A shake of his head, a slide of his thumb across my lips. "Nah, I'm teasing. It's beautiful, mama. You and me, what we got together? It's beautiful. So beautiful it makes you cry, and that's okay. That's beautiful, too."

He kisses away my tears, his lips tender on my closed eyes. "Swear to god, Nik, I'll never take you for granted. You'll always know down to your fuckin' soul how much I love you."

"So will you," I whisper back, still too overcome to speak any louder.

I grip his shoulders and rest my forehead against his, plant my feet in the wet sand and feel the ocean curling around my ankles, and I slowly rise off of him, pull his softening length out of me. I gasp as I lose him, and his cum immediately seeps out of me and drips down my thighs. I stagger to my feet and take a stumbling step, fall forward into the churning surf and dive beneath the waves, kick along the seafloor until my breath aches in my lungs. I surface, and turn to see Chance lazily breaststroking after me, his eyes greedily licking over my nude form as I rise out of the water to hip-depth. Droplets of seawater drip off the tips of my breasts and sluice down my belly and hips.

Just the plunge in the water has cleaned me off, for the most part, but I know I'll be feeling reminders of us for hours to come.

He reaches me, stands to tower over me, gazing down at me with love like stars in his eyes. "So fuckin' gorgeous."

We play in the water for a long time, swimming along the shoreline, diving beneath the waves, chasing each other. For a time, we laze at the edge of the water together, just reclining where the water reaches our butts in the sand, trailing along our toes as it recedes, silently watching the last of the sun dip beneath the horizon. Purples spring out in the sky, smearing with the pinks and oranges, and the waves slowly calm.

Eventually, Chance takes his feet and helps me to mine. "Come on, mama. Let's eat."

16

Chance

I DRIFT SLOWLY TOWARD WAKEFULNESS, WARMTH radiating through me. Heaven—this must be heaven, to wake up like this. So warm. Feeling so good.

More than good.

Incredible.

Heat washes over me. Through me. More than just heat—fire. But not the destroying kind of fire—the delirious, beautiful, crazy kind of fire. Wetness. Wet fire? My half-awake brain knows that makes no sense, but that's what I feel.

I don't want to open my eyes. I don't want to emerge from whatever dream I'm in. I feel too good.

There's a movement to the wet heat.

My eyelids flutter. Snippets of the world greet me: the woven strands of the ceiling above me; the posts supporting the roof; the sea, the trees, the sky, a pale graying blue of early dawn; the thin cotton blankets bunched at the foot of the bed, rumpled and twisted and tangled; a wild burst of red curls draped in a springy curtain around the sharp angles and delicate curves of Annika's face; her mouth wide open, lips stretched around my cock, sliding upward and upward until I pop free and smack against my belly.

I groan, my hands diving with a mind of their own into the luscious thicket of copper ringlets. "Annika, oh good god, Jesus..."

Is this real?

Am I dreaming?

Good lord. I close my eyes, but the sensations continue—she takes me in her mouth, sliding down my shaft, her tongue slithering against me. Her small soft hand clutched around my base, squeezing, pumping. Another hand cupping my balls, massaging, gently squeezing, teasing them with her fingernails.

I open my eyes again, and it's real. She's there. She's lying alongside me, feet in the air beside my head. Hair loose in a profusion of wild red curls, bouncing when she bobs on my cock a few times.

She pulls off of me again and turns to look at me, curling her fingers around my erection as she meets my eyes with the brightest, sweetest, most loving smile I've ever beheld. "Hi there." Her voice is soft, quiet.

I can't summon words, only a lost, helpless groan.

Her fingers drift up and down, lightly circling my shaft, barely touching, while her fingernails claw delicately over my balls, dragging, trailing, tracing, teasing. Fuck, that feels good. Her fingernails never stop playing with me as she pulls my cock away from my body and gives it a long, slow, loving lick up the underside, up to the glans, and then flicking her tongue tip against the slitted hole. All at once, then, she wraps her mouth around me, sliding me in, in. Sucks around me, bobs up and down—with her mouth as wide as it can go, she can still only take the first few inches before I hit the back of her throat.

And then she surprises me. Cupping my balls in a firm grip, she slides her mouth further down my shaft in achingly slow increments, not inch by inch but millimeter by millimeter. I feel myself enter the tightness of her throat. She shimmies backward and leans closer to my body and lowers her chin to open her throat, and keeps taking me. And more. And more.

"Oh fuck, oh fuck, ohhhh…*fuck,*" I hiss. "You don't have to do that, baby."

She hums, a long moan around me that sends delicious vibrations through me, but doesn't stop. She takes more. Slow, so slow. She doesn't make a sound. I feel her breath huffing through her nose onto my skin, a warm bath of air on my shaft. Both hands cup my balls now, massaging and squeezing.

I ache. Her mouth and throat are tight and wet and hot—more than I can handle. I can't take any more. But I don't want it to end. I want to feel this forever, her beautiful mouth, her clever soft hands.

"Oh fuck, Annika. Jesus, your fucking mouth."

Another groan—*"Mmmmhmmm?"*

"Fuck yes, fucking heaven, honey. Please don't stop. Feels too fucking good."

"Mmm-mmm."

"You won't stop?"

"Mmm-mmm."

"Promise?"

"Mmmm-hmmm."

And now she can't take any more of me—almost half my length is in her mouth and throat, more than I thought anyone could take. I groan, a ragged, broken sound. She pulls backward the merest amount, and then her mouth nudges against me. Another slide backward, more this time. Then back toward the root. Further, now. Again, and again, sliding further back each time before gorging deep, until her lips suction around my glans and her tongue swirls in maddening circles against my tip.

The pounding heat she's building within me crashes to a crescendo, pressure throbbing in my balls and bashing through my cock until I'm grunting with the effort to hold back, wanting to make this last as long as possible, wanting to feel her incredible mouth around me until the last possible instant.

She knows I'm there. She takes as much of me as she can in one slow, smooth movement, then swallows around me with a rippling of her throat muscles around my shaft. That is my undoing.

"Oh god, oh fuck, oh my god, Annika, Nikki—oh fuck, I love you oh god I fucking love you—" I have no idea what I'm saying, the words torn out of me beyond my control. "I'm coming, I can't stop it, oh fuck, Nikki, I'm coming—oh fuck oh fuck ohhhhhhh *fuck*!"

She swallows around me as I detonate inside the hot wet wonder of her mouth. I hear her gulp, and then she's bobbing on me in slow, methodical, steady slides of her lips down the length of my cock, taking my cum as it bursts out of me. Her mouth retreats to suck around my head, and stars burst and blink behind my shut eyes. Her massaging fingers squeeze around my balls as I orgasm, massaging and kneading, and I swear she somehow manages to suck and squeeze another orgasm out of me. I arch off the bed, and she takes my unexpected movement in stride, waiting until I've settled back down to the bed. She wraps one hand around my shaft and pumps me hard and fast, and her other hand squeezes my balls, one finger laying against the very root of my sac and driving in, where I've never been touched before, almost but not quite pressing into me. When all I do in response is groan helplessly, spasming up off the bed again, she does push the tip of her finger inside me, and the clashing exploding mind-melting intensity of my orgasm splinters and expands into exponential universes of ecstasy hitherto unknown.

Another spasm of cum is wrenched out of me, and the stars bursting behind my eyes multiply until I'm spinning, dizzy. I'm floating, I'm flying.

And still she doesn't stop.

She milks yet more out of me, bobbing down unexpectedly as far as she can and then back to sucking around my head again, pumping, tongue licking in swirls, her fingertip pulsing in and out of me, pushing this endless orgasm further and further with ruthless enthusiasm.

A breath I didn't know I was holding explodes out of me in a gusting groan, and my spine bows, arching me off the bed.

Finally, just when I think maybe I can't take any more, she releases the suction of her mouth around my cock, taking me in her hand and stroking my length, caressing simply for the sake of affection, kissing here and there on my shaft. Slowly, carefully, she pulls her fingertip out, and now my entire body is limp and boneless and I'm gasping, panting breathlessly as if I'd just finished a ten-mile uphill ruck with full gear.

She rests her cheek on my thigh and gazes at me with that sweet, tender love in her eyes, a pleased, proud, cat-got-the-milk smile playing on her lips. She's still idly caressing my cock, more for her own pleasure at merely touching me than for any other reason. "Hi there."

"Jesus." It's a raw, hoarse grunt. I'm still spinning.

She giggles. "Good?"

I stare at her, boggling. "*Jeeee*-sus, Nik."

She giggles again. "Did I break you?"

I rub at my face, my eyes, shake my head to clear it of the stars and the dizziness. "Yes." I let out a groaning sigh, shaking my head again. "What—god, I can't even talk. What prompted that?"

"I woke up and you were hard. So...I gave myself a little present." She rubs her hands up my thighs, around my cock and up to my belly, back down to my thighs.

"You gave *yourself* a little present?" I let out a bark of laughter.

"Mmmm-hmmm. That was for me." She gives me that smile again, nuzzling my now-soft shaft with her nose, kisses. "I wanted to give you the best blowjob you've ever had."

"You're not making any sense. *You* wanted to give *me* the best blowjob I've ever had...as a present to *yourself*?"

She laughs, a light trill. "Yep."

"How is that for you, rather than me?"

"Well, you see, I woke up horny, and you had a beautiful hard-on. And I was just laying there listening to you sleep, looking at this huge, gorgeous cock, and I just... wanted it. I wanted to taste you. Touch you. Make you come harder than you've ever come in your life." She shakes her head. "I don't know, Chance. You've done something to me. I always had a healthy sex drive, you know? Like I was a normal teenage girl, did all the usual sexual explorations. Hooked up in my early twenties. But my focus was always volleyball. My training. My team, and then Kelly. The games. Tryouts. I never really felt the need for a boyfriend, and sex always came second to my game. And then all that shit happened, and it all shut down. *I* shut down. And now you've woken me up, and it's like..." A shake of her head, looking for the right wording. "It's like all that time I was shut down and ignoring my body and not having sex, it wasn't *gone*, it was just...simmering. Like a pot set to boil but on very low heat. And now that I'm aware of my body, aware of my sexuality, I mean, it's like it's all coming back. All the time I was shut down, all that need was building up and gathering inside me, and it's all expressing itself *now*. With you. Does that make any sense?"

I shrug, nod. "Sure. I get that. But what you just did... babe, fuck, I fuckin' swear I saw god himself."

She laughs. "That's exactly what I wanted." She frowns, an adorable quirk of her lips and furrowing of her brow. "I can't explain what I was feeling, other than it felt like a craving. *That* kind of a craving, except instead of drugs, I needed you. I needed your cock. Your cock is my drug, now."

I laugh, shaking my head. "Well, babe, you can get your fix of *that* drug whenever you want."

"And do you have any idea how happy that makes me? How happy *you* make me?"

"Yeah, I do, because you give that to me, too. You make me happier than I ever knew a person could get."

She just smiles again. "Also, honestly, Chance...part of it was simply that you have the most perfect, the most beautiful cock I've ever seen in my life, anywhere, ever, and I just had to...worship it." She shrugs, a svelte, sleek roll of one shoulder.

I rumble a husky laugh. "You sure know how to make a guy feel good about himself."

"You *should* feel good about yourself, Chance."

I let heat spark in my eyes, and circle her ankle with one hand. "Speaking of feelin' good…" I haul her slowly backward toward me by her ankle. "Think it's your turn to see Jesus."

She twists onto her back as I drag her toward me. "Chance, I just wanted to—"

"And you did. Now it's my turn." Her ass comes to rest on my chest, her feet on my shoulders, and I trace a finger down her seam—she's soaked with pungent desire. "Feelin' hungry, mama. Need to eat."

Her eyes go hooded, flutter, close briefly. "Chance…" it's a breath. A plea.

"You this turned on by suckin' me off?" I ask, trailing my finger between her lips, gathering essence and smearing it onto her clit. "Fuckin' soaked, baby."

"Yes," she gasps. "I've always liked giving head, but with you…" she pauses to moan, biting down on her lower lip as I tease her clit, slide my finger inside her, back to her clit. "With you, I…oh fuck, that feels good—with you, god, making you feel that good turns me on like crazy."

I grasp her wrists and pull her upright to sit on my lap, sitting upright to meet her. She gazes down at me through a curtain of ringlets, eyes heavy-lidded with desire, cheeks flushed. Her breasts hang in front of my face, overfull, heavy, perfectly tear-drop shaped, nipples hard and erect and begging for my mouth. I oblige, fisting her hair and cupping one breast as I flick my tongue against the other. She moans, gasps, cups my head against her.

The intoxicating scent of her need-drenched pussy

beckons, a siren song I cannot resist—and don't try to. I lie back down and pull her up my body until her sex is above my face. She tucks her shins under her butt and gazes down at me, her hands resting on her thighs. I hold her eyes as I bring my mouth over her opening, and watch with eager delight as her eyes slide shut and her brow furrows and her mouth hangs open.

At first, I just kiss her sex, my mouth fusing to her lips and tasting her essence. She writhes, moaning. "Please, oh god, Chance, I love your mouth. Eat me, baby."

I rumble a laugh, and give her a flick with my tongue, my laugh turning to a pleased groan when her sex floods with a renewed torrent of need, soaking my mouth. Another flick with my tongue, and a hungry slide of my lips.

She grinds against my mouth, throwing her head back with a loud whimper. "Chance, god, fuck, yes, yes. You like the way my pussy tastes, baby? You love it as much as I love your cock?"

God, her dirty talk makes me crazy. My cock stiffens as I taste her, listen to beautiful dirty encouragement drops from her mouth. She cups her breasts, lifts them and lets them drop, then pinches her nipples and twists hard.

I growl my affirmation, showing her how much I love her pussy instead of answering with words. I devour her, then. Mercilessly, I ravage her clit with my tongue, build her to the quivering cusp of climax and then slow, mouthing her lips and kissing her sex and teasing her until she's writhing and grinding with frustrated desperation. And then I send her flying all over again.

I run my palms up her belly and grasp her heavy tits— she grips my hands and presses them against her breasts as if forcing me to play with them. I twist and pinch and flick her nipples, caress the pendulous delicious weight of them, and I edge her closer to orgasm and back away, again and again. I torture her this way, to the edge and then stopping, until she's mad and wild with need.

Her eyes are blazing, her hips ceaselessly grinding her sex on my mouth. "Chance, goddammit, please—please let me come. I can't take it anymore. I need to come, baby. Please."

I pinch her nipples until she cries out in protest, and at that moment, I send her over the edge, thrashing her clit with my tongue until I feel her tumble into climax. Her spine arches and her head flings back, shoving her tits forward and roughly scraping her pussy against my mouth with desperate force.

"Oh fuck, oh *fuck*, Chance, yes—*yes*, fuck yes—oh my fucking god I love you I love you I love you, don't stop, baby, please fuck don't ever stop!"

And then she can only scream, riding my mouth hard and fast, her hands in her hair as I pinch and release her nipples in time with her thrusting sex.

Finally, she can come no more and slumps, gasping, shaking all over. Sliding down my body, she cups my face in trembling hands. "Chance. Oh my god, honey." She wipes at my mouth, giggling, and then kisses me, a deep, slow, thorough kiss, her tongue sweeping my mouth. Breaking, she rests her forehead on mine. "Wow. Just...wow."

Lifting up with palms braced on my chest, she gazes down at me. Speaks not a word, but reaches between her thighs, finding my aching, straining cock. She fits me between her lips, hesitates a beat, another...and then impales herself on my cock, taking me to the hilt in one slow slide of her wet, hot sex.

She leans forward, breasts smashed flat on my chest, cups my face, kisses me, and sets a rolling rhythm of her hips. Her mouth never leaves mine, sometimes kissing and sometimes just breathing with me, our breaths mated, heartbeats in synch. I meet her rolling rhythm with rough thrusts of my own, gripping her hips and pushing and pulling. Her whimpers fill my mouth, my ragged grunts huff into hers.

Everything before this was discovery, release, exploration, connection. This is something else. There's no desperation, no hurry, no chase to completion, no tangling or rolling or shifting positions. No dirty words, no filthy exhortations. Not even declarations of love, or gasps of encouragement.

Just our bodies uniting, our souls merging. Her, and me, becoming us.

I feel her quaking above me, and I wrap my arms around her shoulders and waist and crush her to me, claim her mouth in a wet hungry kiss. She spasms around me, and sobs into the kiss but doesn't break it, and I let my own release build and explode in perfect harmony with hers. My bones turn to jelly, my veins liquefying into raw flowing heat. Our movements are as one, climax into climax, sobs mating with groans, gasps marrying with grunts.

It is endless.

Time is nothing. We come together for an age, an eternity.

And when it's over, we lie together, still joined, breathing together in the dawn silence.

17

HOME

Annika

WE SPEND ALL THAT DAY AND THE NEXT lazing in bed, eating, swimming, and making love. His appetite for me is voracious, and his need for me has his big beautiful cock hard for me again and again, no matter how many times we've fucked already.

I've never known pleasure such as he gives me. His mouth, his fingers, his cock...he's magic. He wakes me in the middle of the night with his greedy mouth on me, and carries me out to the beach with a blanket over his shoulder. He spreads the blanket on the sand and he fucks me gloriously senseless beneath the stars.

We wake in the warmth of dawn, there on the blanket, spooning. He's behind me, and we make love like that, lazily, slowly, gasping into the pink light of the Hawaiian sunrise.

There's no more talk of the past. No more secrets to share. Nothing to unburden, no demons to face.

Finally, on the fourth morning, we pack up and shut down, taking care to leave it better than we found it. Chance loads up the boat and pushes off, and we say goodbye to our little getaway before heading back to the real world.

———— ◆ ————

After more than twelve hours of nonstop travel, we reach Las Vegas and Club Sin well into the small hours of the following morning. The club is closed by the time we arrive, the parking lot mostly empty except for a few cars left by people too drunk to drive home themselves. Chance leads me to the side entrance and down the stairs directly to their personal quarters below the club.

We find the gang all gathered in the common area, bottles of beer cracked and being drained, glasses of whiskey clinking, voices overlapping and laughter ringing.

Myka sits on the counter near the range, her arms draped over Rev's shoulders as he leans his back into the V of her thighs—she holds a half-empty beer across his chest, and he has a bottle of whiskey in his fist. Kane sits facing Myka and Rev, his back to the table, and Anjalee sits on the table behind him, her legs under his arms and her hands idly toying with his hair—a glass of red wine sits on the table beside her, and he rests a glass bottle of fancy distilled sparkling water on her knee. The four of them are having a chaotic overlapping conversation, Anjalee and Myka talking while Rev and Kane have their own conversation. Solomon, Silas, and Saxon are clustered together on the couch, playing a first-person shooter video game— occasionally, one of them will curse or laugh or snap some insult at one of his brothers, but their attention is rapt. Cigarettes and joints smolder in an ashtray on the coffee table, tumblers of whiskey clustered around a mostly empty bottle of high-end whiskey. Lash sits on the far end of the couch, away from the brothers, watching them play and nursing a bottle of beer.

Kane is the first to notice our entrance. "Hey, Chance—missed you, buddy! Annika, good to see you again. Come on in, ya'll. Grab a drink and hang out with us."

Chance beelines for the kitchen area, leading me by our joined hands. He's careful to go at a pace I can match with my bum leg. He and Rev collide with an audible crash, embracing as men do, with violent smacks on the back.

Rev claps a palm to the side of Chance's face, a rough gesture of masculine affection. "Good, bro?"

Chance nods, glances at me, resting a heavy hand on Rev's shoulder. "Best I've ever been, and then some, brother."

Rev yanks him back in for another hug. "Glad to hear it."

Myka takes a swig from her beer, and then hops down from the counter—she's wearing an almost indecently short black mini-skirt with a tight white tank top, a black sports bra beneath it, and calf-height lace-up combat boots. "So, Annika. Do we have a third woman around here? Anj and I could use some more estrogen around here. All this testosterone is exhausting, you know?"

"I…" Except Kelly, I've never really had any real female friends. "Yeah. I'm…I can't think of anywhere I'd rather be than wherever Chance is."

Anjalee holds her wineglass by the bowl in both hands, smiling at me over the rim. "Awww! That is so very sweet. Chance is a most wonderful man, very kind. It is good to know he will be receiving the love we all know he deserves."

Kane squeezes her knee. "Well said, honey."

Myka clomps over to me in her hard-heeled boots and pulls me into a hug. "Welcome home, Annika."

A moment later, I feel Anjalee wrap her slender, delicate arms around me from the other side. "Welcome, indeed."

I feel my nose sting and my eyes burn. "Thanks. I . . . thank you."

They release me, and Myka grabs me by the arm and pulls me toward the bedrooms. "Anj, grab a fresh bottle of red and some glasses. Time for girl talk!"

I glance at Chance over my shoulder, and he grins at me. "Welcome to the Broken Arrows, mama."

Anjalee is right behind me, a bottle of wine in one hand and three goblets in the other. I find myself sprawled out on a king-size bed in one of the rooms, surrounded by photos of Rev and Myka in various settings—in the club during the day, facing each other across a beer pong table; in front of a farmhouse surrounded by a huge group of people I assume are Myka's family; here in the common room, Myka straddling Rev on the couch, her hands framing his face as he gazes at her with a look of the purest love, while she throws her head back in laughter. There are other photos of Rev from his military days, a camo bucket hat hanging from a nail, a shelf of books, a bureau, and a free-standing brass-framed clothing rack on locking casters, full of Myka's clothing. The small room is packed to the gills, but it manages to feel cozy and homey rather than overstuffed.

Myka and Anjalee cluster around me on the bed, and

Anjalee pours wine for all three of us. The door is open, and I can hear Chance's laughter bellowing out, loud and carefree.

"So." Myka leans toward me. "I'm dying for some gossip."

I laugh, shake my head. "What gossip? I just met all of you."

She leans closer yet, whispering. "No, like, details. You and Chance." She grabs my knee, shaking it. "Is he packing what I think he's packing?"

I blush. "Um." I glance at Anjalee, but she's waiting for my answer with wide, eager eyes. "Yes? I mean…" I can't help a breathy giggle, as I decide to throw myself into this newest experience—girl talk; Kelly and I weren't the type of friends to giggle together over boys. "Whatever you think he may have, down there?" I widen my eyes dramatically. "Multiply it. By a *lot*."

Myka covers her mouth with her hand, coughing laughter. "I mean, I know what my man has, and I'm gonna guess that Chance is even bigger than him. And my man's got…well, let's just say that if you see me walking funny sometimes, he's why."

"Kane leaves me quite deliciously sore," Anjalee puts in, then rests a comforting hand on my other leg. "If your Chance is so very well endowed in the manly department, you must be quite sore indeed, after three days alone in Hawaii with him."

I laugh but don't otherwise answer. There's a bit of silence then. Strangely, it's companionable, not awkward or strained.

"I think I'm going to like it here," I say. "I haven't had any real friends in a long time."

"No?" Myka says, the larger question in her voice.

I nod, shrug. "Yeah, I sort of alienated everyone in my life. That's what Chance and I were doing—he was helping me make amends with people."

"Did you?" Anjalee asks.

I nod. "Yeah, I did. It was...so intensely cathartic. Like, the process of apologizing and admitting my faults and all that to all the people I screwed over and pissed off really helped me forgive myself and move on. I think I can actually have a relationship with my family again, and with Kelly. They all live over on the West Coast and I'll be here, but...there's the opening, now, where there wasn't before." I look at Myka, and then Anjalee. "I'm just thankful that you guys seem so welcoming, I guess."

Myka clinks her glass against mine. "This place, the people here? We're sort of becoming a family." She glances at me. "Has Chance explained anything about this place? What it is?"

I shrug. "Not really." I finish my wine, and Anjalee pours more, finishing the bottle between the three of us. "He showed me a tattoo over a brand and told me he'd taken an oath not to kill anyone ever again, as part of his 'terms and conditions,'" I put air quotes around the phrase, "of living here, what he called the Broken Arrow compound."

Myka nods, sips. "Yeah. So, all the guys who live here—Rev, Chance, Kane, Solomon, Silas, Saxon, and Lash—are guys who've been through hell and back, and for various reasons cannot or will not return to normal, everyday civilian society. I only really know the stories behind why Rev, obviously, and Chance and Kane are here. The others are still sort of a mystery. I know some of the basic outlines because of that fun little sharing circle we had, but the brothers are not very social or forthcoming, and Lash is...well, he's a total enigma. Even what he shared didn't shed much light on who he is." She sips again, considering. "They're all outcasts, sort of. Products of violence and trauma and the worst the world has to offer. This place is sort of their haven. The owner, whom no one but Inez has ever even seen, rescued them each from their individual situations, brought them here, gave them employment and a home where they're safe, and a group of like-minded men who understand them, and will not judge, no matter what horrors lie in their pasts."

"And how did you and Anjalee end up here?" I ask.

We swap stories then—over another bottle of wine. I learn about Myka being kidnapped by Rev's enemies and her subsequent rescue, and how Kane helped Anjalee confront and escape her controlling parents, and then how she helped him face his past and find forgiveness from the man who raised him, after Kane got his daughter killed in a drunk driving accident. I give them the story of my volleyball career, the accident and my injury, addiction, recovery, my debt to Alvin, the whole thing.

It feels good to talk about it. They don't look at me like I'm a freak, or an abomination. There's no pity, no judgment. Just acceptance. Understanding. In a couple hours of conversation and sharing, I feel almost as close to Myka and Anjalee as I have anyone else—they have their own traumas, and they get me. We're all here together, in this exclusive club of fucked-up people.

Family. Not by blood, but of choice. I choose Chance, and these people are choosing me as well. No secrets, nothing harbored or hidden. It's all out there, good or bad.

By the time we've finished our various stories, I've been awake for more than twenty-four hours. But...I'm happy. Content. Ready to start this next phase of my life—with Chance, and with this ragtag bunch of misfits and fuckups and addicts and men stained by blood and violence, and the women who love them.

I'm home.

EPILOGUE

A WOUNDED BIRD

Silas

I T'S BEEN A QUIET COUPLE OF MONTHS. THE
compound beneath Club Sin is a hell of a lot louder
and more active than ever, with the addition of Annika
to our group. The three women are thick as thieves, always
huddling together and cackling and talking, glancing at
their men with those secret, sweet smiles. Chance is pretty
much the same after his little trip with Annika, except he
smiles more, laughs more...and he and Annika actually
leave the compound together for dates and adventures.

Bully for him.

And Rev.

And Kane.

I always assumed "happily ever after" was fairy tale
bullshit, but I guess for some lucky motherfuckers, it can
be real.

Just not me.

I see Sax and Sol watching the three couples, and I see
the jealousy. I see it. They want that shit, too.

Not me.

No fuckin' way. Some needy bitch clinging to me,

needing me, riding my jock about leaving the toilet seat up and all that shit.

No.

I visit the girls in Hel when my physical needs get to the point I can't ignore them and my own stupid hand isn't doing the job anymore. Mostly, Lydia. She's hot as fuck, with that bottle-red hair and those big pale tits, and that mouth like a fucking vacuum. She doesn't ask questions, doesn't try to sweet talk me, doesn't share her own shit, and doesn't pretend like it's anything other than what it is between us—me paying her to scratch the itch.

Speaking of whom, I haven't been to see her in a few weeks—since Chance and Annika got back. The club's been busier than ever, and I don't like to make a regular habit of it. I pay her, of course—top dollar, even though she offered me a lower rate due to my status as a Broken Arrow. Nah, I'm not taking advantage like that. But, I'm feeling the need.

After the club closes, Sol and Sax head to their rooms, as usual. I think they both visit Hel, just like I do, but we don't talk about that. Lash, ever the lone wolf, vanishes into his room as well. Rev, Chance, and Kane all hang with the girls in the common room, and I take the opportunity to slip away unnoticed. Not that I'm ashamed or anything, I just keep my shit private. Toro and Taj are locking up the gate between Hel and Fisticuff, and waiting to escort the girls to their cars. Chance usually does that, but now that he's with Annika, he's passed the job to others, and has pushed the role of lead enforcer in Hel to Lash. He wants to stay away from the ladies, I guess. I get it.

The girls don't live in the rooms they lease from the club—those rooms are working quarters only. They all have their own private apartments throughout the city, and are provided an escort from their cars into the club and back out to the parking lot at the end of the night. They work set hours, too—for the club, at least. What they do in their own time is up to them, obviously, but they only work at Sin from 8 p.m. to 4 a.m.—an eight-hour shift.

It's after four, by now; most of them, once the club is closed and the patrons are gone and the doors are locked, spend some time at the bar in Hel, having a few drinks, talking, and relaxing before going home.

That's where I find Lydia, clad in her loose, gauzy, sheer, black robe that obscures precisely nothing, lounging at the bar, sipping a martini and laughing with Sindy and Karma about who knows what. Toro and Taj each have a bottle of beer and a cigarette, but they're off in a corner together, providing presence and security and waiting for the girls to be ready to leave.

I prowl up the bar between Sindy and Lydia, tap the bar top with a knuckle. "Yamazaki, neat—two fingers."

Danni gives me a chin lift of acknowledgment, pours my drink—more than two fingers, because she's nice like that. I toss her a fifty and wave off change, and she goes back to sipping her own drink and chatting with Candi and Brie at the other end of the bar. I never get tired of the sight of Danni—what straight dude could? But I pull my gaze from Danni's bare, glitter-dusted rack to Lydia.

"Hey." I lean my elbow on the bar, sip the whiskey, and give her a look.

She smiles at me, takes a slow sip. "Silas. It's been a while."

"Busy. The usual."

She nods. Her expression is knowing. "Things okay?"

I shrug. "Sure. Same as ever. You?"

She twirls a crimson lock of hair around a finger and takes another drink. "Oh, fine. A busy night. I'm kind of tired."

I push away what that really means with practiced ease. "Another night, then." I take a pull from the Yamazaki, and it burns like gold and sunshine going down.

She shakes her head, touches my chin. "I've always got time for you, Silas, you know that."

She finishes her drink, stands up, and takes me by the hand. "Come on. Bring your drink. I'll take care of you."

She leads me down the hallway to her room and locks it behind us. It's a small, simple room. Black vinyl floors that look like wood planks. White walls and ceiling. A small en-suite bathroom. A queen-size bed, with a small chest at the foot end. Lydia has a few abstract art prints on the walls, a small red leather love seat opposite the bed, and a bedside table with two drawers.

She leads me to the love seat and gently pushes me onto it—I let myself fall backward into it with a heavy plop. Straddling me, she brushes her fingers through my hair, touching my stubble with gentle fingertips.

That's what I like about Lydia—she makes seduction seem natural, gentle, and easy. With me, at least. I wouldn't know about anything else.

She brushes her robe off, clad now in nothing but a lacy white thong. Kisses my neck. Peels my shirt off. Descends slowly to kneeling between my thighs, kissing down my chest.

Reaches for my buckle.

I'm ready for her, knowing what those hands and that mouth can do, and eager for it. Needing it.

She's got me in her hands, using that soft, gentle touch.

My phone rings—it's a dumb phone, and only a handful of people have the number—my brothers, Inez, and... my mother.

It's not my brothers, and I just saw Inez while closing up the club.

Which leaves only one person who could be calling me.

I freeze solid. My heart hammers in my chest, and Lydia stops her strokes, looking up at me. "Silas? What is it?"

I swallow hard. "I gotta take that."

"Now?" She sounds disappointed.

Fuck me, but I wish that was real, instead of her just being damn good at her job.

"Yeah. Sorry." I stand up, a little too abruptly, and she rises with me, frowning at me in confusion as I buckle my pants around my raging hard-on. "Wish I didn't."

The phone stops ringing. A beat of silence.

"Are you okay?" Her voice is quiet.

The phone rings again, and I fish it out of my front pocket—*mom*, says the caller ID on the front screen of the clamshell device.

"Shit," I growl. "I gotta go, Lydia."

She unlocks the door for me. "I'll wait around a bit longer, if you want to...resume."

I shrug. "Just go home, Lyd. Another night."

She nods, donning her robe. "Okay, Silas."

I open the phone as I step into the hallway. "Hello? Ma?"

Silence greets me, and then I hear a sniffle. A rough, shaky breath. "Si, baby?"

"Mom. What's wrong?"

"He…" a sob. "I couldn't take it anymore, Si."

"Mom—what *happened*?" I snap the words, harsh, angry.

"I couldn't take it anymore. I've taken it for twenty-five years. I can't take anymore. I didn't want to do it, Si." Her voice is faint. Trembling. "I killed him."

"Who? Dad?"

"Yes." It's a whisper.

I'm stunned speechless, shocked into unbreathing silence. "You…*what*?"

"I shot him. He wouldn't stop, Si." A sob, a sniffle. "I had to—I couldn't help it. I'm sorry—I'm sorry."

I'm jogging for the Broken Arrow area, pounding on my brothers' doors. "It's okay, Ma, it's gonna be okay."

Sol and Sax huddle near me, listening, asking me what's wrong with their expressions.

"Ma, listen to me. Call the police, okay? Call 911. It was self-defense."

"What the fuck, Si?" Sol demands.

I cover the mouthpiece. "Mom killed Dad." Back to the phone, to Mom. "Are you hurt?"

"He wouldn't stop, Si." She coughs—it's a wet sound. "I hurt, baby."

"Hang up with me, call 911, and then call Robert. Don't answer any questions the police ask till Robert is there, got it?"

"Si, I…" I hear a shuffling against the mouthpiece on her end, a loud clatter, a faint, distant sob, and then she's back. "Max, oh god, Max. I'm sorry, Max. I didn't mean it. Why didn't you stop? Max, oh god, oh god…"

"Mom?" I can't swallow. My gut is a void, an empty pit.

I know this feeling. Something bad is about to happen—something worse.

A sob, from Mom. Then, her voice. Faint, quavering—hollow, as if something integral to her being has been sapped away. "Silas?"

"Here, Ma," I croak. "I'm here."

"Tell your brothers…" a pause, and a sound as if she's panting and keening through her teeth. "I'm sorry. I wasn't strong enough. I lost you. Tell your brothers I'm sorry."

"Ma, hold up. It's okay. Gimme a few hours and I'll be there, okay? We'll all be there, all three of us."

"It's too late, baby."

"Mom, no."

"I'm sorry, Si. I love you." A brief, tense moment of silence. "Tell your brothers I loved them."

"MOM!" I shout it, so loud my throat scrapes raw.

BLAM!

Clatter.

Silence.

I hold the phone to my ear. But I know what's happened. What she did.

The phone slips from my fingers. Hits the floor.

Sax and Sol are staring at me.

"Si?" The question is on Sol's face. In his voice.

Instead of answering, I spin on my heel and smash my fist into the wall—it goes through the drywall and splinters the wooden stud; I'm roaring, screaming.

Sol pulls me away before I can punch the wall again;

I don't feel pain, even though I can see my fist bleeding, and know I likely broke something.

My pulse hammers in my ears, and I can't pull a breath into my lungs.

There are no thoughts in my brain.

Sax bear-hugs me from behind and Sol pins me from the front, his arms going around me and Saxon.

None of us speak.

There's nothing to say.

———— ◆ ————

Dressed in black jeans, combat boots, black open-neck button-down with a black leather jacket, I stand in the rain, watching the backhoe fill in the first grave—Mom's. Dad's is beside hers, waiting. Her casket gleams in the rain, dark wood with shiny metal trim on the outside; mounds of rich black dirt and runny brown mud obscure the casket bucket by bucket.

Robert, the family attorney and executor of their estate, handled all the arrangements. My brothers and I drove through the night and stayed in a hotel in Boston under fake names, met with Robert for a quick, discreet reading of their wills.

Everything was left to the three of us, split equally, the house and grounds in Beacon Hill to be sold and the proceeds split between us. There's a hefty pile of stocks, bonds, IRAs, and a host of other financial bullshit which none of the three of us give a single fuck about—it's old money, Boston Brahmin money, and we don't really want anything to do with it. We collectively decide to let the investments stay as they are, and just handle them later—the proceeds from the sale of the estate, liquidation of other physical assets, and liquid assets in bank accounts are still gonna amount to fucking mountain of cash. Not that we need it.

Sol and Sax have already left, taking the Club Sin G-Wagen back to Vegas the moment the service was over. I told them I was gonna stay—I wasn't ready to leave yet. Not sure why. There are plenty of cars at the house, and I technically own all of them, so I can grab one later.

After I'm done here.

I need to watch to the end.

After a few minutes, Mom's grave is a slight rise of black loam at the foot of her headstone: *Elisabeth Carey Cabot, beloved wife and mother, 1965-2022.*

The backhoe maneuvers over to Dad's grave and pushes at the pile of dirt, knocking it into the grave and onto Dad's casket with a loud pattering that turns into thuds. I hold up my hand for the backhoe operator to stop; he does, bringing the bucket to rest on the pile of dirt and removing his hands from the controls.

I move up to the edge of the grave, staring down at the casket—his is cherrywood. "Fuck you. You fucking *bastard.*" I snarl the last word.

I spit into the grave, and it smacks onto the wood with splat, a splotch of white. It's not enough.

Without thinking, I unzip and cut loose a stream of piss onto the casket. It's chilly enough that my piss steams.

There.

I roll my hand to gesture for the operator to resume.

"Like that, huh?" the man says; he's older, short salt-and-pepper hair, thick salt-and-pepper stubble, wearing a baggy pair of dirty jeans and a ripped, stained Patriots hoodie.

I just nod.

"I was overseas when my old man croaked, but if I'd'a been here, I'd'a pissed on his grave, too." He resumes filling the grave.

I watch until Dad's grave is filled, and then I turn away and walk out of the graveyard.

The rain is cold, slanting sideways, cutting against my face and neck like wet knives.

I like it. Suits my mood.

I reach a road big enough to have taxis after several minutes of walking, and I give the driver the address. I still know it, even after ten years of absence. I can feel the taxi driver's sense of awe as he pulls up to the huge wrought iron gate.

"You live here?" He's a Southie, I can tell from his accent.

"Used to," I grunt.

Robert told me the code to the gate, so I hop out and punch it in; the huge black gates—ten feet tall with spear-like spikes at the top—swing inward. I hand a hundred-dollar bill to the driver and head through the gates without a word or backward glance. Another code from Robert gets me into the garage.

The sea of cars is, honestly, impressive. Dad was a serious collector. The garage is more of a temperature-controlled warehouse than a garage, containing at least fifty highly collectible, extremely expensive classic cars—the first six cars I see equal at least a million dollars.

I walk between the rows of gleaming, polished metal, touching a hood here, a fender there. Mercedes, Ferrari, Lamborghini, Pagani, Hispano Suiza, BMW, Ford, Chevy,

Dodge, AMC…there's something of everything, and each one is most likely rare in some way.

The car that catches my eye is an Aston Martin DB5—silver, just like James Bond drives in several movies. That's the one.

There's a locking key box on the wall near the door to the house, with another code. I find the right keys after some hunting. Fortunately, the DB5 is near the doors, so I don't have to do any tedious rearranging.

There's nothing in the house except bad memories and old nightmares, so I don't bother going in. I just pull the Aston Martin out and close the door with the clicker I find in the glove compartment. The gates open automatically as I approach, and close behind me.

I breathe a sigh of relief as I put the monstrous old house in my rearview mirror. I blank my mind, just like in the bad old days, when I had to do something unsavory for my former crime syndicate employers. Don't think about Mom. Don't think about that last fucking phone call.

Blank mind.

Just drive. Out of Boston. I don't know fucking where. Don't care. Anywhere but here.

———— ◆ ————

I've left Massachusetts behind and I'm somewhere in Pennsylvania—the sticks. Farmland. Miles of barbed wire and clusters of cows grazing. Hayfields. Silos. The occasional little farmhouse, with an old barn, one of those lights hanging from the electrical wire over the dirt driveway.

I fill the gas tank at a gas station so old and behind the times that it doesn't even have pay at the pump. I grab a package of beef jerky, a liter bottle of water, and a Styrofoam cup of old, bitter, burnt coffee.

Keep driving.

Blank mind.

No memories, no thoughts. No feelings. Fuck, please god, no feelings. Feelings are toxic. Feelings are the enemy. Lock that shit down tight, way down deep inside a box. Wrap the box in chains and padlocks, and toss it into the Marianas Trench of my cold, black, bitter, broken soul.

Just drive.

Past midnight. No fucking clue where I am, except still in the goddamn boonies. West Virginia, maybe.

My headlights pierce the night—it's pitch black out here, with an endless wash of stars against a black sky. A deer crosses ahead of me, pausing on the other side and watching me, its eyes shining silver in the darkness.

A farmhouse ahead, the obligatory light glowing orange amber, illuminating a patch of the dirt driveway, a pole barn, and a battered old truck.

Off in the distance, on a rise, small yellow squares indicate a house. Here, a high fence runs parallel to the road, six feet high at least, with barbed wire rolling across the top. Clearly, someone likes their privacy.

A huge gate, this one chain-link, manually operated. Oddly, it's ajar a few inches. Some security.

I'm in an almost Zen-like state, and I almost hit her.

She's half jogging, half stumbling on the shoulder of the road. Holding her ribcage. My headlights give me a snapshot of her—fairly tall, slender, willowy. Auburn hair, long, the tip of the braid dancing just above her ass. She's wearing an ankle-length skirt, the kind ultraconservatives make their women wear. Denim, or khaki material, hard to tell from the brief glimpse. Long-sleeve shirt—not enough for the chill in the air this time of night.

I keep going.

Not my fucking problem.

I glance in my rearview—I can just make out her shadowy shape behind me. She stumbles, falls, catches herself on her hands, scrabbles to her feet and lurches into an agonized, desperate run.

Fuck.

Fuck, fuck, fuck.

I jab my foot onto the brake pedal and slew the car onto the shoulder. Neutral, parking brake. Leave it idling. Hop out. My taillights bathe the road in a dim red glow, exhaust curling in the light.

She halts several feet away. Arms around her ribs, gasping. Not crying audibly, but I see the tears on her cheeks.

Good fucking lord, she's stunning.

Exquisitely beautiful. Her features were crafted by a master artisan, and she is his opus. Symmetrical, all perfect curves and delicate angles. Wide almond eyes, dark, brown or gray. Even in that conservative, almost Mennonite or Amish getup, it's clear she's got a hell of a body. Slender, svelte, but with enough curves to make a man dream of her.

She's trembling, staring at me. Silent.

I gesture at the car. "Get in."

She shakes her head. Not no, I don't think, just…unable to process what I'm saying. Or, unable to even speak.

"You're hurt. Running from someone." I take a step

toward her, and she shuffles backward with a terrified whimper. "Hey. I won't hurt you. Trying to help."

She's been beaten to hell. Her lip is split and bleeding, her nose is bleeding, and a bruise darkens her eye. The way she's holding her ribs makes me suspect they're bruised at least, if not cracked or broken.

And yet, she's breathtaking.

Seeing her beaten, battered face cracks open a memory.

His foot slams into her stomach, and she can't even gasp or cry. Can only curl in on herself, mouth open and flapping, eyes leaking tears. Or, they would, if they weren't both swollen and bruising. He hauls her up to her feet... and backhands her, a vicious bone-jarring crack of his knuckles against her delicate cheekbone. She stumbles backward, twisting away, still not able to breathe from the kick.

I tackle him from behind, try to get my arms around his throat. I almost manage, but I'm not fast enough, not strong enough. I'm only ten, after all. He hurls me over his shoulder and his foot batters into my stomach, sending me rolling...

I shake my head. Here. Now. Side of the road, looking at a beautiful, beaten girl.

Fuck no.

I hold out both hands toward her, palms out, like I'm trying to approach a skittish horse. Voice quiet. Low. "I'm not gonna hurt you. Okay? You need help. There's nothing out here in any direction for miles."

She twists to look back the way she came—the partially ajar gate. "I..." her voice is a hoarse, scraping whisper, barely audible; she looks back at me. At the car. Longing yet terrified. "I can't."

I approach another step, and she freezes, not even

breathing, so I halt again. "If you're trying to escape who-ever did *that* to you…" I gesture at her, and then the black ribbon of road disappearing into the darkness whence she came. "You won't do it on foot. Not with broken ribs."

"They're not broken," she whispers.

"Sounds like you know from experience."

She doesn't answer, but she doesn't need to. I see the answer on her face. "Just leave me." It's another whisper, shaky and thin.

I shuffle closer—three feet gape between us. I take another step, and she shuffles backward, almost hyper-ventilating. "Not gonna happen."

"Why?" The question escapes, it seems, unbidden. Immediately, she drops her head. "I'm sorry—I'm sorry." Her voice cracks on the second *I'm sorry*.

I blink at the sudden apology. "Wait, hold up. Why what? And what are you sorry for?"

Shakes her head, chin dropped to her chest, visibly shaking all over. "It's not my place to question. I'm sorry."

"Jesus fuck." I'm starting to get a vague sense of what she's running from. I point at the car. "Look, lady. I don't know if you're aware of what you're up against, out here. There isn't anything but fuckin' cows and fields for miles in every direction. Nearest anything is a gas station, and that was ten miles back the other way."

She swallows. Doesn't answer.

"You ever walk ten miles before?"

She shakes her head. "No, sir."

"No sir," I echo. "Shit."

She trembles. "Sir?"

"Quit calling me sir. Jesus." I look away, exhale sharply, look back at her. "You need medical attention." I look down at her feet; they're bare. "Fuck me running. You're barefoot?"

She wiggles her toes. "I didn't have time to get shoes."

"Well, you're not going far in that state." I gesture at the car. "Just get in."

She stares at me. Blinks back tears, the nods submissively. Takes a tentative step forward. Another. Not looking at me, shaking like a leaf, her chin tucked against her chest, eyes downcast, she rushes past me toward the car. Getting away from my presence as quickly as possible.

She opens the door gingerly, folding herself into the seat—it's obvious each movement causes her pain. Once seated, she folds her hands on her lap and waits. Head down. Eyes down.

God, what did they do to this girl?

I close her door, taking care to do so gently, moving slowly. She still jumps when the door thunks closed. I slide behind the wheel, put it in gear, release the brake, and drive away. She watches in the side view mirror, rapt. Waiting.

I glance at her. "Hey. You're safe now."

She shakes her head. "He won't let me go."

"Your husband?"

She shakes her head but doesn't answer.

I drive in silence for a while, and then glance at her. "I'm Silas."

She doesn't look at me. "Naomi."

I chew on a million questions, but only ask one. "Got anywhere to go?"

A slight shake of her head, eyes downcast.

"Can you look at me?"

She turns her head slightly toward me and meets my eyes. "Yes sir?"

The "sir" bugs the shit out of me, but I've gotta take this fucked-up situation one step at a time. Right now, that's the least of my worries.

I reach out a hand, slowly. "I'm gonna see if you've got a broken nose. Okay?" She pulls away, a sharp, abrupt movement, and I drop my hand. "I won't hurt you, I promise."

She lifts her shoulders, turtling. "It's not broken. I'm okay."

I bark a huff of laughter. "Darlin', you're far from okay. But if you say it ain't broken, I'll believe you." I glance at her midsection. "The ribs?"

Another shake of her head. "Fine."

"Not fine." I frown in her direction. "Take a deep breath."

She glances at me, as if assessing, and then I sense resignation in her. She sucks in a breath, but can't fill her lungs all the way before her breath hitches, and she breaks off the inhalation with a soft cry of pain.

"Cracked, at least," I say.

"No doctors. No hospital. Please." Her voice is soft, but desperate.

"Why?"

A roll of her shoulders, a shake of her head.

I growl in annoyance. "I've got no problem avoiding a hospital, but I gotta know why."

"They'll take me away. Put me in jail."

I frown. "What? Why? What'd you do?"

She looks at me in confusion. "They're filled with sinful men of the world. They'll take advantage of me. Take me away."

I growl again. "That's horse shit, Naomi. Lies they

told you to keep you prisoner." I glance at her. "Whoever *they* is."

She shakes her head. "I shouldn't be here. I shouldn't be in this car with you."

"You'd rather go back?" I ask, frustration creeping into my voice. "I can turn around and bring you back there."

The terror in her eyes at this suggestion breaks something inside me. "No! Please. No. Please, no. I'm sorry. I'm sorry. I shouldn't have questioned you." She shrinks against the window, shaking all over, as if I'd lifted my fist toward her.

"Hey, whoa." I glance at her, trying to soften my tone. "I told you I won't hurt you."

"It's my place."

I snap my head around. "Your *place*? To be hurt?"

A shake of her head—this one means she can't possibly explain it to me, and can't even try.

"Jesus, Naomi."

"You take the Lord's name in vain rather liberally, Mr. Silas."

I quirk a grin at her. "Sure do. Don't like it?"

She rolls her shoulders. "It's not my place to tell you otherwise. I'm sorry for speaking out of turn."

"You apologize for everything." I eye her. "You don't need to apologize to me. Not for a damn thing. Not ever. You're not gonna make me angry. I won't ever touch you unless you allow it. That's a promise, okay?"

She stares at me, uncomprehending. "Sir?"

"Sir. Fuck, quit calling me sir. I'm just some guy, all right? I don't own you. I'm not your superior or your better, or anything. I'm just Silas."

"Yes sir." She realizes her gaffe, and blanches. "I'm sorry."

I can't help a laugh. "All right, all right. Don't hurt yourself."

I switch my grip on the wheel, guiding it with my left hand and resting my hand, somewhat heavily, on the gear shifter. It's an abrupt movement, and she lurches away from me, shrinking against the door. She's panicking, panting.

"Jesus, you're more skittish than a day-old horse." I eye her, thinking. "Look, you can't—" I trail off. "Shit. I can't expect you to not be afraid of me. It's obvious you've been abused your whole life. You've got no reason to trust me."

I pull my Glock from the holster at the small of my back, moving slowly. I twist it to grip it by the barrel and hand it to her. "Take it."

She stares at it like it's a snake. "Why?"

"You think I'm gonna hurt you, shoot me."

She moves her gaze from the gun to my eyes. "No, I…I…"

I place it on her thigh without making contact. "It doesn't have a safety, and it's loaded. So, you know, keep your finger off the trigger."

"Wh-why?" Her voice shakes.

"Put you at ease, a little."

She places her palm over the weapon, pinning it in place without actually taking it, staring at it. "I don't understand."

"I don't want you to be afraid of me. That'll help you trust me. You know I won't touch you without your permission, 'cause you can just shoot me."

"Why…" she trails off, and then seems to find the courage to ask the question. "Why do you have a gun?"

"Some folks out there don't like me. It's for protection."

She looks at me for a moment, breathing carefully, shallowly. "Are you kidnapping me?"

I laugh. "I just gave you my gun."

"Oh. Right." A lick of her lips. "Where...where are you taking me?"

"Hell if I know. Away."

"Well, where are you going?"

I shrug. "I dunno. I..." I debate what to say. "My parents both just died, and I'm...still processing."

"I'm sorry."

I bat my hand as if smacking away her question. "Yeah. Thanks."

"What—" She shakes her head. "I shouldn't question."

"You're allowed to ask me shit, Naomi. I won't bite."

She studies me. "How did they die?"

I almost regret opening myself to the questioning. "Um. Well. My...my dad did that—" I gesture at her. "To my mom. My whole life, her whole life. A few days ago, she snapped. Shot him, then herself."

She gasps. "Oh. Oh my. I'm...I'm so sorry."

"Yeah. I was...I was on the phone with her when she..." I swallow hard, clear my throat. "Yeah."

"Silas." It's the first time she's said my name. It's a breath, and the sound of my name on her lips makes something in my chest thump, makes my skin tighten, makes my lips tingle. "That's awful."

"Hasn't been fun."

"Is that why..." she pauses to slow her breathing; she seems to be fighting panic just engaging in normal conversation with me. "Is that why you're helping me?"

"Part of it," I answer, honestly.

"And the other part?" She's getting a little bolder with the questions.

"Couldn't leave you alone, hurt and scared, on the side of the road. I'm not a good dude, Naomi. But…even I've got some ethics. Not many, but some."

"Why are you not good?"

I shake my head. "That's a big question for another time."

She bobs her head in a shy, subtle nod. "Of course."

I glance at her again, stealing a surreptitious scan of her face—blood is crusted beneath her nose and on her chin, her lip is puffy and split, and the bruise shadowing her eye is darkening with every passing moment. She needs to get cleaned up at the very least, and I'd feel better examining her ribs myself. I'm not sure she'll allow me that close, though.

I've been driving for more hours than I can count at this point, and while I could probably keep going, just looking at Naomi makes it clear to me she's in a lot of pain, terrified, exhausted. She can't go much longer.

The fuck of it is, I have no clue what to do with her. I can't be responsible for this girl—woman? Another glance; she appears to be in her early twenties, so at least I can't be charged with abducting a minor or some shit. Not that I'm particularly worried about that—I can handle myself, and I damn sure know how to avoid the law.

But what the hell do I do with her?

I chew on what to do and wrestling with what I've gotten myself into for the next hour of driving. Naomi is perfectly, utterly still the entire time. Her hands are folded on her lap on top of my Glock, head ducked, eyes downcast, shoulders hunched up around her ears as if waiting for a blow any moment. She barely breathes.

In all my life, I've never seen such preternatural still-ness in a human being. It's fucking freaky. She doesn't look out the window, doesn't fidget, shift, sniffle, change posi-tions, nothing. Just sits there.

Finally, the lights of civilization cast a glow on the horizon—I'm on a rural county highway rather than a free-way, so there are no signs to tell me if there are any gas stations or hotels. As we approach the town, it becomes apparent it's a tiny little place. We pass a gas station, now closed, a general store, a hunting and fishing supply place, a local dive bar watering hole populated with a handful of older model pickups. And, thankfully, a twenty-four-hour drugstore and a motel. The motel isn't much to write home about, but it's somewhere to stop for the night.

I pull into the drugstore first. Naomi doesn't react at all.

"I'm gonna grab a few things. You need anything?" I turn my torso to face her, careful to move slowly, keeping my hands far from her personal space.

She shakes her head, not looking at me.

"You sure? Hungry? Thirsty?" Her gaze snaps to me, and I hear a rumble of her stomach; I laugh. "Yeah, you're hungry, but you're too scared of me to say so."

Her eyes are wide, and she's breathing hard, panic panting. God, now what?

"What do you like?"

A shrug of her shoulders.

"Potato chips? Pretzels? Soda? It's a drugstore so it's not like I can get you a real meal. Everything is closed at this time of night in a podunk place like this." I wait. "No input?"

"I don't know." It's another of those barely audible whispers.

I sigh. "All right. I'll grab a few things and you can decide." I gesture at the gun. "I won't be gone long. It'd be best if you stay in the car. If you get scared, come in and find me. Okay?"

She's shaking all over, fully panicking now. "I…I…" Her little pink tongue slides across her lower lip. "May I come with you, sir? Please?"

I nod, and hold out my hand, palm up. "Sure. Whatever you're most comfortable with. Can I get the gun back? Not safe for you to carry it out in public."

She scoops it up in her palms and proffers it to me, palms cupped together with the weapon in her hands. In taking the gun from her, my fingertips brush her palms, and she gasps, yanking her hands to her chest as if burned.

I suppress my irritation, reminding myself that she's probably never known a gentle touch, or anything but violence. It's not her fault, and it's not me. It's just the situation.

I shut off the engine and headlights and pocket the keys, exit the car. Naomi doesn't get out, seems to be waiting. With a sigh, I round the hood and open her door for her. Moving slowly, she gets out and moves a step away, waiting with hands folded together in front her, head bowed, as I close the door. When I take a step forward, she assumes a place a step behind me and to my right. When I slow my pace as we enter the store, she holds that position, behind me and to my right.

A woman's place is behind the man, I would assume she's been taught.

I halt just inside the drugstore—it's a little mom-and-pop place, not a chain; the rows of shelves are tightly packed, filled with junk food, snacks, soda, sports drinks… the usual. The cashier counter is to the right of the entrance, the wall behind lined with bottles of liquor, cigarettes, and chewing tobacco. The druggist counter is on the back wall, a metal grate closed and locked, the light off. Behind the cashier counter lurks a young man with long greasy dark hair and a patchy beard, wearing baggy ripped jeans and a huge black hoodie. He watches something on his cell phone, earbuds in his ears. He ignores us totally.

I glance at Naomi. "You can walk next to me."

"Yes sir."

I again suppress a sigh. "I'm not telling you to. I'm saying you can do what you want. You can wait here. You can walk next to me. You can wander around the store by yourself and pick whatever you want. I'll buy it for you. You can walk out of the store and not come back. You're your own person now, Naomi."

She shakes her head, hunching her shoulders up around her ears, looking panicked again. "I know my place." Her voice is quiet as ever, shaking with fear.

"Your place is wherever and whatever the hell you want it to be," I growl, unable to contain my frustration.

"Yes sir." Agreeing blindly, purely out of fear and conditioning.

I sigh. "Come on. Walk wherever you want to walk."

She keeps her place behind me and to my right, following meekly as I grab a bag of Doritos, a bag of pretzel twists, more jerky, a case of Coke, and an eight-pack of red Gatorade. Naomi expresses no interest in anything, just follows with her head ducked, hands folded, skirt hiding her steps so she appears to float, so graceful and smooth is her gait.

I bring my armload of purchases to the counter, and the kid pauses whatever he's watching and starts ringing me up without a word, let alone removing his earbuds. I notice Naomi's gaze wandering to the rack of magazines and chocolate bars lining the front of the cashier counter—specifically, her eyes fix on a Hershey bar.

"You want that?" I ask, pointing at the chocolate.

A shrug of her shoulders.

"Do you?"

Another shrug, and now she's shaking again.

"Naomi." I keep my voice quiet, and as gentle as I can make it. "You want the chocolate?"

A hesitation, and then she very subtly, very fearfully, dares to nod, once—and then turtles, as if terrified this expression of a desire will get her hit.

I reach in front of her to grab the Hershey bar—my shoulder brushes her hip. At the contact, she shuffles backward with a sharp inhalation through her nose, hands raised in front of her face, shaking all over.

I straighten, moving slowly, lifting the bar of chocolate. "Whoa, easy. It's fine. You're fine." I set the bar with the rest of the purchases.

The kid looks up finally, glancing at Naomi; his eyes widen when he sees the state of her. His eyes flick to his phone. To me.

I hold up my hands, palms out. "Hey, I didn't do that to her. I'm helping her."

He looks at Naomi. "He tellin' the truth?"

Naomi doesn't look at him, but nods. "Yes," she whispers.

"Sure?"

Another nod.

The kid shrugs, reads off the total, asks me if I need a bag. I decline one, pay with cash. Carry the stuff out to the car, set them on the hood to open the door and pull the seat forward so I can place them on the minuscule back seat.

A diesel engine idles somewhere nearby, but I think nothing of it. A door opens, creaking, and then closes with a harsh slam. Still, I think nothing of it. Not until I hear a soft whimper from Naomi.

I toss the last item into the back seat and straighten, glance at her. She's not just trembling, she's shaking so hard it's almost a seizure, shuffling backward, eyes wide, tears pooling in her eyes.

I follow her gaze.

A huge red pickup truck idles halfway in the parking lot, halfway in the road. It's older, well-cared for, with a suspension lift and knobby mud tires. It's mud-splattered, with a long whip-like radio antenna bent from the hood and fastened to the rear bumper. There's an LED light bar across the roof of the cab and a bull bar with a winch in front of the grille.

A man stands outside the truck, glowering at Naomi and me. Rage distorts his features, his hands fisted at his side. He's in his sixties, lean and hard, with gray hair in a lank ponytail and a long, thick beard at his chest. He's wearing hunting camo and knee-high boots.

"Get over here, *now*, Naomi Ibsen." His voice cracks like a whip.

She freezes in place, and I watch her gaze flick to me,

to the man I assume is her father. "Please, Papa. I…I…" she can barely form words, she's so terrified.

I step in front of her. "I don't think so."

"This is none of your business," he snaps, not sparing a glance at me. "She's my daughter. My *property*. I say she's comin' with me, so she's comin' with me."

I frown. "Property? She's a person, and a grown-ass woman. She doesn't have to do a damn thing she doesn't want to."

He ignores me. "Naomi. Last chance. I gotta say it again, your punishment will be far worse." He glares at her, his expression ugly, vile, mean. "And you already earned yourself a world of hurt, girl. Ten days in lockup, you come now. Make me say it again, you'll be in there a month."

I palm my pistol with practiced speed, cup the butt and take a prowling step toward Naomi's father. "I'll kill you where you stand, old man. Look in my eyes and ask yourself if I'm bluffing." I turn my head to angle a look at Naomi, without taking my peripheral vision off the old man. "Naomi. Get in the car. Unless you want to go with your father. You make your own choices. You stay with me, I can protect you."

"You're *mine*, Naomi. You'll come with me. You'll do as I say. *Now*."

I don't bother trying to answer his command. I just keep my pistol trained on his T-box.

A long, tense silence.

Naomi edges toward the passenger seat of my car, fumbles for the handle without taking her eyes off of her father. "Goodbye, Papa." She opens the door and half falls in, shutting the door on the corner of her skirt.

Her father's eyes are full of hate and murder as they meet mine. "You'll pay for taking what's mine."

I meet his gaze with a cold, baleful stare of my own; I've stared down mafia dons, hired assassins, and South American cartel warlords. This pathetic fuck doesn't even register. "She belongs to no one but herself. Come after me, you'll find out exactly who you fucked with. This is your only warning, old man. Don't fuck with me."

I turn my back on him deliberately, pistol at my side. Swing behind the wheel, start up the DB5. I keep the pistol in my right hand as I put the car in reverse, back out into the road facing the way I've been heading, and then put it in first. Her father is still standing by his truck, watching. I roll down my window. Rest the pistol on my left elbow, draw bead, and fire once—his back left tire pops, deflates. Naomi jumps at the crack of the gun, gasping,

He doesn't react, but the hate and rage on his face intensifies.

Jesus. No wonder she's so afraid of everything, if this is the monster who raised her.

I drive away.

"He'll kill you." I can barely hear her.

I laugh. "He can try."

"You don't understand. You don't know him."

I give her a cocky grin. "And honey, you don't know me. Trust me when I say he won't hurt you, or me." I let the grin fade, let her see my confidence. "He'll never lay a hand on you again. You have my word."

She looks at me—we pass under a streetlamp, and I can make out the color of her eyes in the dull orange glow. They're gray. Not just gray, but the layered dark shades of a storm cloud. Her hair is pure auburn, a burnished reddish brown. In the sun, I bet it'd be more red. It's so long—in a thick fishtail braid, it hangs over her left shoulder and curls on her lap. The end is tied with a faded piece of red fabric torn from a larger swath. Not even a real ponytail holder.

"Why?" Her voice is stronger, a little louder. "Why are you helping me?"

I shake my head, roll a shoulder. "Honestly, I'm asking myself the same question. But I am. I will. I'll protect you, Naomi. You're okay now. You're free."

She blinks rapidly at me. "Free?"

I nod. "Yeah. You're free."

She swallows hard. "I just didn't want to hurt anymore," she whispers.

I reach out a hand toward her, but she shies away, and I drop it back into my lap. "You won't be hurt anymore, Naomi. I fucking swear."

She just looks at me. Assessing. She meets my eyes for a moment, and in that moment, I see behind the curtain—I see a woman who has just done the most courageous thing I can think of.

Something that took balls of fucking steel.

And that was just her escape. Getting in the car with me just now? Defying her father to his face?

I can't imagine the courage that must have required.

I find a huge well of respect for her filling up inside me. I don't know what the hell I'm doing, what I'm going to do…but I just know down to my balls and bones that my future is tied up with hers.

Why, how, hell if I know. But I feel it as surely as I know the lines on my palms, the angles of my face in the mirror.

I'm starting to understand Rev, Kane, and Chance a

little bit, suddenly. Not that I'd ever say that to them, not after I was so openly derisive. But…I feel drawn to her.

And more than anything, I feel a fierce, feral, violent drive to protect her. To make sure no one ever hurts her again.

It's something in her eyes. In her stillness. In her fear of everything around her, every twitch of my hands. She shouldn't be so afraid. She's too beautiful to be so terrified, so deeply hurt.

She's a wounded bird who deserves to fly.

I'll take care of her.

Protect her.

And god help anyone who gets in my way.

ALSO BY

JASINDA WILDER

Visit me at my website: **www.jasindawilder.com**
Email me: **jasindawilder@gmail.com**

If you enjoyed this book, you can help others enjoy it as well by recommending it to friends and family, or by mentioning it in reading and discussion groups and online forums. You can also review it on the site from which you purchased it. But, whether you recommend it to anyone else or not, thank you *so much* for taking the time to read my book! Your support means the world to me!

My other titles:

Preacher's Son:
Unbound
Unleashed
Unbroken

Delilah's Diary:
A Sexy Journey
La Vita Sexy
A Sexy Surrender

Big Girls Do It:
Boxed Set
Married
On Christmas
Pregnant

Rock Stars Do It:
Harder
Dirty
Forever

From the world of *Big Girls* and *Rock Stars*:
Big Love Abroad

Biker Billionaire:
Wild Ride

The Falling Series:
Falling Into You
Falling Into Us
Falling Under
Falling Away
Falling For Colton

The Ever Trilogy:
Forever & Always
After Forever
Saving Forever

The world of *Wounded:*
Wounded
Captured

The world of *Stripped:*
Stripped
Trashed

The world of *Alpha:*
Alpha
Beta
Omega
Sigma
Gamma
Harris: Alpha One Security Book 1
Thresh: Alpha One Security Book 2
Duke Alpha One Security Book 3
Puck: Alpha One Security Book 4
Lear: Alpha One Security Book 5
Anselm: Alpha One Security Book 6

The Houri Legends:
Jack and Djinn
Djinn and Tonic

The Madame X Series:
Madame X
Exposed
Exiled

The Black Room
(With Jade London):
Door One

Door Two

Door Three

Door Four

Door Five

Door Six

Door Seven

Door Eight

The One Series
The Long Way Home

Where the Heart Is

There's No Place Like Home

Badd Brothers:
Badd Motherf*cker

Badd Ass

Badd to the Bone

Good Girl Gone Badd

Badd Luck

Badd Mojo

Big Badd Wolf

Badd Boy

Badd Kitty

Badd Business

Badd Medicine

Badd Daddy

Dad Bod Contracting:
Hammered
Drilled
Nailed
Screwed

Fifty States of Love:
Pregnant in Pennsylvania
Cowboy in Colorado
Married in Michigan
Christmas in Connecticut

Goode Girls
For a Goode Time Call…
Not So Goode
Goode to Be Bad
A Real Good Time
Goode Vibrations

Billionaire Baby Club:
Lizzie Goes Brains Over Braun
Autumn Rolls a Seven
Laurel's Bright Idea

Club Sin:
Rev
Kane
Chance

Standalone titles:
Yours
The Cabin
The Parent Trap
Wish Upon a Star
Big Hose

Non-Fiction titles:
You Can Do It
You Can Do It: Strength
You Can Do It: Fasting

Jack Wilder Titles:
The Missionary

JJ Wilder Titles:
Ark

To be informed of new releases, special offers, and other Jasinda news, sign up for Jasinda's email newsletter.

jasinda wilder

CPSIA information can be obtained
at www.ICGtesting.com
Printed in the USA
BVHW030916120223
658360BV00006B/108